THE SPACE BETWEEN BREATHS

KELLIE SCHORR

Brother Mockingbird

Library of Congress Control Number: 2024952726

Cover Design by: Alexios Saskalidis
www.facebook.com/187designz

For information please contact:
Brother Mockingbird, LLC
www.brothermockingbird.net
ISBN: 978-1-960226-26-6 Paperback
ISBN: 978-1-960226-27-3 eBook

To Cathy, who turned "my dream" into "our dream" and
loves me every step of the way.

1

This is my fourth life in the same body. It will likely be my short-est, but not the most painful. It has certainly been the loudest. The beeping of the heart monitor, a rhythm not as steady as the nurse would like, would be meditative if it wasn't lodged in a cacophony of overhead announcements, doctors shouting orders, EMT's calling out vitals, and the handcuffs clanging against the metal rails of the bed. The clamor of reporters screaming questions and ordering their cameramen to get closer finally fades as security pushes them away from the ER doors. Although answering the unanswerable has been my job for most of my life, I won't have to answer them. Not now. Not ever. Everything is red.

"Bitch!" Keith Allen screams from across the room. At least, that's what it sounds like. It's the only somewhat discernable word he's howled since our ambulances arrived together at Mountainside General. That's better than poor Officer Johnson. He hasn't made a sound. I don't know about Lieutenant Rhodes. I think she may have gone straight to the morgue. Any other city would have the good sense to take us to different hospitals, the victims and the violator, but not Oakland. It's a small town. A prison town. I know all about prison towns. This is the only place they've got.

"Sit still and see what moves," Shastri Nolan told me back in my second life, when I could sit at his feet for hours, listening to his teachings with the concentration of a hawk and the heart of a tigress. That's what I hate about spiritual gurus. They can never just say "Here's what happened" or "Yes, I did it." They start by relating some story from their past, and by the time you figure out that the clues are inside the story, they switch gears, leaving you to figure it out.

"Prep OR two and get Kensling in there from respiratory."

"Doctor, she's..."

"Get a pressure pack on that. Up the oxygen, her saturation is low."

"What's her condition? Is Allen dead? Can I get a statement?"

"Get that reporter out of here, NOW!"

"Surgical Associates says Dr. Hart is on his way over. Who is he taking? Him, or her?"

The problem is that in this room, in this life, everything is moving. Except me, of course. Maybe I should look for what stays still.

"NOOOO!!!" I hear Keith, his fleshy, sweat-stained body still strapped on a gurney, shriek before a curtain opens and he's wheeled away for a much-needed surgery. A nurse smiles at the thought. I feel her glee. That's probably not a good thing. But hey, I didn't take the final shot. I'm an avowed pacifist, a teacher of compassion and reason. I'm a woman of peace. Everybody knows that. Besides, I'd already taken a bullet through the back by then.

I float through the icy blue air ferried from one room to another, consciousness hovering somewhere just beneath the surface of my ventilated shell: my spirit aware, my flesh cold. The clattering of the steel rails and hard rubber wheels on polished tile makes an ominous milepost. Things are "touch and go" the surgeon says to the cop. When I somehow make it through the lengthy operation, I'm moved to a private room in the ICU while my body sits at the roundabout of fate, choosing a path. They won't let another patient near me until they know who they're dealing with.

"Lylarose!" A voice draws me out of morphine dreams. Penelope's here. That must have sent the reporters into a feeding frenzy. I imagine them squawking like seagulls at a fish fry. "Ms. Fine! Ms. Fine! Ms. Fine!" Not that she'd mind. She spoke to me in her real voice, not that fake, slightly Southern accent she puts on for the masses. "Can you hear me?"

I shift my eyes toward her but I'm not sure they actually move. The absence of Keith's caterwauling allows the nurses to go back to their normal range of chatter and care plans. They finally get around to scanning the armband hastily attached to my wrist and the labels stuck on the chart, the table, the cart, and some tech's sleeve. Doesn't really matter if I live or die, billing needs to charge someone for my care. That's one thing that doesn't move.

"I'm here. I'm here with you," Penelope says in a whisper as if that increases the spiritual likelihood of my understanding. "I am present in this moment with you."

"Ms. Fine?" The nurse asks, in equal parts curiosity and awe. "Are you *the* Penelope Fine?"

"I'm not important right now, but yes," she answers, her sweet, faux-friendly mini-drawl returning as her volume rises. "I'm Penelope Fine."

"I'm so honored to meet you," the nurse bubbles as the bells clatter and echo off the institutional beige walls. Alarm fatigue. That's what Marian called it when you work in a hospital so long each warning buzzer fades into the background until you barely hear it. It doesn't really matter that my blood pressure just tanked and a siren is going off by my ear. They can only hear the calm, confident voice of that pretty, blond bestseller with perfect eyebrows, a stunning silhouette, and a permanent spot on Oprah's Top 250. "I've read all your books."

Penelope nods. Of course she's read all her books. You don't make the Times list repeatedly if people don't read them all. In what will likely be her last selfless act during my fourth life, Pen turns the attention away from her glory and points at the monitor.

"Why is the machine doing that?"

"She's dropping." One nurse scurries out and two come in with a needle to stick in a tube. They talk about orders and maximum dosages, stabilizing something, and signing off for one another until the machine calms back down. I watch Penelope stare with a fixed gaze at the monitor as if, by her will alone, she can bring me back from the brink. It must have worked because the beat goes on.

Penelope's expertly polished fingernail runs across the handcuff likely belonging to the officer standing in the hall drinking old coffee and checking his watch. Shift must be nearly over. "This isn't necessary."

It's not a question. It's a pronouncement, fitting of the empress.

"Dr. Gentry is officially in the custody of the Oakland County Sheriff's Office," the nurse advises while her smitten fan heart collides with her sense of moral outrage and duty. "I'm afraid only they can make that determination."

Surprised I've lived into the night, Penelope texts furiously in a recliner by my bed. Another sleepy cop sits right outside the door, and the questions grow more severe.

"Are you related to Dr. Gentry, Ms. Fine?" The night nurse asks, curling her lips as she looks down on my shrinking, immobile body.

"Lylarose is my teacher," the author answers. Soft. Honest. Almost humble.

"Seems to me you should put your faith in better people." The nurse with a brutish square haircut, sharp eyes, and a large golden cross around her neck, actually snorts as she checks the tubing and fake-accidentally kicks the bed to see if it jars me. "Trust God and not man."

"Don't bite the hook, Pen. Don't bite it, little fish." I project my thoughts, my energy flowing toward her in bright amber waves. My lips will not move. "Swim away, swim away."

She says nothing. Good girl.

"How in the world can a woman like you follow someone like her?"

Penelope smiles with genuine affection as she peers into my dimming eyes, seeing herself grow and laugh, cry and change. She swirls in warm sepia memories of my searing lessons taken to heart, and the clear truth she chose to ignore. The pride she has in her awakening shatters with the blinding realization that strikes us both at the same time.

I'm the villain.

How did this happen?

2

This was my first life in this body. Endless light shocking every fiber of my small skeleton with electric bolts of being. There were no walls, no forms, just a rolling landscape of polished steel. There was no gravity. There was just me. Infinite.

That's what I imagine it was like. I don't really remember being born, no matter what that school psychologist said. What I do remember, most clearly, is sitting on our porch in South Dakota when I was six, sucking on my inhaler as beads of happy sweat rolled down my reddened cheeks. I had been helping my father pull weeds in his garden, if "helping" means standing over assorted green sprouts that all look the same and asking repeatedly, "Is this a weed?"

My chest tightened and I walked to the shade, fishing the inhaler out of my too small Garanimal shorts (hippo + hippo means you match!). My mother appeared on the porch with a glass of sweet Southern lemonade, almost as deep and rich as her all-too-real Appalachian twang. My labored breathing turned to donkey honks. I'd had enough asthma attacks by then to make us all pros at it. Dad left the garden, reluctantly, and joined us. I sat there clutching my chest and blurting like a rusty lawnmower attempting to start. My parents stared blankly at me, waiting to see if my breath was going to catch and let me whir back to life, or if I'd just die there on the porch and be carted to the dump like last year's weed whacker.

Finally, the motor engaged. I slumped back in my lawn chair

enjoying those first wonderful minutes of pure, unlabored mid-summer air. My father mopped his brow, took the lemonade my mother brought for me, and drank half the glass before setting it down. We hovered there - the engineer, his wife, and their sickly, disappointing offspring - locked in the perpetual uncomfortable silence that was our home.

"Virga," my father mumbled.

"Huh?"

"Virga," he said again. "It's the streak of rain that hangs in the sky before it falls. The day you were born the air was so thick with virga I thought surely you would be a thunderstorm."

"Really? Wow." I looked at the sky with new awe. Did it hold the sticky heaviness of my life in its airy expanse? Was that a celebration or an omen? Did the universe know I was coming six weeks too soon with lungs that would never catch up? Did it care?

"Oh, for Christ's sake. We lived in Tampa, Lawrence. There was virga every day," my mother scoffed as she turned on her heels to leave, satisfied that I was going to live through the afternoon. Nice families don't let their kid die on the porch without watching. "Lylarose, those shorts are practically at your privates. Whether you like it or not we need to go shopping."

"Yes, ma'am." Even at six, I hated to go shopping.

"Growing like a weed." My father drank the rest of my lemonade.

"Am I a weed?" I asked, remembering the fun of our garden time lost in inhaler mist. He chuckled.

"Probably. But I won't pull you just yet. Let's see if you grow a flower first. If you're pretty, you can stay."

"I don't think I'm a thunderstorm," I confessed. My parents were powerful giants with so much bright red energy I always felt like an empty paper sack when I was near them.

"No. You're an everyday summer shower, Lylarose," he said, stepping into the yard. "The kind that waters the earth and makes the plants grow. You'll do."

That's pretty much everything there is to know about me. I'm an everyday summer shower, and I make the plants grow. I forged a life of watering the tender human souls of wounded ragweed and thirsty crabgrass until the day I became a scythe.

3

"This is Laura Lindeman on special assignment for *News Now!*"

Penelope's beloved iPad blares the internet news site from the radiator anchored to the ICU wall, where she set up a power dock and mini ground-control station. I keep electronic devices limited and out-of-sight at the Virga Center for Meditation and Renewal, simply known as "Virga." Now that I'm out of commission, she seems to be trying to feast on all of them at once. If she's not tapping at her laptop, she's texting, scanning, or chatting on some screen. Maybe that's why news people always appear to be breathless and shouting. They know it's a competition. No one is simply sitting and watching just one thing.

"Chaos reigned this morning at the Maryland State Penitentiary at Bowles Pass where gunfire erupted during a counseling session between Dr. Lylarose Gentry, the accomplished psychologist and meditation guru to a clientele of A-List stars, and Keith Allen, an inmate convicted of the murders of two women, one of whom was the legally recognized wife of Dr. Gentry. One correctional officer was pronounced dead at the scene, and another died en route to care. Dr. Gentry and Keith Allen were both rushed to Mountainside General Hospital in Oakland and are listed in critical condition at this time."

The picture changes from an aerial view of the prison, taken by helicopter, to the circular driveway and heavily guarded automatic doors of the hospital. The cameraman manages to capture Ms. Lindeman's good side with a flattering down-angle, the hospital marque, and the burly state police guard outside the door all in one shot, while filtering out the other fifteen news vans gathered around the parking area. They didn't give these guys enough credit for good lens work.

"I'm standing outside the ER of Mountainside General and, as you can see, they've closed off the emergency corridor to the press, but no other casualties from the prison appear to have been admitted. Local police and specialists from the state board of prisons are actively investigating the incident and will not comment about what happened at this time. However, an anonymous source disclosed to *News Now* that Dr. Gentry is the alleged shooter and is believed to have acted alone."

"Ms. Fine," a nurse whispers from the doorway of the dim room. "Here in the ICU we don't allow devices which emit that much volume. We need to keep the room quiet for the patient and other patients on the floor."

By "other patients" she means Keith who, like me, is lying dormant in a guarded room across the nurses' station from mine. The only difference is he's being purposefully kept on medical sedation. My mind is doing this by itself.

"Keep logging on or follow our Social Media feed for live updates. I'm going to stick with this story until all the facts are clear. Remember, for internet information updated by-the-second in real time, set your browser to *News Now*!"

"I'm so sorry." Penelope reaches over and swipes the mute button, much to everyone's relief. "We're protected from media interference here, right?"

The nurse looks at the police officer standing by the door and back to Penelope. "It's a secured floor right now, yes."

"Good, because the last thing Lyla needs is a bunch of click-whores rummaging through her medical charts." Pen holds the iPad up for the nurse to see. "Look at those boots. Who's she trying to channel? Soledad O'Brien dressed like Shania Twain for Halloween?"

The nurse smiles and walks back down the hall. Whether my stay in this room, or this life, is one more hour or another week, it's going to be something no one here is likely to forget.

The key to meditation is to focus on your breath. Inhale. Exhale. There is nothing else. No bills, no court summons, no presentation due next week, no mountainous laundry pile, no parent-teacher conference, no breaking news, no broken hearts. Just you. Inhale. And you. Exhale. It's that easy. And, that hard.

The breath is our center, the bridge between the three stages of our being—the personal (I breathe), the interpersonal (you breathe), and the collective (we breathe). No matter our politics, religion, occupation, social class, or mental status – we all breathe. By putting our attention on the one simple act we have in common, the illusion of our separateness disappears. Assisted by machines, I breathe; Keith breathes. Two people perpetually locked on the opposite sides of pain and power are now the same – nothing but breath. The problem is most people won't see either of us on the inhale, or the exhale. They see us in the space between the in-breath and out-breath, and there in that fleeting second of breathlessness, they will assign our blame.

The space between breaths is where love begins and babies are created, where patience has a chance and hope is nourished. It's also the home of my age-old friend, Death.

Near the midnight hour, when the nurse has finally gone on a break, the cop's wife drops off his dinner in a fast-food bag, the grease from that burger causes an oil slick in the disinfected air. This afternoon, when he put on his uniform, neither were prepared for him to spend his shift sitting outside the door of today's top story. She peers into the room the way people look at a shrine, from across a threshold, not daring to enter, but yearning to draw out just enough of the sacred to give them a lift when life lays them low. I can't tell if she is looking at Penelope or me, not that it matters anymore. For this one night, we are equally famous. He's been given strict orders to call the homicide division "as soon as she wakes up." Funny, I've been about the business of awakening my whole adult life, and now, when it's needed more than ever, I'm not sure that I will.

The chair squeaks as the barrel-chested man tries to tiptoe all 275 pounds of himself into the room. The lights are low and he manages to kick a crash cart placed not too far from the bed.

"Sorry, sorry," he whispers, his hand in the air as if he's the one being arrested.

They both look at me to see if that is the magic bullet which will break my slumber like a prince's kiss. It isn't. I could have told them that. I stopped believing in magic the night my second life ended in a pool of my beloved Marian's blood. That is, until today. There was powerful magic today.

"Ms. Fine?" He kneels down beside the recliner.

"Yes." Penelope never imagines people want something other than to confirm her existence.

"I...um...my wife thought...well...we...well, our daughter..."

She taps her shoe against the tile floor, the red lacquered soles echoing her impatience. Oh my Buddha! That woman. She wore Louboutins to my emergency!

"Say again?"

He reboots and stiffens his back, his hand with a death grip on the prize.

"Our daughter is graduating from high school this year, and my wife wants to give her this book as a present, and if it's not too much trouble, I was wondering if you could sign it. Please?"

He holds up a newly purchased reprint of *You'll Be Fine: A Guide to Making it in the Big World*. It's the book that started it all. A series of quick-wit essays she tapped out and gave to her then boyfriend's sister, who just happened to work for a gift book publisher. Who knew the world was so desperate for another graduation gift? She nudged Dr. Seuss' perennial favorite, *Oh, The Places You'll Go*, over just enough to find a place on the top shelf.

I once heard a coach say it's not good for a baseball player to hit a home run on his first at-bat. It ruins his swing. He tries to hit another every time the ball comes toward him until he's known as a strike-out king and sent packing. The nearly instant bestseller didn't ruin Penelope's swing. After essays about her book tour (*Travellin' Fine*), her marriage (*A Fine Romance*), her little girl (*The Baby's Just Fine*), and her divorce following the accidental death of her child (*Far from Fine*), it was pretty clear that first home run had ruined her very life.

The burgundy day she collapsed on the floor of her guestroom during our session at Virga, finally feeling all that pain in a shattering clarity punch to the heart, it took me more than an hour to put enough of her emotional pieces together so she could sit in a chair. After a hiatus to regrow the soul she'd cannibalized for her slice of fame's pie, she was on Good Morning America pushing her latest release, *Back to Fine*. That one didn't just mess up her life, it also left a pretty hefty dent in mine.

I went from being an unknown meditation teacher living a quiet, uneventful life to guru-to-the-stars faster than Marian could kiss me goodbye when she was running late for work. I knew then Penelope wasn't destined for change. Even now, when she opens up the little laptop she carries in that gargantuan Balenciaga leather tote, I'm terrified she's probably writing an outline for *A Fine Mess: My Mentor, Meditation, and Murder*.

"Well, there's a relic," she smiles sweetly, taking the book in her hands and running her fingers over the cover. She remembers the hasty, carefree young woman who wrote those platitudes grounded on nothing but days with cloudless skies. "I'm surprised they still sell this."

"Oh yes," the man with a dusky complexion and soft brown eyes under his regulation cop haircut nods. "We can't wait for her to read it."

Penelope fishes out a brand new ultra-fine point Sharpie, conveniently placed near the top of the pile in her bag, and opens the cover. Just as she removes the cap, her eyes scan my body lying trapped on the bed, covered in tubes, IV lines, and surgical tape – my own version of sackcloth and ashes. For a moment, I think she can sense me rolling my eyes sarcastically, even though they haven't moved. But, no. She's not thinking about propriety. She has commerce on her mind. She doesn't always get money, but if Penelope Fine gives you something, even a signature, she's gonna walk away with more.

"What's your daughter's name?"

"Courtney." His smile outshines my blood pressure monitor in the low light. The mission is successful. His wife will be so happy.

"Is it Courtney Brault?" She points at the name on his badge. "You know, blended families these days."

"We aren't blended. First marriage, only child."

"Have you thought about more?" She circles like a hawk.

"Um...no...I work nights and my wife teaches. We also...you know... are...a little past the age to deal with a baby."

"I lost my daughter when she was three," Penelope says. Shameless hustler. She uses the awkward silence the way a bad magician appears and disappears in fake smoke.

"I know. My wife, um, read that book, too. I'm...very sorry, ma'am."

She nods, silently accepting the condolence. His compassion is high, and his guard is down. The well is primed. Now to draw the water. She positions her pen above the page and stops.

"Officer Brault, I hate to ask, but is there any way you could remove those handcuffs from my teacher?"

"Um, well, no..." He looks at the blank opening page of the book.

"You mean you don't have a key?"

"Oh, no, I have the key, of course. It's just protocol to keep a suspect secured until questioned."

Penelope circles the pen in the air, writing nothing but offering everything to the imagination.

"Dr. Gentry is still a suspect? I think they should have cleared this up by now. If your wife read my last book, you'd know Lylarose Gentry is one of the most life affirming, non-violent people on the planet. She once designed an international meditation summit for representatives at the UN. It's simply not possible for her to kill someone." Still not one mark on the book. She had to shift it on her lap so he didn't accidentally salivate on it.

"It's problematic, Ms. Fine. At this point we know very little. We do know the wing commander, the first armed responder, shot Dr. Gentry because it appeared she was holding a weapon at the time."

"He shot her through the back."

"Well, a perp can kill you without facing you, ma'am. She could have turned around at any moment and fired at him. There were already two officers down when wing command entered the room.

Law enforcement is trained to respond at the suspicion of a weapon and to use deadly force. There is no such thing as 'shoot to wound.'"

"Appeared? Suspicion? Was she holding the gun or not?"

"They are doing an analysis on the gun and the scene now, but, due to privacy laws guarding the inmate's rights, the counseling pods have no in-room surveillance. With both Inmate Allen and Dr. Gentry unable to give any context to the situation, it may take a few days to a week to know exactly what happened. This isn't CSI, ma'am." His eyes open wide as he realizes she hasn't signed yet and he is treating her like a common crime show addict. "What I meant to say is that there is some confusion as to whether Dr. Gentry or Inmate Allen had the weapon or what was happening. She remains a suspect until forensics tells us otherwise."

"Keith Allen would make more sense. He was probably assaulting her. This was his plan since the moment he asked to be counseled by Lylarose under the guise of healing together. He threatened to sue the state if they wouldn't let him meet with her. That man hates women, you know." Ever the writer, she begins to change the narrative in Officer Brault's mind, which is currently as blank as the page she's supposed to be signing.

"Yes, I know."

"She is just another victim of Keith Allen's misogyny. I think it is cruel to have one of Allen's victims cuffed to a bed when all she is trying to do is survive. It must be very uncomfortable for her."

"The suspect is in a coma. I don't think she is bothered by the restraints."

"I am." Penelope holds the book open with her elbow but puts the cap back on her pen. "I am bothered by the word 'suspect' as well."

"If I take these off..."

Officer Brault still thinks he can bargain with her even though he's already fishing in his pocket for the key. That's adorable.

"...and something goes wrong, I'm going to hold you responsible, Ms. Fine."

"I promise you." She takes the cap back off the pen. "If Lylarose wakes up, pulls out all these IV lines, extubates herself, and walks out of this room, I will happily spend the rest of my life behind bars. At this point, I'd go to jail just to see a glimmer of hope in her eyes."

The cuff snaps open with a ceremonious click. The next sound is the Sharpie scratching across the soft cover's page.

The room fills with bright yellow sunlight, even though it's nearly one in the morning. Officer Brault's glow will last until he gets home, where it illuminates their bedroom so undeniably, his wife will be lifted from her slumber to behold the shimmer of their momentary brush with a celebrity.

"Dear Courtney, I wish you a life of high adventure and no regrets. Best of luck! Penelope Fine."

4

I know things. I can't tell you how or why. I just do. I once told Marian that when I die, I want to be cremated and have a gold plate on my urn that says "I knew this would happen."

"You are so fixated on dying." She threw her hands in the air, tired of hearing about my impermanence.

"I'm not fixating on dying. I just enjoy fantasizing about being cremated."

"Why?"

"Because, I'll finally be warm."

I've been cold since the day I was born. Even in the Northern Virginia summers at Virga, where the humidity makes the trees perspire, I carry a jacket in my car and keep a blanket by my chair. Our family made cross-country moves every two years as I was growing up. With every move I thought we would finally be in a place where I would be warm. It never happened. Even when we lived in Douglas, Arizona, where 110 is an average July day, I was cold. Cremation, it seems, will be my last chance for a warm fate.

My father was a senior design engineer for a company that built large-scale properties like megamalls, amusement parks, and prisons. Mostly, during my childhood, he built prisons. That figures. The problem with prisons is the projects are always built in tiny brackish-water counties with small populations, set ways, and narrow bank accounts. "Prison Trash" was what they called us. They hated us because they needed us. We had money, education, stories from other places, and the freedom to pick up and leave when the job was done. They had crappy flat land, generations of disappointment, and no plans to go anywhere. The jobs that the new prison promised would keep these towns afloat when the farmers had a rainy year or the coal mine was on strike, so we prison trash were a necessary evil they seldom cared to admit. Even now, as much as the nice, homespun residents of Oakland, Maryland hate the caravan of press trucks setting up all over town, this will triple their income for the year.

Heading up the design team, my father would be one of the first on a site. He'd scout the town, find a house to buy, and send the truck to pick up our lives and drive us to the new place, leaving the old house in the hands of a realtor. My mother didn't even throw away the packing barrels. She just stored them for the next time. While I lived with the perpetual hope of moving to warmth, my mother saw every new town as a chance to arrive at happiness. It never happened.

"One of those prison trash kids," the school secretary said, motioning to me with her thumb, as if I wouldn't realize she meant me. I was eight when we left South Dakota and moved to Elverta, a small California town close enough to Sacramento to access big city things like doctors and the ballet, but far enough away to lack manners. "Needs a psych referral."

"Oh sweet Lord, I just processed that one last week. Already in trouble," the other clerk tsked her tongue and shook her head, causing her big hair to inflate as she grimaced, the color of her energy matched the plum lipstick she had on her teeth.

"I'm not in trouble," I said mildly. At least that's what Mrs. Naughton said when she walked me to the office.

"You're not in trouble, honey. I just want to let a special kind of doctor talk to you for a while. I think you have some abilities he's going to find interesting. The counselor will give you a referral and they will call your mom to pick you up," Mrs. Naughton said as she nodded reassurance. Her energy colors, a pretty teal and white mix, were bright and steady. She believed what she was saying. That made me want to believe it, too.

"Do they have to call my mom?" I asked, hopeful there was any other way to do this.

"Don't worry, Lyla." She patted my boney shoulder with a meaty, confident touch. "You didn't do anything wrong."

Great. That placed the odds of getting my ass kicked for the interruption to my mother's afternoon at 50/50. It depended on what she was doing when the call came in and what mood my dad brought home from work. Green mood or yellow, a talk or a shrug. Orange, over the arm of the living room sofa for a few swats of disinterested parental correction to shut my mother up. Red, it would be the belt – anywhere he could hit me while I curled up into the smallest ball possible in a corner. Maroon – the blood red, dark seething fury. Dear Hera, don't let it be maroon.

I had not yet been introduced to organized religion, and went directly from my dinosaur stage to worshiping the Greco-Roman gods I saw in Saturday afternoon fantasy movies. Hera was my deity of choice when I lived in Elverta. Of course, at that point, I would have prayed to a turkey sandwich if I thought it would keep me from the belt.

"You can't blame these children," the big-haired clerk said as she put a piece of carbon paper between a white and pink page and rolled the whole thing through the typewriter, carefully lining up the keys with the lines. The click-thump of the typewriter's cylinder was an oddly comforting sound. I miss it. "These prison trash parents drag them from town to town. They grow up on construction lots with rough men and the nastiest kind of language. No home, no church, no extended family. I had one girl who couldn't even tell me the name of the street she lived on because she'd moved so many times. It is abuse, I tell you, raising kids like that!"

The girl she was talking about was Susan Hyson and her inability to remember her address had nothing to do with the fact her father worked as a site foreman for my dad's company. Susan couldn't remember her new address because she was a dipshit. Plain and simple. As early as eight, I marveled at how the most obvious answer was always overlooked in favor of a more interesting alternative. People do love their theories.

"What's your name, sweetie?" The woman asked, slowly and clearly, as if I hadn't heard all of the other sewage that just poured from the plum lipstick hole in her face.

"Lylarose Gentry." I saw her colors shift from plum to pale pea green. Confusion always looks like turtle skin through my eyes. "L-y-l-a-r-o-s-e."

"One name?"

"Yes, ma'am."

"Do you know your address?"

"Yes, and I know yours."

Clack-Bang! The typewriter carriage slammed to the other side and she turned to look at me for the first time, mouth ajar in an expression I would eventually learn meant I'd taken one step over the line. Or, maybe, ten.

"What did you just say?"

"I live at 221 Seneca Avenue, Elverta, California, 95626."

She turned back to the typewriter trying to fill in the space before her short-term memory lost the numbers. She mumbled to the keys. "Seneca Avenue? Fancy dancy, little rich girl."

"You live at 3349 Rockhill," I said, purposely projecting over the tapping. "Apartment 3B."

All sound stopped.

"What the hell?" She looked at me, the eight-year-old prison trash kid who just spouted out her address as easily as I spelled my own name even though I've only lived here a week. "How do you..."

A sharp claw like a hawk's talon dug into the flesh of my arm, sending a lightning bolt down my spine. My eyes winced and I gasped, quietly, before my breath came back. The talon withdrew leaving a stinging silent warning in its wake.

"I'm Peggy Gentry, what seems to be the problem?" My mother asked, her deep Southern diphthong a sharp contrast to the fast California up-speak the ladies in the office all used. The clerk's pale skin and wide eyes made the entire room seem comically large. If my mother's nail prints hadn't been rising on my skin, I would have laughed out loud. My mother accentuated the word "seems" and lifted her pitch on the word "problem," using that drawl to weave her own spell on the outmatched clerk.

"She....I...my...," the woman stammered as my mother shifted her feet on the mustard-yellow, seventies carpet. "Mr. Travis, the counselor, will explain everything. I'll have the referral typed out by the time you're finished with him."

She was speaking to my mother, but she never took her eyes off me. I tried to smile to give her a little comfort. It would be years before I realized that when you reveal secret information to people about their life, their habits, or their innermost thoughts, smiling at them in reassurance actually increases the creepy factor. A lot.

The counselor explained that Mrs. Naughton thought I was too "advanced" for the third grade class and might be suited for promotion or a special program. They wanted me to see a child psychologist in Sacramento that specialized in these kinds of matters. My mother gripped the side of her chair so hard she nearly warped the plastic.

"That's just way kind of you," my mother said, her words so full of syrup you'd think he was a stack of pancakes. "Lylarose left third grade in South Dakota, and she will continue third grade here. I promise you there won't be any trouble."

I nodded while her Brooks Brothers heel pressed down on my foot under the chair. No trouble. No trouble at all.

"She hasn't been any trouble, Mrs. Gentry, and if our psychologist thinks third grade is appropriate, we will be glad to readmit her. However, we can't place her anywhere until we get his evaluation."

I shuddered in my seat. My mother didn't lose often, which was a good thing because she didn't lose well.

"Let me tell you something," she said, a hiss replacing the drawl. "We move every two years. I can't be putting this kid in every special program you podunk schools develop for the three students with an IQ over one hundred you have in this town. She's not going to be your doctoral thesis or some picture you can point to and take credit for years later. My son, Barry, is brilliant and he graduated without special classes. Lylarose can do the same. Just sit her in a desk, and teach her whatever she needs. If she's a problem, call me. My husband, the senior engineer of that big prison project in the valley, will correct her at home."

I watched as the counselor's colors dimmed until he sat in front of her looking like a piece of uncooked bacon. But, I gotta hand it to the guy, he stood his ground.

"It's policy," he said, rising to encourage us to leave. He pointed to the door with an overcorrected 52-degree angle, allowing him to keep an arm between his body and the volatile menace that was my mother.

We walked out of the office so quickly I didn't have time to smile at the horrified clerk again. My mother just grabbed the form out of her hand on our way through the door. I planned to mention that the clerk's paycheck was in a windowed envelope on the tray beside her typewriter, and that's how I knew her address, but the moment was lost, like so many things, in the wake of Hurricane Peggy (as my dad called her). I left the clerk without explanation, staring at me as we careened down the hall. I figured it would be okay. After all, like my mom always said, "A little fear isn't a bad thing."

I crawled into my mother's Chevy Caprice, my tiny feet hanging over the edge of the gigantic seat, and fumbled with the seat belt buckle that was larger than my hand. The car still smelled like engine oil from the leak I mentioned to my father yesterday, and pretzels she must have been eating on the way to the school. I breathed a sigh of relief. It didn't smell like a man. I always knew my mom was having another affair long before my father figured it out. Her colors would be all over the place, and her car smelled like the beery sweat of men who were not my dad. I never mentioned it to her, but I always knew. She knew I knew. She'd narrow her eyes, and I'd stare out the window. A little fear isn't a bad thing.

"I can't..." I began, fumbling with the buckle that I couldn't seem to get into the slot. She took it from me and pushed my hand away, clicking it easily. I was in awe of her power.

"Advanced, my ass," she said, craning her neck to look behind her as she backed the land yacht out of the parking space. "You're as dumb as a stick."

I nodded.

"Now, Barry. He never had these kinds of problems in school. I never had to pick him up in the principal's office. Barry always had..."

I phased out at that point. Her color had gone back to beige with the red sparkles she got every time she talked about Barry—or, as I called him after I read *The Lord of The Rings* in seventh grade, "The Precious."

My mother grew up in a small Southern town with a small Southern family full of Southern ideas in Southern Tennessee. She was notably intelligent and, I discovered when I once stumbled upon a high school photograph of her, unusually pretty. Only five foot two, she had a perfect hourglass figure, chestnut brown hair with a natural wave, bedroom eyes, and full ruby lips. When she graduated from high school she did what every bright, attractive girl in her neck of the woods was encouraged to do— she married a good steady job. The fact that the good steady job came attached to a man with needs, ideas, and requirements didn't really dawn on my mother until the ring was on her finger and he moved her out of Appalachia to the first new house in a litany of motion.

At first, decorating the house and learning all the cocktails and social graces required of a company wife filled her days with interesting challenges. By the third move, when the same old couples with the same old stories camped at her table, playing gin rummy with fake smiles while their bratty kids ran around the yard tearing up the begonias, her enthusiasm for being the senior engineer's wife had drained dramatically. My mother's life became an overcast metronome of doing her marital duty in the bed of a man she really didn't like and waking up to another day of upper middle class malaise.

Then, the sun muscled its way through her dreary existence and made glorious love to her. A beam of light, so amazing the earth most probably stopped spinning for a few seconds just to behold it, shone on the perfectly manicured lawn of a little house in Jacksonville. Or was it Middleton? Or South Elkstown? I don't remember where it happened but it was a miracle nonetheless. Barrett Lee Gentry was born. All hail.

Barry gave my mother the one thing all the good jobs, bowling trophies, progressive dinners, and grabby quickies with strange men in a photo booth could not provide—a reason to live. A mop of stark blond hair and an oddly angular chin gave some folks the idea that he might not be "all Gentry," but my father never denied Barry as his.

"After all," he joked with the foreman of a project, "Possession is nine-tenths of the law."

I, on the other hand, was clearly a Gentry—tall and thin with impossibly straight black hair, baby blue eyes, bright mind, small hands, and a slow and steady manner. My father looked like a nerdy Dean Martin. I was his awkward, uncool, offspring—more scared mouse than Rat Pack. Still, there was no doubt I was my father's daughter in every way; a fact my mother held in evidence against me for the rest of my life.

In the family photos produced before my birth (which is almost all of our family photos—the camera seemed to have disappeared after I was born), my father can be seen standing by his wife with his arms to his side. Barry is standing in front of her, my mother's arms wrapped tightly around him as she smiled. She had such a pretty smile. The Precious was a "boy's boy"—riding bikes and throwing water balloons at the neighbors. He built houses out of Lincoln Logs so he could kick them over and once broke a little boy's nose by jumping off a high-flying swing into the poor kid's face. But that was okay because, boys.

He was never hit. He was barely scolded. My father said, "Boys need a different kind of discipline, Lylarose." Truth is, my mother wouldn't have it. Nobody spanks The Precious.

I discovered "discipline" for Barry consisted largely of sitting in a chair for five minutes or being grounded for a week when he was in high school for getting caught looking through a girl's window while she undressed. I'm sure he wasn't grounded for looking, but for the fact it was a trailer park. Nice families don't voyeur across the tracks. Even then, my mother's protection of her perfect boy was outshone by my father's raw social influence. They didn't have to pick Barry up at the police station. Oh, no. The cop drove Barry to our house and apologized to my father for the inconvenience of his visit.

I don't remember that, of course. I was an infant. You see—the dark clouds that gave way to the sun of Barry's arrival took a little over fifteen years to gather enough strength to return. When they did, on a cloudy day in Tampa where the air was thick with virga, Barry was nearly sixteen, and I came into the world six weeks premature. By the time I remembered more than just blobs of bright colors that turned out to be people, Barry had graduated high school, somehow, and was working on a corporate farm that my father bought controlling interest in as a way to secure his son a future.

I've only seen Barry a handful of times. Once, when I was in middle school and he married his first wife (my mother's tears pushed a local river over its banks), at my father's funeral, and when Barry had a heart attack, his third wife found me on the internet and asked me to travel to Minnesota to help her handle my mother (erroneously thinking that was possible). Barry made it through that okay. Even cardiac arrest retreats from the momma bear when The Precious is in peril.

I've never been jealous of Barry, except that he escaped the Gentry house so much earlier and easier than I did. It's not like we are really related. We have the same last name, the same sweet tooth, and the same habit of recalling where we lived when we tell a childhood story. We were raised by the same Lawrence and Peggy Gentry, and yet, by very different people. I always say, "My mother had an only child, and then me." I don't hold anything against him. It was not his fault he was born a sun god, and I came out as an inadequate rainy day commoner with asthma and corrective lenses. It took getting a Ph.D. in Psychology and reaching my second life, but I eventually came to accept—it wasn't my fault either.

"Okay, Lylarose," Dr. Greaves said, pushing his too-long greasy brown bangs over his bald spot. "I'm going to give you a list of three words to remember, and tomorrow when you come back to finish your testing, I will ask you..."

"Apple, table, penny," I said, looking over my shoulder through the tiny door window at the lady doctor who was impatiently pacing back and forth.

"What?"

"They gave me that test when we moved to South Dakota. The words were apple, table, penny."

"How old were you then?"

"Six and a half."

"I see, well your..."

The door flew open.

"I'm sorry, Harold, but you've had this room for over an hour and the rest of us need the equipment. Can you finish this in my office or go back to your own?"

"Five more minutes, please." His colors were still pulsing yellow—the more he talked to me, the faster he pulsed with excitement, just like the doctor in South Dakota. But light pink slices, like cracks in a window, appeared when the lady doctor showed up. "Lylarose, I have some blocks over on the table I'd like you to arrange in certain shapes for me. Let's go sit there."

"You never told me your three words." I wanted to help him out. That morning, when he sat in his office talking to my mother about the testing, he was trying to be nice and she cut him off without hesitation.

"If you think I'm bringing her here every day for a week you're out of your mind. It might surprise you, Dr. Greaves, but real people have lives that don't accommodate your agenda. You can have her today and tomorrow, and if that is not satisfactory, I am very sure my husband will be happy to talk to someone in the school system about your inability to properly dispense your duties. Write your report and get her back in class."

White shards of lightning shot through his whole body. He was afraid of my mother. I instantly bonded to him and took him as a friend. I didn't want him to get in trouble because he forgot to do the memory test. Friends don't let friends screw up because they have a crush on the lady doctor.

"That's okay, I think you got that one. We'll finish with the blocks and move back to my office."

"We should go to hers." I pointed to the little window where the lady doctor was holding up her wrist and tapping her watch.

"Why do you say that?"

"It's bigger, and it smells better."

"How do you..."

"Your office smells like cigarettes, and your roof has ten panels across and four panels on the side. She has those white peppermint candies in a bowl that make it smell good, and I thought maybe I could get some." Friends tell friends the truth, right? "And she has 15 panels across and 6 panels on the side."

His pink aura turned reddish brown. The yellow pulse got stronger. I guess I shouldn't have mentioned she had a bigger office than he did. As a kid, I didn't yet understand that office size meant more than floor space and ceiling panels.

"I don't smoke in my office, Lylarose." He stiffened. I might be talking too much.

"The coat that you smoke in is hanging on a hook on the back of the door, and it makes the air in the whole office smell." Definitely talking too much.

"I see. Well, let's go to Diana's office, then."

"But I didn't make the shapes for that test."

"You got that one."

He opened the door and the lady doctor flopped both arms down on her legs as she rose from the bench in the hall. Beside her sat a bored little boy in thick round glasses who looked every bit the prisoner, as I did.

"Finally!"

"I'm going to wrap up her auditory in your office. If you finish early, come and sit in," he said. Then he leaned over and whispered in her ear. "You're not going to believe this kid."

She must not have finished early (or, by the look of the gray snakes she emitted, she didn't want to deal with him) because she never came. He gave me a handful of the peppermints, and I spilled the beans about the colors, the sounds, the smells, and everything I could cough up about the way I experience the world. From my earliest days, I was a shameless candy whore.

That never changed. I'd probably wake up for the cops right now if someone waved a Snickers under my nose.

"If you tell one more person that bullshit—the only colors you're going to see are black and blue!" My mother had hissed in the moving van on our way to California. I hadn't mentioned anything about them until I told Dr. Greaves. He was my friend. He wouldn't sell me out.

"The subject has hypervigilance, heightened sensory perception—particularly olfactory and visual clarity—as well as an audiographic memory and advanced spatial and mathematical acuity. Subject is diagnosed as having optical synesthesia with similarity to the Grapheme-color spectrum indicated by visual phenomena involving colors and shapes emitting from other people. Subject would require a more intensive research methodology than two afternoons to explore the phenomena, although it appears to be a genuine and naturally occurring experience." My father read the report as we sat in audience at the kitchen table a week later.

"Jesus Christ," my mother muttered, reaching for the Bacardi cocktail she brought to the table with her. Other than when my father would announce we were moving (again), he had only called a full family meeting at the table three times: the day we received the psychologist's report, the day my parents told me I was gay, and the day I decided to go to college.

"Settle down, Peg. She's got synesthesia, not syphilis."

"There's a cure for syphilis," she retorted.

"What's syphilis?" I asked, reminding them I was still in the room. That's never a good idea.

"You told him about the colors, didn't you?" My mother snarled. "What did I tell you?"

"Not to talk about the colors."

"What did you do, Lylarose?"

"I talked about the colors."

Solemnly, I stood and pushed my chair in, looking at the arm of the couch in the living room, since it was likely to be my destiny in a few minutes. I turned to the hook by the fridge where the wooden paddle hung. Might as well get this over with.

"Sit back down, Lylarose," my father said, suppressing what I thought was a chuckle.

"I'm not getting a spanking?"

"Kid, you don't need a spanking," he sighed a weighted, weary breath. "You need a filter."

"What's that?"

"A filter is like a screen in your brain that holds back things you shouldn't say to other people. Most folks develop one as they get older, but you're going to have to get one now."

"Why do I need one?" I asked. It was an intriguing idea at the time.

"Because nice families don't have circus freaks for children!" My mother cried in a shrill shaking tone.

I nodded. I spent most of my young life hearing about what nice families didn't have or didn't do. I would be in my thirties before I figured out what they actually had and did.

My father talked to the psychologist and negotiated a truce. Dr. Greaves recommended I be placed in fourth grade so Elverta Elementary could save face with Mrs. Naughton, and my parents would allow me to go to Dr. Greaves for extensive testing at a future time "once I was settled." Of course, Dad assured my mother, the prison would be finished and we'd live in another town before that time ever came. Going to fourth grade meant I would graduate at 17 instead of 18, which wasn't unheard of, even if Barry was nearly 19 when some poor, paid-off principal handed him a diploma.

Later that night, I rose from bed and looked out into the sparkling expanse. In my mind, I connected the stars into something that looked like a giant scroll of parchment in the sky—just like the kind they wrote on in my favorite movie, the Disney "Robin Hood" with the little fox. Another constellation made a huge quill. Guiding it with my small fingers, I wrote in elegant script—for an eight-year-old—the following letter:

"Dear Dr. Greaves,

You are not my friend.

Lylarose Gentry."

It was my first break-up. Closing my eyes, I blew a small and steady breath until the letter was gone, presumably delivered by the cosmos. I was confident Dr. Greaves would get it. Didn't everyone receive star mail?

I still wasn't sure what a filter was, or how I was going to get it into my brain. Eleven months later, when I woke up in the recovery room of the Elverta Medical Annex, I knew exactly what it was, and it had been firmly sown in place. I also met a new friend. Its name was Death.

5

Siddhartha, a son dearly loved and sheltered by his kingly father, never saw sickness, death, or unhappiness until the day a chariot driver took him down the wrong road—or the right one, as the case may be. There, the prince saw the hidden ones—impoverished, sick, and dying. His fragile worldview was so shattered, he left his wife, his children, and his kingdom to wander with a group of ascetics, starving while seeking the truth. Only when he was near the end of his ability to live did he learn there was a middle way between grandiose and gaunt. Then he was the Buddha. The world did not care. The suffering did not immediately end. The crops still needed harvesting, the animals needed milking. Nothing had changed, and yet, everything was different.

I'm afraid that's what Penelope is going to figure out as she keeps her vigil by my bedside, putting everything on hold to stare at the monitor and beg each doctor who comes into the room for information, intervention, or hope. What have I discovered trapped in this comatose shell awash in a river of denial and damnation? The same lesson. There is a middle place between alive and dead, awake and asleep. I've been here since the day I looked at the open, empty eyes and stiff, unbreathing body of the first and only person who ever really loved me, and told the police officer, "Yes, that's my wife."

To the rest of the world, nothing changed, and yet, now—as the scrolling text under every news anchor's head in the state is revealing tonight—everything is different.

I have to admit I'm touched by Penelope's devotion to me in the sad state of affairs in which I find myself. It wasn't hard to follow a guru who taught in nice clothes at an upscale retreat center, filling the air with spiritual confidence and words of wisdom. It's a lot harder to place your trust and devotion in an unresponsive body with a small hole in the back and a gaping wound the size of a fifty-cent piece airing out the front. Particularly when that body is on a high-railed bed in a guarded room where the air smells like antiseptic death, and the only words are the hissing of the vent. She believes I still have something to teach her, even now. Let's hope she's right.

"Ma'am, you can't go in there! Ma'am! Ma'am!" Officer Brault shouts.

"I want to see my husb...oh. It's her."

"Ma'am!"

"It's alright, Officer Brault, she can come in. I don't mind," Penelope says, batting those soft eyes and wrapping him in an energy that looks like purple ribbons. Honestly, Pen is the only woman I've ever met who sheds such beautiful colors with her false words. With other people, their colors always showed me they were lying, and I would be on guard. Pen's are so pretty, I know she's lying, but I just don't care.

The cop looks straight into Penelope's face. He doesn't turn to stone. He turns to Jell-O, left out too long in the sun. Before Penelope can rise from her chair he retreats back to his seat outside the door.

"It was a woman problem," he'll joke to the correctional officers from the prison guarding Keith Allen's door. "So I let the women handle it. And that Ms. Fine...she's a woman who can handle it."

"Pat-ric-ia A-llen," Penelope sings, each syllable injects more acid into her smile, like botox, with a higher degree of poison. "You've come into the wrong room, dear. Which is sort of a pattern for you, isn't it? Wrong room, wrong husband, wrong life..."

"You...you...you... and," she looks at my body, "her! That lying bitch. She murdered those guards. She shot Keith."

If Pen was hooked up to this monitor instead of me, not one number would change. Her blood pressure doesn't rise, her volume doesn't increase—even her smile doesn't diminish. Her colors swirl with shiny silver lines, like a sharpened sword ready to split her opponent in two. The Penelope Fine who I always knew lurked just below the surface but had never seen— the vengeful, smart-enough-to-do-real-damage and full of unprocessed grief Penelope Fine—reveals herself in full regalia. There will be no help, self-help or otherwise, for Pat Allen today.

"Now, now, you don't have to keep getting things wrong on my account, Mrs. Allen. I already know you're a complete fuck-up as a human being. To be clear, Lylarose didn't kill anyone. I'm sure of it. Your husband, on the other hand, has two murders, a conviction for attempted rape, and countless cases of client molestation on his eternal docket. Maybe you should look in your own pitiful pocket before you start handing out verdicts."

"We're divorced," Pat says, retreating to the wall and putting her hand near the red button used to summon a nurse. I don't blame her. If I had a coiled blond cobra stretching out its venomous hood in front of me, I'd hold on to the call button, too.

"Is that why you're here? To see your ex-husband and go over some divorce decrees? I hope you aren't expecting a conjugal visit. I hear that might be off the table."

"He's still the father of my children," she whimpered.

"Bullshit."

"He is!" She fumbles for her phone as if pulling up Facebook pics of her kids with their enormously high foreheads, doughy complexion, and wide cheekbones would prove paternity and charm the serpent.

"I don't question that he planted them in your belly." Penelope advances two more steps toward her prey. The whole exchange is like watching an old episode of Marlin Perkins's "Wild Kingdom," where you're pretty sure his assistant, Jim, is about to die. "I just doubt that the reason you're running up and down the ICU looking for any room with a cop in front of it is because Daddy's late for dinner."

"You don't understand me," the prey whispered.

"I don't just understand you, I know you. I knew you the minute I saw you enter that courtroom with your drawn face and tear-swollen eyes, in your Alexander McQueen dress and dollar store soul. I saw the prosecutor lay out the series of lies you told to the police, even after Keith was arrested. I saw you justify standing by your man as countless women read harrowing victim statements of their pain. I was sitting on that shitty wooden bench holding THAT WOMAN'S hand when they showed the photographs from her wife's autopsy and described your husband's fingerprints on her throat. While Lylarose was teaching us that every human being has a core of basic goodness and deserves our compassion, even a morally bankrupt opportunistic wench like you, I watched you argue with a victim's mother over whether he 'really hurt her that much.'"

"They were trying to sue the practice! I had to protect my family. I have to look out for our money. That's all we have left." Pat spits words in her direction, flinging them like dirt at a rock fight. She knows it is not enough, but it's the only weapon she has. "And 'that woman' you're standing up for...she's a liar. She told me she was going to empower him to face what he did. She said they would work through this together. She was going to give him the courage to make a life in prison and get off the sex offender ward—so I could bring our kids to visit. The high and mighty Dr. Lylarose Gentry, guru extraordinaire, queen of compassion. Nothing but a common thug! She was..."

"She was in a secured counseling room with a lot of bullets and no cameras," Penelope says, the truth as crisp as the air from an ice cream freezer. "That's all we really know right now. I don't care what you hear. I don't care what you fantasize. I don't care what the bloggers broadcast. The only murderer in that room belonged to you, and I hope you wear him like a shroud until the day you die."

Pat manages to get almost completely to the door before the tears fall down her cheeks. I never noticed this before, not in court or in my office, when she pleaded with me to counsel her husband—the man who murdered my Marian—but Pat has the most beautiful hazel eyes. Deep with desire, haunted by regret.

"I trusted her," she whispers, pointing to my prone body.

"Well, sweetie," Penelope answers in her fake cadence, patting the extra two pounds the hospital food seems to have added to her taut tummy overnight, "I trusted Diet Coke. Looks like we've both been had."

6

My favorite word is "chiaroscuro"—the interplay between darkness and light. In a world so full of color and activity, the stark contrast of a black and white photo draws the soul and pleases it with brutal distinction. With eyes that screamed in Technicolor from the time I was born, I find respite in the simple beauty of dark lines.

"Don't tell your father you bought him socks," my mother said for the twenty-third time. Even after the pediatrician told her I can remember almost everything I hear, she repeated her edicts to me with the constancy of that watch on 60 Minutes that always seemed to be counting down the seconds of our lives. "It's a surprise."

"I won't," I said, again. It was the first Father's Day present I think either of us had actually purchased for my dad. Barry wasn't much on Father's Day, but he did Mother's Day like a champ. At the crossroads between toddler and child, I could finally run with glee to my father when he came in from work and greet him with some earth shattering news about flutterbys or what I had for lunch. He always accepted my breathless trot toward him with openness and more than a little gratitude for the fact I could walk at all.

Our family stories were filled with encounters between my mother and her beleaguered pediatrician, Dr. Ralston. I talked early and clearly, far outpacing my physical development. I couldn't walk, I couldn't seem to hold things without dropping them (that's actually still the case), and if left unattended for more than a few seconds, I would indelicately fall on my ass. My mother's favorite Dr. Ralston story happened on one of the first trips she made to discuss "the problem with Lylarose" after a cocktail party where a toddler my age ran rings around me while I sat on my rear talking nonstop. As the story goes, Dr. Ralston held me on his lap and addressed my mother in that matter-of-fact fashion men in the late 1960's used to speak to women.

"I promise you, Mrs. Gentry, you will not have to carry her to kindergarten," Dr. Ralston affirmed as I batted his arms.

"I'm not so sure about that. She crawls on her elbows everywhere she goes. It's ridiculous she isn't standing on her own yet. I don't know if she's sick or just lazy, but something is wrong with her."

I continued to flail and giggle, squirming and smiling. He wrapped a protective arm around me and launched into what my mother described as a "condescending diatribe."

"I think you need to face some facts, Mrs. Gentry. Lylarose was born six weeks premature with underdeveloped lungs and an erratic heartbeat. It is possible, well...probable... that she is going to have some cognitive...um...disabilities. Maybe even some mild retardation..."

"Tick. Tock. Tick. Tock," I gurgled at the doctor, slapping his watch with my tiny hands.

"Really," My mother said, her drawl making that a four syllable word and her fluidic deep voice turning it into a challenge.

"Tick. Tock. Two o'clock."

"What did you just say?" He asked me.

"Tick. Tock," I batted his watch, which was probably exactly like the one my father wore. "Two o'clock."

My mother reports that, at that point, the doctor looked at his watch and discovered it really was two in the afternoon. He turned sheet white, open-mouth stared at me with raised eyebrows, and stammered, "She can tell time?"

"Of course she can," my mother glowered as she pulled me off his lap. "Can't all intellectually disabled children read a watch before the age of two?"

Victoriously, she left his office and rushed home, anxious to get on the phone and tell the other company wives how "that pediatrician" got his comeuppance at the hands of her lazy, underdeveloped child.

The next day, like he did every day, my father came home for lunch at one, ate, and played with me. He picked up his briefcase at ten minutes til two, tapped his watch, and said, "Tick, tock, two o'clock. Bye, bye, Lylarose."

How my mother would cackle as she related this tale, crowing at the doctor's shocked face and the fact it just happened to be near two o'clock when he saw me. I always liked that story because it is one of the few times in her tales I actually did something right. It also reinforces what I tried to tell Marian every time she would start in on all the things I "know." Sometimes, I am smart. Mostly, I'm just lucky. What we call "genius" is usually a right place, right time kind of thing.

A few years later, after a day of Father's Day shopping, my mother was finally convinced I could keep the sock secret and started dinner. When that watch my father still wore said ten minutes after six, he pulled into the driveway.

"Don't tell him about the socks!" My mother shouted from the kitchen (twenty-four). I was still undamaged enough that I didn't wait to see what color he was before I greeted him at the door. I just ran with wild abandon, jumping in the air on the assumption he would drop his briefcase and catch me.

"Dad. Dad. Dad. Dad," I chanted. "Dad!"

"Lylarose!" he said in an equally excited tone. "What's new?"

"I'm not gonna tell you," I bubbled. When your dad is six-foot-four being lifted in his arms is a lot like ascending in a rocket ship.

"You're not gonna tell me what?"

"I'm not going to tell you I got you socks!"

"DAMMIT!"

My mother thrust her hand on her forehead. My father just laughed.

"Tell you what, Lylarose. Let's sit down in the den and you can 'not tell me' all about it."

Sometimes I'm neither smart, nor lucky, but it works out okay anyway.

⌒⌒

"We bought the socks from the blue man," I related to my amused dad. It probably wasn't the first time I'd used a color to describe someone, but for some reason it caught his attention.

"Who? A man with a blue shirt?"

"No, the blue man. He had a white shirt and this." I pointed at my dad's tie.

"His face was blue?"

"No," I frowned, squinting and trying to project a picture of the man into my father's head. To my great regret, the "brain fax" has not yet been invented. Why doesn't science ever work on important things? "The man was blue. He was nice."

"Soooooo, when you saw him, he looked blue?"

"He WAS BLUE!" I stomped my feet. "BLUE. BLUE. BLUE."

"Dinner." My mother stuck her head in the den to see the interrogation. If I blurted out about the socks, what else might I be telling him?

"Where'd you buy the socks I don't know about?" Dad asked.

"Jesus, that kid," my mother chuckled. "Harringtons, why?"

"What kind of man was the clerk?" My father's colors were a steady light green, which I hadn't yet identified as a sign of his confused, curious state, but my mother started sparking red. That color I knew all about.

"You can stick your accusations in your ear, Lawrence Gentry!"

I bit my lip as the energy in the room swelled with anger and sprayed a mist of resentment and anxiety in the air. The generator ramped into full spin, ready for an emission, or an explosion.

"All I want to know is what he looked like, Peg. It's not about that." His voice dropped two octaves and his breathing was slow and rhythmic.

"He looked like a clerk. Like a man. Like the millions of men I deal with in the world every day that I don't go home with! What do you think he looked like?" She was spitting her words forward, but backing into the hall at the same time. I could understand that. I wanted to back away, too.

"Lylarose said he was blue." Yellow flag. Situation resolving, but drive with caution.

"Lylarose says a lot of crazy shit," my mother advised him with the authority of a woman who spent every day with me, not just "after work and weekends" like my dad. "At the bowling alley, she described Phyllis as the purple lady, and in Ralston's office, she called the secretary 'green spots' and said another kid was a Creamsickle. Then he puked."

"Don't you think that's something?" He asked, his green hue returning. He looked into my eyes as if he could reverse the lens and see through them himself. Oh, if only that were possible. "What color is your mom?"

My mother's default color was a deep beige or dusky candlelight.

She sparkled pinkish-red when she talked about Barry and developed dull gray lines when my father was in the room. Don't get too comfortable, though. She could turn crimson in the blink of an eye. Hurricane Peggy always hovered at the brink, waiting for the first bad wind to blow. Still developing my color pallet, which was stuck at the primaries, I had no word for the glow that I saw around her. I tried to think of something the same color.

"Mamaw's eggs," I said. My father's mother was a subsistence farmer in Tennessee who collected eggs from her chickens each day and left them in a basket on the counter. The deep beige shells, so different from the stark white eggs we usually ate, always caught my attention. My mother opened her arms wide and flashed the same victorious smile she used on Dr. Ralston.

"I look like Mamaw's eggs. That's just perfect. If you keep talking to her, you're going to look like a bucket of coal or Jennifer's cat. She just wants attention—which you give her in spades. If you stop listening, she'll give up this load of crap and straighten up."

"I suppose," he sighed and got up for dinner, reaching his hand down to take mine as we went to the table. "She's so convinced, though. She really thinks the clerk was blue."

Silent dinner was followed by silent television watching and then silent night after my bath. I went to Dad's study, where he was working on a blueprint, to say goodnight. He put his giant hands on my shoulders and knelt down, looking again into my eyes.

"What do you see?" He whispered.

"You, Daddy!"

He laughed and shook his head. "Okay, then."

My mother tucked me into bed as she did each night, pulling the sheet as tight as she could and securing it under the mattress. It was a lot like sleeping in a straitjacket.

"I asked you to keep one secret and you couldn't do it," my mother said with a disappointed sigh.

"I'm sorry," I replied. The moment having passed, I didn't really understand what she was talking about, but those two words always seemed to go a long way with her when she got that tone.

"There's an easy way, and a hard way, Lylarose. One way or the other, you're gonna learn to keep your mouth shut."

Three moves later, two weeks after I turned nine, and eleven months past the day Dr. Greaves affirmed, to my mother's dismay and my father's satisfaction, that I really was seeing something, I learned that lesson. I learned it the hard way.

"Get your pole and a box of bobbers. Grab your jacket, I don't want you complaining about being cold the minute we hit the lake," my father said. It always took us a few months to get settled in a new place. I knew we finally arrived when my father pulled out the map to scout out fishing holes and bought a license for the two of us. I adored fishing with my dad. Partly because he would be relaxed and use the time to tell me all about birds, fish, and hydraulic prison door lock systems, and partly because my mother never went. He ruminated, and I split my concentration between listening and trying not to cast into the trees. I don't want to tell you how many bright red and white bobbers on fishing line I left hanging overhead. Let's just say, the birds must have thought there was a barbershop in the sky.

"Lyla's such a tomboy," the company wives slurred when they saw me in a baseball cap I took from my dad, carrying a tackle box and babbling about big, juicy worms.

"You can take the man out of Appalachia," my mother would

snark to her friends, "but you can't take Appalachia out of the man. Now, I discover, he's putting it into the kid, as if she doesn't have enough trouble."

The older I grew, the less the colors assaulted my senses. They went from a glowing shield of light that all but blocked a person from view to an outline of sorts I could see if I looked for it, but could block out most of the time. A vibrant emotion could make them undeniable, but for the most part, I had control. It followed the sad pattern of our culture. Children arrive in the world full of daily miracles and fiery magic. We use every means at our disposal—socialization, shame, school, prescriptions for Adderall—to stamp it out, all the while paying $150 a ticket to watch an illusionist in Vegas, until his secrets hit the internet, and we cry in despair that there's no magic in the world anymore. The colors were still with me, but I was less the circus freak my mother feared, and more the beneficiary of the insight they provided.

Climbing into the seat of the white company truck with a camper shell on the back, I looked at the scrawled fishing permit he had thrown on the dash. It was a clash of worlds when an omnipotent man like my father had to get a paper permission slip to go fishing, just like the one at school when we had to go to the bathroom. Adulthood didn't seem very different from elementary school, only they were less accepting of the powers that be. We fished for about an hour when I started a natural disaster, by wheezing.

"I'm...um...I'm..." I gasped, tapping the pockets of my jeans frantically. "I..."

"Lylarose? Where's your inhaler?" My father asked, pretty casually considering his child was holding her chest, beating at her clothing, and clearly not getting any air.

"Gl...glo...ah." I shook my head, flailing my jacket to show him it wasn't in my coat or the pockets of my jeans. My mind's eye showed me the exact location of my inhaler. The kitchen counter, beside the bowl of peaches, underneath the cabinet holding the plates Barry made in ceramic class that I wasn't allowed to touch. At home. "Gluh..."

Gasping and frantic for any air, the warm sun of the afternoon dimmed as the whole world narrowed around me, loud ragged constriction of my lungs howling out a hurricane warning that I couldn't clearly hear over my desperate attempts to stay alive.

"Glove box! Don't go anywhere," he said, finally catching the fear in my eyes as the rapid inhalations made me light headed. Don't go anywhere? The only place I was about to go was the afterlife. Since we didn't believe in heaven, the river Styx would be my destination, I assumed. Panting and nearing the pass-out line, I shook my jacket pocket. A half-eaten cinnamon Jolly Rancher stick and seventeen cents fell out on the ground by the worm bucket. Great. I'll at least have some coins for the ferryman. Maybe if he liked to fish, the worms would get me a better seat.

"It's not there!!!" My father shouted as he slid back down the hill with a bottle of coke and a screwdriver in his hands. My mom was right. Brilliant people can be very stupid. "What do we do?"

I held up one finger on my right hand, the left still massaging my chest and trying to get the elephant to move. Then two. Then three. "Cou....cou..."

"Cou? Count. Count to three?" He looked around to see if there were any campers, or magicians, in the recreation area but alas, none were to be found. "Okay, okay. One, two, three!"

Presto chango! I can breathe! HOONNNKKK! Oh wait, I'm dying from lack of oxygen.

I shook my head no. If I was going to live, I would have to take matters into my own trembling hands. I grabbed him by the arms and made him look me in the eyes. I mouthed words as best I could, trying to get him to say them aloud in a breathable rhythm that was less of an atonal blues riff and more like a waltz. Time for the little magic I had left. I silently said the incantation in my head and nodded with the beat.

One...two...three...

Breathe...with...me

One...two...three...

You...and...me...

Black hair to black.

Blue eyes to blue.

Gentry to Gentry.

Father to daughter.

"One..." I mouthed. I waited two beats. "Two..."

He caught on. Finally.

"One," he said with me, picking up the waltz. "Pause, pause, two, pause, pause, three."

Yes! I nodded emphatically, taking the biggest swell of air I could get yet.

"One...two...three..." He said again, his attention locked on target. Over and over, he repeated the numbers as I steadied my breath to his rhythm, finally catching an even flow until my lungs released.

"I'm okay," I whispered, a tear from the breathless surge stinging the corner of my eye. He was still chanting. I had to pick up the volume, "Dad! I'm okay."

"Where'd you learn that?"

"The babysitter in Marfa. She used to do it with me when I couldn't breathe."

"Good memory. Thank heaven for that."

He leaned back and used his hand to put his sweaty mop of black bangs back in place. I heard him gasp as if he too had been holding his breath. We sat there, just breathing, for a time. It was one of the most spiritually connected moments I've ever experienced. The calm before the storm, as it were. Eventually, he spoke.

"My god, Lylarose. How could you forget your inhaler?"

"It's in the kitchen. I forgot to pick it up. I'm sorry."

"You should be. You gave me quite a scare! Seeing as that medicine is required to save your life, I think you're smart enough to keep it with you, young lady."

"Yes, sir," I said in a husky whisper. I looked down at the Coke and screwdriver, then slowly shifted my eyes back to his. I was not going to be lectured on survival intelligence by a man who brought those items to an asthma attack. He nodded and laughed.

"Okay, you're right. We need to have some kind of system in place to make sure this doesn't happen again," he said. When I tell this part of the story (the only part I ever tell, until now) to my friends who also have parents who are engineers, it brings hearty laughter. Leave it to an engineer to come out of a medical emergency talking about a "system." I've often thought we needed a Twelve Step Group—Adult Children of Engineers. We'd all show up to meetings with duct tape, a spreadsheet, two screwdrivers, and string.

"There is supposed to be an inhaler in the glove box. Your car and Mom's. But the one in Mom's expired, so I think she took the one out of yours."

"Why didn't she just buy another? We used to have a box of those things around."

"I dunno. That was South Dakota. I don't think the store here sells them in boxes. Mom doesn't like to shop for them a lot."

"Well there has to be a pharmacy that can sell us more than one at a time."

"Denise Gibson has asthma. You can ask her dad the next time he comes home for lunch with you."

"Is Denise in your grade?"

"She is now." Moving to new places where everyone has lived there forever and already has established "best friends" meant the prison trash kids were pretty much stuck with each other. Projects would take some away earlier or bring them in later, but we were just as locked together in this life as the company wives, only less boozy and hair sprayed.

"What did you mean by the next time he comes home with me? Phil Gibson doesn't come home for lunch with me."

"Oh," I shrugged. "I thought he came home with you because he was at the house before I got home from school yesterday."

"You saw him?" During the asthma attack, I couldn't see colors because I couldn't see much of anything. But now my dad's were getting stronger, and the red dots I thought were from our scare were growing. I kinda wished we could go back to just breathing.

"No, sir."

"Then how do you know he was there?"

"The house smelled like that beer. Not the kind you drink that smells like car fluid, the kind he brings over that smells like bread dough."

"You mean Coors?"

"I dunno. It's the one you can't buy here. It smells like the bread Mamaw makes before it's all the way baked."

"Coors." In the days before you could get Coors everywhere, Phil Gibson made quite a profit hauling cases of the stuff in the trunk of his car. His sister lived in Denver so he had a ready excuse if he got stopped. A lot of the men in the company were willing to pay good money for a box of that beer. I don't think my dad ever paid though. Phil just gave him some because my dad was his boss.

"So you think he was there when you were at school because the house smelled like Coors?" So much red seeping into the mix. Shut up, Lylarose. For the love of Hera, shut up.

"I thought he came home for lunch with you because the smell was really strong and Mom was deep yellow, which she usually is when she's...um...well...been with...people."

"Your mother was what?"

"Deep...um...happy. Just really happy."

"What was she doing when you came home?"

"Laundry."

"On a Friday afternoon?" True to engineer ethics, the Gentry house had a standard laundry day. It was Tuesday. "Was she washing her clothes?"

I shook my head.

"Your clothes?"

Another shake. He was leaning close to me, his face flushing to match the outline emanating from his skin.

"Towels?"

"Maybe."

"Yes or no, Lylarose," he demanded. "Did you see her with the laundry or not?"

"Yes, sir. She was folding."

"Was it bathroom towels?"

"No, sir."

"Then what was she folding?"

"Sheets."

"From our bed?" There were no other colors now, just red. Dark, brown, day-old-blood-red.

"No, sir. The ones in Barry's room."

"I see."

Barry's room was already a sore spot with my father. Every house we moved into after Barry left home had a room dedicated as a guestroom solely for him to visit. Except, he never came. When she begged, cried, and bribed, he always found a reason he couldn't make it. Still, the room was full of stale air, empty dressers, and a made bed. If guests stayed with us, they sometimes got to stay in Barry's room, but my mother really had to like them.

"Can you breathe now?" He said, already standing and reeling in the fish hook that lost its bait long ago. I nodded, pulling in my little bobber I'd managed to cast at least ten feet from shore. I had been sure that cast was going to net a big one. I nodded to show I felt better.

"Get your jacket on, and get in the truck. We're going home."

He drove in silence, an agitated maroon ball, taking corners too fast and hitting the brakes only when we got right up to a stop sign. I pressed my body as close to the door of the truck as I could get. I'm surprised I don't have the Ford insignia permanently burned into my skin. We pulled into A&W Root Beer and the truck screeched to a halt. Back then, it was one of the only places with a drive-through window.

"One Junior Burger and a root beer," my father said in a dangerous monotone, throwing some cash at the girl in the window, his mind clearly elsewhere. I thought of mentioning that Mom liked cheese on her Momma Burger and onion rings instead of fries, but one look at his red face told me it was not a good time to be helpful. Mom was on her own. Turns out, he didn't order for her anyway.

We pulled into the driveway, and my father parked the truck sideways, blocking her car in the double-sized concrete slab. I got out and went to get the tackle box from the back. He stopped me.

"Leave it," he said. He pushed the A&W bag into my hands. "Go to your room and eat."

"In my bedroom?" I asked, aghast. There were a lot of rules about food in the house I was raised in, and not eating in my room was one of the first.

He put his hand on my shoulder and squeezed just hard enough for me to focus on his short, clipped words. "Take this bag. Go to your bedroom. Do NOT come out until I call for you. Do you understand me? Do. Not. Come. Back. Out."

"Yes, sir."

I started toward the door, but he was going to the side of the house where the trash can was. Stupid asthma. We were having a great day and nothing had made any sense since that first honking gasp.

"Can I get my inhaler?" I called toward him.

"I'll bring it to you. Go to your room. NOW!"

Not known for speed or agility, I managed to break an Olympic sprint record on my way down the hall. I sat on my bed holding the fries as carefully as I could, so I wouldn't drop any and get a grease stain on my bedspread. My father opened the door. He slammed my inhaler down on the student desk.

"Here. I don't care what you hear. I don't care what you want. Don't come out of this room, Lylarose." He was in such a hurry he didn't even give me a chance to say I understood. He reached for the doorknob. In his hand, the same one he had my inhaler cradled in, was a crushed beer can that read "Coors."

Blue. The luminous silky blue of the midsummer sky, wrapped around my small battered body like a blanket, enveloping me. My screaming had stopped and the stark red blood pouring over me was covered by swaths of blue. I began to levitate, the blanket of blue locked around me like my mother's tucked-in sheets. There was so much noise, and yet no sound. I couldn't hear, I couldn't see. I floated through the air in that beautiful blue. It was, without question, the most peaceful, transcendent event of my entire life. I was completely calm, free, and warm. So very warm.

"This is death," was my last cogent thought. "I'm so happy it's warm."

Bright, searing white light in a sharp room full of angles and tile. Hissing machines and cacophonous beeping. People scurrying around speaking in hushed voices. The clacking of three-ring binder clips right by my ear as the light moved out of my eyes.

"Sorry about that, honey," a melodious female voice said before another clack. "Didn't mean to shine that in your face."

The clacking stopped and my eyes closed again. I retreated into the darkness looking for my lost blue.

"She's waking up, get her parents and the doctor," the voice said again.

Forcing my eyes open against the pressure, like they taught me to do in swim lessons, I broke the surface and emerged, feeling a rush of cold air. I heard the doctor before I saw him. He had a deep voice, heavy with concern but lilting with happy relief.

"Lylarose? Lylarose? Can you hear me?"

I nodded. I tried to lift my hand to block out the terrible light, but it seemed to weigh fifty pounds. I couldn't move it. I squinted against the light. The room smelled of pine cleaner and latex. This was not heaven, the underworld, or the river Styx. I shivered in the brutal air. I was alive. I turned my head to see the form of a person standing over my bed fussing with my rhinoceros arm.

"You're a lucky little girl," he said.

"Phil Gibson! Oh my god, Peggy!" I heard my father shouting as I took another small bite of my Junior Burger. I had only managed to get half of it down before the quiet murmuring turned to full-scale warfare.

"There wasn't anyone else," my mother screamed back. "Get your head out of your blueprints, for once, and look around this shithole, Lawrence. It's worse than Marfa! I needed someone who bathes on a weekly basis!"

"You need a shrink!" My father retorted. "It would have been bad enough if you picked someone from another department, but my own employee? I'm supposed to look at him every day knowing he fucked my wife! How the hell can I have any authority with a man who's got nothing but your open legs on his mind? Do you know what you've done?"

Something hit the wall. I didn't know if it was glass or ceramic. I didn't know who threw it, but the shattering echoed through the house with enough force to stop my appetite. I put the burger in its bag and placed it on my desk. Unfortunately, while the burger didn't get much play, I managed to drain the root beer.

"Can you hear yourself? This isn't about you, Lawrence. The whole world does not revolve around your damn job! Why do you think I have these needs? I'm nothing but another fucking tool in your box. I schmooze the bosses, feed the wives, bowl with clients, and keep this place a palace so you can get ahead. It's always about you!"

"You might be a tool, Peggy, cause you sure fixed us this time!"

He shouted. The sharp stinging in my midsection increased with the volume of my parent's blustery exchange. I was trying to hear the fight, but the only thing I could pay attention to with any surety was the fact I really needed to pee. My mind, traitor that it is, aided my predicament by tracing my day in reverse. I didn't pee at A&W, I didn't go at the lake, in fact, the last time I used the bathroom was before I got in the truck to go fishing. That was a juice, a coke, and a large root beer ago.

My mother let out some kind of primal roar, louder than the tornado sirens when they lived in Oklahoma, and there were more shatters of glass against the wall. Hurricane Peggy hit with maximum force. I searched the room frantically, looking for a jar or bottle or something. My room, subject to regular maternal inspections, didn't have much in it, or anything I disliked enough to want to pee in. And, let's face it: if eating in my bedroom was against the rules, peeing in it was definitely across the line. I had to get to the bathroom.

"You fucking egghead!" My mother was yelling. I pressed against the door trying to figure out where they were in the house. "I'm not a slut. You're the company whore here, Larry! You!"

Crash, crash. Two more items bit the dust. I closed my eyes and brought up mental images of the house. If I could figure out what she was throwing, I could figure out where she was throwing it from. The china hutch was in the dining room but she wouldn't break her mother's dishes over Phil Gibson. More ceramics from Barry's high school art class were in his room, but there's no way she was wrecking a treasure from The Precious. In the living room, we had a shelf with vases from the Marshall Islands where they lived when Barry was small. It had to be them. If I stuck to the side hall, I could run past the door and they'd never see me. I really needed to go.

I doubled over and grabbed my crotch with one hand and the

doorknob with the other. Carefully, so gently, like a person putting the top piece on a house of cards, I turned the knob and cracked the door. The rumbling of my father's "rational voice" bubbled like a stream and made a smooth, hypnotic wave for my mother to follow. They had passed the "whose fault it was" part of the fight and seemed to have moved to the "what do we do?" time. Surely, it was safe to pee now. Well, actually, it didn't matter if it was safe or not. Time was up. It wasn't a question of whether I was going to pee. It was just a question of where.

I slipped into the hallway, making sure to close my bedroom door so it would look like I was in there. Positive they were still in the living room surveying the broken vases, I took a few quiet steps past the door and put my back against the wall. That was when I saw it. A shattered ceramic mug that once said, "Mom" laying in the hall. I looked over my head to see the mark on the wall where it hit. The person doing the throwing had been my father. What better way to hurt the woman who hurt you than to desecrate the shrine of The Precious?

I realized if they fought in Barry's room, they would be facing me. I raised my eyes. There was my father, leaning up against the empty dresser. I saw my mother's leg—she was sitting on the bed. I tried to turn to go back to my room, but my father shifted and looked straight at me. There were tears on his cheek. I froze.

"Lylarose!" He snarled, wiping his eyes. His hand was on his belt buckle before I could get a signal from my brain to actually reach my legs. "I told you to stay in that room!"

"I...uh...I..." I heard the awful jangling of that buckle and the swip, swip as the belt slid through the loops of his pants. A flood of urine ran down my legs. "Noooooooooooo."

He stopped long enough to see the puddle gathering on the floor beneath me.

"God. Damn. It!" He screamed. I ran down the hall as fast as I could, and hit the closed bedroom door with a thud. Before I could get the knob to turn, he was on me.

Heavy full-armed lashes of the belt tore into my skin. I whelped and got down, curling up as the stinging leather bit my flesh over and over. I tucked my legs in, welts already rising on my calves. Lash after lash, the leather smacking me echoed like the snapping of trees being broken by marauding giants. I put my arm up to shield my face from the onslaught. A clunk, not a slap connected with the bone of my wrist. It was the buckle. He was so enraged, he hadn't folded the belt, or managed to grab it properly. He was beating me with the buckle end. I had to stop this.

"Dad!" I cried out. I shifted, exposing my unbeaten side so I could see his face. There was no one in his eyes. Just the anger of a thousand bees built up behind them, mindlessly lashing out until the stinging stopped. If I could grab the belt, I could show him he had the wrong end. Biting my lip, a lash hitting the back of my thigh with enough force to push me against the door, I reached up to grab it just as he began a furious downswing. The heavy metal of the buckle smashed into my palm. I did it! I grabbed the buckle. Just as I curled my finger around it to get a better grip he pulled his arm back in a rage. He was six-foot-four, 250 pounds, running on pure adrenalin and standing over me. I was nine.

The buckle sliced through my finger like the ripping of a T-shirt. My mother might be a category 4 hurricane, but at that moment, I let out a cry of pain so jagged and raw the actual core of the earth imploded and every volcano spewed lava over the whole world. Blood poured down my arm as I shrieked, the universe going instantly dark.

"Lawrence!" My mother's shrill voice was the last thing I heard as I slumped against the door. Then it was blue. The whole world was blue. Death was blue. It embraced me like a lover. It promised me for-ever. But I left it at the altar, saying only that we could be friends, and walked back down the aisle into the bright white light of my first life.

I was a lucky little girl.

"I've seen bicycle chains tear open a hand before, but this one left an exceptionally smooth cut, and enough of your finger to be re-at-tached," the surgeon said, showing my parents the stitching along the meat of my third finger as the nurse prepared to put on a new dress-ing. "Fortunately for your daughter, the chain must have been pretty clean because the wound shows no signs of infection."

My mother cooed at him, giving a shot of pure, 100 percent proof Southern charm. "We feel so fortunate that you were the sur-geon on call. You've done an excellent job with our Lylarose."

He smiled at her. They always smiled at her. My dad just looked down at me and winked.

"As for you, Miss Lylarose," the doctor said, with that adult-to-child superiority that made me want to sit up in the bed and stab him in the eye with the bendy straw from my water cup, "the next time you want to check the chain on your bicycle, you let your dad help."

"I sure will, sir," I said with a big smile, playing the rube in an Andy Griffith sitcom. Not only did I wake up with a filter that would hold all of my insights inside my head where they couldn't hurt any-one (especially me), I also got a bag of masks so I could wear whatever face pleased power, just like my mother's. Later in life, that bag would get me into the Maryland State Penitentiary at Bowles Pass with a plan and a weapon.

I wasn't shocked by how easy it was for my parents to pass off a wounded child, covered in urine, welts, and blood, as a bicycle accident. Elverta was a small town that needed the prison, at the price the company quoted them, and if it meant turning a blind eye to an indiscretion, well then that would have to be done. In fact, we were prison trash, and we'd pack our trucks and be gone as soon as the building inspector placed his seal. Why get involved? It was easier to agree it was a random accident. If it was really child abuse, let the next town deal with it.

It wasn't what they believed, but what they didn't believe that made my heart hurt late at night when the masks were off and the filter loosened. They didn't believe an intervention into the middle class vagabond family was worth the risk. They didn't believe the system designed to protect me would do anything more than send a social worker, take a statement, and at best, recommend my father take a six-week class on anger management. They didn't believe getting involved would make a difference.

They'd rather cling to the myth of bicycle accidents, the power of a fifteen-minute social service interview, and the assurance that once they grow up, the kids can sort all this out by themselves. They'll hold that thought until a New York lawyer and his battered wife beat their adopted daughter to death in a ratty apartment no one would have ever guessed was theirs. Then the city will regretfully ask, "Where was social services?" and file the issue back inside the "What is wrong with people?" folder for later review.

We fight all the time over what people believe. It's what we don't believe that's killing us.

"When you're discharged we'll go home, get back to normal, and we won't speak of this again," was my mother's final edict as she pulled the top blanket back to re-tuck the hospital sheet. I struggled to get my good hand out from under the restraining linen and reach for the blanket.

"You want the blanket?" My father asked, secretly untucking the sheet my mother used to lock me in the bed.

I nodded, straining again to pull it around me. "I'm so cold."

"Well, that's normal," he chuckled, lifting my cast and placing the blanket underneath it. He smiled one of his best smiles, as pure relief shone from his weary eyes. At that moment, I realized how scared he must have been all along. That evening, when my mother left me in his care to go bowling with the company wives, my father pulled the chair close to my bed and pointed it toward the door so he would see if anyone was coming in. I'd had food, soda, pills, and vitals. If there was ever a safe time to clear the air—this was it.

"What happened last Saturday," he started, his head pointed in my direction but his eyes made contact with everything in the room but me. "That went wrong."

That was it. It's not the only time I've heard that sentence. When a cell block foundation cracked under the weight of the girders—"foundation went wrong." When the electronic door locks didn't synchronize so as one side of the room was locking inmates in, the other side was letting them out—"doors went wrong." It was Lawrence Gentry-speak for "I'm sorry" or "I'm responsible"—"That went wrong."

I nodded, eyes focused on my casted hand with my third finger prominently braced and sticking out (boy, did I have fun with that—I got to give everyone the bird for almost four months, and there was nothing anyone could do about it). I wasn't as disappointed in his reckoning as I expected to be. What was he going to tell me that would make this okay? There were no magic words to wipe away the stark reality of the experience. So, "that went wrong" would have to do.

"Your mother and I have done a lot of talking," he said, more confident in where this conversation was going than where it came from. That's something you learn when you move all the time. It doesn't matter how much you love or hate a place, you'll soon be somewhere else. So, move forward. "We've made some changes."

"Changes?"

"I put in for a new project. Remember that special kind of plastic-glass I told you about, the one they are going to make entire pods out of? I'm going to head up the first see-through cell block. How's that for cool?"

I smiled and nodded for him. Our lives had been dictated by the company for so long it never dawned on me his career ladder wasn't the most important topic of this or any conversation. "When are we moving?"

"Next week," he said. "So you won't have to go back to Elverta Elementary, but you will be in 4th grade in Colorado."

"Colorado? Is it nice?"

"Very. Good fishing there." He paused and looked down at the cast. "When you're ready, of course."

"Will Mom like it?"

He took a deep breath. "That's the other change. Part of the reason your mom is...well...unhappy...sometimes is that she never really gets time to herself. So she's going to start taking long vacations during the summer months, and maybe some weekends through the year as well. You'll stay on Mamaw's farm when you're not in school. Mom just needs a little space to…uh…be herself."

"Alone?"

"Well, she might make some friends on her adventures. But, it's her time, and she can do whatever she likes. I'll be working, which is what I like, and you'll be helping Mamaw, Uncle Luther, and Bud with the farm. You're gonna learn so many good things."

His body surged with bright energy. He really wanted me to love this plan, even though it wouldn't make much sense to me until I took Intro to Human Sexuality in college. Then I realized my parents were secretly pioneering an open marriage long before something like that had a name (nice families don't screw around!). I just hoped the plan was going to make my parents happy, and every summer, I got to be in the safest place in the world—my grandmother's farm. So—Colorado, or bust!

I can't say I noticed my mom being much happier as she unpacked the barrels and set up the big new house, which had both a "Barry room" and a standard guestroom. What I did notice, particularly as I went through being "the new girl" with her casted middle finger stuck in mid-air, was the lack of other prison trash kids. It was a small project, and we were there very early. When the crew started arriving and the company wives came over to meet my mom and see the house, I didn't recognize anyone. They were a whole new crew. We never saw Phil Gibson again. It was the ultimate proof of their power. If you made my parents really mad—they could (and would) make you disappear.

I didn't tell my father, but I went through some changes too. I stopped chattering happily about the colors, smells, numbers of items in a random box, and sharing casual observations about everyday life. I embraced my new filter as a safety device for everyone around me and became a silent connoisseur of life. When I stopped talking, except for when I was asked a question or was with someone I truly trusted, an amazing thing happened. Everyone started talking to me.

Another thing occurred on the day that started out as a fishing trip and ended with me blanketed in the warm blue cocoon between worlds. I lost my fear of death. I have never courted death. I don't long for it. I don't set an extra plate at my table and beg it to drop by for dinner. But I've always known, when death comes to me at last, it will find a friend.

7

"If they want their damn money back, give them the money, Topaz. I can't do everything. I'm here with Lylarose and trying to get the police to clear this up. You are going to have to handle the center. That is your job, isn't it?"

"Should I refund the ongoing memberships, or just the people who came for the retreat with her this weekend? Are we canceling the rest of the retreats? Should I put something on the website?"

"Why don't you just write 'We regret to announce our guru is in a coma and has been falsely accused of multiple murders, so 'Meditation Monday' will be postponed."

"You're not helpful."

"Then stop calling me!"

"So, it's yes to anyone who wants a refund for Virga memberships or future classes, and no to changing the website until we...um until we know...?"

"Until we have the police statement clearing her of this. Don't jump ship. I need you."

"I'm not. I know she, I mean, she doesn't even..."

"If this drags on I'll get my PR guy to write something for the site until it gets settled. Just smile, give the refunds, and Namaste your little ass off. This will pass."

"What if someone wants a refund from a class they've already taken?"

"If they want money back for wisdom she already gave them, tell them 'no'—because they clearly didn't get any."

"What do I tell them about the crime tape all over Lyla's office, and there's still cops..."

"Sir! STOP where you are!" Officer Brault's raised voice shreds Penelope's ability to think strategically.

"Gotta go, Topaz. You're the Director of Virga. Direct."

A distinct Appalachian twang far more annoyed and real than anything Pen could produce comes from outside the door. My heart jumps when I hear it, although the monitor doesn't seem to change.

"I showed you my ID. Do you need a blood sample? I'm going to see my niece, and I won't be stopped. Not by you. Not by anyone."

Penelope walks heel-toe, letting the fancy shoes give both cadence and warning of her approach. "What's all this noise?"

"Sorry, Ms. Fine. This gentleman wants access to Dr. Gentry and I was explaining we have had to increase security. After Mrs. Allen got in there, it was decided we need to tighten control."

"Pat Allen couldn't find the right room, the right man, or her ass with both hands. This gentleman..." Penelope gestures toward the rumpled old man in worn jeans and a gray flannel long sleeve shirt over an old school undershirt. He looks and smells like he'd driven all night just to get here in time. "...is clearly in the right place."

Without waiting for Officer Brault to agree, she motions for the man to come into the room.

"Thank you, ma'am," he says, his sweet voice and backwoods manners lighter and higher pitched than I remember. "I'm Bud Gentry, Lyla's uncle."

"Of course you are," she replies, running her fingers through my raven hair, revealing the emerging white strands underneath the surface, and looks up at his salt and pepper ten dollar haircut. His eyes, calm as the deep blue sea, twinkle when he sees me.

"My daughter, Tammy, paid cash money for some DNA type test

to trace our family history. They said we originated from Galway, Ireland. It's a seaport town. It said Galway folk have hair of black, eyes of blue, and are salty as hell. I don't know that I believe all that. I've nary gone out of Tennessee, except to take my family to Myrtle Beach, but that's what they said for the money."

"I wouldn't doubt it for a minute, Mr. Gentry."

"You can call me Bud, Miss..."

"Fine. Ms. Fine. And you can call me Pen. That's what Lylarose calls me."

"You're her..." Bud gestures across my body and hers with vague broad movements in a hysterical attempt to nonverbally ask if we are lovers.

"STUDENT!" Penelope overcorrects him. "I am one of her students, and I don't know if she'd agree, but I think of myself as her true friend."

I agree, Pen. I do agree. I'm sorry I can't tell you that now. I'm sorry you may regret it.

Bud slides a chair close to the metal rail of the bed and puts his hand on mine. His fingers are soft, not at all like the calloused farmer's hands he used to have. His touch though, still filled with love. A circle of Caribbean blue emits from his body and rolls over me like waves gently lapping up on a beach.

"What does the doc say?" He asks, glancing at Officer Brault.

"Wait and see. That's all any of them will commit to at this point. She lost a lot of blood and required extensive surgery. Now, it's just a matter of time. She might wake up; she might never. The longer she's out, the less likely she is to come back."

Bud nods and squeezes my hand. How I ache to squeeze back.

"If anyone can defy the odds, it's our Lyla."

There's a tear perched on the corner of Penelope's eye. She

catches it with her finger and pushes it away before it can smear her expertly made face.

"I'm afraid Dr. Gentry never spoke much about her family. It's really nice to meet you."

"Lyla never spoke much, period," he says, leaning back in his chair, moving his hand to my leg, but never letting go. "She could listen, though. Boy howdy, she could hear things no one alive could make out. Heart things, you know?"

"Oh, I know," Pen chuckles.

"I only ever saw Lyla in the summers when she was just a young thing. Her momma would drop her off each June and pick her up mid-August. My brother, Lawrence, her daddy, stayed home to work. We used to laugh because Lyla was such a city girl. She had nice clothes and fancy sneakers, and her momma said she had to eat Wonder Bread bought from the store. Ma Gentry always called it 'square bread' because we only ate cornbread from the pan and the loaves we got at the Winn Dixie looked like boxes to us. Well, Ma would send Luther out to get one loaf of that square bread for Lyla, and make sure her momma could see she had it. Then, when her momma left the next day, Lyla would say, 'Y'all eat that—I want some cornbread' and all the cousins would dig in on that square bread. It was like a dessert.

"Lyla was a touched little girl, and I mean that in a good way. She could feel things, appreciate things, we never noticed. She'd talk about how the jars of canned food from the pantry hissed when Ma Gentry opened them and say they were whispering secrets the food had stored up. Every time it rained, she'd get into bed, even if it was noon, and listen to the rain hitting that old tin roof on the farmhouse. She said it was nature's music and the prettiest song she knew. She could pull beans for two hours and tell you exactly how many were in the bucket. She never seemed to think much on herself, but I can tell you all of us on the farm thought the world of Lyla."

"All of us at Virga do, too." Pen chokes, looking at the ceiling to keep another threatening tear at bay.

"It's because of Lyla my wife and I ever got together. You see, Cindy worked in Mountain City as a teller at the bank. No one ever accused the Gentry family of having much money, but we did get funds from selling crops and a government check for my Uncle Seth who got wounded in the war, so I would go to the bank at least twice a month. If I could manage it, I'd surely end up in Cindy's line. I was taken with her from the moment I saw her, but I was a farm boy, one of those 'Gentrys,' and I didn't think she'd have anything to do with the likes of me. I'd talk to her and say how nice she looked or remark on her pretty handwriting, but I was too shy for much else. Every night, I'd pray to God she would notice me and that she wouldn't have some other man's ring the next time I went to town.

"One day, after chores were done, I saw Lyla sitting on a rock by the trickling branch that ran behind the barn with a blanket wrapped around her shoulders. I asked her what she was doing, and she said she was having a picnic and listening to the water bubble over the rocks. She said the branch was telling her a story. I sat down beside her and got real quiet. I didn't hear nothin' but the same old water trickling I'd heard my whole life. Then Lyla said, 'Uncle Bud, whatever you want—I think it's waiting on you.'

"She couldn't have known about Cindy. I didn't tell nobody 'cause I didn't want my brothers to tease me. If anyone else had said it, I'd just laugh and push them in the water, but not Lyla. She was different. I sat there with her, listening to the branch, and I was overcome by the spirit. Now, I was raised in the church, but I've not been much of a holy man. Still, it was like the spirit was just there with us.

I knew Lyla's folks didn't cotton to religion, but I couldn't help myself.

"'Will you pray with me, Lyla?' I asked her.

"'I've never done that, Uncle Bud. You'll have to show me how.'

"'Oh, it's easy,' I said. 'You hold my hands, and close your eyes, and I'm gonna ask God for something, and in your head, you just tell God that you agree. 'Cause the Bible says if two or more agree, it will happen.'

"'Okay,' she said. I took her little hands in mine, and I prayed the Jesus out of that stream. I told God how much I loved Cindy and how I'd give anything if she'd love me back, and I asked God to make it so. Lyla nodded the whole time. When I was done praying, I let go of her hands, and she just looked at me with them bright eyes peeking out from under her bangs. Then she stood up.

"'What do we do now?' She asked me.

"'Wait and find out if Cindy loves me.'

"'Where is she?'

"'Oh, she's in Mountain City at the bank,' I said.

"'Let's go ask her.' Lyla was ready to get in the car.

"'No, no! We can't go askin' something like that. That's not how it works. We just gotta wait and see if something happens. It's not instant, Lyla. It's like if you see the bus and you want to catch it. You pray to God to catch the bus, and you watch to see if it stops so you can get on.'

"She crossed her little stick arms and looked me straight in the eye. She said, 'If you pray to catch a bus, Uncle Bud, you should run.'

"The more I thought about it, the more right that sounded. So I gathered up some money around the house and went to the bank to deposit it. When I got to Cindy, I was so overwhelmed I could barely breathe. I just kept thinking of what Lyla said. So I told Cindy there was a pretty little picnic spot by a branch on our farm, and my young niece says if you listen real close, the water will tell you a story. I said if she had some time and didn't have some other fellow needing her attention, I'd surely like to take her there.

"Cindy smiled as bright as a full moon. She said, 'I've been hoping for so long to do that very thing.'

"Forty years, three children, and six grandkids later, we still stop by the old farm house now and then and go listen to that branch. I don't know what story it told Lyla, but the story it tells me and Cindy is our own."

Sweet silence fills the room for nearly five minutes before Pen speaks.

"That's a beautiful story," Pen says, putting her hand on his, on me.

I summon all the strength my still body could offer and send a thought to her with enough power behind it to shatter concrete.

"If you use this story in one of your books, I will kill you, and I won't need a gun to do it."

I don't know if she hears me, but she swells with violet affection and goldenrod respect for him. Let's hope it holds past the afternoon.

"That man, the one who they say Lyla... he's the man who killed her...um..."

"Yes. She had been meeting with him every two weeks for a few months as his spiritual counselor. She wanted to use her gifts to get him to understand his crimes, and himself. She was trying to help him. Like she did you. Like she did me. She left the center with her mala, her singing bowl, and her prayer shawl. It wasn't any different than any other day at Virga, until the police cars showed up."

For the first time since he entered my hospital room, his colors of love and concern transforming the institutional blank walls into a garden, my Uncle Bud takes his hand from me and wraps Penelope's tapered fingers in his warm embrace, one hand on each side of hers. He's the same uncle who could slaughter a pig one moment and carry a butterfly on his arm the next. He embodies the basic goodness of the simple, loving family my father's job and my mother's disdain kept at a distance. He is every pleasant memory from my first life, wrapped up in an aged, confused, heartsick man.

"Pen," he whispers, almost reverently. "Did she do this?"

For the first time in her long vigil, tears flow freely down Penelope's face, taking at least $200 of makeup with them. She doesn't wipe them. She doesn't blink them away. She drops her shield just long enough to put her arms around my uncle and hug him as hard and long as I would if I could move. With her tears, truth falls from her lips.

"I don't know."

8

Keith Allen sits straight up on his side of the yellow line that runs across the floor, the table, and the walls. There are always a few beads of sweat on his forehead right below the combed-over glob of moist black-brown hair. A couple more gather around the cheesy moustache that would have made him a god in the eighties, particularly when he told the ladies about his waterbed and Beta video tapes. Now, his upper lip looks like a grease stain on a yellowed tablecloth someone tried to hide with a potted plant. He isn't sweating because he's nervous. You'd have to have a conscience for that. He's sweaty because the air vent on the inmate's side of the yellow line doesn't quite work, although the visitor's side cools just fine.

He lifts his hands, showing them to the guard, then places them palms down on the table. I don't have that requirement, but I place mine flat on my side of the line as well. It creates a sense of similarity, thus inducing trust. He's a therapist, too. He knows exactly what I'm doing. He imagines we are chess opponents, equally matched. He must think I'm the white side, because he always lets me start first. Little does he know, while he's been moving his bishop in position to protect the king, I've been sacrificing my pawns, one by one, to open a pathway for my queen to go straight for his jugular. No castling. No long diagonals. No check. Just checkmate, you son of a bitch. The king is dead. Long live the queen.

"How's your world?" I ask.

"How's yours?" He replies, knowing the vague question is simply a counselor's opening move.

"Busy. I've got two new students interning at the center, and I'm writing an article on the healing powers of certain chants to combat insomnia."

"Losing sleep, Dr. Gentry?" His eyes sparkle. He's drawn me out.

"Sometimes. Most nights I drop into bed after evening meditation so tired my eyes close before I hit the pillow. Other nights, not so much."

"What do you do on those other nights?" He whispers, as if the guard standing with his back against the wall on my side of the line can't hear anything below the volume of a jet airplane. "Do you kiss her pillow and tell her goodnight? Do you reach down between your legs? Do you touch yourself, the way she touched you? Do you moan her name in the moonlight as your fingers dance in little circles, putting more and more pressure until you feel her right there with you, pressing you down on the mattress?"

I yawn. "You're making me sleepy, Keith, with all this bed talk. I don't know what you have to do for the rest of the day, but I have no time for a nap. Let's meditate, shall we?"

I turn my hands on the table so my palms face up. The singing bowl mallet, a decorated cylinder concealing my perfectly balanced, hand-sharpened ice pick, is just an inch away. I can grab it any time I want. It's so close. I'm so close. So close. His arousal puts him off balance when I break his entrancement. He shifts his legs. He'd love to drop at least one hand under the table to play a little pocket pool and adjust himself, but there's no way Officer Johnson would allow it.

"I've been meaning to ask you something," he stares at my fingers, trying to distract himself from his urgent business below the table. "What the hell happened to your hand?"

"My hand?"

"That's quite a scar you're sporting."

I lift my middle finger in the air giving him a full shot of the bird. I have to admit, that felt great.

"My finger was nearly severed by accident when I was nine."

First rule of the long con—don't lie to the liar. Keep it brief but keep it real, until the end game is on.

"What kind of accident?"

"Oh, you know, childhood accident. I'm sure your kids have bumps and bruises they've earned from falling off swings or soccer."

He nods. "They do. David has had two casts from soccer already. Ellen's more careful."

"Girls usually are."

"Except you, apparently." He motions toward my hand, awash in his superiority.

"Apparently."

"You know what's funny? I made it through childhood without one scratch. I didn't even have acne as a teen. No cuts. No stitches. The Reverend and Mrs. Allen never got so much as a call from the school about a bloody nose on their boy. I didn't have one mark on my body until this."

He runs his hand over the thin line that snakes across his cheek just above the jaw. When they scraped her fingernails in the morgue, Marian had half his face embedded under them. Good job, my love.

"Welcome to humanity, Keith."

He reaches out toward my hand, he wants to touch my scar, feel my pain. He's been feeding off it since these sessions began, but I'm not giving him enough today. He's hungry. He's jonesing for the ache I carry inside. I flex my hand, pulling just out of reach. He lunges, his finger brushing across the raised edge of my flesh.

"ACROSS THE LINE, ALLEN!" Officer Johnson shouts, sending Keith back in a jolt, his hands once again on the table. The sound bounces off the walls, creating an echo from my singing bowl. The moment lost.

"Officer Johnson, we've talked about this before," I say, pointing to the door. It only took two sessions for the guard to interrupt our 'counseling' and give me a reason to ask the warden for permission to send him outside the secured counseling pod when necessary. I always knew the day would come when it would be necessary.

"The C.O.'s are there for your protection, Dr. Gentry," Warden Hummel argued.

"Trust me, there is nothing Keith Allen can do to me that would be worse than what he's already done," I replied. "The journey of compassion-based healing has to be unencumbered. We need safe, focused space. I would be forced to tell a judge you were denying Mr. Allen a proper counseling environment."

We made a deal. If a session was intense, or interrupted, I had the right to request my 'protection' stand outside the door and peer through the glass window until I stood, signifying I was ready to leave. Sometimes I let him stay through the whole session. I'm pretty sure Johnson is some kind of earpiece for the warden. He's the only guard I've ever had, and he is always interested in what we say. If this works, what a story it will make. "Guru Heals Wife's Killer in Pioneering Prison Program," the papers will say. That's not gonna hurt Hummel's campaign for governor, now is it? Maybe he'll publish an article in a professional journal. If this fails, Warden Hummel wants to be the first to know so he can push the blame through any door but his own.

Keith is always placed in the room before I arrive and removed after I leave with the stipulation he must remain seated on his side the entire time. He complains he has to be strip-searched before and after every session. I have to admit, that makes me feel good.

"Scar is smoother than I expected," he says as soon as the guard closes the door from the outside.

"It's old."

He flashes that sardonic half-smile he likes to give me right before he taints Marian's memory for his amusement. His pores always emit a faint smell of garlic when he's aroused. I wonder if his wife found that bothersome.

"Like her skin. I was surprised by how smooth your wife's skin was when I had her neck in my hands. I'm sure you felt that way about her, too."

The mallet is in my hand ready to reveal my true purpose. I grip the handle to keep from dropping it. Now I'm the one sweating. I raise it slowly, carefully.

Goooooooonnnnggggggg.

It clashes against the side of the singing bowl. My scarred hand drops back on the table.

"Let's begin with meditation."

Red and blue lights alternate, creating a visual assault designed to move any car out of its way. They clear three police cars through the winding wooded path. A small sound, like a wounded antelope moaning, can be heard as the bark of the oak trees reflect the blinking primary colors before the cars turn on the narrow gravel road leading to the main house. The sound gains pitch and volume, becoming a shrieking hawk screaming as it dives toward its prey. It cuts through the quiet of Virga; a drill to the skull.

I imagine the chaos their arrival must have caused the middle-aged ladies in their ninety-dollar yoga pants sitting on cushions in the yard devoutly following their breath. Inhale goodness. Exhale alarming police activity. I can see the scene so clearly as I listen to Penelope describe it over the phone to the one person I least expected her to confide in. She leans back in the hospital recliner, her posture, like her psyche, taking a beating from the long wait for truth.

Pen was stretched out on the hammock by her guest house lazily petting one of the center's cats, probably the large black and white female with a purr like heaven and the white paw of Satan ready to claw you to ribbons on the first misstep. They have so much in common, after all. The lights drew her eyes from the horizon. Pen started running to the main house before the noise shook the blossoms in the Zen garden. She was at Virga the night there was only one car. The night a uniformed man held up Marian's driver's license for me to see. A few years before that, the writer was at a bookstore sitting behind a card table, signing copies for her fans, when the lights showed up to escort her to the airport and her daughter's body, lying dead in an emergency room two states away. From vast experience Pen knows what it means when the lights arrive.

She hopes to cut them off at the narthex but she's too slow. Two officers are already in the main house, looking in meditation rooms and the lecture hall. Another two are running to the small house Marian and I lived in before the rest of the center appeared on our land. Luka skitters out of the kitchen and clings to Penelope like a terrified chipmunk, the one that hawk is screaming for.

"They say we have to leave the building. They say it's an official..."

"Go get Topaz." Pen gives calm and clear orders. "The rest of you, go to the yard. If you're a guest and have a car here, go to town for lunch. Follow instructions. Do what they say."

The fact she used Topaz's real name probably clued everyone around her that the end of the world was imminent. A no-nonsense, take-no-prisoners director who kept the books balanced and the center functional, Topaz had the unfortunate distinction of not being a "people person" in a workplace where personhood was the topic at hand. I always thought of her as an intelligent dreamer, but others did not share my view. I stopped counting the number of complaints I got about her when the decorative abacus in my office ran out of beads.

It all came to a head the day a group of Tibetan monks stopped by the center to do some teaching and make a mandala on their tour of the U.S. She worked tirelessly for weeks, running roughshod over every excuse, question, or idea until their arrival at the center was flawlessly executed. Standing in the doorway of the main house, I bowed with great respect to the gentle Master and his students. He spoke with rolling, soft, breathy tones in broken English, whole enough to be understood most of the time, and gestured at my students with gratitude. To my eyes, he was bathed in golden light, pure and refined. I was overtaken. I clumsily put my arm out and pointed toward the director.

"She is the person who has made this possible," I said, hoping to draw his attention to her so I could recover from my pounding heartbeat. He bowed to her.

"What is your name?" He asked with that beautiful rollercoaster inflection.

"Topaz," she said, somehow managing a smile.

"Top-ass," he said, bowing to her, and encouraging his students, many of whom spoke no English, to do the same.

"Top-ass, Top-ass," they all chanted repeatedly, bowing and smiling.

I'm pretty sure I'm not the only one who had scars on my lower lip from biting it. When the weekend was over and we held the teachings of the Master in our hearts with great affection, the monks, like the sand mandala that blew away in a night's wind, left us. The director's new name? Well, let's just say it wasn't as impermanent as she'd hoped.

I was sitting in my office one night, using the Dremel drill to hollow out the wooden tops of the singing bowl mallets so the covert blade of the ice pick would slide right in, when I heard two students trying to decide whether or not to leave the meditation cushions out for the next day.

"She's in there, let's just ask," one said.

"Do not disturb the teacher," Luka said, carrying my tea tray. "Go ask Top Ass."

The students giggled and ran to the admin building. I pushed the ice picks under some papers and kept the drill and wood out, frowning as if I was engaged in an intense artistic endeavor. Which, in a way, I was. Make no mistake, vengeance is an art form all its own.

"What was that commotion?" I asked, bowing and thanking Luka for my tea.

"Oh, the students had a question," she muttered, clearing away the afternoon serving.

"Did you send them to Top Ass?" I asked, not looking up from the wooden cylinder. She nodded, small dots of beige uncertainty that I might be angry appeared around her. "I think I know what she will say."

"What?" Luka always looked at me like the next word from my mouth was going to be the combination of a bus locker containing the holy grail.

"Whatever the hell she wants," I laughed. She laughed, too. Once you let someone know it's okay to be a human being and you're not going to judge them for it, the rest of any relationship is a breeze.

The day the lights arrived at Virga, Penelope stood in the doorway to that very office, arms extended to cover the frame, watching the cops move from one room to another, taping off areas they planned to inspect later.

"Ma'am, I need you to exit the building right now."

"Why? What's happened?"

"I'm sure someone will answer your questions outside, ma'am."

"I'm Penelope Fine, and you are?"

"I am asking you to leave the building, ma'am."

"I'm not going anywhere until you tell me what this is about."

A detective flipping through notes in a leather bound notepad steps up to the hindrance with Topaz at his elbow, her usually stern eyes spinning like plates on sticks, threatening an avalanche of shattered china.

"What's going on here?" Topaz demands to know. It's really the only way she knows how to talk.

"I'm not moving until I get an explanation. That's what is going on."

"I will remove you by force, if necessary," the first officer says. Pen smiles with the same grin that black and white cat gets right before her claws come out.

"You clearly don't know who I am, which is okay." She cocks her head to one side and continues to smile. "But I should warn you. If you lay one finger on me, you won't just make the nightly news. You'll be on TMZ."

The officer steps back and takes a second look.

"Penelope, just move," Topaz sighs.

"Penelope Fine?" The officer with the notebook looks up.

"Yes!" She opens her arms as if she is going to embrace him.

"The Maryland State Penitentiary at Bowles Pass has you listed as the next of kin and emergency contact for Dr. Lylarose Gentry. Is that correct?"

"Yes. Where is she? What's happened?"

"I need to speak to you in private," he says, giving Topaz a sideways glance.

"STEVE!" A third officer runs up with an iPad and shows it to the detective. "We found these on a table in the house."

Penelope dodges to the left to see the picture on the iPad, giving away access to the doorway she knew she couldn't hold forever. Three wooden mallets are lined up beside the bowl I used to eat my morning oatmeal. The carnage happened so fast Luka hadn't had time to clear the breakfast dishes.

"Those are for the singing bowls," Topaz blurts out. "They begin and end our sessions."

The officer flips the screen with his finger to reveal a closer view. The tops are from the singing bowl set. The bottoms are wooden handled ice picks, sharpened to a laser point.

"Just like the one at The Bowl," the officer says to his superior, using the nickname for the prison Warden Hummel hates with the same fire Topaz feels for hers.

For once, Penelope Fine stands in stunned silence, her mouth half-open. Her mind half-shut.

"I've never seen..."

"Ms. Fine, please come with me," the notebook cop says. "There's something I need to tell you."

Ten minutes later, the warrant shows up at Virga with two more cars. Penelope doesn't stop them because she's already in her SUV, driving as fast as she can while checking in with her publicist on the way to Mountainside General Hospital. She spills that last detail to her unsurprised listener as she talks by my bedside.

"Of course, you called Stacy," he says with a sigh heavy enough to break a tabletop.

"It happened so fast, Bill," she replies, trying to catch her breath from the long description. This phone call is more than she's said to him in years. "I just left the center in their hands. I'm here with Lylarose. I'm not sure. I don't know what to do next."

"I know you love her, Penelope," he says. He was always the calm one. "Probably more than you've loved anyone, except Rosie, of course, but..."

"I loved you, too, Bill. I just didn't know how to...to..."

"That's not what I'm saying. What I'm saying is maybe it's time to let her go."

"I can't do that."

"You did it with me."

"That was different. You know it. How dare you?"

"You said in your book letting go of our marriage gave you space to put your heart back together."

"I didn't leave our marriage. You left me. Remember? You were probably right to do so."

"Sure. It gave you more material. Turned it from a sad story to a tale with an epic villain. Rosie gave that book its heart. My leaving gave it full-blown good vs. evil. For the rest of my life, I'll be 'the man who left Penelope Fine by the gravesite of her child.' Never my child. Always yours."

"That's not what I meant to happen, and that's why I can't let go of Lylarose. She knows my spirit, my truth. She knows I didn't mean to hurt you. She knows I'm so..."

She wants to say 'sorry' but it won't come out. Not now. Not, maybe, ever. If she says it, she'll melt like the Wicked Witch of the

West in a rainstorm. At least, that's what she believes. What we believe is all the truth we ever see.

"This whole thing is going ugly fast, Penelope. Since you say you're about honesty these days, let's have some. The media is all over this. I heard Laura Lindeman on some show comparing her to David Karesh, a façade of harmless spirituality hiding murderous intent. This shitshow is going to drag your guru through the mud, and if you don't let go of her now, it will drag you right along with it. Then you'll lose the real love of your life—your fine career."

"They're wrong, Bill. All of this is wrong. She didn't do this. She couldn't. As you pointed out on several occasions during our marriage, I don't really know that much about anything. But I know this, and I am going to prove it."

"You called me for advice, and that's my advice: Get out of this, now. Do what you do. Walk away. Write a book. Make a million. Don't look back."

"I never told you, but I'm happy for you and Jeannie. I mean, I'm glad you have someone."

"Goodbye, Penelope."

9

The thing about change, the soft underbelly of our existence, is the fierce independence it holds, even as we erroneously believe we can control it. A baby's conception, a misunderstanding, a memory, a sin, a job ending text, a bomb, a kiss, or a death—they all have buttons on the speed dial of change. Best we get used to that. Best we learn to answer the phone when it rings, because the real message is often lost in the static of life's interference.

Colorado turned out to be a good transition for my family. The project only lasted eighteen months, but the cell block was such a success my father was given a raise and choice of assignments. He picked a multi-security level, large-scale prison compound planned for the New Mexico desert. The project was a five-year commitment, which meant I could begin, and end, at Farmington High School.

The promise of an uninterrupted four-year stay gave me the incentive to make real friends and get invested in the chess club—something I had never been able to do with my in-and-out education. In a world where reputation was everything, I was finally getting the chance to be someone other than "the new girl." My best friend, Annie, and my small group of nerd herders were the kind of friends who would have really listened to me, if I ever had something to say.

The "vacations" my mother took allowed her to work out whatever needs she had, which largely seemed to be the need to be away from me and my father. When she was at home, she was still absent most of the time, lost in her own thoughts or the tangled plots of her 'stories' that started with "Capitol" at noon, breezed through "As the World Turns," and ended each day with a "Guiding Light." She continued to bowl and hold dinner parties, but the hurricane dissipated into a few blustery afternoons and the occasional biting wind. I got too tall to be put over the arm of the couch and the belt came off my dad's waist more as a reminder than a promise. It was just as effective. The sound of a buckle jangling or the leather swishing through a loop gives me the cold shivers to this very day. I made poor Marian dress in the bathroom with the door closed for our entire marriage.

There were a few slaps and pushes, but on the whole, the Gentry family settled down to a new pattern of disconnect punctuated by the occasional casual cruelty.

"Ow!" I exclaimed as the door to the plate cabinet hit me in the forehead. I was standing there drying dishes when my mom purposely opened it, pausing to enjoy the satisfying thud against my skull.

"Peggy," my father sighed. The roles had reversed. I was the good one, the one he shared his blueprints, dreams, and gardening tips with, and she was the brat. "That was not necessary."

My mother looked at me and shrugged. Her drawl started with a deep exhalation, then she said to my father, "Menopause and puberty shouldn't live together."

"What does that mean?" I asked my father when she adjourned to the TV room.

"It means she's planning another trip," he said.

It was Annie's mom who did the right-of-passage kind of things for me that a mom normally does for her daughter. The day I came out of the bathroom with a spot of blood on my underwear, I told my mother something was terribly wrong.

"You're supposed to be so smart, why don't you already know about this?" She said and turned back to her TV show. In those days, when tampon commercials weren't seen on prime time and before the "awareness culture" that trumpeted every female issue with a megaphone, it was easy for me not to have one clue as to what was going on. Nice families don't talk about periods.

I put some toilet paper in my underwear and went to Annie's. When I saw the paper was no match for the next few drops, I quietly told her mom I was experiencing spontaneous and unexplainable blood loss, and if we could go to a hospital without bothering my mother, that would be best.

"Oh, sweetie!" Mrs. Harwood wrapped her arms around me. "You're a woman!"

"No, I'm bleeding. Right now," I said. Once again, I was having a medical emergency, and the only adult present had no idea what to do! I was very probably nearing the river Styx in ruined underpants, and she wanted to have a philosophical discussion about gender? At least she didn't offer me a Coke and a roll of duct tape.

"You started!" Annie shrieked. "Oh my gosh, I'm so jealous! I've been waiting to start forever, traitor."

After a trip to the drug store and a delirious conversation about pads, belts (those days are gone—change, it's a good thing), tampons, and hygiene, I was fully set for the next forty or so years of female life. Personally, I didn't find it as entrancing as Annie did, and a few months later when she finally started, she confessed it was not as cool as she imagined.

I arrived home to find my mom immersed in her shows. The TV had become her in-house lover. It would never leave her, yell at her, or expect her to plaster on a smile and feed six couples in the name of career advancement. When she moved, it would go with her. When she lost her temper, it would find her. It had the kind of perfection no one in our house, not even Barry the Never-Present Sun God, would achieve. I had this fleeting hope my new physical reality might create some kind of connection. We never did too well mother to daughter. Maybe we'd be okay woman to woman.

"I started my period," I mumbled.

"Enjoy it," she replied. "Just don't get pregnant."

I blushed. "I...um...don't think that's gonna happen."

"You'll never get a boyfriend with your flat hair and boring complexion. You'd think that girl and her mother would teach you to shade or highlight or something other than makeup and mascara. Plus, what boy wants to date a pair of jeans? Get some skirts, Lylarose. The other girls in your school don't look like urchins..."

At that point my mother started reciting the one artistic endeavor she made in her life, an epic poem dedicated to her only daughter, entitled "Why Aren't You Like The Other Girls?"

"I don't want a boyfriend," I said. "And every time I try to curl my hair it goes flat in like an hour."

"Of course it does, Lylarose. Everything about you is flat," she said, then looked at my boobs, in case I had magically forgotten them or managed to escape my teen discomfort about the large statement they made on my otherwise thin body. "Well, almost everything. Those might help you get him, but they won't help you keep him."

"What?"

"Never mind," she said. "Just remember, trying to catch a boy is not a good reason to have a baby."

"Why did you have a baby? Me, I mean. Not Barry. Why did you have me?"

In that moment, there were no masks, no colors, no filter—just a pure, desperately honest question. To her credit, my mother turned off the TV and looked me straight in the face to give me an equally honest answer.

"If abortion had been legal where we lived, I wouldn't have."

"Oh."

The wall of silence that followed was one of the few times I didn't feel comfortable in the quiet. We just sat there with the raw truth between us.

"You couldn't have found someone who…"

"Nice families don't have back alley procedures, Lylarose."

"Yes, ma'am." I made my way to Dad's study where he was going over plans for a common room that fed into different cell blocks. I was going to ask my mother if she could have found someone to raise me, someone who wanted me. But her answer pretty much covered it all. Nice families also don't give away their kids like a pricey coat that didn't look like its picture in the catalog. At least, in her view of the world.

"Hey, Dad," I said. "Mom's watching TV. I'm going to my room."

Whatever the reason, he asked me to stay with him. Maybe it was the pall of my mother's truth, hanging from my spirit like wet newspaper on a clothesline, or maybe it was just the fact that I spent so much time at the Harwood's, he was starting to think his whole life was filled with absentee voters.

"You can relax in here if you want. I'll show you the plans for the Special Housing Unit."

"No thanks," I said. "Some other time."

"Or, you could watch some TV." He pointed to the small television that was one of my mother's castoffs. "I think 'Facts of Life' is coming on."

"Okay," I said, nestling down on the couch as he turned back to his drafting table. "Don't want to miss the Facts, and I think Mom's watching something else."

"Are you okay? I didn't even have to bribe you with a candy bar."

"Do you have a candy bar?"

"No," he laughed. "User."

"You brought it up," I answered. His mood was bluish green, light and solid. He reached over and turned on the TV, the knob clicking until it landed on channel 8. As the show reminded us to take the good and take the bad, I must have forgotten I detached my mental filter when talking to my mom, and it wasn't screwed back in yet.

"I don't know why I like this show," I muttered. "It's the same story every week. They are fighting over some boy, then the pretty one does something mean, and the black one or the fat one has to show her that it's mean, and the housekeeper talks to them, and they all become friends until the next show when they are fighting over a new boy."

"That sounds accurate," Dad said, not looking up. Yet.

"It's dumb they fight over the boy. If I went to that school, I'd fight for Jo. She's really the prettiest."

"What did you just say?" Now he looked up.

"I mean, Blair's pretty, but she's like—'beauty shop pretty.' Jo is totally 'I wake up this way' pretty—you know—natural."

"So you like the motorcycle girl?"

"Well, duh. Who doesn't?"

"Like a 'crush?'" He asked.

"No, like I think she's cool. I don't have a crush on Jo. That's weird."

He nodded. We watched the girls get into a tizzy about the boy who was helping the maintenance man. Well, I watched. Dad just seemed to be staring at me. When the show was over, I excused myself and went to bed.

Silly Dad, thinking I had a crush on Jo from "Facts of Life." She was too tomboy, too gruff. She'd be an awesome friend, but she was kinda bossy. Besides, I already had a crush—or at least someone I liked to imagine kissing me at night when I hugged my pillow before going to sleep. There was no way "Facts of Life" Jo was ever going to replace my true love—Miss Beadle from "Little House on the Prairie." She was the most beautiful woman in the world, and if I might confess, a great imaginary kisser. I told her all about my period before our goodnight kiss. She liked my newfound womanhood. I did, too.

"When you finish the dishes, sit back down at the table. Family meeting," my dad said, the outline of his feelings bristling with sparks.

"What did I do?" I asked. I no longer feared the punishment, but I did like to know the "why" that went along with it.

"Nothing," he said. "Don't be scared."

"Are we moving?"

"No."

"Then, I'm not scared."

"Lylarose," he said with a low whistle. "If I had to tell your mother we were moving again—I'd be scared."

I wrapped up the dishes, stowed the placemats, and made sure the plastic floral centerpiece was put back in the proper place. We sat there, the engineer, his wife, and their sickly disappointing teenager, staring at each other waiting for someone to chase the silence out of the room before it suffocated us all. I remember pulling myself out of my body and looking at our family from above. It was the kind of moment an old-school illustrator would have drawn for an article on kitsch Americana. Not Norman Rockwell, though, more like Charles Addams.

"Lylarose, your mother and I have some serious questions and I think we just need to clear the air."

"What did I..."

"Has a teacher been touching you?" My mother blurted out.

"Um...what?"

"Like the P.E. Coach? Has she been in the locker room with you? Did she help you take a shower? Small towns like this are full of perverts."

"I don't go to P.E., Mom," I said, fishing my inhaler out of my pocket and shaking it toward her.

"What about the chess club sponsor? Has she been trying to teach you something special?"

"Mr. Vaughn is a 'he.' Not really, he just keeps saying I'm too careful. I castle too soon."

"You spend a lot of time with that girl's mother..."

"Peggy! The Harwoods are not in question here," my father admonished.

"What IS the question here?" I asked. This was all so surreal—even for my family.

"We're just trying to make sure you're okay, Lylarose. We love you," my father said. If my mother rolled her eyes any farther back in her head, she would have swallowed them.

"I'm fine," I affirmed.

"Do you like girls?" My mother asked.

"Sure," I said.

"You see!" She spit the words at my father who put both of his hands up to calm her, like the horse whisperer.

"Do you like boys?" My father asked.

"Yeah. Lots of my friends from science club are boys," I said. "I pretty much like everyone."

"Okay," my father leaned over and looked in my eyes as if the answer was written there in blue calligraphy for him to read. "If you were going to hold someone's hand, or kiss them, would you want it to be a girl or a boy?"

Miss Beadle! Oh my gosh, how did they find out? I'm not the only one with extra-sensory powers in this house.

"Uh...I don't...really...think about it," I said. Oh, Miss Beadle, I would die before betraying you—my golden-haired school marm.

My father let out one of those long "I'm-getting-tired-of-this-young-lady" sighs. "Try harder, Lylarose. IF you were going to kiss somebody romantically, would you rather kiss a girl or a boy?"

"A girl."

"Oh, Jesus," my mother wailed.

"They smell better, and they have softer voices," I added. That would help, right?

"Okay," my father said, nodding sympathetically. "It's going to be okay."

"She's already got problems fitting in, Lawrence, now this?"

"I fit in fine," I said. "I have friends, good friends."

"White trash and losers!" My mother threw her hands in the air.

"Well, who do you hang out with?" I challenged her, clearly okay with meeting my friend, Death, sooner than later.

"Enough!" My father pointed a finger at both of us. "That's enough."

"Lylarose, do you have a teacher or friend who is a lesbian?"

"I don't know that word," I said. When you come from a violent home, curiosity is often the first casualty. The less you know, the better off you'll be. Between all the moving, keeping up with my home-work and house chores, and making sure the filter stayed secure, I hadn't had much time to learn about social things like how to walk in heels, which side the fork goes on, or sex. There were no LGBT clubs in my school. Hell, that wouldn't even be an acronym for another twenty years. The only gay person on TV was the guy from "Three's

Company," and he was just pretending. At a very sheltered thirteen, I didn't even know what he was pretending to be. I just knew it made the grown-ups giggle.

"A homosexual," he said.

"A what?"

"Hoe-Mo-SEX-ual," my mother said phonetically, only with her accent it sounded like a 45 RMP record played at 33 RPM—on Mars.

I shook my head.

"A woman who has sex with other women," my father finally said.

I frowned. "Sex? Like, sex, sex? Get you pregnant, past third base, sex?"

"Yes," he said.

"You can do that?"

"Oh my God." My mother put her head on the table. Looking back now, I can't decide if she was so upset because her daughter was a lesbian, or just that stupid.

"I think it is very possible," my father said, leaning forward and using the same voice he used when he told me why I shouldn't play with electric wires or wax the car in the sun, "that you are a homosexual. A lot of people call that 'being gay.' And when a woman is gay, she is called a lesbian."

I nodded. Wait until I go to bed tonight and tell imaginary Miss Beadle I am a homosexual gay lesbian. She'll be so surprised!

"Okay," I said. I waited for the other shoe to drop, but there didn't seem to be one. My father reached out and put his hand on top of my left hand. He never touched the right, where the scars of his wrath reminded us all of the valley we walked through to get to this point.

"You have the rest of your life to figure out who you are and who you love. You don't have to do that right now. I just wanted you to know the words, and make sure we all understood where we are with this."

"Okay."

"There's just one more thing and it is very important," he said.

There's that other shoe.

"You're not dating some slutty girl from that school while you live under my roof, missy!" My mother erupted. She was glorious in her pronouncement. I was delighted and intrigued that there were slutty girls at my school, and they would date me.

"Peggy! I said that's enough." Just once I would have loved to see my father walk HER to the couch and tell her to bend over. "Lylarose, it would be better if you didn't date until you were much older."

"I don't want to date. I have too much homework and chess club."

"Good, but that's not the important thing. The important thing is this: you can never tell anyone what we've talked about at this table tonight. Don't tell them you are gay. Don't tell them you like girls."

"Why?"

Another sigh.

"Because people will hurt you, Lylarose."

"I don't understand," I said. All these years later—I still don't understand.

"Just keep your mouth shut."

"Yes, sir."

Other than the occasional snide remark from my mom, the topic never came up again. Imaginary Miss Beadle evolved into Daisy Duke, then Molly Ringwald, and by the time I was ready to graduate from Farmington High, she had become full on Kim Basinger—legs and all. Dad was right. I had the rest of my life to figure it all out. Maybe, by then, there wouldn't be people in the world who wanted to hurt me just for liking girls.

THE CIRCUIT COURT FOR MONTGOMERY COUNTY,
MARYLAND
THE STATE OF MARYLAND
v.
KEITH W. ALLEN
Defendant
CRIMINAL CASE NO. 6 -57-12587
Whereupon proceedings in the above titled action commenced
before:
THE HONORABLE WILLIAM J. PIERCE, JUDGE
FOR THE STATE:
VIVIAN PRESCOTT, Esq.
HOWARD WILSON, Esq.
Deputy State's Attorney
50 Maryland Ave.,
Rockville, MD 20850

FOR THE DEFENDANT:
EVAN HARRIS, Esq.
Harris, Eggleston, and Wells, Inc.
234 Munfield Ave., Ste 71
Rockville, MD 20851

... Page 139

DIRECT EXAMINATION

Q: Mr. Allen, did you know Nanette Muntreat prior to the events
of May 21?

A: Yes.

Q: In what capacity did you know her?

A: She was my client for a brief time.

Q: What is her sexual orientation?

A: Sexual orientation is somewhat of a myth. It can be fluid and hard to determine.

Q: According to her intake form at your therapeutic practice, her family and friends, her girlfriend, her Facebook page, and the bumper sticker on her car, what is her sexual orientation?

A: She is a lesbian.

Q: Did you know Marian Fitzwater prior to the events of May 21?

A: No.

Q: Did you know Stephanie Rawls prior to the events of May 21?

A: No.

Q: You stated in your deposition that you saw those two women coming out of Babes Bar and Grill as you were engaged in forced sexual penetration with Miss Muntreat in the parking lot behind the bar. Is that correct?

A: It was consen...<inaudible>

MR: HARRIS: Objection. Inflammatory.

MS. PRESCOTT: That's the charge on the plea he took, Judge. Don't like it, don't cop to it, but in the eyes of the law, that's what was happening.

THE COURT: Sustained. Rephrase the question, Ms. Prescott.

Q: What kind of establishment is Babes Bar and Grill?

A: It's a bar.

Q: What kind of bar, specifically?

A: A lesbian bar.

Q: So when you admit you saw Marian Fitzwater and Stepahnie

Rawls walking our of a lesbian bar, is it fair to say you thought they were lesbians?

A: I didn't think about them at all. I just saw them come out of the back door of the bar.

Q: That's when, according to several witnesses, Miss Muntreat started screaming for help. When they ran to her aid, you shot Ms. Rawls and strangled Ms. Fitzwater to death after she attacked you in defense of her friend?

A: Yes.

Q: Mr. Allen, did you once publish an e-article supporting the use of sexual conversion therapy?

MR. HARRIS: Objection! There is no hate crime stipulation on any of the charges.

MS. PRESCOTT: Withdrawn.

MR. HARRIS: I object to this entire line of questioning. Ms. Prescott is attempting to characterize Mr. Allen as someone who fits the prosecution's script. She is not questioning the witness prima facie and is simply trying to muddy the water.

MS. PRESCOTT: In a case where every victim is a lesbian, Your Honor, I'd say the waters are exceedingly clear.

10

Personal strength has nothing to do with the clothes of power, efficacy, or status. A judge's robe, a cop's badge, an actor's makeup, a warrior's armor, a teacher's book bag, a runner's medal—none of those show the kind of fortitude one requires to get through the journey. Strength, true inner strength, is naked. It is the courage to open your real, raw, beating heart and touch it with your own finger, leaving a print that will never smudge, even as you risk disrupting the rhythm. Unimaginable strength is when you reveal that uncloaked, defenseless center of your being and let another touch it, too.

It took everything I had to let Marian touch my heart. I questioned the sanity of it more than once. Yet, even then, I knew it was the most brave and important thing I would ever do. I'm so glad now, because in my dark third life, through the lonely howling hunger for light, her fingerprint was all I had to guide me.

"There's still time to send in your video for the *News Now* Nightly Poll. Did Lylarose Gentry kill two officers and shoot Keith Allen, or was she an innocent bystander? Tell us what you think. Here's some of our latest:"

"Criminals got too much rights," a man in a trucker's hat and a plaid shirt says into his phone. His hands shake and his cigarette stained forefinger keeps showing up on screen. "State shouldn't be paying to feed and house that murderer. Death penalty for everyone that kills. That would cure this country in a hurry."

"There's no way," a woman with a fading black pixie cut showing silver roots, ruby red lipstick, and way too much mascara says as she bats her eyes. Her lashes must weigh a quarter of a pound. "I went to a mindfulness seminar where Dr. Gentry was one of the speakers. She was so calm, and really funny. I didn't expect her to be so funny. There's just no way someone that peaceful could be a cop killer."

"Cops are corrupt these days," a college-aged man wearing a *Resist!* T-shirt standing in front of a craft beer sign opines. He probably spent more time grooming his ridiculously stylized beard than in an actual political science class. The video, produced with a bluish filter and high angle shots, holds the marks of a budding filmmaker. "Whatever they say she did should be questioned and investigated. Power lies. Of course, she had power, too. Maybe she did. She probably did. But the cops are still lying."

"She's a Buddhist teacher, and he's a convicted murderer," a young woman in a lab coat with her hair pulled back in a severe bun and black plastic framed glasses says. She has a half-annoyed look that is probably her resting face. "Occam's razor. The simplest explanation is usually the right one."

The segment anchor's face fills the small video feed like an invading alien with a giant head. "Lylarose Gentry: Innocent or Guilty? What do you think?"

Penelope reaches over and bats the iPad into submission with an impatient grimace while she yammers into the phone.

"Over by that Buddha with the garden lights, the one who looks like he's doped up, there's a little ceramic frog. The spare key to my guesthouse is inside. The travel kit is in the hall closet already packed with makeup. Look in it and make sure the compact is a neutral palette, if not, there's some in the bathroom, grab one. Also, there's a little golden bag with bamboo brushes. Make sure you get the long handled ones. The short ones are harder to control and I don't need streaks on my face right now. I'm trying to hide the stress, not draw a road map to it."

"Wait a minute, Penelope...key?"

"Topaz, keep up! I have a long list of things I need you to bring. Would it be better if I just texted them?"

"The guesthouse doors don't lock from the outside. They just have that little chain. Remember that time the risk management lawyer got into that huge argument with Lylarose over guest safety versus spiritual openness?"

"I remember him arguing, then leaving with prayer beads around his neck telling Cineque he wanted to sign up for her yoga class. Lylarose just bowed as he walked away."

"So she put that gate on the grounds and those little door chains but not locks on the doors. Except, I guess, yours?"

"Do you think serious paparazzi are going to be deterred by some rebar and wire designed to blend in with the woods? The last thing I need is Joe Camera from Daily Star pawing through my underwear drawer."

"But it's okay if I paw through?"

"If my vibrator shows up on "Cheap Thrills of the Rich and Famous," I'll sue your ass so hard you'll be doing standing meditation for a month."

"Please. I have ten dollars and fifty-seven cents in savings. You can have it. That's why I'm coming to the hospital, remember? To get you to sign a few checks from the Virga Foundation so we can pay the staff in case more memberships go bye-bye."

"Since you are coming, you can bring me some clothes and necessities. I don't know how long I'm going to be here, and the traffic in this so-called 'secure floor' is heavier than I-405 on a Friday afternoon in LA. I can't stay in these clothes forever."

"Since you've already been photographed in them," Topaz coughs.

"What? I came in through the nurses' parking garage and I haven't left this room. What photograph?"

"I'll send you a link. Let's just say they didn't get your best side."

Pen alternates between typing a novel of the things she wants Topaz to haul to the hospital and looking at her phone for the link to the picture. She grinds her teeth as the blue bar snakes across her screen. When it hits the other side, the first picture she sees on the glorified gossip site claiming to be "today's news" is a full portrait shot of her with her arms wrapped around my uncle Bud. The angle is straight on, and if I'm not mistaken, there are some Photoshop tears in addition to her real ones, a little more layered agony than her face truly displayed. She can't complain too much, though. Whoever added the tears used a nice filter for her hair and added some form flattering curves along the waistline. Guess he thought making her look good would reduce the likelihood of a lawsuit.

"Family Bids Goodbye to Beloved Guru."

"Friends and loved ones pause to grieve the imminent death of renowned meditation master Dr. Lylarose Gentry. Dr. Gentry was one of four people removed from The Maryland State Penitentiary at Bowles Pass with gunshot wounds Thursday morning. Gentry was meeting with Keith Allen, the man convicted of killing Gentry's wife and one other."

The photo credit belongs to a freelancer, yet the byline reads "Laura Lindeman." I suspect she's the one who's been causing the publicist to blow up Pen's phone until she blocked Stacy's texts. For

Penelope, that's a lot like shutting off a main artery. I'd like to think it was the minimization of Stephanie, Marian's best friend since nursing school—the "one other" who died with her that night—which caused Pen's anger, but it's more likely she's just mad about the picture.

"What the fuck is this?!" She throws her phone in the lap of the door officer, nearly knocking him out of the chair he had leaning against the wall.

"I...um...I don't know, ma'am. I...um..."

"Are you protecting us or not? Any two-bit jackass with a camera can apparently get by you. I want someone in charge to explain exactly how the hospital is going to keep this kind of cluster fuck from happening again and I want to speak to them now!"

"Lens stalker pretended to be a drug rep. Stood at the nurses' station and took half a memory card before someone noticed his sample case was emitting light," the detective says, walking up to the door just in time to save the terrified guard from her hissing fury.

"You again," she shakes her head. "I remember you from Virga but I don't remember your name, Detective..."

"Mesa. Detective Steve Mesa."

"Are you in charge of this investigation?"

"Noooo, no. No." He waves his hands as if warding off an evil spirit. Only a risk addict or a fool would want to head up this investigation. "I'm just the scene manager, in charge of evidence collection and follow-ups. I got a report when hospital security picked him up."

"After he sent the pictures to *News Now*?"

"He must have had some kind of app that sent a few out before they took the memory card from him. Evidence, you know."

"What I want to know is which one of your officers is feeding Laura the Leech information about this case before I am being told? I am Dr. Gentry's legal guardian. I shouldn't learn these things from the internet, even if they are bullshit."

"That's pretty much it, Ms. Fine," the detective nods along with her staccato recitation. "Anytime you read 'sources close to the investigation,' it means one of two things—they heard support personnel chatting at lunch, or they pulled the whole thing out of their ass. You'll be glad to know actual cops don't talk to the press until an arrest is made and all evidence is filed with the court."

"So this part that says, 'sources say there were four different prints on the gun' is some butt nugget and not a real statement?"

"That one is real," he shrugs. She would pick up on the one truth in the whole story. Good girl, Pen. "One of our ballistic guys has a big mouth."

"So there are four sets of prints?"

"Yes, ma'am. Preliminary, and I can't stress that word enough, analysis shows them to be Officer Johnson, who was the owner of the service weapon, Inmate Allen, and Dr. Gentry. The fourth set of prints is unidentified at this time."

"When will it be identified?"

"Tomorrow, or never. You're pretty media savvy. Don't tell me you haven't heard of the myth of fingerprints."

Penelope crosses her arms and waits for him to tell her. The silence is much less painful than admitting to a stranger out loud there's something she doesn't know. His colors include a playful ocher, which swirls in a half circle. He's thinking of waiting her out, but he's got things to do, and he's already deep into overtime.

"So," he begins. "In the movies, fingerprints are easy to find, can be identified within twenty minutes, and always get the right person. That's all legend. Truth is there are very few real fingerprints on anything. There's a million smudges, partials, and print overlays that mess up identification. You can pull a hundred fingerprints from a room and only end up with two or three valid samples. Then, unless you have a matching sample, such as Allen's on file at the prison or Dr. Gentry's from her credential application, you're pretty much stuck with an unknown digital file. Fingerprints don't open or close many investigations. They are just another dart to throw at the wall and hope you hit a target."

"I see."

"The fourth set could be Officer Johnson's wife, who handed him his gun in the morning as he was getting dressed, or his neighbor who held the weapon once to see how heavy it really is."

"Or it could be a person who took that gun from Officer Johnson and killed those people. Someone Keith Allen got to help him escape, or rape, or do whatever the hell he had planned."

"If it was another inmate's prints, we would know."

"Lylarose got in the prison. Visitors get in the prison. How many people like the 'fake drug rep' who took my picture got in as well?"

"I'm not here to debate case scenarios with you Ms. Fine. I'm here to ask you some questions."

Pen sits down in one of the straight-backed visitor chairs instead of the recliner. She has no intention of letting her long legs or pretty face pacify this guy. She's a stone mountain he's never going to climb.

"I wasn't there. She didn't do it. Why don't you go look for the real killer, or are you still looking for the one who got O.J.'s wife?"

Detective Mesa remains unimpressed. Abuse is free, and he can get it anywhere.

"With that out of your system, I'll give you the easy ones first, like your guru's feelings about Mr. Allen or any plans she might have shared about his demise. We are operating on the assumption he was the ultimate target. The other two were collateral damage."

"No one was 'collateral damage' to Lylarose Gentry. Her world view, her practice, were all about having a heart that saw every person as being filled with value, worthy of comfort and peace. To deny the foundational goodness of another being is the road to suffering. She'd never enter that willingly. She even reached out to Patricia Allen after the trial and offered her a list of counselors who specialized in helping kids whose fathers go to jail."

"Is that how Dr. Gentry ended up counseling the man who killed her wife?"

"No, he asked her to do that. Sent her letter after letter. She ignored them at first. Then Patricia came by and begged Lylarose to consider it. Keith was the one who petitioned the warden to make it happen, threatening to sue if he was denied the right to the spiritual counselor of his choice."

Detective Mesa holds up a small picture in front of Pen. The man is a middle-aged blond, with bright eyes and extremely white teeth showing through a confident smile. He's wearing the same starched brown uniform shirt all of the corrections officers at The Bowl wear.

"Have you ever seen this man at the Virga Center?"

Penelope draws close and makes an overdramatic point of staring at the man's face. She goes so far as to take her fingertip and trace his jaw line before shrugging.

"I've never seen him in my life, and I don't pay attention to the guests at the center."

"But you do live there, don't you?"

"No, actually I don't. For a detective, you're not very good with facts. Maybe I should see your badge."

"So that's not your guesthouse like..." he flips a few pages, just to prove he has been paying attention. "...Topaz Williams, the director, said it was?"

"Oh, it's my guesthouse, but I don't live there. That's why it's called a GUEST house. My world is a big and busy place, Detective

Mesa. Sometimes I have to get away before I'm buried in the avalanche. I stay at Virga for personal retreat. Hence, I don't pay attention to others. I'm going there to get away from the crowd, not join it. I've been staying there a little more since Marian was killed. I know about grief. I thought I might be able to help."

"The man in the picture is Brent Johnson, the correctional officer shot to death at The Bowl. Did Dr. Gentry ever mention him to you?"

"No. She never talked after she came back from counseling Allen. She'd enter her patient notes into the computer, go to her house, and close the door. I assume she had to shake off the horror of sitting in the same room with that murdering asshole."

"So you never saw Johnson, and she never mentioned him? Were you present for any conversations or overhear any phone calls where his name might have come up? Did you see or hear anything odd?"

"What do you define as odd?" She toys with him; the cat seeing if she can get more out of the mouse than just a pounce and a kill.

"I define this whole thing as odd, Ms. Fine. It stinks like a four-day-old fish sandwich. A situation a licensed psychologist like Dr. Gentry should have never agreed to participate in, a proposal Warden Hummel shouldn't have approved, and a corrections officer who shouldn't have been anywhere near that room. It all adds up to odd, or worse."

"Lylarose was there as a teacher, a spiritual guide, not his psychologist," Pen reminds the detective. She's bristling at the idea I violated my professional ethics, while simultaneously ignoring the fact I took an ice pick disguised as a meditative tool into a prison and floated out on a river of blood. Isn't the human mind wonderful?

"Brent Johnson was a perimeter patrol officer. They are the only corrections personnel allowed to carry service weapons because they do not work in close contact with inmates. He doubled as a transport officer, so he also had a handgun, not just a perimeter rifle. He was one of only four armed officers on the premises that day, and he was standing watch over a counseling session in a secured room three feet from an inmate. That doesn't make any sense."

"Maybe he was covering someone's shift. It's not always a conspiracy, sometimes it's just coincidence." Penelope smirks as she drops the quote from her latest book in front of him like a veil of verbal lace. The detective discards it with a shake of his head.

"Johnson was assigned wing duty every time Gentry and Allen met. When we looked at the assignment roster, it showed he requested that particular station. Transporters get a bonus every time they take an inmate off the grounds, but he took himself out of the running for extra pay to stand in a room listening to psychobabble? Unlikely, unless he was getting better money for being there from somewhere else."

"If you think Lylarose was paying him off for some reason, you're barking up the wrong guru. She has very little money of her own. Lyla left her practice the minute she could afford to spend all of her time at Virga. They lived off of Marian's salary and what little profit the center made each month. Marian always handled their finances and after her death, Lyla passed it all off on Topaz. Once her bills are paid there's probably not enough money in her bank account to take a three-day vacation, let alone buy off a guard."

"She is the sole owner of a major property in one of the most expensive counties in Northern Virginia. She counsels celebrities and CEO's. I find it hard to believe she's the working poor."

Penelope wags her finger at the investigator.

"She may own Virga, but it's paid for by the Virga Foundation, which takes in all fees and covers expenses, staff salaries, and county taxes."

"She still has control of that money."

"No. As I'm sure you are already aware, I'm the director and primary benefactor of the Virga Foundation. I started it to maximize some kind of profit margin and keep the place open. My accountant has a proxy and works with Topaz on all the details, but the money begins and ends with me. Lyla wants nothing to do with it. She's not even on the check card at the bank. She never wanted there to be any questions about her profiting off the dharma or the donations. She gets a salary, like everyone else."

"So you're telling me the famous Dr. Gentry is actually broke and unable to manage the assets of her own million dollar center?"

"It would never dawn on her that she's broke. Lylarose doesn't have anything she doesn't need, and she needs very little. She doesn't care about money. She doesn't want fame. She hates attention. She's not driven by ego, status, or ambition. Any glamour or reputation she has is probably my fault, and believe me when I tell you she isn't happy about it."

Penelope's already perfect posture stiffens as her spine wraps a sheath of metal around the tender cords. She hasn't noticed he's taken control of the conversation, nor does she understand the more armored she becomes, the weaker her position grows. Openness is the real power position. Vulnerability is strength.

"She just wants to help people, teach people. Her way is a different way. If you're ever going to understand this case, you have to understand her past, her heart, her practice."

"Look, I admit I don't get it. I don't know jack about all this woo-woo stuff. I know she trusted you more than anyone in her life. Surely there was some clue she might have given you to help us figure out how this all went so wrong."

"Trusts me? She knows me at my deepest level, Detective. She can see past my denial, my pain, my projections, and my outright lies.

She believes in me, she teaches me, and in a way, I think she cherishes our time together, but the one thing Lylarose Gentry does not do is trust me."

"Well, that's interesting, because she left everything to you, Ms. Fine. The Virga Center, the property, her money, the cats on the grounds, and even her wife's ashes. I doubt a woman as smart as she is would give her life's work to someone she didn't think would do the right thing. So, I'm gonna ask you one more time..."

"I..." Penelope looks at my body, eyes narrowed. I can't tell if she wants to thank me or choke me. I've been getting a lot of that today. "I didn't know, Detective. Honest. She must have changed her will after Marian died."

"What was her..."

"Enough." Penelope points to the door in a perfect imitation of Wonderland's Queen of Hearts. "I'm not answering another question. I'll give you the name of my lawyer when I figure out which one I want to use. You can talk to him or her. Now leave."

"You have more than one lawyer?"

"Do you have more than one notebook?"

"I can take you to the station for questioning. You'll be able to call one of your representatives from there."

Penelope's smile returns. "Really?"

She draws it out, the way my mother used to when the hurricane warnings started to sound.

"Oh, yes."

She reaches behind her and, without even looking toward the window, opens the curtains to reveal the street below where reporters are doing face shots and promo tests. Boom operators and tech guys sit on folding chairs in front of their vans eating fast food from the local Tastee Freeze and talking on their phones to angry wives or disappointed lovers. The tiny town resentfully hosts a carnival of false eyelashes and wireless mics all parked right outside the automatic glass doors of Mountainside General Hospital.

"Well, when you haul me out of here make sure to spell out your full name for them, if you can do it over my screaming and dramatic crying. You wouldn't want the Internet trolls to harass some other poor Steve Mesa because they got the wrong guy. And, since you're apparently not too media savvy, here's a clue. Don't get caught on camera talking to Laura Lindeman as you take me out. Because when I sue you, I'll use the clip as evidence that it was probably you who told her all those lies about my teacher in the first place. You can be convicted of slander, even if Lylarose dies. At the very least, it will cost you your badge."

Detective Mesa takes a deep breath, turning from the window, his head down. He's at least confirmed she was telling the truth. I might teach her, but I don't trust her.

"You win, Ms. Fine. I thought you wanted to know what happened, but I see you're really only interested in having your way."

"Maybe the truth is my way," she counters, still motioning toward the door. He goes out with the same controlled saunter he walked in with, only the vibrant semi-circle around him is now a dull gray blob.

"By the way," he says, taking Pen's cell phone from the door guard and tossing it onto my bed. It hits my shin and bounces against the rail. "This officer isn't sitting here to protect Lylarose Gentry from the press. He's here to protect the rest of us from her."

Eight months before I graduated from high school, the big change loomed around the corners of our house like a thief who lived in the attic and came down every night to steal our food. It was time to think about pulling out my traveling shoes. Only this time, the move was up to me.

"Table," my father said, sticking his head in my bedroom where I was lying on the bed in the dark, staring at the ceiling and listening to Christopher Cross sing the virtues of "Sailing" from that album with the pink flamingo on the cover that everyone on the planet seemed to own.

"What did I..."

"Nothing, Lylarose. That's the problem. Nothing." Lately my father seemed to be a blur of charcoal colored routine and burnt orange practicality. "Kitchen table in five minutes."

"Yes, sir," I said. I scanned my room to see if my mother's morning inspection turned up anything that would cause this. By that point, we had been through three psychologists, two full IQ tests, and several placement exams, and they still thought I was stupid enough to leave incriminating evidence in my bedroom? I couldn't imagine anything I had or hadn't done, at least that would be kitchen-table quality.

My mother, who acted more like a reprimanded teenager than I did, fidgeted in her chair. She kept looking at the beige telephone on the kitchen wall and then her watch. My father motioned for me to sit down and made a "stay" gesture toward my mother. He walked out of the room, leaving both of us trapped and curious.

"Are we moving?" I asked.

"We better not be, or the next trip I'll be taking is divorce court," my mother responded.

"I'm a little surprised that hasn't happened yet."

SLAP! A quick, stinging blow landed on my cheek. Oh, geez, I forgot to put in the filter.

"Watch your smart mouth, Missy!"

"Yes, ma'am."

I didn't so much forget my filter as I had left it in the corner of my mind for some rest. As soon as I made it through dinner, I'd go to my room and mentally take off my filter with the same amount of glee I felt taking off my bra. I'd bathe in the freedom of just being me until the morning, when fate forced me to leave my teen cave and rejoin society.

"Do you know what this is about?" I asked my mother hoping to force the hot echo of that slap out of the room before my father came back with whatever he had planned. Besides, if we were going to be cellmates, we might as well get chummy, right?

"You, of course," my mother snapped. "If there's something wrong in this house, you can bet your bottom dollar it's about you."

Maybe solitary confinement would be better.

My father returned with a cardboard box and sat it on the kitchen counter. My mother shifted, looked at the phone, sighed, and rolled her eyes.

"Can we hurry this up?" she asked.

"Just a moment," he said. "This is important enough to do correctly."

"If you'll check your calendar, you'll correctly remember it is the fifteenth of the month, Lawrence. I'm not giving up my time with my son over this, whatever it is." She stood up and went to the phone, took it off the hook, listened for the dial tone, and put it back.

"I'm aware of your phone call," he said, then quietly whispered in my direction. "I should be, I pay for it."

I bit my lip. Apparently, Dad's filter was a little loose tonight as well. Barry's on-again (I need money), off-again (too busy to call, Mom) communication with my mother created such havoc in our lives. While his first wife was still in the hospital, two days after their second baby was born, Barry abandoned her and the kids, transferred her things to a storage facility, changed the locks, and moved his current mistress into his house. This meant he didn't answer the phone in case it was wife number one, the court attempting to collect child support, or the soon-to-be ex-husband of the mistress, who was soon-to-be-wife number two. I guess I should call her Shari. Nice families don't number their spouses.

My mother couldn't call Barry, and he didn't call her. When Hurricane Peggy used one of her "vacations" to make a surprise visit to his house (accidentally meeting future wife number three while he was still married to wife number two), an agreement was quickly reached that he would call her the fifteenth of every month. He would let the phone ring twice, then hang up so he didn't have to pay for the call. My mother would then run to the bedroom phone and call him back to hear all of his latest triumphs. After several missed fifteenths set off tropical storms in our atmosphere, and Dad grew tired of having to wait for a third ring to answer the phone, my father managed to reach Barry and make a new deal. Suddenly the calls came every fifteenth, and I noticed an envelope missing out of the box in the den on a monthly basis. My father eventually confided in me that he told Barry he would mail him $200 every month he called. He would also take $20 off for every day that he was late.

"Barry does better with a system," he said.

My dad. Saving the world one system at a time.

"I just know he's going to call," my mother said, as my father motioned her back to her seat. "Hurry the hell up."

My father went over to the box he brought to the table and pulled out a hammer, some lipstick (I noticed it was a tube of mine, not hers), and a ballpoint pen. He set them on the table in front of me. I thought he was going to show us the layout of his new prison block, so I prepared for my mother's agitation to boil over in a tsunami of "I don't give a damn about your stupid job."

"Growing up on a farm, you don't get a lot of career choices," my father began. "It's pretty much 'do you want to plant potatoes and shovel horseshit on this piece of land, or do you want to get another piece and plant potatoes and shovel horseshit there?' I was young, and I was stuck. It took World War II to give me other options. The Army put me through school so I could join the Corps of Engineers. When I got home after the war, your grandfather expected me to pick up the shovel and go right back to the horseshit. I said I was going to continue to work as an engineer. He told me a real man can't make a living with a pencil. I joined the company and proved him wrong."

My grandfather died of stomach cancer before I was born, and the recollections of his uncompromising life views were only stories to me. I tried to shrink my father down into a young man, but it never quite worked. There was no way to displace his power.

"I had to fight for where I am. I had to fight for where you are. And it's killing me to watch you sit on your butt and throw it all away."

"I don't understand," I said. "I haven't thrown anything away."

My mother looked at her watch and the phone.

"The school counselor told me you weren't applying to any colleges. That you told her you weren't sure you wanted to go. What do you call that?"

"Lazy ass," my mother mumbled.

"Um... I call it...figuring out what I want to do, I guess. I don't know if college..."

"What you need to know, missy, is that the clock is ticking to your eighteenth birthday, and you better have an income, or you can sit in the Sears parking lot eating your chess set while you figure it out, because at eighteen, I'm breaking your plate."

"Peggy, don't help."

She rose, red in the face, with one finger pointed at me and the other positioned between my father's eyes. "Lawrence Gentry, you're the one who has me sitting here. Don't you..."

RIIIINGGGGGG

One Ring.

RIIIINNGGGGG

Two Rings.

A pause. This was more than a pregnant pause. It was a quadruplet carrying moment ready to explode from the gut like that guy in "Alien" with just as much mess. No third. She bolted from the table.

This was the only time Barry ever helped me out.

"Anyway," my father said, "that's the reason for the display. Here are your choices: You can do manual labor—honest, hard work for little pay. You'll end up just like my mother did, a weathered soul— old before your time. You can play the supportive wife to a rich man, like your mother has. With your sexual proclivities, that would take quite a bit of acting, and you'd probably end up even less happy than her. Or, there's the pen. You, like your father, can make a living with your mind. Your amazing, misunderstood, entirely under-challenged mind. If you want to use the pen, you gotta go to college. One of these things is going to be covered in your fingerprints, Lylarose. This is the time in life when you decide which one it's going to be."

"I'll talk to the counselor tomorrow," I croaked. "When I turn eighteen, will you really throw me out and not feed me, or is that just mom-talk?"

"I hope you'll be far away in a dorm with a scholarship and a monthly meal card by eighteen," my father said, dodging the heart of the question like a pro.

"Oh, Barry, I'm sure your father and I can send you a check to help with your car," my mother said, purposefully loud enough for us to hear. I watched my father's colors devolve from forest green to maroon, deepening with every second. His hand seemed to be pulling into itself, creating a fist where there was, only moments ago, a lesson. He would never in his life hit my mother. That wasn't going to help me in the slightest.

"I'm going to my room now," I whispered.

"That's a good idea," he nodded slowly, his face as red as the rest of him. We went down the hall together. I turned to the left, to shelter. He went to the right, into the path of the storm.

"Lylarose," he said, right before I closed the bedroom door.

"Yes, sir?"

"Go to college. Get out of here. For all our sakes. Get out of here."

"My dad would be so horrified," I told Marian the day we opened a bottle of champagne to celebrate the completion of the main meditation building at Virga. We were in the large common room. She unboxed each new cushion, wincing at the chemical smell as they came out of the package. I placed them in a semi-circle around my own, well-used, meditation seat.

"Not enough locking doors and steel bars for his taste?"

"He wanted me to make a living with a pen, and here I am, gainfully employed by sitting on my ass."

"In dreams alone have I imagined such a job," she replied, rearranging my cushion placement by pushing the seats farther apart, an act surely driven by her imagining the germ-filled inhale breath of the collective exhales. Some folks just aren't made for the challenges of community.

"You weren't made for a sitting job," I countered. I'd never known a woman less able to sit still than my wife.

"You weren't made for the prison of a pen," she answered. "You need to be free to think and to teach. There's no cell in the world that's ever going to hold or satisfy your soul."

She was wrong about that, of course. One of the very few times in her life Marian was wrong. I found the only satisfaction in life worth living for, and dying for, in the space between breaths at the secured counseling cell of The Bowl. There I was filled. There I was freed. There I was found. My fingerprints on everything, and no way to explain.

11

Gong.

I bang my weapon against the singing bowl with a short, quick snap of my wrist, allowing the tone to bring me back from the cosmos as it has so many times before. Only this time, I wasn't following the breath to a place of calm and clarity. I sat there the entire ten minutes, mentally jamming my ice pick into the fold of his neck, right under the tracheal plexus. Again. Again. Again.

"Can I ask you another question, Dr. Gentry?"

"You're certainly full of curiosity today, Keith, but as I like to say, any day could be your last, so put all the food on the table and eat like tomorrow isn't coming."

"Do you always meditate with your eyes open?"

"Yes."

"Why?"

"Because closing your eyes is what you do when you're asleep. It's a time for dreaming and blissful imagining of things the way you want them to be. Meditation is about being awake. It's a time for hard truth and breaking the illusions that keep us captive in a world of sorrow."

"Sleeping isn't all it's cracked up to be. It can bring the nightmares out," he says with a little dragging hiss. He projects menace with every word, disappointed with my lack of apprehension. There's nothing he can do to me before Officer Johnson would come back into the room, my knight in uniformed armor, his purpose clear.

That's why I need to be fast. I've got a limited window to pull off the mallet's wooden sleeve, bring my left hand back to the handle, providing reinforcement of the scar-damaged right, and make a fatal lunge with enough force to open the artery. No time for a speech. No time for the why. No time to make him look me in the eye and see the abyss he forged by his own hands, the black hole in the universal fabric that I pray sends him into some sort of conscious oblivion. It's a masterful Zen koan—to send him into timelessness, I have almost no time.

"Are you having nightmares?" I ask him.

"Only during the day," he chuckles. "Look around. You know why they call this place The Bowl? Because this is where nightmares come to take a shit."

I finger the handle of the mallet as he talks. If I have to sit here and listen to more whining about how much he hates prison life, I might just cut the session even shorter than I planned. Not yet, though. Johnson's still too interested. It takes a good ten minutes of babble before his eyes gloss over and he starts fidgeting with the tiny cell phone he illegally has in his secondary cuff holder. The wing supervisor is Rhodes. She's a stickler for the rules, not very popular with any of the other C.O.s. She'll give him shit if he gets too distracted. That's bad news for me. Turns out, it'll be bad news for her, too. I'm so sorry, Officer Rhodes. You were not in the plan.

I've watched countless crime documentaries where the killer walks around the house leaving bloody footprints, lets their cell phone ping off every tower on the getaway route, or stops by McDonald's with a dripping axe in the front seat of the car. I say the same thing every time. "How can they be so fucking stupid?" Now, I know.

When you plan a crime, particularly a murder, you have your whole life to imagine every detail. You walk through it step by step. You practice with the weapon—transporting it, concealing it, aiming it, claiming its power as extension of your will. You study the layout. You know what you want to say. You know how you're going to do it. You know what you'll be wearing—the gloves, the loose fitting clothes, the throw-away shoes two sizes too big. You plan every single moment the way a mother counts her newborn's fingers just to make sure they're all there.

What you don't do is plan the time after. You might have a vague idea of what you're going to do with the body, or how you're going to get out of the alley unseen, but really, those are quick afterthoughts not well attended. You can't plan what you don't know, and what you don't know is the avalanche of emotions, colors, force, and shock which feeds into your bloodstream that transforming moment when a life spills out on the ground. You become blind to the cameras, the neighbors, the walls. You're so numb you don't feel the blood seeping into the folds of your clothing, clinging to your hair, nestling under your nails. You unplug from the system, and the translator in your head shuts down with the rest of the lights, so things like stop signs, witnesses, and warnings have no meaning. As I will discover, no matter how carefully you chart your course, the storm of your inhumanity is going to collide with an unexpected front that will push you right off the map.

"I suppose I should thank you," Topaz says as the elevator doors open, and she sees Penelope standing by the door cop. "Carrying this shit will save me billions on a personal trainer."

"She's with me," Penelope tells the jittery officer who's still reeling from her earlier tirade. At this point, Godzilla could walk into the room with Aquaman speared on a trident like a cocktail weenie and the guard would allow it.

"Robyn and Luka are on the way," Topaz gasps. "They've got the rest of your stuff."

"Who's Robyn?"

"One of the students who didn't burn her membership card, demand all the money in the world as a refund, and flee to another religion in the dead of night."

"Has it been that bad?"

"It leveled off. Your celeb friends were the first to bail. Didn't want the backlash when the story gets slow and reporters start naming members as a way to squeeze every last drop of outrage out of it. Fuck enlightenment, they can't afford to lose 'likes.'"

"They're not my friends," Pen says, her commitment to living an authentic life bursting through the need to be the best and brightest in every conversation. "Celebrities don't really have friends."

"Honey." Topaz drops the heavy makeup case and gym bag full of accessories. "Save it for Lyla."

At the mention of my name, Topaz turns and takes her first good look at me. She puts her hand over her mouth, closes her eyes, and opens them again in the hope it will somehow look better than it did the first time. It doesn't.

"Lyla," Topaz gasps, as she puts her hand on my arm, then runs the back of it over my cheek. The contrast between her dark skin and my pale visage makes the world stutter for just a moment. In my immobile state, my flesh has become nearly translucent. "She looks so small."

"It's the hospital socks," Pen gurgles, trying to control the rush of emotions bubbling up as she stands witness to the oddly tender touch of Topaz on my brow. "Hospital socks make everyone look small."

Pen's colors shift abruptly from her usual sparring periwinkle to burnt orange. It's not my socks she sees, but the little white booties with ruffled lace edges Rosie wore to the park that day. Bill tried to get her to wear her sandals but she wanted her "momma socks" because Pen was on the road. She was still wearing them when Pen entered the curtained off bay in the emergency room. Her tiny shoes must have fallen off as Bill rushed her screaming and choking to the ambulance that jerked to a halt at the edge of the grass. Rosie's body, swollen with bee stings from a nest she wandered into, her face already discolored, went limp in his arms. His. Arms. EMT's gave the small girl enough epinephrine to treat a horse, but it was too late. No one at the park had an Epi-pen. Bill wouldn't have known to ask for one if they had. By the time the police car picked Penelope up at the airport to rush her to the ER, there was nothing left for her to do but mourn.

"I didn't know, baby. I didn't know," Pen moaned, gathering Rosie in her arms. The toddler was cool and not quite stiff, but losing flexibility rapidly. She hugged her daughter so tightly, as if she could somehow draw Rosie back inside her body and give birth to her anew. When she looked down and saw the white socks on the bluish legs of her precious girl, a cry came out of that woman that dwarfed every sound on earth in its horror and desperation. There was no word, no image, no color that could hold it. Rosie was gone. Pen missed the signs of a venom allergy. She missed the chance to rush her child to care, to breathe for her, to fight for her, to challenge fate in a match of wills over her. She missed the moment of death. She missed her daughter's life.

"The records are all safe, yes?" Topaz asks, taking in all the numbers on the monitor, as if she had any idea what they could possibly mean. Surely they add up to something, right?

"Huh?" Pen's mind goes through whiplash as she's yanked forward through time, from that fluorescent emergency bay to this clattering dimly lit hospital room where she plans to wait for my death like a stalker at the bus depot. This time, she won't look away, she won't give in, and she won't be late.

"The membership records and files of those who have taken classes or counseling from Lyla, they're secure, right? They can't be hacked and end up as the sidebar of *News Now*?"

"How should I know?"

"Your fucking nephew was the computer tech who did the work, remember?" Topaz lets me go, subconsciously aware she probably shouldn't berate my student while holding my hand. "He's some kind of computer god."

"Oh, Jeremy. Yeah. He's not a god, though, or a tech. He's a hacker who uses his skill to keep people like him from doing what he can do. He could be a great programmer, but he's sorta a ne'er do well. He needed money for one of his costumes, and Lyla gave him the job. You know her soft spot for 'creatives.'"

"Costumes? Oh, Lordy, here comes today's top story."

"He's a professional cosplayer. He goes to conventions dressed like comic book characters. Those costumes can run thousands of dollars. Anyway there's not a program he can't break into, and if he did our system, no one can get anything out."

"Maybe the cops should hire him. They've asked everyone on staff if we knew Lyla's password. They said they can send her computer to the state lab to break the encryption but that takes time and they want to clean this up fast."

"Why are they wasting time on her computer? Do they think she has a Word document in there called 'My plan to murder Keith Allen?' or 'Revenge.docx?' Everyone knows she didn't do this. They're just trying to pin it on her because a fast answer is better than no answer."

Topaz inhales deeply and lets the air out like a slow mist. She looks at the monitor again. "Well, the three passwords they tried were Buddha, Virga, and Marian. So they need all the help they can get."

Pen sits back down in the recliner and leans it all the way back. For the first time, the small lines snaking from the corner of her eyes are visible to the casual observer. Every wave of information washes more sand from the beach. She needs this to end. It's only a matter of time until she's lost to the erosion.

"I'm kinda surprised it wasn't Marian," Pen says wistfully.

"Me, too."

12

"What are your plans for the center?" Topaz asks. She hates waste. Money, time, pizza crust—everything in her world has a proper and quick use. Beating around the bush is for the ungrateful, and she won't have it.

"Um...I don't know...I'm guessing you heard..."

"She left everything to you? Of course I heard."

"Fucking big mouth cops."

"I heard it from Luka. Investigators are turning Virga upside down looking for evidence. She showed them where Lyla kept her paperwork. She asked me if we should call you because your name was on a document. Turns out she was one of the witness signatures on the will."

"Luka knew?" Penelope glances over at me, giving the best case of side-eye ever given to a woman in a coma. I'd giggle, if I could.

"Luka knows everything about Lyla and 'Miss Marian.' She was at Virga with them before Lyla hired me to run the center."

"She was what? Their housekeeper?"

"I don't know. I just know the only person on earth who possibly took Marian's death harder than Lyla is Luka."

"You know," Penelope looks through the open door to make sure the quiet little cook isn't standing outside. "Marian is the only name I've ever heard her say. It was always 'The teacher' and 'Miss Marian' but no one else gets mentioned."

"She calls you 'The Movie Star.'"

"I know!" Penelope sits forward, happy to brush the heaviness of the situation away for a few moments and engage in some girl talk, even if it is with Topaz. "I've told her a hundred times I'm an author, not a movie star. She makes me sound like Ginger from *Gilligan's Island*."

"Girl." Topaz waves a hand in her direction. "Please. Ginger? Nah. You're just a young version of Mrs. Howell."

Penelope's eyebrows raise as her brain loads a cannonball into her mouth and readies to return fire.

"I wouldn't talk, Mary Ann."

"Mary Ann? Really?"

"At best."

"Well, Lovey, assuming Thurston didn't get all of your money in his divorce settlement, what are your plans for the center?"

"Isn't this a little premature? I know she's been out for longer than Dr. Gonzalez would like, but her mind, it's so strong, so able...if anyone can come back..."

"Come back, and go to prison," Topaz sneers. "Whatever her future is, the center is not going to be part of it. We need to rename it, rebrand it. Get a new guru."

"You don't know that." Pen's eyes narrow like a cat extracting her claws into the arm of the sofa as a preview of things to come if you touch her vulnerable belly too quickly or too hard.

"You've got to see this for what it really is. You can't just sit in this room and write a new ending. Her life as we know it is over. You can't run from this."

"I know all about running. I've run from far worse things than this. Trust me when I tell you, running is not what I'm doing here."

"Then we need a blueprint. Offer her up to her fate and move forward on our own. We can't do that until you admit the truth. Live or die, she's not who you thought she was. She's not who any of us thought she was. She's our past, not our future. Come back to the center with me so we can minimize the damage. Leave the night watch behind."

"Never."

"She killed them, Penelope."

"No."

"Yes."

"We're talking about Lylarose Gentry. The woman who keeps a bug cup in every room of the center so spiders can be relocated instead of killed. The woman who stops the car, no matter how late she's running, to carry turtles across the road. The woman who answers every question, listens to every person, wishes on stars, and heals hearts so broken she has to use pieces of her own to put them back together. There's just no way."

"She agreed to counsel him."

"She was trying to help."

"Because she intended to kill him all along."

"It was his fucking wife who came to Virga and begged her to do it."

"She made that weapon."

"There has to be another explanation."

"She got the guard's gun."

"There's no proof. Mesa says he wasn't even supposed to be there with a gun."

"She murdered those people."

"You sleazy Judas. How can you even say the words? You have meditated beside her for years. You've seen her live the precepts she teaches. Topaz, you work with her every day. You know her!"

"I know a woman sick with grief. A woman who stopped sleeping, stopped eating, stopped smiling. I know a woman who put her whole heart in the arms of another and lost everything she had, including her mind. I know an intellectual fortress so tall and strong that when it imploded, the shattered pieces came down like meteors, and the whole village was buried beneath them. Don't you understand? I've been crushed under one of those rocks, too. Don't you see I'm bloody, and broken, and exhausted from pushing the weight of this off of me so I can breathe? It's not just you, princess. We're all aching. We're all trapped. We all need rescue. And we aren't going to get through this until we accept the truth. If you really believe the things she taught you, then you have to awaken to reality and face the facts. She's guilty."

"Get out of this room."

A soft voice, so airy and sweet you'd think it was the sound of fairies landing on crystalline flower petals, flutters through the sickly gray energy clogging the room in a choking fog.

"The teacher," Luka says, gently placing the clothing bags on an empty chair before rushing to my bedside. She makes soft cooing sounds and covers my body with pure energy like cool water, refreshing my soul and everything else in the room. She pauses and looks at me as slowly and deliberately as she slices mushrooms; so paper thin that they disappear the moment they hit the pan, leaving only the flavor of their goodness behind. She drinks in my spirit and her surety covers my entire body with peace.

"We managed to get it all up here in one trip." Robyn's deep, hearty announcement provides the rock for Luka's water to crash upon. She drops a large suitcase with a thud. "Are you moving in?"

"Hopefully, I won't be here that long," Penelope says. "Thank you for your help, um..."

"Robyn Brooks." She reaches out to offer Penelope a clumsy

handshake, not unlike a sweaty politician reaching for a donor. The stocky woman with rough hands, no makeup, and a haircut aptly named 'sheer and shave' smiles broadly. Penelope offers a limp-wristed, garden-party hand tap in response. If Luka is the scent of sea spray on a crisp morning, Robyn is the salt of the earth rising from fresh ground on a humid afternoon. "I'm so glad to meet you, Ms. Fine. I see you at Virga on Fridays when I go to Dharma and Donuts, but I never wanted to disturb you. Luka says you're there on remembrance."

"Retreat. I'm doing a personal retreat," Penelope adds, trying to keep an eye on Luka but unable to avoid Robyn's intruding nature.

"When Topaz suggested I come tell you what I told her, I was so happy because meeting you has been a dream of mine."

"Topaz brought you specifically to talk to me?" The corners of Pen's Cheshire cat smile start to rise. Someone's gonna get it.

"Yeah. I was telling her those cops are full of shit, and she said I should come and let you know what I had to say, in case it helps with anything, you know?"

Luka kisses me on the side of my forehead, in the soft space above my eye. I'd trade my oxygen line just to feel it for a second.

"She is between worlds," Luka says, intertwining her fingers in mine, careful not to jar any of the tubing keeping me connected to this life.

"Do you think she can hear us?" Robyn asks. "I always wondered that. Like, can people who are checked out actually hear what we're saying and stuff—it's just—they can't answer?"

"Of course, she can hear us," Luka says. "She's our teacher. She hears the words we say, and the words we don't. She hears us now like the trees and rocks of the earth hear us, silently understanding more than we even know we say."

Penelope looks over at Topaz and silently mouths the word "Judas."

"They've done brain scans with patients in a coma that show they can hear," the nurse says as she hustles over to make sure Luka didn't dislodge anything important. The bags on the pole are only half empty. She fusses with some buttons on the monitor, creating noise but not change. Her presence is message, not medicine. "Some patients move from coma into what is known as a 'minimally conscious state' in which they have consciousness about what is around them, even though they can't participate. That's why we try to limit the amount of people and activity in the ICU."

Boom goes the dynamite.

"They just came by for a quick visit. They'll be leaving soon," Penelope assures. She's too tired to put on her public accent, but the nurse responds to the few pieces of glitter the author has left in her charisma case.

"Alright, then. Just remember, you should always assume a patient can hear you. Keep it positive. Speak love."

The nurse leaves as Penelope reaches for her phone to tap out that last sentence in her notepad. Whatever book she ends up writing, that's sure to be her "fine advice." With the progress she's made, I'd like to think she'll attribute it to the ICU nurse who said it, but I don't. That's okay. The nurse didn't say it to be in the liner notes of the next great self-help tome. She said it because sometimes helping the patient means healing their loved ones first. That's something Marian said.

"So anyway, Ms. Fine," Robyn begins with her recently chastised indoor voice, but regains full volume by the second sentence. "I was telling Topaz, the cops are full of shit."

"Yes, you mentioned that."

"See, I wasn't always into mindfulness. I spent most of my life mind blowing, or at least mind drugging, you know? Anyway, that's how I met Dr. Gentry. I was in a halfway house after I got out of prison, and she came and did a speech about using meditation to forgive yourself and connect with your true goodness. I asked what happened if you dug in your heart and there wasn't any goodness. Lyla just laughed and said, 'Then you're not a bad person, you're a bad archeologist, cause it's in there. Keep digging.'"

"Prison." Penelope's fake smile, like her accent, is so faded it barely registers on her face. What is obvious are the persistent daggers her eyes keep throwing toward Topaz.

"That's why I wanted to meet you. I went through the shit as a kid, and then I turned around and piled it on everyone as an adult. When I couldn't deal with it anymore, drugs dealt with it for me. I tried rehab, methadone, even Jesus, but I just couldn't get free. I decided to cash my check, and bought enough smack to stop all the pain, you know, forever. I got picked up before I could even get the needle in my arm. I had so much powder on me I got busted for possession with intent to sell, even though the only place I was planning to take it was hell."

Luka shudders when Robyn says the word "hell," and her normally quicksilver aura ripples as a rock breaks the surface of the pond. I don't blame her. Once you've been through hell, that word never sounds casual again.

"I did three years of a five year sentence. It was hard going, but then they got your book, *Far from Fine*, in the library. I read about what you went through, and how you got through it, and I followed your twelve-step system "Terrible to Terrific" all the way. We even had a group meeting in the common room once a week to go over it and support each other. By the time I got out, I was ready for life, you know? Anyway, I want to thank you. Your book was the key."

"I'm so glad it helped you." Penelope pulls the recliner back to its upright position and begins to stand. I once told her that being forced to listen to the constant praise for the book she sold her soul to write is her karma, and the only thing one can do with that kind of karma is accept it, and learn. Some lessons in life are set on eternal repeat. They're usually the ones we need the most.

"Just listen," Topaz whispers, pulling Pen's sleeve to hold her in the chair.

"Yeah, so, like I was saying, I did three of five, and while I was in, there was this chick who was found guilty of killing her grandmother. Drug money, you know? But her lawyer had the appeal going strong because they never found the old lady's body. She meets with her priest in the confessional room they have set up. You know, a safe room."

"Like the one Lyla was in?"

"Yeah. Well, she got in bad with a roughneck on our wing and was worried she was gonna get killed, so she tells this priest every-thing. I mean, like, everything. And he can't tell because, you know, priest. Two weeks later, the lawyer drops the case because a 'sniffer dog' on a 'random exercise' just happens to dig up grandma under some wild mushrooms in the woods."

"Why am I listening to the ID Discovery channel?"

"Shut up," Topaz says with the authority of a woman who's raised two boys to become excellent, well-disciplined men.

"Then one of my podmates got busted for dealing prescription drugs she got from this music minister at her church who was also a pharmacy tech. She never ratted him out cause it was a short sen-tence, and they were hot and heavy, you know, besides the drugs. So he got clergy clearance to see her in the counseling room, and they were talking about getting back to business once she was out. A few weeks later, the pharmacy installed some surveillance and guess who got picked up with a pocket full of rockets? That guy."

"Robyn, I've been sitting with Lyla since the police came to Virga. I'm very, very tired."

"Don't you see?"

"No."

"Seeing clearly has been a problem for Penelope, lately," Topaz interjects.

"You shut up."

"That secured counseling room is bullshit. They claim there's no cameras, no sound, because of our rights, but every secret I ever saw go in one of those damn rooms came out in the wash. Suddenly, cops who know nothing are brilliant. The answers to questions just fall out of the sky. Everyone inside knows the room they tell you is safe is the most jacked-up room of all."

Penelope leans forward. "You're saying there are hidden cameras in secured rooms like the one Lyla was in?"

"Thank you, Buddha. Someone finally pulled the sword from the stone." Topaz makes a deep bow to Robyn causing Luka to giggle. Me too, in spirit if not body.

"Yeah."

"Why don't they just release it then? If I leave a bad tip for a waiter, it goes viral in 20 minutes. Why wouldn't a tape that shows exactly what happened in that room get out? And if they know what happened, why are they taking computers, collecting fingerprints, and spending piles of budget money trying to figure it out? Maybe your prison was leaky, but I don't think that's the case here. They are working too hard to solve this case to have the answer in their pocket all along. But, thanks."

"It's not out because it can't get out."

"Are you kidding? That skank, Laura Lindeman, has been waiting for a case like this since the Casey Anthony trial bought Nancy Grace her own island. I could get a story about Lyla on *News Now* before the elevator hit the lobby."

Luka releases my hand and takes the final seat in the corner of the room. She lets her fingertips glide across Pen's shoulder, seeing if she can transfer my presence to her. "You know how the teacher tells us 'Stop thinking like you think?'"

"What?"

"Egg-zactly!" Robyn catches the ball that sails over Pen's head. "You're thinking from the outside. Try thinking from the inside. They can't let the tape out because if they admitted that the secured counseling room is being monitored, they'd be violating about a million prisoner rights, and every inmate who talked in the room could..."

"Go to court and get their charges dismissed."

"So they have to do the work and make it look like they solved it without the help. You know how, when you get a puzzle, there's a picture on the box? That's what the recording is. It's the picture they secretly use to put all the pieces together. And if they don't like the picture, they can make a new one out of the pieces and put the box in a furnace."

"So if there is a picture on the box, how can we see it?"

"I'm an ex-smack head, not a strategist," Robyn says before her eyes fill once more with stars. "But I bet you can figure it out."

The nurse makes another pass, and Topaz catches one hell of a glare before she breaks the party up. Walking to the door, Pen catches her by the arm.

"I don't get you, Top Ass."

"Of course you don't."

"First you tell me I need to accept that Lyla massacred three people, then you bring this woman here to tell me how to prove she didn't. What the hell?"

"If Robyn's right, and there's evidence of what happened in that prison, you're the perfect person to find it. You've got power. You've got money. You've got connections. If the cops are lying, and she didn't do it, you can spin that bullshit into gold. If they aren't, and you end up watching her blow holes in your faith, then you can move on with your life and do what it takes to save the center."

"So this is all because you don't want to lose your job?"

"Don't be so disillusioned. I'm just thinking like I think."

Four students look at the same pale, tube-covered body that once was their teacher. Topaz's mouth forms a snarl of anger and disgust, merely the fruit of her brutal disappointment. Penelope's eyes show desire and fear. She wants there to be a camera in that room. She wants to see that video, and she's terrified of what it may show her. Robyn gives me a confident "whatever you did, I got your back" kind of nod. Luka looks at me the same way she does every day. It's the way she appeared when she brought me tea, or told me an appointment was waiting in my office. It's the same expression she had the day she found me on the living room floor, hugging the vase that holds Marian's ashes, my mouth propped open in silent lock-jawed sobs. The same one she had the day she caught me in the kitchen, mercilessly stabbing a block of ice with no glass nearby, jamming the hand-sharpened pick into it again, again, and again. I've been at least ten different people during my third and most horrible life, but I never changed in Luka's eyes.

"May we come back later with some tea for the teacher?" Luka asks.

"I don't know if that's a..."

"Yeah. Luka can make you a salad or something, Ms. Fine. You know, because, hospital food," Robyn adds.

"Pot stickers?"

"Pot stickers." The two visitors nod in agreement.

"That would be wonderful."

There are journeys of the heart, battles of wits, and wars of the mind, but the stomach is always going to win.

"Luka, what do you know about Lyla? Do you know where she's from? Why she never talked about herself? Is there something we should know? Something that could help us? Something in her past?"

The cook shakes her head. I have a filter. Luka has a vault.

"A long time ago I asked the teacher how to let go of the past, and she told me she had no experience in that," Luka says as her eyes mist over with memory. "She said she did not have to let go of her past. It let go of her."

13

Whether you go to college, see the world, or just work while you try to find a path that suits you, seventeen through twenty-three is a fantastic time of life. You know everything. You have nothing. You'll try anything. Your regrets can be carried in a backpack. Your hope is a mountain. When the acceptance letters and scholarships rolled in, just under the deadline due to my late filing, I did what everyone expected. I listened to where my parents wanted me to go, said nothing, and chose a college in the opposite direction. I kept the science major dad had advised but soon discovered it was the scientific art of understanding people that called to me.

"We are moving to Indiana in three weeks. Why am I standing in this shit-shack cubicle in California, Lylarose? Do you have an explanation as to what in hades I'm doing here? Because I would really like to hear it."

"Beats the hell out of me, ma'am." That was my first thought. Fortunately, the filter was locked in with tight screws, and it managed to stop the words before they slid down my tongue. "Um...I don't know why you're here, Mom."

"I'm here because the counselor called me, Lylarose. She called me because she said you changed your major from biology and pre-med to the department of psychology. PSY-CHOLLLL-O-GYYYY." She spit words at me with such disgust the air dripped with the mucus of her immune system rejecting them. "Your father couldn't leave work, or he'd be here with me to talk about how disappointing and ridiculous this is. If he had any sense, he'd have brought his belt along."

I backed away from my tiny desk and slowly eased to the other side of the dorm room cot from my mother. If I needed to, I could step diagonally and put Shawna's cot between us as well. For now, one bed-length seemed to be enough. Late at night, I often sat in the darkness pierced only by the stereo lights, listening to slow jazz, wondering what our mother-daughter relationship would be like when I was too old to hit, too big to be bossed. I realized, standing by daylight in the dorm room, wearing a Mills College sweatshirt, and looking for an object to hide behind, that I'd never be a grown up in my mother's mind. If I was President of the United States, she'd stab a secret service agent just to get close enough to slap the words right out of my smart mouth. Or, she'd screw him. Whichever was faster.

Speaking slowly and carefully, fully aware that Tina, the world's meanest RA, and the rest of the women's dorm hadn't been given a hurricane warning and were unprepared for the chaos, I tried to calm the storm. "I know I changed my major. I didn't know they called you about it. I don't understand that part, ma'am."

"You're underage. You're still seventeen. They had to call us for permission."

"Did you give it to them?" Please, please, please let her have done the right thing.

"Of course not. Don't be absurd."

"Mom..."

"Don't 'mom' me, missy. If you don't want to be a doctor, you can be a researcher or a college professor. If you don't enjoy biology classes, you can be an engineer, or a statistician. I'll pay for you to transfer out of this hippie hellhole to a real school where you can major in physics or mathematic theory. The one thing you are not going to do with your time and my money is become a goddamn psychologist."

"I don't want to fight." I raised both arms and inched a little closer to Shawna's cot. "But I'm here on a full scholarship. It's not your money. In fact, I'm the only person on this floor who isn't getting any parental support. I'm the only person who..."

"It's the principle, Lylarose. It was my money that raised you. It was my money that put clothes on your back, shoes on your feet, and those twenty-dollar-a-pop inhalers in your mouth. Everything I have done has been an investment in your future." She looked around the small dorm. "And, my god, what a poor return I've gotten."

At that moment, what I wanted—more than a bag of groceries, or a new set of tires on my rattletrap car, or air in my lungs when the asthma elephant crushed my chest—was to remind her that it was my father who had the paying job in this family, and she only had the money for her "investment" because he invested in her. Maybe his return wasn't so good either. But the room was small, and there were innocent people in the hall pretending to read posters on the wall who were listening to every word. Practicality before pleasure. Safety before sass. If survival was my religion, I was a high priestess by seventeen.

"I don't want to be a doctor, or any of those other things. They are all great jobs for someone, but not for me. I want to understand people, and I want to help people understand themselves. People talk to me all the time about everything. I want to use that for something good. This is what I've chosen to do with my life."

"Really? Well you've never been very good at picking what to do with your life, have you? At six, you wanted to be a paleontologist, and at twelve you wanted to work for Atari as a game tester. It's always been dreams and patty-cake with you, Lylarose. It's time for you to grow up and face the music. Helping people understand themselves is never going to pay your rent. Get your ass back to biology."

"I'm not going to be seventeen forever," I said. She turned and looked at me, mouth pressed closed, jaw locked, flat hand pulling back. I straightened up and looked her straight in the eye. That's the thing about temporary insanity. It isn't temporary at all, really. It's a slow rolling boulder gathering mass, inching closer every day to the edge of the cliff.

"What did you just say to me, young lady?"

Now or never, Lyla. Stand up to her now or serve her forever. Just like your father.

"I said I'm not going to be seventeen forever. I'll keep taking the basics that are required for both majors. When I am of age, I'll just change my major anyway. I am going to be a psychologist. Not because I can't get a man—or a woman—to support me. Because it is what I want to do. It's...it's...who I am."

"You think this is going to make everything better?" She hissed, low and virulent. Her accent was completely swallowed by the bile in her mouth. "You think you are going to become some kind of social services warrior swooping in and taking kids out of their bad homes the way you prayed they'd come for you? You think it's going to make your scars go away if you hold their little hands all the way to foster care? Forget it, Lylarose. No one came for you then, and saving others won't help you now."

This was her greatest guilt in my mind. Even after this discussion, when I would lie awake, or try to meditate, or write a journal entry, I would come back to this moment. I can remember the smell of RA fundraiser popcorn wafting up from the front desk, the bleak, faded wallpaper with roses behind my mother's head, the way Shawna half-ass made her bed and left the crinkled blanket under the coverlet, and three drops of rain—then four—on the window. I remember it all so clearly. For most of my life I thought this was the highest horror I would ever endure. She knew.

I always thought the beatings, the berating, the late night rallies, the early morning lies were a rollercoaster she didn't buy a ticket for. I thought she, like my father, just found herself strapped into the tumultuous ride, and later, when she looked back at the slides, she thought we were just an average family on vacation having fun, even if it didn't feel like it at the time. But no. Standing there analyzing my career decision, she revealed the stark truth all too clearly. She knew they had damaged me irreparably. She knew it was abuse. She knew I needed—I prayed for—a rescue. She knew it was wrong. All along, she knew it was wrong. She knew our family was a living hell. She put her daughter through it anyway.

"I don't want to be a child services worker," I said, sticking with the facts until I could process the rest. "I want to be a trauma recovery therapist. I want to work with people who endured something terrible or who lack the life skills to cope with their challenges."

"What a bunch of hogwash. Surely you have a higher goal in life than helping the crazies go to a grocery store between flashbacks. That's what you're talking about, right? Helping all these "adult children" learn how to put on their boots and take responsibility for their own life? Let me tell you something, Missy. Once you take the car keys, you're responsible. It's not Mommy or Daddy or mean Aunt Sally's fault you're fucked up. They can sit on your couch and whine their ass off, and it's nobody's fault but their own."

"You don't see the pain people are going through," I said, using all my powers to keep from crying in front of her. I hadn't mentioned the colors to my mother since I got the filter. I had never told her what it felt like to hear and see the sorrows of others every time I go out the front door. An elderly woman in the grocery store tells me she's exhausted from watching TV until 2:00 a.m. because she can't figure out how to go to bed now that her husband is gone. A girl in my poetry elective confides in me that she told her mom about her dad touching her, and the mom did nothing. A dear friend who made me laugh, and gave me extra food when he could, swore me to secrecy then informed me he was diagnosed with **GRID**. Nineteen years old, full of life, love, and music. He was dead before they renamed it **AIDS**. Strangers, teachers, friends, lovers, the whole world is a Jackson Pollock painting in my head pleading for mercy, and I can't just ignore it.

"People are hurting. Men, young gay men, are dying daily. Women, wonderful kind women, are struggling. There is a need for someone who listens. Someone who sees things clearly. Someone who can help them to help themselves. I don't always know why, but I am that person. At least, I'm one of them."

"Don't be so dramatic. When Barry was your age, young people were taking LSD and jumping from windows, but he didn't become a drug counselor. Rise above the riff-raff, Lylarose. Whatever this gay plague thing is, it probably serves them right. They made choices."

"If sexual indiscretion deserves the death penalty," I started, lifting my eyebrows and cocking my head to the side. I didn't get to finish that sentence. I didn't have to. If she was accusing me of making mountains out of molehills, she would have been right. Because I just took her little bubbling pit of upper middle class snobbery and turned it into Vesuvius.

"You listen to me, you spoiled brat! I'm not the one with my head up my ass, throwing away the future for the cause of the day. Who do you think you are? Robin Hood? You want to live in the gutter with the rest of the homos, spreading around god-knows-what because you feel sorry for them? Go to it. You want to blame parents for the child and the rich for the poor? Do it! You want to live in blinders and think the world should be kittens and candy land? Have it at! Scrape all your pennies together each month to pay the rent and wear clothes from the second hand store if you want. But don't come crying to me for money when you've got nothing but a dollar in your pocket and disease on your hands."

"I won't," I said in a low, stern cadence. "That's Barry's job."

SLAP!!!!! The red, fiery sting of her palm across my cheek echoed through the room, and probably the rest of the dorm. My neck whipped to the side and my vision blurred when my glasses flew off and landed on the floor with a clatter. I slumped to the ground, clutching my face. I felt the motion of her arm pulling back as her body sucked every molecule of energy from the room. She was going to hit me again, and this time, she wouldn't stop with my already swelling cheek. She'd break every bone in my face before that hand stopped descending on me over and over again. She sucked air in through her clenched teeth, hissing and building herself into a perfect storm. She stepped forward, her arm back as far as it would be. I put my hand, my scarred, painstakingly repaired hand, in harm's way once more to soften the blow. She bared her teeth like some kind of wild beast and...

"So! You're Lyla's mom?" The chipper, hyperactively fast voice, about three octaves too high, shattered the moment—unexpected lightning causing everything to freeze. "I'm so glad to meet you. I'm Shawna Tewes, Lyla's roommate. I'm sure she's told you all about me."

The silence after the strike was profound. My mother stood there, her arm still raised in the air like a mannequin from *The Twilight Zone*. Slowly, I pulled my extended hand back to my body and took a few grateful breaths of air, made crisp and clear by the flash of Shawna's appearance. Shawna had one hand on her hip and the other extended, as if she was greeting my mother at afternoon tea instead of interrupting a near death experience. Finally, my mother dropped her arm.

"Get up, Lylarose. Don't make a scene." She was still hissing, but her accent had returned. She kept her back to Shawna for as long as she could. I was worried that when my mother did turn around, her eyes would slice my roommate in half, and she'd fall in two pieces on the floor. Shawna withdrew her ignored open hand and managed a weak smile as my mother looked her up and down, mentally collecting ammunition from her hand-me-down dress to her over-styled eighties hair. The number of Shawna's flaws ticked off in my mother's head so loudly we could all hear the clicking.

"I...ah...I think Lyla might need some ice for that cheek," Shawna mumbled.

"That is the beginning of what Lylarose needs," came the severe response. Shawna winced and pulled back, the way you do when you open the oven and all the heat rushes out to scald your soul. Mom turned around to face me one last time. "Don't call. Don't write. Don't ask. Don't bother."

And with that—she was gone. No phone calls. No Christmas cards. No nothing. At some point, my father retired from the company, and they moved to a little town not far from the farm where he was raised. He promised her it would be their "forever home," and she bought a new set of luggage and learned the route to the Knoxville airport by heart. He gardened, she traveled. Or so I heard in the newsy notes my aunt Cindy would send until arthritis took her hands.

Shawna followed my mother—at a safe distance—out of the room and down the hall, ensuring the storm was actually over and not just retreating to gain momentum. I managed to get off the floor and was sitting on my cot when she appeared with a sandwich bag full of ice cubes she stole from the RA freezer without permission. She wrapped it in a Mills T-shirt and held it against my cheek until I could hold it myself.

"Are you gonna be okay, Lyla?"

"Yes," I whispered. What choice did I have? What was there besides being okay?

"Your mom is so...so..."

"Yeah."

"Look, I know that was none of my business, and I shouldn't have busted in. I just thought..."

"You're either really brave, or kinda dumb," I said, my voice returning to its soft, steady tone. "Either way, I'm glad you were here."

"I really stood up to her, didn't I?"

I chuckled, which made the swollen side of my face howl and tighten. It was the last time I was ever slapped in the face, and the only time I actually deserved it. Barry wasn't here to explain or defend himself. I shouldn't have brought him into it. Shawna shouldn't have been drawn into harm's way either, but I felt less guilt about her involvement. She made a choice she was proud of.

"You looked like seventies Wonder Woman standing there with your hands on your hips. All you needed was the spin and that bad disco music in the background."

"That's high praise coming from Robin Hood."

"You heard that?"

"Are you kidding? The History Department across the street heard that."

"I don't know what to say about this."

"You don't have to say a damn thing."

Later, on our way to the dining hall, Tina the RA watched us go by the desk. She gave a low whistle as I passed. "Gentry, with that for a mother it's no wonder you never talk."

I just kept walking, but Shawna—who was always better at giving advice than following it—spun around, put her hands on her hips, and flipped her hair like Diana Prince getting ready to transform. She pointed majestically at Tina.

"Shut. Up. Bitch."

Then, she leapt through the doorway singing, "Wonder Woman..."

My smile made my face hurt all the way to dinner. Her friendship, that rock steady, always ready friendship, would be the safe harbor for me a few years later, when my first life came to an abrupt, bloody end.

14

Penelope arranges her necessities, turning this little beeping cave of well monitored stasis into an impromptu dressing room that makes her look like a refugee from an explosion at Bergdorf Goodman's, and heads once more to the bathroom—the only private space the officer stationed at the door will grant her unless she's willing to leave the room. She stops and faces my body, always hopeful. Never assured.

"If I spend much more time making phone calls in the potty, the next *News Now* headline is going to read 'Author gets C-Diff waiting for Beloved Murder Guru to Die.'"

Well, at least she's kept a sense of humor about things. She shakes her phone at me, not unlike what she would have done to her own teenage daughter if things had gotten that far.

"I'm going to find that tape, Lyla. If there is one. And when I do, I'll watch it...I'm gonna...well...don't disappoint me, okay?"

The hiss of vent seems to answer, but neither one of us knows what it's trying to say. She closes the bathroom door with a sharp click, just as the officer answers his phone and begins scribbling in the tiny notebook he fishes out of his pocket. If I were granted the power to talk, even for a minute, I'd tell Penelope three quick things:

I am so proud of you.

I'm so sorry.

The walls in this place are made of fancy cardboard and the bathroom is not as private as you think it is.

"Hey, Trin, It's Penelope."

"Honey, how are you? How's Lyla? What's going on? Greg says the paparazzi have you trapped in the hospital like some kind of wild fox and you're probably chewing off your own foot."

"No, no...no foot chewing, yet. I'm here by choice, but there is a whole hunting party on the street below. I'm sitting with Lyla."

"How is she doing?"

"Not so good."

"Sorry, love. The news is saying crazy things. What happened?"

"It's a long story, Trin, but I think you can help me sort it out."

"Anything."

"When you did the research for your mystery series, did you get any information from Bowles Pass, they call it 'The Bowl,' or any of the prisons here in Maryland?"

"No, sorry, hon. Greg does most of the legwork on those. You know what they say about college professors—we don't die, we just change our specialty to research. He used the prisons upstate. If you need something done, I can ask him."

"That's okay, thanks anyway. I need some information about this specific prison and the warden there, Hammer or Hallum or Humble or something, but I need it now."

"Penelope Fine, come on down!"

"What?"

"I have three interns from the English Department sitting around my office playing Zip-Zap or some damn game on their phones. I can have anything on the web sent to you in about an hour. With a little more time and some free pizza, they can give you the world."

"Fantastic. I need to know anything they find about the prison, floor plan, how it's built, when, by whom, and everything about the warden, his social media footprint, political affiliations, awards, headlines, anything."

"Moving over to the fiction aisle with me?"

"Oh my god, Trin, I wish this was fiction."

"Are you okay?"

"Yes."

"No, I mean, really. You're not, well, you're..."

"I'm not going to take a bunch of pills and wake up in your brother's bed and breakfast puking my guts out."

"Hey, now, that's not what I meant."

"It's exactly what you meant. And no, I'm not there. The reason is lying in this room fighting for her life, and I'm not even sure why. I'm confused, but I'm not hopeless."

"You'll tell me if..."

"Thanks for the info. Can you send it to my private email? The public account is way too hot right now."

"You got it. Love you!"

"Same."

Penelope flushes and washes her hands, considering herself a master of illusion. Still, she jumps when she opens the door to see the police officer standing right in front of it.

"Oh my gosh!"

"Sorry, Ms. Fine, I didn't mean to scare you or..." he gestures toward the toilet. "...get in your business."

"That's okay. I'm a little raw right now. Emotionally! I mean, emotional right now."

"Well, Detective Mesa called and asked me to give you the latest on the case. He said you wanted to be updated on any developments."

She nods as he tries to decipher his own handwriting.

"The room analysis has been completed, as has Dr. Gentry's clothing. They are still working on her body scraping."

"What about Keith Allen's body? Did they scrape it too?"

"Um...I don't know, ma'am. I'm just reading what he told me."

"I'm sorry, Officer. Go ahead."

"The majority of the blood found on Dr. Gentry's clothing, other than her own, was consistent with the wing supervisor, Cecilia Rhodes. It was determined Rhodes was shot at close range. There were a few spatters of Corrections Officer Johnson's blood on her clothing, not consistent with being near the victim when he was shot. Her clothing also contained Inmate Allen's blood, which is expected since the bullet that hit Dr. Gentry was a through-and-through to him."

"Did she shoot him? Did she shoot any of them?"

"Detective Mesa didn't tell me that. Two weapons were found at the scene. One was a stabbing implement brought into the facility by Dr. Gentry. There are two sets of prints on that: Dr. Gentry and an unidentified print. The other was C.O. Johnson's service weapon. There were four sets of prints found on it: Dr. Gentry, Inmate Allen, C.O. Johnson, and an unidentified print. The two unidentified prints do not match each other. C.O. Rhodes was a direct contact officer. They don't carry weapons, but her Taser and control implements were undisturbed in her belt.

"All four had gunshot residue on their persons, probably because it was such a small room. That shit goes everywhere. Dr. Gentry also has a burn mark on her neck, likely from a hot casing, and a laceration on the webbing of her right hand, which shows she was holding the gun and cut by the slide."

"What does that mean?"

"You don't know very much about shooting, do you?"

"Buddhists and guns don't really go together."

The young officer looks over at me and tries not to smirk.

"Well, Johnson was a transporter, so he carried a Glock 9mm

in a Blackhawk SERPA III holster. That means it can't be grabbed. He has to disarm the holster with a combination of clicks to release the weapon. The Glock has a slide on the top that takes the bullet through the chamber and ejects the casing."

He turns his finger and thumb into a schoolyard "cops and robbers" game piece. He probably played that a lot growing up. He was always the cop.

"If you hold the weapon incorrectly, once you fire, the slide quickly goes up and back, which will nip the webbing of your hand. After the bullet fires, the Glock ejects the casing, which is hot. Guns don't get hot when you fire them. Casings do. There's not an experienced gun owner in the world who hasn't had a "hot shot" wound when the casing accidentally ends up hitting some skin. I once had a casing jump inside my shirt through an open collar. Boy did that hurt! Then, my girlfriend was furious because she thought I had love bites all over my chest."

The young officer snort-laughs as Penelope emits a gentle giggle like an impressed sorority girl waiting for him to take her out for a burger and some beer. I have some convincing masks in my bag of tricks, but nothing like she's got. Her face simply shape-shifts into the right expression.

"If he had a special holster, how would Lylarose have gotten his gun?"

"She could have overpowered him once he drew his weapon."

"Officer, really?" Now it's her turn to snort. "Look at her. She gets winded doing the downward dog pose in yoga."

"Or he gave it to her."

Penelope winces. She tries to hide her reaction but it's about as noticeable as one of the faces on Mount Rushmore blinking. I've talked people into new places, better habits, and profound turn-arounds in my time. Could I talk my way into a gun? You betcha.

"Inmate Allen had a broken nose and defensive wounds on his hands, including a bite mark on his forearm. A forensic dentist will have to do a comparison, but the detective says it appears to be Dr. Gentry's. She has no visible defensive wounds on her body, other than a bruise on her wrist. Detective Mesa has yet to confirm who actually had control of the gun at the time wing command entered the cell."

"Is that it?"

"That's all he has for now."

"None of that makes her guilty."

"Yes, ma'am." The officer says, returning his notebook to his pocket. "None of it proves she's innocent, either."

"In this country, you have to prove someone guilty, not innocent," Penelope says.

"In court, maybe. Reality doesn't need a lawyer. It just is what it is."

Pen nods in agreement. If nothing else, she's at least grown enough in her spiritual journey to stop fighting with the truth when it's staring her in the face.

"Can you contact people through that thing?" She points to the microphone on his shoulder.

"Just dispatch. I do have a phone though."

"Good. I'm ready to answer some questions, but I'm only willing to talk to the top people in charge. No junior grade detectives, no technicians, not Mesa. I will only talk to the warden and the person in charge of the investigation. Can you do that?"

"Sheriff's office doesn't have any say about what Warden Hummel does, ma'am, but I can ask the lead detective to be here."

"I want the warden, or there's no deal. And give me at least two hours. I need a nap."

"Yes, ma'am, I'll tell them but..." the officer shakes his head and opens the case to his phone.

"But what?"

"Well, if you don't mind me saying so, ma'am, I know Steve Mesa. He was my training officer. He's a good man."

"It's not personal. My time is always in high demand, so I'm used to making it count. Talking with the warden and the person in charge, without going through the middleman, is the way I make things count."

She's the first celebrity he's ever seen up close. He'll tell his friends about it for the next ten years. Stars—they just aren't people like the rest of us.

"Besides," she adds, looking once again at my still form on the bed. "Good people? They can surprise you."

The first guru in Tibet was a man named Padmasambhava. With his consort, Yeshe Tsogyal, he taught dharma to the resistant Tibetans, battling cultural hatred and evil spiritual deities in an effort to bring the people to compassion and truth. He endured outrageous weather, and defeated water dragons and fire wielding demons, not to mention backstabbing court politicians trying to make themselves irreplace-able to the king. Through his concentration, his patience, and his power, he prevailed. He built the first monastery at Samye and found-ed the Nyingma school, the oldest tradition in Tibetan Buddhism. Side by side, Padmasambhava and Yeshe Tsogyal taught for over 50 years, giving wisdom, healing people, and creating esoteric practices thought to be more magic than meditation. He is often called the Second Buddha.

When it was time to leave Tibet, he despaired the truth of his teachings would be mangled by malevolent spirits and greedy intellectuals, so he and his consort used all their powers of mind, body and energy and did a miraculous thing. They hid the wisdom in its unadulterated form in rivers, trees, rocks, and weeds; then in animals, and finally the deepest parts of the minds of human beings. In one ancient story, the guru raised a young girl from the dead, just to tell her a great truth, then allowed her to die again and rejoin the cycle of rebirth. It is said, generations later, her reincarnation discovered the teaching deep in her mind and brought it to the world. This hidden wisdom is called *terma*, and to this day, there are people who dedicate their lives to finding it.

Over time, the concept of terma broadened to include the hidden wisdom that lies in all of us and the nature around us. The way a walk in the woods can soothe and comfort the most stress-addled mind? Terma. That moment when you didn't know how something worked, but you took a guess and it turned out right? Terma. That weird déjà vu you feel when a teacher or a friend tells you a fact, and you nod because it just sounds so right. You don't know why, you just know it's true. Yep—terma. Hidden knowledge is waiting all around us, patient for the moment when we connect to it anew. When you don't know the answer, when you can't find your way, never despair. Terma is there.

The colors I see don't give me terma. They just act like a flashing neon sign alerting me to its presence. With every action, there is reaction. The price I pay for holding the treasure map of terma is being a beacon for people who simply can't hold their secrets anymore. Marian always treated it like a game. I'd come home, drained and over-talked, and she'd take a guess.

"The teller?"

"Not today."

"The doorman?"

"Nope."

"The lady behind you?"

"He was a guy. It's his weekend to pick up the kids, so he's getting out money because those kids bleed him dry. He spends all weekend entertaining them with movies and go-carts when what he would really like is just to chill out with them at home. His ex complains if they don't come back with two T-shirts and a Facebook pic."

"Did you get milk?"

"Yes."

"The guy at the diary case is getting a divorce."

"No, but the woman who works in the floral department is having her brother over for Thanksgiving, even though he's a useless jerk, because it will make their other brother jealous."

"How was your flight?"

"Late."

"Lady on the left?"

"Going home from visiting her sister for the last time. They had a fight over politics, and the only thing they agreed on during the stay was that they were never very close, and it would be better if they let each other go. She's not upset about it in the slightest. The sister is a liberal who would vote for Mickey Mouse if he offered her free health care."

"Viva Mickey!"

"The guy on the right worked for a computer company. Going home after a sales pitch to a client. Really tired of the travel on the job, but the pay is great, and it's the only way he gets to see the world since his partner is too freaking cheap to go anywhere but Cancun on vacation, and they've been there four times. He thinks the partner is screwing around but doesn't want to accuse unless he can prove it."

"I thought you sat on the aisle."

"Oh, I gave that seat up to a lady traveling with little kids so they could all sit together because it's the first time the youngest one has flown, and he's had such a hard year because of a bully in his third grade..."

"STOP!"

"Welcome to my life."

"Quick! What am I thinking right now?"

"That I need to leave my suitcase on the floor, take a fast bath, and tell Luka I'm home because you're starving to death, and she won't feed you without me."

She'd fawn and wrap her arms around me, kissing me with her signature mix of urgency and familiarity.

"You really are amazing."

"Yep, I'm made of fairy dust and stars." I'd lean toward the bed, swiveling my hips and lifting my eyebrows. "Wanna send some star mail to the airline about that flight delay?"

"After dinner," she'd pull away. "I'm near death."

We'd laugh, and eat, and laugh some more. She'd tell me some gory ICU story, and I'd pretend to listen. I'd tell her about my teaching, and she'd interrupt me to add more bloody facts to the ICU story. Eventually, as the night wore on, we'd make our way back to the bedroom, and write that star crossed letter together after all.

She asked me once if I thought the "talk-to-me button" was a blessing or a curse.

"Neither, really. It just is."

"Buddhists are so boring. Catholics, we know how to answer that question. If I heard all the personal shit you hear, I'd have to go to confession once a week, just to tell the priest the scandal. He'd love it! I'd get absolution by the bucket. So, for me—total blessing—with curse-like sprinkles on top."

I never really thought of my synesthesia or the avalanche of personal revelations I endured to be a curse until the day Keith Allen buried me in ash.

"My mother used to keep cheese in her purse," he said. Hands on the table in the gray concrete room, a shrug from his shoulders was the only movement he'd attempt. We were still new at our biweekly dance. I watched as his pock-marked face got fatter on hefty portions of self-pity and prison food. He likely saw me shivering, withering into a cavern so deep my cries could not produce an echo. The ice pick hadn't yet made its maiden voyage into this barbed wire Escher painting. There was still hope, then.

"I'm sorry, what?"

"My mother kept cheese in her purse," he says again, frowning with disgust.

"That's unusual. Was that for luck or something?"

"It was to eat."

"Oh, you mean when you were a small child, your mom kept a baggy of snacks for you?"

"No. When I was a teenager; my whole life, actually." Keith's eyes go up and to the left, his body emits an over-ripe lemon smell with the hue to match. "It was so humiliating, I hated eating out. I hated being anywhere with either of them."

"Because of the purse cheese?" I was so guarded against anything invasive that I filtered out vital information. Every word he said was a threat or a clue sent through the metal detector of my mind like the visitors processed into The Bowl. My scanner is more effective than theirs. No murder weapons got past my ears as easily as the one I carried into the heart of this prison.

In my second year as the main student of Shastri Nolan, when my relationship with Marian was still as new as it always felt to me, I took on the job of managing the slide projector for his beginner's class. The monastery had one of those carousel projectors that clicked off the slides with the touch of a remote that was so un-remote it was wired to the machine. A broad shouldered man, with a silver rim of hair around his bald crown and an obviously broken nose that surely had a tale to tell, Abel Nolan was more suited to working at a loading dock than teaching the mysteries of the dharma. In his youth, he'd been in the Army and then a trucker before taking refuge in the three jewels. His voice, laden with every cigarette he smoked in his two-pack-a-day habit until he found his path to a Buddhist retreat (by way of a hippie girlfriend), bubbled like molasses over low heat. He took me down a hall to a small closet holding a wheeled cart. On it, besides the projector, was a 2 x 4 block of wood painted white. Stenciled in black letters, it said "SACRED."

"You put the little feet of the projector all the way down, then set it on the board," he explained. "It will put the slides in the perfect place for the screen."

I nodded without question, eager to show my respect and cooperation. I used the SACRED board for months before I had the nerve to ask about it. Finally, when the curiosity cat had ripped up half my mental carpet and ruined the blinds, I brought it up.

"Master, I understand the purpose of the board. It serves to lift the projector. But what makes it sacred? Has it been covered in mantras? Was it a gift from a great teacher?"

"Yes, Lylarose," he gurgled. "Every year, the Dalai Lama himself climbs a forbidden hill in the mountains of Dharmasala, cuts down a holy yew tree, and makes me a 2 x 4."

There's "slip on Jell-O in the cafeteria" dumb and "right in front of your face" dumb, but there is nothing in the world like "the teacher just used sarcasm" dumb to boil your cheeks and make you laugh at the same time.

"So, not a priceless relic then?"

"Home Depot, $2.99."

"I see."

He let me walk nearly to the door before I heard his gruff rasping cadence cut through my mortification.

"People fear the sacred."

"What was that, Master?"

It was one of those moments, like so many I had with him, where the room filled with electricity, like bristling air before lightning. The wisdom he gave me was always preceded by the sparks of its promise. His voice a distant, unmistakable thunder.

"The sacred. People have a natural fear of it. They're afraid to touch it. Because if they do, they run the risk of putting a human fingerprint on the divine. Even though most people make god in their own image, not one of them wants the responsibility of giving the holy their identity. There is so much progress we could make, so much good we would bring to sentient beings, if we would only learn that it is our touch, our interaction, our attention, which makes something sacred in the first place."

I stood there, conscious of everything I had touched that day, and everything I hadn't.

"Anyway," he chuckled, the twinkle in his eye marking a return to blue skies. "A 2 x 4 puts the projector at the correct height. I tried to keep one on the cart, but people would take it. Lama Tisdel used one to prop open his window. One of the students used another to mark the boundaries for a lawn game. I couldn't keep a damn board in the place. So, I painted that one and wrote "SACRED" on it. It's been here for three years."

The first day I planned to meditate with Keith, I walked up to the metal detector in that stolid soulless entry hall which prophesied not doom, but merely oblivion with institutional surety. I carried my singing bowl packed in a clear plastic box. I was still new to The Bowl, and the guard's eyes undressed me as surely as his hands lifted my visitor badge for inspection. In the shuffling cattle line of sagging exhausted women here for a few hours with a still-loved husband, and the wheezing breath of polyester-print, geriatric ladies arriving for a chance to talk to a wayward son, I stood out. I was a sure and solitary woman who didn't avert her eyes or feel embarrassed about where I was or the act that brought me to visit the sex offender's unit. He wasn't my lover, my child, or my friend. He was my anger. He was my pain. I was not ashamed to see him here. I was glad, even though it would never be enough for me.

"It's a singing bowl. The shape is designed to ring in such a way as to align the heart and open it to the universe," I said, handing the box to the guard. He held it with both hands, peering through the plastic as if he were looking at the Holy Spirit in a zoo. I went through the detector, and he handed it back to me, nodding the all-clear to the next guard. He hadn't opened the lid. He hadn't shaken or disturbed it. He could barely breathe holding it. And I knew. As long as it didn't stand up and shout "Murder!" I could bring anything on earth into this prison if it was cased in a hallowed plastic box.

People fear the sacred.

✿

"Every time we'd go out to eat, my mother would bitch at the menu," Keith continued. "'Look at this! A dollar extra to make a hamburger a cheeseburger. A dollar! For a slice of cheese. We are not paying that.' My father would just nod in agreement. A minister in a small town where everybody talks about everything knows not to argue."

"I understand small towns." I nodded. "I remember reading that your father wasn't the first minister in your family, is that right?"

"I come from a long line of holy rollers, it's true," Keith said, the body of that statement dressed in regret. "Some of them might have even meant it. The cloth goes back six generations of Allen men, until me, of course."

"You studied to be a minister but dropped out of your M.Div. when your first wife divorced you, and you went for a Master's in Social Work instead. I'm sure that didn't make your mom very happy if the price of cheese sent her over the edge."

"It wasn't the divorce that pissed her off, it was how to explain it to the church. It was always about the church. I didn't even want a fucking cheeseburger. I would have been happy with a plain old hamburger or a slice of pizza. But no. The church, the almighty church, needed to think we were doing swell even though the fine-feathered flock paid my father a birdseed salary. So she'd tell me to order the hamburger, then, when she thought no one was looking, she'd take this gross slice of generic American cheese with tobacco from her cigarettes, mints, and purse gunk stuck to its wrapper and put it on my burger so they thought my parents paid for the upgrade."

His words turned in their cask from the sweet wine of yesterday to the vinegar he's stored in their place. In that moment, he was not a murderer or a man, he was a small boy, trapped inside layer upon layer of social expectation, like a nesting doll in hell.

"Someone was always looking. When we lived in the parish house, my mother would buy expensive food and put it in the front of the cabinet so when she went to get the coffee creamer, they'd see we only ate the best. Behind it, though, was the store brand cans and crap she fed me and my dad. We only got the good stuff when it was expired, or when my dad lost his position and we had to move to another church."

"Did you go to many new churches?"

"Every couple of years. Same pattern. He'd be the 'new minister,' and the church would be elated. Everything he said was profound, and his sermons stirred the spirit. Then he'd run through the six or seven good sermons he had and start chewing the fat in the pulpit, talking about God, guns, and giving donations. Attendance went down. Deacons started sending suggestions. My mom would begin going to the ladies' bible study just to make sure they weren't talking about us. My dad would figure out what they wanted to hear and feed it to them until they were so full they vomited up his contract. In one church, they didn't even tell him he was fired. They had a late night elder's meeting, and when he got to church the next day, his key didn't fit in the door. The church secretary handed him a box with his crap and said, 'the Lord has directed us to someone else.' It was all such bullshit."

"Your dad must have had faith that he was making a difference in some way."

"No, Doctor, you don't get it." Bitter chuckles drip venom on the line between us. "My father didn't believe in any of this shit, neither did my mom. It was all just a show in a lime green cotton blend suit with a K-mart tie and football picks written on the back of a Sunday Bulletin. The only time we ever prayed at home was when we had company. The only god in our house was social admiration. My mother married my dad because he was a generational reverend with nowhere to go but up. My grandfather passed the mantle to him, and he tried to give it to me. Christine messed that up. I should thank her. The divorce freed me from that life of lies."

"But you still ended up with a life of lies, Keith."

"That's the one thing I did manage to learn while all those crappy-ass Vacation Bible School weeks swallowed my childhood summers whole. If you have the right credentials, you can do anything, touch anyone you want. Counseling is nothing but ministry, without the pressure to hold your shit together two hours every Sunday morning."

"Really?"

"My first was in fifth grade. I don't know why I waited so long. I was a true believer as a kid, I guess. I was sure there was a hell, and if I was a bad boy, I'd roast my little white ass there. Eventually, I realized I wasn't just some sinner wandering the playground. I was the golden calf."

"People worshiped you?"

"Not the people. I've never had too much luck with them. But when you get lifted up on a weekly basis by the high priest and his wife, there's bound to be some jewels thrown your way. Tracy Hill was in my grade at school, and her family went to our church. She was a little dark-haired girl, shy, straight A's, good citizenship, not unlike you must have been, Dr. Gentry."

He licks his lips as his imagination lingers on my breasts. One side of his mouth curls upward as he mentally tastes the meal my dignity would make. Better than Christmas dinner.

"One day I got Tracy to follow me into the changing closet behind the baptistery. I yanked my pants down right in front of her. She screamed. I told her that since she saw my penis, she wasn't innocent anymore. But if she took off her top, then we'd be natural, Adam and Eve before the apple, and she'd still be unblemished like the lamb."

"Did she do it?" I croaked. My hand dropped from the table. I used every cell in my body to keep a non-judgmental look on my face while my younger self mentally kicked him in the throat with every word, seeking justice for a little girl I'd never known, and yet knew all too well. My soul was slathered in oozing, toxic waste.

"She was going to. She started to cry and tentatively tugged at the hem of her top. I remember feeling so hard, as hard as you get at that age. Then the fucking janitor came in the room, and she fled, babbling that she just wanted to be pure. The church board called a meeting that night. My mom threw a fit, screaming about how my dad was going to get fired because I couldn't keep my pants up. But then, at the meeting, out of nowhere, another side of her came out."

"Just like the cheese from her purse."

"Exactly. She stood up and pointed at Tracy's parents. She brought up how they didn't give to the mission fund and Tracy's Sunday School attendance record was sketchy, whereas I was there every time the doors were open. After all, what choice did I have? She said it was Tracy who agreed to go to the closet with me to look for construction paper, and she conned me into pulling my pants down by saying she would "show me hers" after I did. By the time my mother finished holding court, I was the victim, the little drummer boy just trying to give Jesus a present made out of true construction paper love, and Tracy was the whore of Babylon in Buster Brown shoes and a training bra."

"Were you surprised your mom covered for you?"

"Not really. The Reverend Allen's wife wouldn't let the water rise until her family walked across on the driest land possible.

"The next day, everyone knew what happened by the end of first period. Tracy went to the nurse and said she felt sick. Her mother took her home. They left church and ended up putting her in some Christian school in the next town over. I found other girls, prettier girls, to do what I said because they didn't want to be hauled off like Tracy Hill. But you never forget the ones that get away, do you, Dr. Gentry?"

He leaned over, the tuna he had for lunch wafting on his hot sticky breath as his eyes narrowed. Sucking the saliva off his cracked lips, he made no effort to hide his desire. He curled his words, tinted with need and menace.

"The worst part is...I never got to see those little rosebuds she had under her shirt. My whole life they've been the most perfect boobs in the world. The breasts I never got to see. You've got a good shape for a woman your age, dark hair, and a shy smile. You wanna help me? Pull up your sweater and show me your tits."

"THAT'S ENOUGH, ALLEN," Officer Johnson growls. Keith flops back in his chair. I don't move. I don't react. I don't give him what he wants. Truthfully, I don't give a fuck what he wants.

"I'm fine, Officer Johnson. Please don't interrupt," I said. If I had one thing to do over, well, I would have done everything differently. But in that moment, if I had something to do over, I would have been nicer to Officer Johnson and seen him as a person, an ally, not just a means to an end.

"At that precise moment, when she started to lift her top, I heard the call to the ministry."

"So you decided to follow in your father's footsteps for the power?"

"And the pussy."

"How unfortunate you didn't achieve your goal."

"Well, I got them both, I just had to find another angle. Christine had the makings of the perfect minister's wife, then she took golf lessons, so we could schmooze on the course with denominational leadership, and fell in love with the bar-back from the 9th hole. That chick, she was hot. I don't blame Chris. She wasn't invested in me anyway. Didn't have the glands for it, you know?"

"So, you married Patricia. I assume she had the 'glands' for it?"

"She's not very good in the sack, but she's gotten better over time. I was never really after her body. It was her brains I wanted. She's a business genius. I told her there wasn't a Baptist church in the world who would hire a divorced minister, at least not at that time. She said to change my major to counseling. It's the same job, only less Jesus and more billing. Of course, it wasn't long until I had my own practice. She took care of the office, and I took care of the ladies. It was like an assembly line of produce running right through my fingertips. I just had to pluck the peaches I wanted. I got my life on the right side of the channel, and Pat was the ferry. Simple as that."

"That 'ferry' is the mother of your children."

"Yeah, normal life with all the trimmings. As a bonus, I figured when I was too old to get it up over some doe with a sad story, I could retire, and my kids would take care of me. It was a good plan, until your wife fucked it up."

I cough in my hand, hoping Officer Johnson understands it as an invitation to get involved if that festering sore of a human being dared to profane Marian's memory once more. In the beginning, that was the line. I got used to it, eventually. If you want to reach the end zone, you're gonna have to cross all the lines.

"It was you who murdered her, remember?"

"You wanna know why I like to fuck with you lesbos?"

"WATCH YOURSELF, ALLEN," Officer Johnson says, right on cue. Looking back, I realize he was distinctly agitated from the moment Keith started talking about his own wife, not mine.

"Actually..." I say, staring the rapist right in the eye, seeing nothing but a coffee colored fog between us. "...I would. The prosecutor had several witnesses lined up to show you had a grudge against your first wife for ruining your career plans but that never sounded right to me. The judge ruled the argument inadmissible, and I didn't get to hear your answer. I'd like to hear it now."

"Do you think it will help you save me?" He taunts.

"I doubt it will even save me. Maybe we should just move on." I motion to the officer that I'm ready to go.

"They fight," Keith blurts out, desperate to dump his bag of snakes on the table. He's been sitting on it far too long. "Mentally, if not physically. They fight and they hurt and they die inside with every violation. It's such a rush."

"I would imagine most women and men fight being violated."

"Not like you girls. Why do you think heterosexuals molest little boys?"

"They're pedophiles?"

"The fear!" His arms go up in a "touchdown" gesture. "From the time they are born in this culture, girls are taught to be pleasing, sexy, and open, or if they're ugly—grateful for the attention. The same daddy who tells his little princess she can be an astronaut subconsciously communicates that she better look good and be willing to open up if she really wants it to happen. He does it with every TV show he watches, every action he praises, every joke he makes in her presence. He's not even aware of it. But when someone compliments her, he'll still say, 'She's gonna be a great wife someday.' Boys haven't been sexualized since birth. When you mess with them, the fear, the shame, is so concentrated it will feed you power for months. The boy is destroyed giving the man his due. Girls, they just cry quietly and go on, accepting it's the price of being born female."

He's a craven, egocentric asshole, but manages to scrape the dreadful surface of experience now and then.

"It's the natural order. Women are empty, until a man fills them with his purpose over and over. It's when the man's seed is sown and he's satisfied that the natural connection ends."

"I'm not so sure it's Pat who is bad in bed," I mumble. Officer Johnson gurgles into his hand, pretending to clear his throat. "So you sexually assaulted lesbians because they reject the natural order as you see it?"

"Their resistance is my ambrosia. Admit it, Doctor, you lesbians live under the illusion you don't need a man to be whole."

"No, but we do live under the assurance that all we have to be is exactly who we are, and we don't need another being to tell us, sexually or societally, who that person is."

"Exactly, and when someone—a man like me—not so attractive, not so smart, but oh, so powerful—forces the natural order on you, the fight you ladies put up could get an entire village high. It's pure heroin."

Colors of lust and depravity swirl on a wave of fluorescent energy, bursting from him like an interrogation spotlight, blistering my inner eye. I feel him pulling at my Buddha nature, my human goodness, trying to get a strong enough grasp to rip it from the shell of my body. He begins to rise, not stand, but rise as if to hover over me like a carrion circling the dead carcass of a deer once caught in the headlights. He draws his words out like a snake coiling around the prey, then goes in fast for the kill.

"That's exactly what I'm going to do to you; you hyper-intellectual, tight-ass dyke. I'll drill a hole in you so deep my seed will come out of your nose."

"THIS SESSION IS OVER," Johnson blares, walking toward

the table as I pull back, my own horror filling the room with the drug Keith craves.

"I'll keep at you," he hisses. "I'll batter your psyche and watch you twist like you're being impaled in front of me. You'll feed me your sweet pain until I'm fat and hard, and I won't quit until you bend over this table for me with tears in your eyes because it's exactly what you've needed all along."

"You're a tragic, flaccid man."

I lean forward, unable to really see anything but the surging black and red cloud of corrupt energy surrounding him. I feel Johnson's hand on my upper arm, pulling me away from the line on the table. It's too late, I'm already across it.

"Let's be clear about what we're doing here," I say, ejecting the words like a nail gun. "You're here because you're so pathetically powerless that torturing me is your only hope of happiness while the cage whittles away the rest of your life. I'm here because I'm so fucking numb that I would do anything to feel again, even endure the dull bloodstained knife of your existence. It's a lot like self-cutting, only the scars won't be so easily seen. So we'll do this dance until you get bored or I get broken. You're going to get tired of the new toy, and I'm going to reattach these severed nerve endings and come face to face with all the pain you've put me through. If that happens, I promise you, this will all end and it will end badly."

"I'm gonna fuck you up so good you won't know Buddha from bamboo," he calls over the reverberating clarity of the moment.

I shake my head as Officer Johnson pulls me toward the door, a smile born of sheer insanity spreading across my face.

"You already have."

I can't see my own colors, but I'm pretty sure that day they were red. Not the angry electric maroon my father emitted, but the bright shocking red of fresh blood. I know all about that red—every one of my lives has ended with someone covered in it.

15

The estrangement from my parents became simply another blemish on the skin of my first life. I didn't mourn them. I didn't miss them, even on a lonely Christmas morning when Shawna's family (my usual holiday haven) took a cruise instead of the traditional turkey dinner, and I splurged on a pizza and spent the day watching a Bewitched marathon on TV Land. Oh, Samantha, your mother's got nothing on mine. I went on with my world, not understanding that my lack of longing was just an illusion masking my near constant state of financial and personal desperation.

Working our butts off at both school and night jobs—Shawna at a grocery store, me as an inventory taker (what better job is there for a hypervigilant compulsive counter?)—we managed to get a third floor walk-up that overlooked a set of dumpsters. It left me just enough money for some ramen noodles and gas to get to work and back. It didn't have air or heat but did have an awesome gas stove, and if we turned on all four burners, the whole place would heat up in fifteen minutes. If we wanted cool air, well, the windows opened. Sorta. Needless to say, it was grand.

On the first day of orientation, for my senior year psych clinical, I felt a slow, dull pain in a tooth near the back of my mouth. I told Shawna all about my first day at Dyson Street's psych ward and how overwhelming it was to see so much pain and confusion locked in such a confined space. The tooth started throbbing again. I ran my tongue over a small lump in the gum and managed to block out the ache while Shawna enlightened me with tales from her adventures in student teaching.

It took almost a week before the small knot with the occasional ping became a constant throbbing menace and had grown large enough to be seen in the mirror when I pulled my lip back to apply yet another glop of Orajel. Within a few days, the applications had gone from the recommended once every four to eight hours to every fifteen minutes, and the bump protruded nearly to my cheek. I started taking aspirin the way busy people look at their watch.

"You've got to do something about this," Shawna said as I rubbed the swollen side of my face.

"I'm trying," I sighed. I went to the student health clinic where they gave me three (THREE!) painkillers and told me they didn't do dental care and I had to seek help elsewhere. The emergency room clerk said the same thing when I stumbled into the hospital rubbing my swelling jaw.

"It may feel like an emergency, honey, but that's not what we do here."

I tried several dentists, all of whom agreed it sounded like I had a nasty infection, but none of whom would see me or do the work without insurance or at least half the money up front. I even went to the dental college, who said they'd love to help, but their coverage would not allow them to let students work on a problem that advanced. It was a matter of liability protection, they assured me. As the uninsured party, I had nowhere to go, nothing to stand on, and no one was protecting me. Finally, I lowered the bar as far down as it could go. I agreed to let Shawna ask her church for help.

The doughy pastor with his Just-For-Men hair styled perfectly took his hands off of his pot belly and placed them on the blotter of his hand-carved mahogany desk, making sure not to wrinkle the sleeves of his Ralph Lauren suit. He nodded sympathetically as Shawna explained I was estranged from my abusive family, working hard for the common good, and needed a little help from above. She also mentioned the four years she worked as their volunteer youth camp counselor and the many sermons she'd heard him give about Christ's call to help the poor. If she hadn't decided to be a teacher, she'd have been an amazing defense attorney.

"I appreciate your passion for the message of Jesus, Shawna," he said, "but your friend is not a member of this church."

"Did the Good Samaritan check for a membership card when he helped the beaten man?" Shawna straightened her posture, slapping her hand on his beautiful leather-bound Bible with gold-edged pages. "Did Jesus ask for a secret handshake before he gave out loaves and fish? What about the meek and poor in spirit, orphans, and all the other 'blessseds?'"

"Even if she was a member or a sister in Christ," he backtracked as I sat there, the burning red on my face matching the blood flowing from Jesus as he hung on the cross behind the pastor's head—dying for me, but unwilling to offer me dental care. "We wouldn't be able to help. We simply don't have a fund or committee for this kind of thing. It would take a majority vote of the board after a period of discernment to establish a policy."

I stood up before he did. I had just enough dignity left to walk out on my own power before being asked to leave. "I understand. Thank you for your time."

"I don't understand," Shawna continued to complain as he walked us to the door of the church. The gentle fall sunshine caressed me when he opened the large arching doorway. It was the only thing that felt warm or natural in this "holy space," and I fed off it as the pastor bid us leave.

"Goodbye, Miss Gentry," he said, his useless hands in the pockets of his fancy pants. "I'll pray for you."

Up to that point in my life, I had been ridiculed, studied like a lab rat, moved, hustled, beaten, and nearly crippled. But I had never felt as soul-strippingly humiliated as I did in the doorway of that church. It would forever alter my karma.

Years later, when Marian brought home a young woman who'd been released from the ICU, battered and sliced open, with nowhere safe to go, no family, no friends, few language skills and even less money, I cleaned out the office in our two-bedroom apartment, bought a cot, and spent the rest of that week's grocery budget on gauze and peroxide. Marian didn't ask, and I didn't argue. It took two months for Luka to be able to walk to the corner market and back, and another three to convince her she would be safe doing so. We didn't have much in those early days, but we had enough sense to know when someone comes to you in that kind of need, they deserve more than a wink and a prayer.

"I know a dentist who takes payments," my boss at California Inventory Service told me when I turned in my count-sheet one night. The perfect job for a student, inventory was quiet, orderly, and I could do it alone. Unfortunately, with Godzilla's tooth infection shrieking at me all day and night, I was never really alone. It showed in my work. It showed in my internship. It was going to show in my grades, which I couldn't afford to let drop or I would lose my upcoming fellowship. It showed in my drooping shoulders and pain-filled eyes. It showed.

"Please call me Cynthia," the dentist's office manager, who smelled like spiced mandarin oranges, said as she placed a stack of papers in front of me. I had to initial every paragraph as she explained I was actually taking out a loan that would be due on the fifth of every month. The payments would be a very low $28.47, and

I could pay it off early for only a minor penalty of $150. She also mentioned that since I didn't have dental insurance, they were using "risk-based" pricing, and interest on the loan would be twenty-eight percent compounded daily. So, by the time I finished the thirty-six-month payment plan and paid for the additional loan-related fees, my $350 procedure would cost me $1,697. Truth is, it wouldn't have mattered if the interest was 500 percent or I knew what "predatory lending" meant or if she said her name was Susie Satan from Hell Mutual. The pain had to stop.

I signed the forms.

Cynthia smiled at my miserable countenance. "Don't you worry, dear. As soon as the head office gets back to us with a confirmation number, I'll have Debra call you and schedule an immediate extraction. You'll feel better in no time."

"Thank you," I said, fighting back the tears. My long nightmare was about to be over. If pursing my lips didn't feel like someone was peeling the flesh off my face with a paint stirrer, I would have whistled all the way home. I stopped by Sure Save, gave Shawna the thumbs up sign, and left a thank you note for my boss. I only had a few more months until graduation, and then I would get a paid internship and my fellowship money for grad school. I'd pay off the loan before it became the size of the national debt. Best of all, I could get back to healing and helping the people in my charge.

The following day, I took more painkillers and sat by the phone with the same chaotic, hopeful energy my mother displayed every fifteenth of the month, waiting for The Precious. In my craving for any second of relief from this blinding pain, I finally understood her frantic need for his voice, even if someone had to pay him for her to hear it. When the phone rang, I lunged at it, lifting the receiver as if I just won the Nobel Peace Prize, or at least the Publisher's Clearing

House Sweepstakes.

"Debra?"

"May I speak to Lylarose Gentry?"

"That's me."

"Hi, Lylarose, this is Cynthia from Doctor Sparrow's office. I'm afraid I have some bad news. We aren't able to offer you a plan."

"I signed everything you asked. I agreed to all your terms."

"Our corporate office ran a routine check, and it turns out you don't have any credit history whatsoever. They decided that it was too much of a risk."

"How am I supposed to get a credit history if you won't give me a loan?"

"If you had a co-signer, maybe a family member..."

"I don't have any family. Can't you increase the interest rate? forty percent? fifty? Take my car as a deposit?"

"I'm sorry, Miss Gentry. You simply don't have enough to work with."

"I'm begging you," my voice raised in pitch as I squeezed my eyes together.

"I'm very sorry."

I cried so loudly a flock of pigeons fell from the sky. I slumped to the floor, my tears making a water mark on the carpet. There wasn't going to be an appointment. There wasn't anything else I could do. I was just going to writhe in this pain until death came with its blue blanket to collect my shuddering body that smelled of disease and desolation. By then, my face would be so swollen I would be unrecognizable, but it wouldn't matter because I'd be demented from the agony. Hell, I was halfway there already and this was only going to get worse. All because no one would just pull this damn infected tooth out of my mouth.

"I don't know what to do," I sobbed to no one. An unlikely pair of voices answered.

"Shit or get off the pot," my mother's drawl filled the room. "No more candy land and patty cake for you, missy. Move your lazy ass and do what's necessary."

Her voice was so clear, so real, I actually lifted my head to see if she had walked through the door. My eyes scanned the sitting room, the nook by the door, the kitchenette. Then they started to focus. The freezer had a bag of ice left from our "apartment warming" party. There were still eight pills in the bottle of aspirin. In the drawer was the new set of silverware Shawna stole from her "hope chest" as an act of defiance against her mother's expectation of Shawna's virginal good-girl wedding night, since that ship had already sailed. Around the world. Several times. The only parts Shawna used from it were some forks, a couple of dessert spoons, and the corkscrew. The steak knives? Those were still new and sharp. We weren't on a steak kind of budget.

"You need a system," my father suddenly advised. "Always have a plan. How are you going to do it? What will you do when it's over? What can go wrong?" If I had him in the car with me on that last drive to the Maryland State Penitentiary at Bowles Pass, things might have been different for all of us, or at least less of a surprise.

"I'll take the aspirin, numb my jaw with the ice, boil the steak knife (my one hygienic thought), pierce the gum to let the pus run out, push until I'm under the tooth, which is loose anyway, and pull up. I'll put a towel in my mouth to stifle the noise and one on the counter for any blood that doesn't go down the drain, and it will be done. I'll buy Shawna some new towels. I don't need a loan for that," I explained to my phantom parents.

If necessity is the mother of invention, desperation is the dad of dumbass.

☙

Hands shaking. Breath ragged. Eyes tearing. Skin sweating.

"I can do this."

"I can do this."

"I can do this."

"Don't half-ass this, Lylarose," my mother said from her frontal lobe seat. The sudden appearance of her voice in my head after three years of silence was a jarring omen of things to come. "Go in deep, and hard. All the way, or sit back down and waste away like the rest of my disappointments."

"I can do this."

"Downward angle, with a correlative amount of pressure," my father advised. "Watch the trajectory and timing. Get your head over the sink quickly to let the pus run out. It's about precision."

"I can do this."

I lined the newly boiled knife blade against my screaming gums. The laser-sharp, stainless steel felt like a firebrand when it first touched the swollen tissue that had already started seeping on its own. I had passed the "degree of pain" point. Everything was agony, there was no worse to be had. Only better. Or over. Either way...

"I can do this."

"I can do this."

"I can..."

"NOW!" Hurricane Peggy howled.

I plunged the knife in as far as I could while my head exploded in pain so sharp atoms were split by the sound waves of my screams. My flesh reluctantly split its sinew and ripped apart as the knife divided my gum line. The putrid smell of disease and iron rose in the air. I pounded against the knife with my palm to drive it in and hung in there long enough to feel the tooth move as I yanked downward on the handle ripping into my own jaw. I'd describe what the gurgling, groaning howl of sure torment sounded like, but really—there just isn't a word for that sound. It's something you only know when you hear it. Pray you never do.

Hanging my head over the sink, I anticipated a trickle of blood and pus to dribble out of my mouth at any moment. Just then, Mount Saint Helens erupted and blood spurted everywhere, my mouth a raging inferno of liquid death. Sticky and noxious, the infected blood poured down my chin, my chest, the tile. I managed to stuff a blood soaked towel in the blazing cavern and turned toward the phone. At the impact of my first footstep, a second eruption of bloody horror poured down my throat, choking me on my own anguish. I crumbled to the floor, a falling tower of a woman.

Where was my friend and the blue blanket when I needed it? Apparently, the sight was too gruesome for even Death to get involved. Death packed up the shop and got out of town. Thus endeth my first life. Abandoned by Death, the same way I left it years before.

I don't recall anything until I woke up, my tongue instantly diving into the hole in the back of my mouth where the tooth had been, now packed with gauze and sporting a fresh row of stitches. The only thing more joyous than feeling that empty space was the absence of pain. I looked around the room. There were two lines leading into my IV, twenty-two white no-slip dots on my hospital socks someone had put on me upside down, and the room felt like it was ten degrees. Machines beeping, phones ringing, body freezing—yep, I was in the hospital. Once again, a very lucky girl. Suddenly, my right hand felt the warmth of a friend enclosing it.

"Our deposit is shot to hell," Shawna said.

"I'll pay you back someday," I promised with my half-ability to speak. My mouth felt and sounded like it was full of marshmallows, much better than the razor blade covered marbles of before. "When I'm rich."

"Put that big ass tooth they cut out of your head under your pillow. I figure the tooth fairy owes you millions."

"They cut out?"

"You should stick to psychology, because your oral surgery skills really suck. You managed to break your tooth and rip it sorta from its socket but the root was still attached. You cut the fuck out of your gums and lip, too. A real doctor had to finish your handiwork. You must have made some serious noise, because Juiced-Up Jonesy across the hall called the police and said someone was being murdered in our apartment. I came home from school right as they were hustling your butt into the ambulance. I had to chase it all the way here. I went back to lock the door while you were in surgery. Jesus, Lyla, there's blood everywhere."

"That went wrong."

"You could have...I mean, oh my god. I could have...lost you."

"I'm sorry."

"Once I convinced the cops this wasn't the weirdest suicide attempt ever, things have been okay. Next time, don't leave an empty bottle of aspirin by your unconscious body when you self-dentisize."

"I thought it would help with the pain."

"It's a blood thinner, Lyla."

"Oh."

Smart people are uniquely able to do the stupidest things.

"I didn't put a lot of research into this."

"No shit, Steak Knife Sally."

"Miss Gentry," a male voice interrupted our talk. I didn't need to turn my head to see him. I could tell by the condescending low drop on my last name that he was the doctor who sewed me up. "How are we feeling now?"

"We are feeling 100 percent better," I said, determined not to back down. It would have sounded more impressive if it hadn't come out like "Werf eeling a hunren persin bettah."

"That tooth was killing me."

"I would love to tell you all about the fifty ways you could have just killed yourself, beginning with draining infection into your blood-stream, but for now, we need to talk about the underlying problem we discovered."

"Poverty?"

"Malnutrition, dehydration, and exhaustion."

"I liked it better when my problem was poverty," I said, watching his dark blues and solid colors morph into pastels as he softened his tone and attitude. He might have thought I was the biggest nitwit he ever admitted, but he liked me and was sorry to be giving me more bad news.

"Me, too. I'm going to have you admitted for a few days. We'll do some intravenous fluid and electrolytes along with strong antibiotics to counter the bacteria you released into your system."

I wanted to hear more of his care plan, but Shawna started mouthing the words "yeast infection" and it distracted me.

"I don't have any money for this," I said.

"I think he figured that part out," Shawna fake whispered, tracing her finger along my stitched lower lip.

"Lylarose," he reached out and put his hand on my arm. It was like a simmering ember of warmth in this arctic zone, so I allowed it without protest. "Your body shows signs of a woman taking care of everything but herself. I understand you're a student, but your body is not made for this kind of abuse. You can't care for others if you won't act in your own self-interest. Do you have parents or family nearby who can help you?"

"She's all I have," I said, pointing at Shawna, "better or worse."

"Oh," the doctor said, raising his eyebrows and looking at Shawna with a newfound, incorrect understanding. "I see."

"I'm her friend," Shawna blurted like a woman possessed. She leaned forward to give the doctor a good glimpse of her cleavage. "JUST her friend."

"Well, Miss Gentry, and 'just friend,' I am going to need a few assurances that you are capable of self-care and willing to make some changes in your life."

"Yeth, Doctor," I said, unsure exactly what I had just promised. Fortunately, the universe had a much better understanding of what it would take to turn everything around.

"Okay, Miss Gentry, let me take a look at that mouth," the nurse said, squinting at the stitches. "That had to hurt."

"Are you going to change the dressing or something, because I can leave," Shawna offered. "I've encountered enough horrible body fluids today to get me through several lifetimes, and I teach elementary school."

"No, I just wanted to see it for myself," the nurse said. She had a stunning combination of colors, passionate and yet calculating, steel colored professionalism lined with warm green circles of endless caring. "When they told me a student from the college tried to extract her own tooth with a steak knife, I didn't believe it. You're gonna be a story around here for a long time."

Nice families don't do their own dental work.

"Do you have any other discomforts? I'll be bringing you a new bag of D5 shortly." She looked at the IV site in my arm and pressed on the puffy skin around it. "Try not to move or do anything to mess up this IV. Day shift said you were a hell of a stick, because you were dehydrated."

I tried to think of something, anything, to say but ended up just motioning that I was okay. I was too tired to make any real sense, and even if I had the most witty, intelligent comment known to humankind, it was going to come out of me sounding like a toddler trying to say hippopotamus.

She looked at the armband on my wrist and matched it to the numbers on the face sheet she had on her clipboard. In the days before scanning, whatever went on the face sheet was the only legal record available. She checked it line by line.

"You are Lylarose Gentry?"

I nodded.

"You were admitted by the ER?"

I shrugged. "I wath patthed outh attha time."

Shut up, Lylarose. Just. Shut. Up.

"It's okay to nod," she said. I was so tragic, even the ICU nurse wanted me to STFU.

I shook my head for everything from my birthday to my blood type. When she got to "Emergency Contact," Shawna provided the rest of the answers.

She gave me one last good look, grimaced, and started to leave the room, stopping by the big white board to grab a green dry erase marker.

"Lylarose. I've never heard that name before. It's beautiful," she said. I smiled, with the good half of my mouth.

"That's not her real name, though," Shawna blurted.

"Oh?"

"Her real name is Robin Hood."

"Really? That's synchronicity." She wrote her name and nurse ID on the white board, but it was blocked by her body until she left the room. "I'll be your nurse for the rest of the night, Miss Robin Hood, and I think we are destined to get along just fine."

Then I saw her name written with confident broad strokes in the same bold green color I noticed when she entered the room.

"Marian."

My second life, my best life, began.

16

"Breaking News at Mountainside General Hospital where Dr. Lylarose Gentry fights for her life after a deadly shootout at the prison commonly called The Bowl. Sources report Warden William Hummel and the chief investigators from the Oakland County Sheriff's office have arrived at the hospital. Our own Laura Lindeman is on the scene. Laura?"

"Thanks, Christy. It's been another tense morning here in Oakland, Maryland as the community, in fact, the whole nation, tries to make sense of the carnage that took place just a few miles down the road. Warden Hummel and two police investigators arrived only moments ago but offered no comment to reporters. Susan Bly, our legal consultant, says it is likely they plan to charge Dr. Gentry with the murders of the two corrections officers and the attempted murder of Keith Allen. If Mr. Allen, who is currently undergoing medically induced sedation due to swelling of the brain, should die, the final charge would be upgraded to murder as well."

"Laura, do they have enough evidence to definitively conclude it was Dr. Gentry who perpetrated the violent attack in the counseling pod?"

"There has been no official comment on what evidence they would use to charge Dr. Gentry, but they need to make the arrest official to prevent any legal maneuvering by her counsel or legal guardian, self-help maven Penelope Fine. Ms. Fine has been in the hospital with Dr. Gentry since this began, and it is expected she's putting together a legal dream team to mount a defense for the teacher she described in her New York Times Bestseller as 'A wellspring of wisdom and compassion so deep and so generous that her presence in your life is alchemy. She can turn the lead weight around your neck into feathers of gold and offer you nothing less than a brand new soul.'"

"We'll keep checking in with Laura, but now—did the guru have a dark side? Our guy-on-the-go, Rob Sturmoski, has been researching the murky past of Lylarose Gentry and files this report. What have you got, Robbie?"

"Christy, I can say after five years of internet journalism, finding facts about the famously reclusive Dr. Gentry has been the hardest assignment I've undertaken. Nestled in the rolling hills of northern Virginia, the Virga Center for Meditation and Renewal sits on thirty acres of pristine woodland, sporting a central meditation and teaching auditorium, guest cottages, classrooms, and the rustic ranch house Dr. Lylarose Gentry shared with her longtime companion, Marian Fitzwater. Here Dr. Gentry is known as a quiet teacher with a confident, peaceful demeanor, sharp wit, and vast interpersonal skills. Yet no one seems to know anything about who she was before she made the jump from being a psychologist in private practice to meditation master and founder of this center.

"We know Lyrarose Gentry was born in Tampa, Florida and attended at least eight different schools before graduating valedictorian of her high school in Farmington, New Mexico. School records for juveniles are sealed, so we have no explanation for the repeated cross-country moves or what havoc they might have played in her life. Later today, I'll share an interview with Shawna Tewes-Johnson, Dr. Gentry's college roommate, who alleges severe emotional and physical abuse played a large role in the famed teacher's childhood. She said Dr. Gentry attributed the suffering she experienced as the key to developing a compassionate heart. But could a troubled past, combined with the murder of her companion, lead to the violent surge that took The Bowl by storm? Stick with *News Now* as we explore..."

Pen slaps at the iPad, as if that will force it to shut up. She and that digital cocaine box are so conjoined it's not unlike watching a married couple fight. She'll accuse and slap, eventually turning it off and demanding it spend the night on the lumpy guest room mattress. It will silently, patiently wait for her to want it for something. Eventually, she'll wrap her needy fingers around it once more and give it another chance. After all, they've been through so much together. But, for now, she holds down the power key until its screen goes black and tosses it into her tote bag. Exiled, for crimes against denial.

She slides a hardback chair beside my bed and holds my hand, allowing her fingertips to trace the deep scars from long ago she surely had seen but never thought to ask about. Her head drops. This isn't a crisis. It's an abyss.

"You could have told me, you know," Pen says, her voice low and sweetly sincere—the voice of heart, not reason; of love, not duty. "I wouldn't have judged you. I didn't come to Virga expecting you to be a perfect person from a perfect childhood. All I needed you to be was slightly less screwed up than me. That wasn't a complicated order. But even if you weren't, Lyla. If you battled memories that I can't even imagine, I would have walked with you through any valley. I wish you knew that. I promise I will walk with you through this one, no matter where it goes."

The main elevator dings, bringing law enforcement to our picnic like so many ants with only one goal in mind: carry as much of the food away as they can before the blanket folds up and disappears. Penelope rises from the small chair to return to her reclining throne in the corner. She leans over, running her finger across my temple, then places her lips there, softly kissing me—like a parent putting a child to sleep.

"I'm so sorry, Lyla."

Of all the things I've ever heard a loved one say—when a husband's hidden cancer progresses too far for surgery, or a brother shoots himself in the parking lot of the mall, or a daughter's upper arm reveals cut after cut after cut—the most tragic, heartbreaking words of all are, "I wish I would have known."

"Let me do the talking," the stocky blond in the business casual Dockers and a beige blazer says right outside the door. Her badge is fastened to the pocket of her blouse, near the sidearm holster. A quick gesture to the left with that unbuttoned blazer and she can show a perp everything that needs to be seen. She smells clean, her morning routine nothing but pure soap and water. There's a slight hint of Oil of Olay, probably to deal with the lines that materialize on her face when she smiles. Otherwise, no makeup. Her hair is bundled and expertly banded to meet department regulation length.

"I'm the one who cleared the center," the middle-aged man, sporting a gym body that keeps missing leg day, replies. His badge is front and center on his polo shirt. They've got a comfort with each other that only comes from time. They work together well, except for when they don't.

"Do I have to explain it again?" She coughs, motioning toward Penelope who is sitting up straight on the edge of the recliner, one long tapering leg draped over the other, chatting with Warden Hummel about his run for governor and the rules of campaign contributions. Hummel's silver hair still has just enough black in it to make him look dashing, like a middling Spencer Tracy. His body holds a couple of extra pounds in the middle, and will fit in perfectly when he retires from political life and takes up pickleball in Florida. Pen arranged the chairs that the door guard brought her to center on her as a focal point.

"What? That writer? I've chewed tougher steak than her for lunch."

"Okayyyyy," the woman sighs. "Let's review. A man is a being with two heads but only enough blood for one at a time. So, when the blood goes to..."

"Detectives!" The warden jumps up, interrupting what was promising to be the most compelling thing I've heard since they wheeled my body into this beeping, lifeless, box of a room. Penelope rises slowly, allowing her legs to completely unfold before she extends her hand forward.

"Ms. Fine, this is Detective Denise Markel and Detective Greg Putnicki from the Oakland County Homicide Division."

"I'm Penelope Fine," she says, pausing for a moment of adoration that turns out to be nothing but an awkward shuffling of feet on the tile floor. "Which one of you is in charge?"

"I'm the..." Detective Markel begins.

"We both are," Putnicki says over his partner. "We're co-leaders of the investigation, ma'am."

"Let's sit down. I have a lot of questions." Penelope glides back to the chairs, dropping her hand to touch my leg and give it a squeeze on the way by. She positions herself close to my body, like a sentinel.

"We're here to help," Putnicki affirms, following her to the impromptu conference corner.

"And the blood has made its choice," the woman mumbles, allowing Warden Hummel to follow her smitten partner before taking her seat. "Actually, we have questions for you."

"Of course you do." Penelope looks Detective Markel straight in the eye. Woman to woman, neither one confused by the pheromones swirling the recycled air.

"Are you close to Dr. Gentry?" Markel starts by opening her notebook, making it clear she is only interested in answers important enough to be written down.

"She is my teacher," Penelope answers. If Putnicki asked, she'd have said the same thing. It just would have taken her two minutes and three hundred words to do it.

"I mean, do you have a close personal relationship, beyond that role?"

"I don't think you understand the word 'teacher,' Detective Markel. In Buddhist tradition, a teacher isn't just someone who gives you knowledge. They invest themselves in you, and you in them. It is a relationship of mutual respect, admiration, and sharing space in the spirit of one another."

"Is it one of sex?" Markel asks pointedly. The men in the room shudder in their chairs. Poor Warden Hummel nearly topples over backwards.

"Detective Markel, that's not..." He asserts, practicing for his campaign persona as a man who doesn't want to offend the LGBTQ community, even if he's also working on an endorsement from the state evangelical alliance.

"Let's back up," her partner inserts himself into the situation. "We are trying to understand what happened, and any context you can add..."

"No," Penelope says directly, never lowering her eyes from Markel's.

Now the bones are on the slab. Markel knows Penelope isn't going to be shocked or jarred into saying anything she doesn't intend to say. Penelope knows who she isn't going to sway today. Still, she'll get two out of three. Not bad.

"We were called here because you wouldn't talk to our scene co-ordinator, Detective Mesa. We were told you are now ready to answer our questions. Is that not the case, Ms. Fine?"

"It is the case. I just want you to answer mine first. My question is: how is it possible for four people to come out of a highly secured prison with gunshot wounds, and no one can tell me exactly what happened? Why are we waiting for some geek with a microscope or two unconscious people to wake up and unlock the vault? Meanwhile, the press is running every rumor and tin foil hat theory as headline news. Dr. Gentry's reputation is being shredded by the second, and you are still back at square one asking about her relationships. Why isn't this moving faster? In fact, considering the damage of the 24 hour news cycle, why isn't this already done?"

"Proper police work happens in spite of the media, Ms. Fine. Not because of them," Denise Markel attempts to take the upper hand back from the entitled princess holding court in Room five.

"Once we have a full understanding of what occurred, we will re-lease a statement that clears up anything the media has gotten wrong," the male detective assures her. "It's sad that journalism has gone from reporting to fortune telling, but a sign of the times. Still, our duty is to find the truth, and that's what this conversation is about."

"Warden Hummel, you know what I'm saying, don't you?" Pen places her hand on my bed, co-opting my silent shell into whatever scheme she's planning to run.

"Of course, Ms. Fine. There are cameras everywhere, and we must always be careful how we appear on them," the warden says, elevating himself to her level, if only for a moment. Instead of three against one, the odds even out to two on two.

"How unfortunate Lylarose was shot in the one place on earth without one."

Warden Hummel stares at the floor, and Detective Putnicki glances in his direction, biting the inside of his lower lip. A blood orange circle connects them for a split second. Detective Markel stares straight ahead. Penelope nods to the men, as if she, too, is in on the secret they haven't shared with their female co-lead, leaving the lone interrogator out in the cold. She whispers to keep the truth just between her two new confidants.

"Are you sure there wasn't any kind of surveillance in there? You know, for the safety of your staff or even you, Warden. Something no one else has to know about?"

"I'm afraid that would be unethical, Ms. Fine. It would violate the inmates' constitutional right to privacy with legal or spiritual counsel. We have a great forensic lab at the state level," Warden Hummel says returning the volume to normal. "If we send them enough evidence, they'll be able to tell you exactly what happened."

"Why don't you tell me?" She turns and challenges the warden, striking like a mongoose grabbing the snake by the neck, her eyes locking his as if she just threw him against a cell wall and slapped on the cuffs.

"I...um...I..." The panicked warden sits so far back in his chair the cheap fabric on the seatback is going to infuse itself onto his spine. Wide-eyed, he wipes the foam from the corner of his mouth and gasps audibly before the pain in his chest subsides. He shifts and crosses his arms in front of his body. A few deep breaths and he's back in control. She was close. But that only counts in horseshoes. "I would if I knew, ma'am, but I don't. That's the Lord's truth."

"We were hoping you could fill in some of the why," Detective

Putnicki segues back to their agenda. Markel says nothing. Her head buried in her notebook, she writes with large block print so her partner can get a good look:

"You guys fucked up this interview, YOU can unfuck it."

"Did Dr. Gentry ever talk about Keith Allen to you?" Putnicki asks.

"The man murdered her wife. She might have mentioned that once or twice," Pen snarls, playing the petulant teen being asked what she was doing with those boys by the railroad track.

"Did she ever talk about her sessions at the prison with Mr. Allen?"

"No. She would never disclose information about a client or student session. That violates HIPAA or some ethics code of her license. She is a moral person and an avid rule follower," Pen says, and glances over at the warden with that grin. "Isn't it funny how the only people who seem to follow ethics edicts are the ones who don't need them in the first place?"

His tight thin lips press together until they have the width of a strand of spaghetti. He nods.

"I know the meetings exhausted her. She would come back to the center, go straight to her house, and not come out until the next day. If she had a class to teach, she'd ask someone to cover it. Eventually, she stopped scheduling anything but a massage on his days."

"Did you see her before she went to her last appointment with Mr. Allen?"

"Briefly. She was walking out with her travel kit, and I told her I had decided to accept an offer to keynote a writing conference set on a cruise. I invited her to come with me, but she just laughed. She's not the boatload of strangers type."

Detective Markel's head jolted as if someone just plugged her in, and she whirred back to duty.

"Can you describe the travel kit?"

"It looks like one of those old green and white Samsonite makeup cases my mother used to have, only the sides are see-through and it's made of plastic. There's room for her prayer shawl, her mala, if she isn't wearing it, the singing bowl, and any books she may intend to use."

"Can you describe the 'singing bowl?'"

"It's a metal bowl, decorated with ancient symbols of peace and compassion. When you hit the side, it makes a deep ringing tone, much more intense than a bell."

"Can you describe what you hit it with?"

"A wooden mallet."

"Can you describe the mallet?"

"Can I do it in the form of a question?" Penelope snickers into her hand, causing Markel to look up from her notebook with a frown severe enough to melt steel. "I'll take 'what's a wooden cylinder?' for 250, Alex."

"This isn't a game, Ms. Fine."

"No, it isn't. And you know damn good and well what a mallet looks like. You've got at least three of them in your possession right now. No wonder this investigation is crawling along like a drunk toddler looking for a nap."

"Okay," Detective Putnicki steps back in, risking the wrath of both Pen and Markel with the same well-meaning act. "So, we are clear that Dr. Gentry took a wooden mallet to The Bowl..."

"Ahem!" Warden Hummel coughs.

"To... the Maryland State Penitentiary at Bowles Pass. Did you ever see her tamper with one of these mallets?"

"No. I live in the guest house, and I'm working on my own issues.

I meditated with her, ate with her, went to her classes, and went back to my room. I have no idea what she did in her private hours. Except mourn."

"Did Dr. Gentry display overt signs of anger toward Mr. Allen?" Detective Markel tries again.

"You mean, like refusing to send him a jar of honey for his birthday?"

Markel's eyes shift up toward Pen. The writer opens her hands and nods.

"Sorry. I know. I'm displaying signs of anger. I'm tired, and I'm scared, and I'm...so..."

"Okay," the warden reaches over and lands a butterfly finger on Pen's shoulder. "We understand."

Detective Putnicki takes Markel's pen and writes on her notepad, "Let me. She doesn't like you."

Markel nods and takes the pen back to write, "She doesn't like you either. You just don't know it!"

"Did she ever mention anything about seeking revenge toward Mr. Allen?"

"No. Lylarose was destroyed when he killed Marian, but through the whole trial, she just kept saying that the key to survival was to create solidness in herself. Keith was outside of her, he didn't matter. What mattered was inside her. She grieved by knowing and bettering herself."

Oh, Pen. You will never know how much I still believe that and how desperately I wanted to live that truth.

"Was she suicidal?"

"No," Pen laughs through the question, seemingly finding her balance again. "When you believe in rebirth, suicide is a waste of time. You may live a million lives, but you'll always be you."

"Did she have any woodworking or metal art skills that you know of?" Markel, still on target, interjects.

Penelope raises her arms and drops her hands by her side.

"I don't know! I am her student, not her keeper. She could cut down a tree, chop it into logs, and impale a few pretentious guests in the Zen garden and I wouldn't know. WHY would it matter? Why does any of this matter?"

Markel leans in, her jaw locked and her eyes laser clear. The air in the room bristles with electricity and the collective rage of churning water that's pressed itself against the dam a little too long.

"Because we found a mallet that had been altered to conceal an ice pick in a room where my brother and sister officers were left dead on the floor. I don't give a fuck about you, your teacher, her rebirth, or that piece of shit rapist. But there's a wife and a husband, two sons and a daughter, a mother and a sister who deserve to know the truth. Now, did she make that weapon herself, or did someone make it for her?"

"I don't know."

Markel closes her notebook with a snap. "Then what good are you?"

Pen turns her attention to the warden. "I know this is hard on everyone, not just me. But why the focus on the mallet? They came in here shot, not stabbed. Why the mallet, and not the gun?"

"We want to have as much understanding as we can about what took place before the shots were fired," the warden explains. "Forensics has the gun. We pretty much have everything we need to know about that."

Penelope shifts in her chair, patting my leg. If she was a dog, her tail would be wagging. She transforms from agitated insider to compliant servant of the inquisition, allowing poor Detective Markel to believe she'd forced the headstrong writer into some sort of submission. She answers question after question about the center, the staff, my conduct during the trial and afterward. She talks about the fight we had after Pat Allen convinced me to see Keith. She tells them the truth about how she came to me for help, eight weeks after her own brush with my friend, Death, where her attempt to seduce it was rejected, and she woke up vomiting a half-bottle of pills and two glasses of Johnny Walker Blue. A nurse comes in to do yet another skin assessment and the officers stand to leave. Markel was at the elevator before the warden could button his jacket.

"*News Now* has been reporting you came to arrest Lylarose. I'd appreciate it if you'd clear that up on the way out," Pen calls.

"Not my job," Markel mumbles, never looking back.

"You've been very helpful, Ms. Fine," Detective Putnicki said, reaching out to shake her hand one more time. He uses one of those gross double-handed shakes. He might as well have been slipping her a hotel room key card. As soon as she could free herself from it, she puts her hand on the warden's shoulders, encouraging him to stay just a moment longer.

"Do you have a card, or a phone number I could have, Warden Hummel?"

"If you think of anything, it would be better if you contacted one of those two. They are in charge of the investigation. I'm only in charge of the internal prison review."

"This is for something different."

"Oh?" His heart spins like a slot machine. You can hear it clicking as the neon lights flash from his eyes.

"Have you ever heard of Trinity Marsh?"

"Yes! Of course!" The cylinder came up with five oranges. Jackpot! "I've read her entire McNamera Mysteries series. She has prison culture down. I love her descriptions of McNamera Penitentiary. She's such a great author."

"She's also a good friend of mine," Pen says with a wink, dropping her voice to its low register. My dad was an amazing fisherman, but he had nothing on Pen. That woman could bait a hook for a leviathan. "We share the same publicist. She's actually co-writing a screenplay for the first McNamera movie, and you know, when you do a movie, technical advice is everything."

"Yes, yes it is." He starts fishing in his wallet for a card to scribble his private phone number on. At this point, she could ask for his kidney and she'd get them both.

"Trinity is in need of an expert she can touch base with quickly, and I'd like to have her call you. I'm sure you could answer some very specific questions she has to make sure her prison descriptions are accurate. I can't promise you a technical advisor credit, but it would be fun, don't you think?"

"You bet! There's a lot of information about prisons you'd have to work there to know. I can certainly help." He handed her two cards, just in case she loses one.

"I'll have her call you very soon, maybe even today. I know she's in a hurry to get this project going. And who knows? If the governorship doesn't work out, maybe Hollywood will be your next destination."

He tries to cool down and get the blush off his face before the door cop sees him, but it does no good. He is sunburnt.

She watches through the door until the elevator lowers him beyond earshot. Her phone connects before she gets back to the recliner.

"Hey Trin,"

"Any change? Did they charge her?"

"I need you."

"Anything. Unless you want to feed me to that mob of starved pervertazzi outside the hospital as a distraction. Even I can't take on that many sharks. Are you able to get out?"

"I'm not leaving this room until she wakes up."

"Penelope..."

"Here's what I need you to do..."

Before I was considered old enough to learn chess, the only game my father liked to play with me was one called "Mousetrap" where you went around the board, setting up pieces of an elaborate Rube Goldberg device to trap your opponent's mouse. I listen as Pen sets her pieces on the board and starts the ball rolling. Warden Hummel's mouse doesn't stand a chance. She tosses her phone in the same direction as the exiled iPad, and returns to my side.

"Don't look at me like that," she says. "Just because you aren't moving doesn't mean I don't know how disgusting you think all of this is. They are slandering you with every update, and that phony baloney warden knows something happened before the shots were fired. Something with that ice pick. That means there is a video, and he's seen it. That's not denial. That's not manipulation. That's a straight up in-the-present fact. You might leave me, Lylarose Gentry, but I'm not letting you go with a lie—even if I have to break every truth in the world to do it."

She takes a deep breath and smiles as the cops change from day to night. Officer Brault leans in and waves, his smile still bright enough to light the room. She waves back with a small giggle, her charm weapon set to "stun."

"What the hell was his name again?"

The ventilator hisses and the steady beep of the monitor attempts to give her a clue. She playfully slaps at my shoulder.

"You're not helping."

No, I'm not. I'm beyond helping. But, apparently, in Pen's devoted, determined mind, I'm not beyond help. Not yet, anyway.

She trip-traps over to the door as if her high school crush arrived to take her to the prom.

"Hello you," she says, twirling around to give him a side hug, until she sees the overly large gun holster attached to his belt. She pats his arm instead as she scans the name off his badge. "Officer Brault, you came back to see me."

"Well, there's only so many cops in Oakland, Ms. Fine."

"Still," she leans toward his chest and curls her voice, "you're my favorite."

A husky chuckle emerges from the smitten cop. "Thank you, ma'am. How's the patient?"

"The same. Nothing changes. They come in, turn her one way, put new bags on the IV stand, and then, two hours later, turn her again. I wish I knew what to do."

"If I was you, I'd pay less attention to this room and more down the hall," Brault says, clearly choosing a side—her side—in this night watch.

"What do you mean?"

"I heard Mrs. Allen talking to the doctor when I came in for change of shift. She wants them to lower his sedation. She's trying to get them to wake him up."

"What does that have to do with me?"

Officer Brandt bites his lip and looks at my body, then scans the hall for anyone who might take notice of his breach of objectivity. "Because there's only two people left alive who know what really happened in that room. Whichever one of them wakes up first is the one who gets to tell the story. It shouldn't be him."

Penelope nods, looking down the hall where a different kind of guard, a corrections officer from The Bowl, sits in the hall, absorbed in his phone. She can see Pat's shadow peeking through the doorway, the backlight making her likeness menacing.

"That bitch is up to no good," Pen says.

The officer makes direct eye contact and his lips turn down into a determined scowl. "Your teacher needs to wake up."

Hot flames rising from the fire of ages sizzle before the line of soldiers, each armored in refined steel caked with the blood of human suffering. The arrows were carved from the bones of the hungry, the envious, the lovers, the dead. Purple cloth dipped in the oil of crushed olive branches was ripped from throne rooms and shrouds to wrap the sharpened end of each projectile, thin enough to let the point pierce the flesh, thick enough to carry fire and hell with it. The bows made of long yew frames arch toward the soldiers. The string, formed from anguish, is pulled impossibly tight. On their side, there are thousands of inflamed, seething archers. On the other, one man, sitting under a Bodhi tree, tapping at the door of illumination.

Mara, the embodiment of pain in the world, prances and cajoles in front of Siddhartha Gautama. He's offered him uncountable riches. He's offered to give the man Mara's own daughters, bearing pleasures no human has known. Siddhartha does not accept. Now he will not offer, but offend. He will impale this seeker with a thousand flaming deaths destined to leave nothing but ash and regret. The seeker never blinks, never stops, never takes his mind from its task. If this is to be the day he dies, consumed by the pain of the world, so be it. All is well.

"FIRE!" Mara screams, watching with glee the arcing doom rapidly descending on the prey. A thousand burning arrows light up the sky in an unholy dawn, their sound splitting the air with a shimmering deadly hiss. Siddhartha inhales the acrid smoke of the impalement hurtling toward him. He exhales his surety that there is no other moment but this moment. No other focus than his breath. The first arrow breaks a small branch of leaves off the tree as it flies toward Siddhartha's heart. Moving faster, closer, the time is now, the heat of the flame searing his skin, the tip of the spear reaches its mark and...a lotus flower falls in his lap.

Soft white petals cascade around Siddhartha. The field is covered in the frail bounty of flowers, raining down like so much grace. The soldiers shriek at the beauty transforming their power into poetic revelation and disappear in a puff of black smoke, leaving nothing but the fragrance of purity in the fresh air. Mara, the hardship of the world rendered to impotent posturing, implodes—shaking the ground, but leaving no scar.

Surrounded in lotus, Siddhartha turns his hands so the palms are down, and gives a confident, rising smile. Slowly, deliberately, he places his palms on the earth. He is the Buddha. Instantly awakened. Permanently enlightened. Embodiment of truth, surrounded by flowers that once were death incoming. He sees not one truth, but four: All life endures suffering, we suffer because we cling to what is not real or not permanent, there is a way to stop suffering, and the eightfold path is the way. There is always a way.

My offering would not be made of fire and oilcloth but water and stone. I stood over the kitchen sink, seeing with my mind's eye that illustrious sea of flowers, waiting for the whetstone to stop bubbling. Once the stone was completely saturated I pulled it out of the sink and wrapped it in a towel, hoping to get it back to the desk in my office before Luka noticed me in her work space and ran to get me something. I can't count the number of times she gently took a knife out of my hand, worried I would cut my thumb off trying to do the simplest thing.

"Teacher, let me do that," she'd say with such generosity of spirit I couldn't be mad, even though I'd tell Marian later, "I can cut my own damn apples!"

"Cutting your own apples is self-efficacy," Marian would respond, curled up in her chair watching some Lifetime chick flick on her laptop, headphones at the ready in case I started to grouse. "Letting her cut your apples is loving her by letting her love you. Which is the greater good?"

"Are you purposely mocking me?"

"I'm not mocking, I'm mirroring."

"That's not...heyyy...that's my job!"

She snickered as she opened her arms to hug me. "Can't cut apples, can't have an exclusive on psych-tricks...you better find something only you can do, or I might fail to renew your contract."

I'd wrap my arms around her, kissing her deeply as that soft red hair fell on my cheek, reminding me with every tickle how incredibly lucky I was—not that she loved me, but that I had her to love.

Scritch, scrap, scratch. The metal of the ice pick grinds against the whetstone, leaving granite residue in the salty drops of my tears. I bought the shortest one I could find, but it was still an inch too long. I had to saw it down, then sharpen it to the strongest, finest point I could bring. Marian's urn sat on the shelf above my head, watching the woman she called "the gentlest giant" crafting the means to avenge my loss.

"I want you to see this," I say to the ashes. "I'm not hiding it from you. I'm not deluded enough to think you would ever approve. I just want you with me, because if there is one argument in the world that can stop this madness, you know it, and you'll tell me. Mare, you've got to tell me."

The urn says nothing.

Scritch, scrap, scratch, scrap. Sharper the blade, cleaner the wound. Was that what I was trying to do? Cleanse him? Cleanse me? Cleanse the world of the stinking injustices of life and death? Cleanse a court system that claims to dish out justice, but even with its harshest penalties, it leaves an empty crater in place of a human soul? I don't know. At the moment, I think the heart I was really trying to pierce was my own, just to feel its beat—even if it was the last one.

The only thing I did not fear was this blade turning into a flower. Funny how fate plays out. Not only did everything in that prison cell change in an instant, but as I was becoming a lotus, the room filled with arrows I never saw coming.

"The four noble truths of the Buddha do not take away suffering," Shastri Nolan explained the very first time I sat on a cushion in his dharma center. "They merely explain that you can stop it. Buddhism is the world's oldest 'Do It Yourself' show."

I chuckled and my hand fell off my lap onto Marian's. I pulled it back as if she were a scorpion. First dates are like that—a ballet of scorpions. It was her fault I ended up in this room, on this path, following Shastri Nolan to a new place, a new life, a new world. I made sure to mention it every time she mumbled when I accidentally put her scrubs in the dryer on high heat with my gym clothes, or she caught me pushing the top of the trash down farther so I didn't have to be the one to take it out.

"It's your fault," I would say. "You could have given me discharge papers and sent me packing like every other patient who tries to pull her own tooth."

It worked. Every time. Apparently I was so pathetic, laying there with my stitched up lip and IV lines, that twenty years later she still softened at the memory.

"We've been waiting all day," Shawna fussed and stomped as the day nurse took out the last IV.

"I don't know what the hold up in your paperwork is about, but you can't go without it, Ms. Gentry. The night nurse will see to your discharge."

Years later, after one too many Jameson-laced hot chocolates, Marian finally admitted she asked the nurse to delay my discharge so she could do it. Sneaky little fox.

"So, besides the antibiotics, you need to take these vitamins to help with your nutrition," Marian said, handing me a hospital bag full of free samples. "Of course, eating would be good, too."

"Yeth, ma'am," I said. I couldn't take my eyes off her, and I couldn't feel anything but the heat on my cheeks as my stupidity and desperation trumpeted itself with every slurred word out of my re-covering gum line. I felt like every time she looked at my chart, it screamed "run away!" and yet, she didn't.

"You might also want to manage your stress a little better," she said, looking out the doorway into the hall. Shawna was out pull-ing the car around. "Are you religious? Your chart has a blank space there."

"No. I'm not anti—I'm just...well, not."

"Oh." She frowned. "That's too bad."

"Why?" Let's face it, if this beautiful woman, who had given me incredible care and unspeakable fantasies, invited me to a meeting of the Church of Satan for pizza night, I'd be a "Pepperonian" by change of shift.

"There's a Buddhist teacher who leads a class every Tuesday for medical professionals. It's meditation and stuff to help relieve our stress. I was gonna suggest you try it."

"I'm just a senior intern at the Dyson Street Clinic finishing up my Bachelor's," I said. "I've got a lot more college to go through before I am a medical professional."

"Well, you're pre-professional. I'm sure he won't mind. He doesn't check state licenses at the door."

"Will you be there?"

"Here's the thing," she said with a sigh, once again looking at the door. "A nurse can't date a patient. That's the law. But here in the ICU, we see hundreds of people, and we can't be expected to remember every one of them. So, if you happen to show up at meditation, and I happen to be sitting next to you, I probably won't even know who you are."

"But...you could meet me, right?"

Marian nodded, her smile shedding bright sparkles that glistened with the same light as her captivating eyes.

"Exactly. And you can't come back to the ICU. No more steak knife surgery for you."

There's something Penelope didn't put in her book. I entered Shastri Nolan's center and took my first step toward enlightenment because a pretty girl asked me out.

Walking into Shastri Nolan's meditation room was like entering another reality. Built out of a converted department store, with classrooms upstairs and offices in the basement, the main floor was huge with sectioned off areas for meditation, study, mantra recital, and mandala work. Gold and dark red wall coverings featuring vibrant art from Tibetan masters adorned the walls. As evidence that

I didn't have a clue as to what I was walking into,I expected pews like a church or chairs in an AA semicircle. Instead, there were aging but serviceable blue cushions with gold trim set out in neat little rows facing a main chair. I made sure to find a seat with an empty cushion on each side, just in case someone decided to talk to me and robbed me of a free space. I wobbled back and forth trying to get my rear in the center of the seat, folding my long legs up like one of those gas station maps you can never quite get back after you open it up.

"I'm Marian Fitzwater," she said, offering her hand as she sat on the cushion beside me.

"Lylarose," I said, even though I had to smile through the stitches still holding my lip together. Her eyes scanned the length of my body. It was the first time she'd seen me in real clothes.

"I'm so happy to meet you, Lylarose. You have a beautiful... name."

After the teaching, we stopped by a diner for some coffee. My head was reeling with the truths Shastri Nolan had given us. I picked up a pamphlet on the way out and vowed to go back for more. Marian rattled and rambled about the challenges of working in an ICU as a nearly new nurse and a host of other topics. Finally, she took an in-breath.

"Where are you from, Lylarose?"

"All over."

"Is that in the Northeast? Allover, Massachusetts?"

"That would be Hanover," I said. I didn't know her aura palate well enough to tell if she was kidding or not. There were so many colors swirling around her, all of them shimmering. "I moved a lot."

"I see. Well, I'm from Richmond, originally. My great-grandfather was with the Irish railroad workers who settled there. But I never rode a train or anything..."

Fifteen minutes later, she was still talking about her adventures, and she'd only lived in two places in her life. She asked me what music I liked and before I could answer, she told me all about the time she went to a Melissa Etheridge concert and was so close to the stage she actually got Melissa's sweat on her T-shirt. She said KD Lang was coming through on tour but she couldn't go because she was sched-uled to work that night. Nurses. The second coming of Christ, rebirth of a Buddha, and extraterrestrial first contact could all be happening in their backyard and they would ask what day, because if they were scheduled to work, they couldn't attend.

"Okay, here's the deal. My coffee is getting cold so I'm going to take a drink and that will give you time to beat your record."

"My record?"

"The highest number of words you've said all night is seven. With a little energy on your part, I'm sure you can beat it."

I nodded. I did all the things they tell you to do before a first date—shaved my legs, brushed my teeth, went over a few good jokes, and screwed my filter in super-tight. Maybe too tight. She took a second sip of coffee.

"Go!"

"Um...ah...let's see...I...well, I think you're ...well...I'm really glad you told me about meditation night."

She clanged a spoon against her cup, making enough noise for the server to look up.

"We have a winner! Ted, tell the woman what she's won. Well, Marian, Lylarose has just picked door number three—another date with you this Saturday night."

I laughed out loud.

"Can you make it?"

"Yes."

"It gives you five days to learn more words."

I put my hands up in surrender. "I'm sorry. I'm not a very talky person. But if you give me another chance, I would really like for you to get to know me better."

"I get it," she said, lining up the coffee creamer cups like bowling pins. "I'm a brushfire—crackling flames, sparks, and heat, but it doesn't last very long. You're an ember. The quiet kind under the wood that glows inside and stays warm forever, even when the camp ranger tries to put you out, you're still there, steady and strong. Together—I think we could roast one hell of a marshmallow."

"That would be fun. I like roasting things."

She rolled a salt shaker in the direction of her cup pins, knocking them all down.

"Um...things...like marshmallows ...not...people. I don't like to hurt people."

At this point, the ghosts of all my ancestors collectively put their heads in their hands and murmured doom in the coming age.

"Well," she said as she stood up to leave. "That's good news. Where should we meet?"

"We could have dinner."

"I'll pick you up, and I'll cook," she said. There it was, out in the open. I had poor nutrition, little time, a rattletrap car on threadbare tires, and no money. Still, she wanted to date me. It wasn't fair to her. She deserved better. She still does.

"I have nothing," I blurted. At least she could say she was warned. She leaned over and kissed me on the cheek. When I turned to face her, she pressed her lips against mine and held my hand tenderly, and yet, so tight. Leaning up to my ear after breaking from the cinnamon coffee kiss I wanted to last forever, she whispered.

"You are everything."

❦

Trip trap trip trap trip trap

As a child it was the sound of the three billy goats gruff going over the bridge unaware of the troll.

Trip trap trip trap trip trap

It was the steps of my mother waiting for her son to call.

Trip trap trip trap trip trap

It was the drip of the water faucet in my low-rent college walkup I never could get to shut off.

Trip trap trip trap trip trap

It was the wooden mallet Shastri Nolan would tap against his leg. Breath in—pain. Breath out—peace. Breath in—sorrow. Breath out—joy.

Trip trap trip trap trip trap

It was the paws of the feral cats at Virga tapping our glass door, waiting for Marian to bring them treats and tender ear scritches.

Trip trap trip trap trip trap

It was the second hand of the clock in the courthouse hall as the jury deliberated Keith's fate.

Trip trap trip trap trip trap

It's the sound of the red-lacquered soles on Penelope's heels walking across the polished tile of my hospital room. Chair to door to chair to me to door. Back and forth she goes, her iPad glued to her hand so she can check her private email with a casual glance while waiting for Trinity's report. This isn't walking meditation. It's spin class. Her mind cycles through the steps she's prepared to take, the people she's willing to risk, the price she may pay, all to prove my innocence in a world where words mean more than one thing. No amount of pacing or plotting will give her what she seeks. Still, she turns on her heels and makes another lap.

"Miss Fine," Officer Brault says, turning toward her as a handicapper might inspect a nervous racehorse prancing in the starting gate. His weary eyes reflect the surface tension of a man who is being worn away from constant footfalls. He shakes his head toward Keith Allen's room on the other side of the hall behind the triangular nurse's station. She opens my door all the way, peering directly into the enemy camp. Looking at Keith, Pen sees the thorn in humanity's flesh, an obstacle to her worldview, and a threat to the truth she requires in order to stay sane in this cascading nightmare. I see a man engulfed in tubes and machinery, his ashen-faced wife, and anxious people feeling the pressure from all sides, just trying to do their job.

"Call respiratory. I want them in here," the pulmonologist says to the nurse as she washes her hands at the sink by the doorway. He emits a sizable exhale, his coloring drab, resigned. He knows he shouldn't try this, but he's run out of ways to say "no." Another nurse, the one who's been turning me every few hours, skitters by our door, pushing the crash cart toward Keith's room. Penelope takes note of the tiny padlock securing the drawers. It's not the only thing shackled in that room.

"What's going on?" Brault asks as the nurse leans against the weight of the cart. It makes sense something designed to do nothing less than save a human life would be a little heavy, secured, and bright red. Life, after all, is a dangerous thing. She shouldn't answer, but he's got a badge and the prettiest brown eyes for a man his age. It's a small town. He's a good guy. "Rapist going down, or are you getting him up?"

"It's just an awakening trial. It will let us know if he's ready to be extubated."

"Then he can talk?"

"Then he can sing, but dancing will take a little time," she responds, just flirty enough to make sure he knows the door to her attention doesn't need a key. Smitten, and harried, it would never dawn on her that he is the one cop in the hospital who hasn't asked when Keith could be interviewed.

Brault looks up at Penelope who has a white-knuckle grip on the door jam. She returns his gaze. She wants to command him to do something to stop this, but doesn't bother. Short of throwing himself FBI-style over Keith's body and shouting "Noooooo," there's nothing to do but watch. Shame, really. I would have liked to see that.

"Mr. Allen? Mr. Allen, we are going to try to wake you up now," the nurse says, more for the benefit of Pat than anyone else, I assume. She has the voice of a kindergarten recess monitor—clear, severe, and yet, full of care. The room is a maze of juxtaposition. The square white IV pump on the black metal rack drips with mechanical precision as the equally symmetrical heart monitor rings the slow steady rhythm of life. It is the highest order descending into utter chaos. Tubing extends with lawless abandon covering the upper half of the bed in a nest of snakes. Wires wrap around each other in impossible to follow knots as they power the equipment then curl around the IV tubing, dripping blissful sedation from the milky white bottle attached to the stark metal pole. The bright blue vent tube is the only one not being strangled in the curling mess of care. That one goes past the surface of bed rails and white sheets, through his mouth into the cavern of his being. As a meditation teacher, I spend a lot of time explaining the importance of the breath. Looking through Keith's doorway will show it in a millisecond.

"He's on 50 mcgs," the nurse tells the doctor who makes note of the numbers on the monitor, medically controlled for optimum healing.

"Is he breathing over the vent?"

"Yes," the respiratory therapist answers, talking to the doctor, but looking at Pat Allen. She's sitting forward in her chair by his bed. Like Penelope, her melting face shows a level of exhaustion most people will never know, but her spine is made of steel.

"Wake him up," Pat says.

The guard in the hall stands up from his chair and starts mumbling into his shoulder mic. The one in the room places his back against the wall and drops his hand to his belt. I'm not sure what they think is going to happen, but if Keith magically rises from his bed the size of Godzilla and starts chewing off the hospital roof, they've got it covered. The nurse puts the IV pump on standby, and everyone watches with tense muscles and wide eyes. Penelope gasps.

"Mr. Allen? Mr. Allen?" The nurse taps on his chest at the first sign of movement. "Mr. Allen, can you hear me?"

"Keith! It's Pat! Keith! Keith!"

The nurse reaches down and takes hold of Keith's hand enclosing hers around it. It's the hand that wrapped itself around Marian's neck as she kicked and scratched and gulped for air. It cared only about silencing her, stopping her, punishing her for the crime of deterring his will, deflating his power. When the force of the gunshot that killed Stephanie recoiled against his palm, he dropped his weapon and reached out with that very hand to grab Marian, who had launched herself at him like a leopard. That thieving merciless hand the nurse is holding once crushed my very heart.

"Squeeze, Mr. Allen, squeeze," the nurse says. "If you can hear me, squeeze my hand."

"It's Pat, Keith. I'm here. Look at me."

"Mr. Allen, open your eyes for me. Squeeze my hand. Open your eyes."

The pulmonologist leans over Keith's body as the heavy lids slide up rusty side rails to open the window of the soul. He jumps back fast when the pupils dart around. Confused and terrified, Keith's eyes flex from person to person, ceiling to side rails. His body buckles in his leg shackles as his hand trembles in the nurse's steady grasp, then breaks free, reaching straight for the blue vent tube. Both cops lurch forward, the tendons in their neck drawn like rubber bands.

"No!" Pat shouts. "Keith, No."

The nurse pulls back his hand, holding it with everything she has.

"Mr. Allen. Mr. Allen. You are on a ventilator. Mr. Allen!"

Wild-eyed and sweating, Keith looks like he's just been momentarily lifted from a pit of boiling oil in the deepest recesses of hell. Panic grips him as he tries to twist and turn, reaching for tubes and flailing with random jerks. What does he see through his roiling reborn eyes? Are they monsters? Hideous beasts trying to hold him down, shouting commands he does not understand and ramming alien tubing down his throat to choke and subdue him? What justice that would be.

"Keith!" Pat presses down on his good shoulder. The one without a bullet hole. He whips his head toward her. A shrill shrieking squall emits from the ventilator, shattering the air like glass, disorienting the cops, but not the nurse.

"Don't bite down!" She shouts over the wailing vent alarm. "Mr. Allen, don't bite down. Open your mouth. Mr. Allen, open your mouth right now."

"Heart rate," the respiratory therapist says, causing the nurse to add one more thing to her multi-tasked battle. She's simultaneously fighting with Pat for space near the patient, holding his hand to keep him from tearing off every piece of tape and tubing he can grab, trying to get him to relax his jaw reflex, and now she's got to play by the numbers.

"Heart rate climbing," the nurse says, still battling Keith's unholy terror and keeping his hands at bay. "135."

"Respiration rate 45," the therapist advises the doctor, who has backed away from the bed and is shaking his head rapidly.

"It's too much," the pulmonologist says urgently, "put him back under."

The nurse hits the switch on the IV pump.

"Resume at 50 and give him a bolus." The doctor looks over at Pat who seems to have lost 10 pounds and aged 15 years in the last five minutes. "I'm sorry, Mrs. Allen. He's clearly not ready."

Keith's body goes limp, relaxing his bite as his eyes close to the world once more. The vent alarm ceases its piercing wail, plunging the room in a sudden, curative silence. We spend so much of our lives looking for magic words, soothing rhythms, siren songs, and yet, all the power and passion of life is best kept in a moment's peace and quiet.

The nurse draws up a bolus of propofol, returning Keith to the land of the lost, as both cops reset their holsters, still agitated, but on balance. The door guard steps into the hall murmuring an update to dispatch.

"When can we try again?" Pat asks the doctor.

"Is she out of her fucking mind?" Penelope whispers to Officer Brault. He shrugs with relief as their eyes meet.

"That was close," he says. Pen nods. She looks back down at her iPad. New Mail.

"Thank you, Buddha!" She says, even though I've corrected her at least a hundred times, that the Buddha, who's not a god, has nothing to do with her daily tragedies or triumphs. She stops by my body, lying steady and still, on her way to her laptop. "That bought us some time, Lyla, but not much. Find your way back, and take the express lane."

The respiratory therapist taps her pager, pretending to have some other emergency to attend. She really just needs to get out of that claustrophobic lightning field before the tension strikes her, too. Pat slumps back down in her seat, and the nurse hovers nearby, making sure Keith's reset is complete.

The pulmonologist leaves the unhappy ex-wife of the sedated inmate with his pocket recorder already in hand. He's so dedicated to dictating his notes he's the first person to pass by my door without taking so much as a passing glance at the murderous guru with the celebrity standby.

"Patient failed the awakening trial..." he says.

Trust me when I tell you, Doc. You got that right.

THE CIRCUIT COURT FOR MONTGOMERY COUNTY, MARYLAND
THE STATE OF MARYLAND

v.

KEITH W. ALLEN
Defendant
CRIMINAL CASE NO. 6 -57-12587

'... Page 164

DIRECT EXAMINATION

Q: Mr. Allen, you have testified before this court that you thought you were going to have a consensual sexual encounter with Miss Muntreat on the night of May 21. At what point did she explicitly tell you she was willing to have sex with you?

A: At her appointment the day before I met her at the bar.

Q: Miss Muntreat testified that she told you that was her last appointment with you. What in that statement suggested she wanted to have sex with you?

MR. HARRIS: Objection, Your Honor. The prosecutor has condensed an entire fifty minute session to one sentence. That's an unfair characterization.

THE COURT: Sustained.

MS. PRESCOTT: Rephrase, Your Honor. Mr. Allen, what words did Miss Muntreat use during that appointment to tell you she was consenting to have sex with you?

A: She didn't use words.

Q: Did she write you a note?

A: No.

Q: Then how did she communicate her consent?

A: It was understood by both of us. It didn't need to be spoken.

Q: I see. Was there any doubt in your mind that this "understanding" might not be correct?

A: No.

Q: Then why did you take a loaded gun with you to the bar? If you thought she wouldn't object, why did you need a weapon?

MR. HARRIS: Objection, leading.

THE COURT: Overruled. Answer the question, Mr. Allen.

A: I had the gun for my own protection. Babes is in a bad part of town.

Q: Then why did you ask her to meet you there?

A: I didn't.

Q: Did she ask you to meet her at a lesbian bar?

A: No.

Q: Was it also "understood?"

MR. HARRIS: Badgering, Your Honor!

MS. PRESCOTT: I'm just trying to discover how much of this

event was clearly communicated and how much was wordlessly understood.

THE COURT: Overruled. Continue.

Q: If you two didn't plan to meet at the bar, then how did you both end up there?

A: I knew she went to a trivia game Babes held on Thursday nights. I went there to speak to her. I was hoping to engage her in a friendship now that she was no longer my client.

Q: A friendship that included sex?

A: Yes.

Q: With a lesbian?

A: Yes.

Q: You must have an interesting understanding of friendship.

MR. HARRIS: Your Honor!

MS. PRESCOTT: Withdrawn.

Q: Mr. Allen, you claim you are not responsible for the murders of Marian Fitzwater and Stephanie Rawls by reason of temporary insanity. You were able to find the bar Miss Muntreat went to for trivia night, patiently wait for her to finish her drinks and walk out of the bar, carry a loaded weapon to protect yourself because you thought it was a bad neighborhood, and engage Miss Muntreat in a conversation about having sex. Those all seem like sane courses of action. At what point did you lose your ability to think and act rationally in such a way your responsibility was compromised?

A: When we got to her car, I snapped. I started acting on impulse. I was confused and angry. I was out of control from that point on.

Q: What caused you to snap, Mr. Allen?

A: She laughed at me.

I've read the transcript from Keith's trial so many times I had dreams where these conversations ran on replay until I woke myself up banging the judge's phantom gavel against the mattress. No matter how often I pour over the words, the story is painfully clear, and permanent.

I can still see Nan Muntreat sitting in front of the court, surrounded by so many wadded-up Kleenex balls that it looks like there was a freak hailstorm entirely located on the witness stand. The mousy brown hair she once considered a short and spiky emblem of her lesbian pride is now long and a little stringy, protectively covering her face with the tilt of her head. The small caliber bullet hole Keith put through her pectoral muscle has since scarred over, but she still winces when she reaches for the glass of water. Her head pivots back and forth in a tennis match as she stares at the prosecutor, her girlfriend, and the rape crisis court advocate. She doesn't look at Keith. She doesn't look at me.

She speaks clearly and quickly about needing a counselor to help her deal with the stress of graduate school and her lack of sleep. Allen was the first name on the list of providers her insurance company gave her. His sessions started light and conversationally, talking about her school, her life, her loves. Soon, he began questioning her reality and her sexuality, eventually offering hypnotherapy as a way to "open the veil." Turns out, the only veil he was interested in opening was the one he planned to rip in two.

"I was taught, 'If you see something, say something,'" she said on the stand. "I heard something in his voice, and I said this was my last appointment. When he walked up to me outside of Babes, I nearly screamed until I realized who it was. I guess I should have still screamed."

The defense went by the patriarchy playbook.

What was she wearing?

How much did she have to drink?

Why wasn't her girlfriend with her?

Why did she leave the bar alone?

Was she clear or did she open herself up to misunderstanding?

Why did she let him get all the way to her car before she told him to leave her alone?

Why did she laugh?

"Because the whole idea of me having sex with him was ludicrous," she said with an acid-tongued chuckle and hefty roll of her eyes. Everyone turned to stare at Keith at that point, to see if her unrepentant mocking would once more send him over the edge. Everyone except me. I just watched her, this young grad school dropout, tenuously holding a thousand shards of shattered glass together in the form of a woman.

When he entered her, the pain of her split flesh cramping in her mid-section, she saw a light. At first, she thought it was just her mind trying to distract her from the horror of this grunting, grotesque invasion. Then, when she heard Stephanie and Marian joking about losing the game on an answer they both should have known, she knew they'd just come out of the back door.

Self-defense classes tell women to scream "fire" instead of "rape" because some people don't know what to think when they hear a woman cry out her assault, but everyone believes in the danger of a flame, no matter how large or small, and will come to help. But there, in the dark backlot of Babes Bar and Grill, when the door closed and the light went out, Nan Muntreat screamed the correct word as loud as her voice would carry. Stephanie and Marian immediately ran toward her. Nurses know what "rape" means.

The gun he had loosely clutched in his hand as he pinned her came alive in his panicked grasp. It cut through Nan's upper body with spark and steel. The last thing she saw was Stephanie turn to run back toward the door before Keith pivoted on his heels and shot her through the neck, the kickback of the gun knocking it out of his piggish hand. The last thing she heard was Marian gasping for air as she kicked, clawed, and buckled in his grasp while he strangled her. Nan lost consciousness before the bartenders responded to the sound of gunfire, and Marian's small body crumbled to the ground in a pool of her best friend's blood.

I've never spoken to Nan, even though she once stood less than three feet away from me. I had Penelope on one side and Mrs. Rawls, Stephanie's mother, on the other. I could smell Nan's guilt through the Bath and Body melon soap that coated her skin. She heard the last words my Marian said on this earth. I have compassion for her. I ache for her. I hate her.

"I'm so sorry." Nan trembles, looking at the wooden rail as Penelope fumbles through the tiny designer purse she brought into the courtroom trying to find a tissue. "I wish I wouldn't have called out to them. If I'd have just taken it; if I'd have just let him finish. They'd still be alive."

"Girl! Don't you be sorry," Mrs. Rawls said, her black Baptist cadence showing her upbringing as clearly as the roots on a fading dye job. "You did the right thing. You don't ever let someone put a hurt on you, put a hand on you, that you don't want. You yell until Gabriel rolls down from the heavens with a sword of fire. My daughter died doing what was right. My daughter died doing what was good. The person who killed her is that sleazy devil at that table over there. You can't die in this regret, girl. You still got life. Live it. The way Stephanie would. Live this life hard and proud and victorious, because he is lost and you are found."

I nodded, watching a mighty cloud of golden mist pour from Mrs. Rawls and embrace Nan, nearly lifting her off the ground. The thing you learn when you've been quiet as long as I have is that if there's something that needs to be said, and you just can't say it— don't worry. Someone else will do it for you.

Q: When the alley lights came on and the bartenders opened the back door, what did you do, Mr. Allen?

A: I ran back to my car.

Q: Were you sane then?

A: I don't understand the question.

Q: According to the timeline Detective Swanson gave the court, you went back to your car, tossed your gun out the window four blocks away, went to your gym, showered, changed clothes, discarded your bloody clothes in a lawn garbage bag in the dumpster behind your gym, and told your wife that you worked out longer than expected. Those, again, are sane reasonable actions. If you lost your sanity when Miss Muntreat laughed at you, when did you become sane again?

A: I don't know.

Q: Could you take a guess?

A: I guess it was the next morning.

Q: The next morning?

A: When I woke up.

17

Officer Brault takes one more look in the room to see Penelope absorbed in the information on her laptop and ensure I'm not MacGyvering my ventilator into a jet pack. Convinced the night watch will sail on smooth waters, he slips in his earbuds and hits the Netflix app on his phone. He's up to season four now, and if all goes well, he'll be well into season five by morning. As soon as he settles back, after a nod to the guard in front of Keith's door, doing the same thing, Pen pulls her phone out of the charger.

"Jeremy, it's your aunt. Are you alone in a place you can talk?"

"Hi, Aunt Penelope. Wow. You should call Mom. She's been trying to..."

"You're the one I need to talk to. Are you at your place? Are you alone?"

"Sure. What's up?"

"I suppose you heard the news?"

"Um ...unless it's about the cosplay entry of the New York Comic-Con going up by fifty bucks, no."

"Okay, do you remember Lylarose Gentry? She runs the meditation center where I stay sometimes."

"Um..."

"You set up their computers."

"Oh—yeah—the pillow place! They have that big room full of pillows and that huge gong. I always wanted to bang that thing, at least once. Yeah, I know her. She's super nice."

"They're called cushions, Jeremy, and yes she is. Well, it's a long story but...never mind. I need your help and I need you to keep this to yourself."

"Okayyyy, what's going on?"

"Do you know anything about the IT systems they use in prison?"

"Oh my god, Aunt Penelope! I already told Mom. That was not my stuff!"

"Jeremy..."

"Seriously, I was just in the car, and I don't fucking know how that bag got in the back but..."

"Jeremy! It's not about that. You know how I feel."

"Did you need some? I got some sweet sativa that ..."

"NO! Well, wait..."

Penelope leans back in her recliner and closes her eyes. How nice would it be if she could sneak into the stairwell for a few minutes and take a comfort hit off something other than those stale packages of powdered donuts the nurses keep giving her? Maybe Officer Brault would like some as well.

"...I'm in a room surrounded by cops. Not a good idea."

"Aunt Penelope, are you in some kind of trouble?"

"Not yet. Listen, my friend Lylarose was in a counseling room at a prison and she...well...she got hurt. I need to know what went on in that room. The warden is saying publicly there was no surveillance, but I have proof there was."

"Dude, of course there was."

"So, if there is a video tape of what happened, can you use your special skills, not related to the plants in your hall closet, to get it for me?"

"Was she in a prison run by the Flintstones?"

"What?"

"They don't make video tapes anymore, Aunt Penelope. They've probably got a digital wireless pinhole system with audio and motion triggering so they don't have to turn it off and on. Any time there's sound or movement, it starts and it feeds the signal into a firewalled file set up on the server with direct access links only. Once you partition the main..."

"Blah, blah, blah. Can you get it?"

"Get what?"

"The tape or file or whatever. Can you get the recording of what happened in that room? I have a report with all the prison specs, approximate time and date, who designed the system, brands of equipment, and even the name of the IT director, if that helps."

"You want me to..."

"Don't say it out loud!" She hiss-whispers. "Just say, yes, I can get you what you want, or no, I don't think I can do this. Don't bullshit me, Jeremy. I'm putting everything I have on the line for this."

"You are so totally my favorite relative, Aunt Penelope."

"Jeremy!"

"Yes. Yes, I can do it. I think. Depends on the system and how much encryption and security they have."

"I don't know for sure. I'll email you what I have. The warden is planning to run for political office, so chances are he's been keeping the prison budget lean and tight to show off his management skills."

"It's probably a low-end system then, and state jobs pay so fucking little, they don't have the head of MIT in there running the show. Some vocational compu-grad most likely. Yeah, I can do this."

"I also have some kind of compressed something or another, it's a recording of a long phone call. Could you put that on one of those little flash things for me?"

"Sure."

"In the email I'm going to put the name and number of my business manager. If you need money or equipment or help, call him and he will get it to you fast. Don't abuse it, though."

"Yeah, okay."

"You know that hundred dollar check I give you every year for your birthday?"

"Yeah."

"Do this for me, and you can add a zero."

"Wowww, okay!"

"Do this for me within twenty four hours, and you can add a second zero."

"Really? Cause I would love some of those laser contacts, and a voice changer for my Optimus Prime."

"Really."

"I'm on it. Don't tell Mom, though."

"Sweetie, I'm not even telling myself. We've never had this conversation. Got it?"

"Yeah."

She looks directly at me, her colors a blur of morbid gray and sparkling diamonds. She's craving, and ashamed, all at the same time. I try to imagine anything that will make it through her determination—a red stop sign, road spikes, or nuclear warhead—and send it her way, but nothing gets across the threshold. She must feel something though, because her mask falls off and her downward cast eyes show a sorrow seldom seen before a deep loss.

"Jeremy, I have been trying to live a more truthful life, so there's something else I guess I better tell you."

"What's that?"

"If something happens—if you get caught or they trace this back to you—I will get you the best lawyer money can buy, but I'm throwing you under the bus."

After a moment of silence, a low chuckle comes through the phone.

"Thanks, Aunt Penelope. I sorta figured."

"Good luck. Talk soon."

She gives me a second look as she starts shifting information from one source to another. With busy hands and a plan in motion, her colors brighten and her eyes sparkle like a green energy meter filled all the way to the top.

A camphor-like aroma filled Shastri Nolan's private teaching room, accentuated by the olive-brown haze that clung to his skin. His eyes, which always flashed a twinkle of brilliant mischief, still gave off a spark now and then, but it drained him when it happened. He hadn't made any announcements. He hadn't altered his teaching schedule, although his personal meditations were becoming more like seated naps. I knew he was sick. He knew I knew. He'd furrow his brow and look at me, and I'd just make a hasty bow and retreat. A little respect isn't a bad thing.

"The time has come, Lylarose," he said, motioning for his assistant to close the door behind us as I melted onto the cushion in front of him. Oh, how glorious were those days when I could sit down on the floor unaccompanied by a symphony of popping joints and snapping bones.

"Time, Master?"

"You've become a settled woman, my girl. You're a licensed professional working for a highly respected practice, Marian has put meat on your bones and love in your heart, and let's face it, I spend more time listening to your answers than answering your questions.

This must be changed."

"I still have plenty of questions."

"As it should be. But not here."

"I don't understand."

"I am releasing you as my student, so that you may be a teacher to others."

"But, but...no."

He raised his eyebrows and dropped his mouth in fake horror. He knew darn well this was shock, not rebellion, but he enjoyed giving his acting skills a workout. His voice thundered with incredulous rage, as if he was the huge floating head ruling Oz from behind a curtain.

"You deny your Master?"

"Um..no, I just...no, Master. Who would I teach? What would I know?"

"You know what you need to know: What's here, what's now, how to tell the truth, how to smell a lie, how to find your center, how to let it go. There is a need for those things embodied in our world. Besides, people do their best work outside of their comfort zone. And I have just the place for you to do it."

"Place? Here at the center? I'd have to talk to Marian about..."

"Not here," he says, then that twinkle lights up his face like someone just came home in the evening and turned on all the lights. He puffed himself up and spread his feathers as the most majestic peacock on the west coast. "Why would they need you here? They already have me."

I nodded, unable to suppress a smile.

"True."

"It was my vision to have a center outside of a city. A place where people could go to get away, with so much beauty that when they went back to their concrete paradigms the countryside was still in their head and their heart. Land costs being what they are in California, I secured some property on the opposite side of the world."

"Tibet?"

"Virginia."

This time I did laugh out loud. "Good, because Marian would never agree to Tibet."

He brought out a set of blueprints and a folder containing contracts.

"So far, I've only got the living quarters built. The plans for the actual center, guest houses, a Zen garden, and walking meditation path will need to be finished by you, I'm afraid. Take your time, build as much as you can and be patient for the rest. Lama Rey Choden has a dharma center in DC. He will help you with the project and give you a space to teach in until the center is done."

"Master this is a beautiful dream, but..."

"Dream? I did this with my eyes open!"

I nodded. What kind of fool fights with her teacher? The foolishest fool to ever fool.

"You'll still need to work, at least for the first few years. But, I'm pretty sure the seat of our government will never have too many psychologists, or nurses. So you both should find open doors along the way."

"I need to talk to..."

"And, and..." he said, rocking back and forth with glee as he rolled open another blueprint with a picture of the finished product attached. "...the main house has three bedrooms, so there will be space for you two, a guest, and that young woman you have been hiding in your apartment like an illegal pet while you stitch her back together."

"You will be happy to know that when the landlord comes over we don't make Luka hide behind the toilet."

"How is she?"

"Coming along. She's learning English at a quick pace but is reluctant to use it. Marian managed to get her to go shopping for some clothes, but it's slow going. She's convinced the pimp who cut her up will see her and finish the job. I can't tell her that's not true."

"The Virginia woods will be the perfect place for her to heal in mind, as she has in body. At least, as much as she will in this life."

His cough was congested and ragged, like the Black Forest was growing in his lungs. We both knew it wouldn't be long before the roots of these suffocating trees wrapped themselves around his heart and tethered his body to the earth, releasing his spirit to the sky.

"I would like to stay here with you until, well...a little longer," I said.

"Stay with me? Nonsense. I am going with you—in your heart, in your mind, in that beautiful memory of yours. There's nothing left to see here, Lylarose. Go. Go and carry me with you on this great adventure. You will see me there, I promise."

Tap, tap, tap. That fat squirrel with the glorious bushy tail pushes its bossy little paws against the screen door in the kitchen with just enough force to make a constant disruption. I lift my head from Keith's trial transcript and grab the third ice pick I've sharpened down to fit inside a mallet head. I don't know why I made so many. I was only going to use one. I just kept making them, as if I could kill Keith the same way I was dying inside, day after day, over and over again. Only someone who has been through devastating loss can understand that an instant, unexpected death is not really as fast as it seems to the heart left behind. It never ends. It is a sudden eternity.

Marching to the kitchen door, I wave the sharpened pick at the squirrel.

"I've had enough of you, old man," I say, motioning toward the little squirrel's heart with the sharpest point I've crafted so far. "You can knock at my door until the wood crumbles, but it's not going to stop me."

Knock. Knock. Knock. The squirrel pushes against the door again, insistent that there be a change in attitude, or the amount of nuts Luka puts in the feeder, as soon as possible. His mouth opens when I lunge at him from inside the door. I'm not sure if he's hissing or laughing. Probably both.

"You know I won't stab you, Master," I say. "I know I won't, too. But that doesn't mean I won't kill Keith. You can come to me as a squirrel or a bird or a damn flaming phoenix rising from the singing bowl with a white lotus in your beak, but it will not stop my fate. So do me a favor and find another student to nag, because I quit."

Just to prove I'm serious, I take a ten pound block of ice from the deep freeze and set it on the butcher block. Looking straight into the liquid brown eyes of my detractor, I lift my arm as far as it will go and ram the sharpened pick into the ice, breaking a satisfying chunk off the corner. I look at the door, smiling with maniacal fury, and stab the ice again, and again, and again.

This is for my love.

This is for me.

This is the future he stole.

This is the past he destroyed.

This is the light.

This is the darkness.

This is the pain.

This.

This.

This.

Sweating and crying, I punch and jab the ice over and over, reducing it to chips of frozen revenge. Stabbing at the heart of that murdering piece of shit, I find the solace I need, at least for the night. I raise my hand as far as it will go for one last strike with enough strength to crack open an iceberg and enough power to release the pressure at the core of my wounded soul. I extend my shaking, aching arm, lean forward to put all my weight behind it and...

"Teacher," a small voice says, cutting through the steel of my convictions with a laser pen. Luka's hand wraps around my forearm and pulls the weapon toward her. Thin strands of dark brown hair cover the raised white marks a knife cut left by her ear. Like mine, her scars are faded, but not forgotten. She's so much smaller than I am, her fingers only fit partially around my arm, yet she has enough leverage to take the pick out of my hand.

"Luka, I..."

"Shhhhh," she says. She puts her finger to her lips and slides the ice from the block into the large metal sink. I watch, breathless tears cascading down my cheeks, completely mystified by her poise. She goes to the refrigerator and pulls out a thawing roast she was planning to make for our guests who demand meat protein, even though it is not on our menu. Wordlessly, she sets the slab of meat on the butcher block and returns the ice pick to my hand, this time angling the tip to stab in and up, not down and through. She bows, then grabs a handful of walnuts she keeps in a bag by the back door, and tosses them to the squirrel, who chases the treasures with sudden glee.

Our eyes meet.

"Your enemy is not made of ice."

The first few raindrops tap against the reinforced glass above the radiator behind Pen's head. Her eyes twitch, warding off the noise so she can dive back into the chaotic half-sleep her recliner allows. Soon the drops become more persistent, pit-pattering a natural wake up call. In her dreamy haze, she squints to see if the nurse is tapping her to give an update on my status. She sits all the way up before she realizes it's just a sun shower—the kind that waters the earth and makes the plants grow.

She goes through her new morning routine: check my monitor, run her hand through my hair and ask me to open my eyes, look at the door to see which cop replaced Officer Brault—who usually creeps away at first light—scan her phone, iPad, and laptop for messages from Jeremy, deleting the pleas from her publicist, logs on to *News Now* to see the dedicated camera they have focused on the hospital's front door, and the scrolling update bar on the sideline titled "Massacre at The Bowl."

"How many people does it take to be a massacre?" She asks me, chuckling with exhausted delirium before stumbling to the bathroom with a change of clothes over her arm and her makeup kit in hand. I hear her tweezers snapping together as they pull a stray chin hair by its root.

"Oh god, I've become a Shakespearean crone," Pen cackles before cramming herself in the tiny shower to wash off the night watch and start a new day. The iPad, acting as a seat holder in her recliner, begins blathering as an upload rolls.

"Warden William Hummel is in the hot seat today as the Prison Review Board questions why he allowed a potentially unstable crime victim to act as the counselor for the man convicted of her lover's murder," Laura Lindeman shouts into the microphone. She's purposely standing in the rain, although the equipment tent cover can be seen three feet to the left. She wants viewers to know she's not only reporting the story, she's personally suffering to bring it their way. Before she can martyr herself farther, the clip switches to a press conference on the steps of the Sheriff's office. They were smart enough to stand under an eave.

"The incident is still under investigation. I cannot make any specific comments at this time," the warden says over the incoming questions hurling through the air like locusts. Detective Markel stands to his right, and a man who looks like he just had a colonoscopy with a lightning rod, probably the sheriff, stands on the left.

Did Keith Allen have the right to deny Gentry as his counselor?"

"I believe it was Mr. Allen who requested Dr. Gentry to work with him."

Markel whispers something behind a folder. The warden nods.

"Warden, was it you who authorized Dr. Gentry to work with Keith Allen? Why wasn't the request denied?"

"All the paperwork regarding that request is currently being reviewed," he says.

"Did Dr. Gentry have a psychological evaluation before permission was given?"

"Dr. Gentry went through the same credentialing process as all counselors. There were no marks against her license and nothing was noted in her paperwork."

"Why was there a firearm in proximity to an inmate? How did Gentry get access to it?"

"I cannot comment until our investigation is complete."

"Are you now confirming it was Dr. Gentry who did the shooting?"

Again, Markel speaks to him from behind the folder.

"I cannot comment at this time."

"Can you confirm our sources that say Dr. Gentry brought a second weapon into the facility?"

"I cannot confirm anything at this time."

"Warden, why hasn't there been any surveillance footage released to the press?"

"The incident happened in an unmonitored area. Footage of the hallway on the wing that holds the counseling pod, Dr. Gentry's arrival, and the event aftermath is currently in the possession of the Prison Review Board. They will release it as soon as the investigation is complete."

"What protection did your corrections officers have against...?"

The sheriff steps in before Hummel shoots himself in the foot.

"Folks, that's all there is to say. Our investigators are doing what they do best, gathering evidence and putting together an accurate explanation of the crime. There will be no more comments from this office until an arrest is made."

"Sherriff Wright?! When will that be?"

"Sherriff Wright, are you close to an arrest?

"Sheriff!"

"Sheriff?"

The conference crashes to immediate silence when a fresh-faced Penelope Fine, resplendent in a short black skirt, candlelight blouse, and sharp tailored blazer picks up the iPad and flicks the screen away like dandruff on her shoulder.

"I swear to you, Buddha, when all this is over, I'll never click on this website again."

Before she can scroll through the rest of the twitter updates, the phone begins vibrating, making her entire electronic empire shake for attention.

"This is Penelope," she answers.

"What did you do?" The deep, severe voice on the other side growls.

"What?"

"What did you do, Penelope? Why do I have Detective Mesa and a forensic accountant standing in front of me with a subpoena for all of the Virga Foundation's financial records?"

"I dunno, Topaz. Have you been dipping into the dharma donut fund again? A couple extra sprinkles for you and the hubs?"

"Laugh it up. I'm glad you're having such a good time over there while I'm drowning in angry students who, by the way, don't share your view of Lyla's innocence. Now I've got Johnny Law with a page scanner going through every record line by line and asking me for answers about things I don't know."

"You're right, Top Ass. It's a party here. IV bag changes, vital sign checks, and at happy hour, they use an antiseptic sponge to wash out Lyla's mouth so the vent doesn't give her an infection. Last night—they almost let me do it."

"Do you know what they are looking for?"

"In Lyla's mouth?"

"No, stupid, in the financial records."

"No."

"Is she better or worse?"

"No."

"I can't hold this together much longer," Topaz sighs. "I'm out of strength. I'm out of ideas. I'm over it."

"Are you out of heart?"

"What?"

"I don't care what you and the others think. I know in my heart Lylarose Gentry did not kill those people. That might be the only thing I have left when this is over, but I have it. It's mine."

"Good for you. The rest of us are trying to pick up the pieces because we live in reality, and the view from here is not that jolly. Do you get the news in there? Chaotic history. Abusive childhood. Estranged family. How can you say you know anything about the woman in that bed? She was a stranger to us all."

"I have no explanation for the woman I don't know. The woman I'm looking at carried me when I couldn't walk and taught me when I couldn't learn. What did she teach me? That as long as I have breath, I have another chance to do better, be better, and that there is a gentle way to do everything, but yelling is usually faster."

Pen laughs at my old joke. It works. Even Topaz snickers on the other end of the call.

"Maybe I should yell at this guy pawing through my Quickbooks."

"Well, it would be a faster way to get arrested," Pen suggests. "You might even beat me into jail. Maybe we can share a cell."

A moment of silence unfolds between these two warriors, ever sparring with each other because they are the same. Pen reaches out first.

"I think Detective Mesa is looking for a money trail between Lyla and the guard who got killed. They think he may have been working with her. I don't know why, and I don't think Mesa is going to find anything, because even if Lyla turns out to be the sneakiest deadliest guru on earth, she's still way too cheap to pay someone for help."

"True that. I'll just let them keep looking then. They asked if Lyla ever used FundFinders for the center or if she donated to it. I said I didn't know. Do you?"

"No. Never heard her mention it. Ask Luka. If Lyla did it, Luka knows."

Topaz emits a crack of cynical laughter dry enough to polish glass.

"Because Luka's such an open book too?"

"Could you try?"

"You try, she and Robyn are on their way to you. She had the travel tea set and Lyla's mug. She said something about promising you pot stickers?"

"Oh thank you, Buddha." Penelope's mouth begins to water even as she speaks. "I need those so bad."

"I gotta go. Listen, if Lyla wakes up, tell her she owes me an explanation."

"Okay."

"And if she doesn't...If she...well, tell her when I see her in the next life, she still owes me an explanation."

Penelope bites her lip and closes her eyes.

"And tell her...thanks for giving me a chance when no one else would. Um... just tell her I said, 'thank you.'"

Penelope nods and drops the call before she's expected to respond with words her strained voice will not allow.

"Well, this round of mascara made it three whole minutes before it was ruined. These days, that's probably a record," she says to me, making her way back to the bathroom for another touch up as warm tears fall down her cheeks like summer rain.

THE CIRCUIT COURT FOR MONTGOMERY COUNTY, MARYLAND
SENTENCING HEARING FOR
KEITH W. ALLEN
CRIMINAL CASE NO. 6 -57-12587
VICTIM IMPACT STATEMENT

THE COURT: Thank you, Mrs. Rawls. I am sorry for your loss. Next statement?

MS. STICKLAND: The Court calls Dr. Lylarose Gentry, spouse of Marian Fitzwater.

THE COURT: Dr. Gentry, you may proceed.

DR. GENTRY: Thank you, Your Honor. Mr. Allen, when I was told this is my chance to face you and convey to you how very much I've lost, and the terrible impact you have had on my life, I did nothing but laugh. It was not the silly kind of laugh that happens when a rare moment of joy filters through the bleak and tear blinded days of my existence without Marian. It was an incredulous chuckle of a woman who knows there are no words for what your depraved act has done to me, and even if they did exist, saying them out loud would call fire from the heavens to rain upon us and raze this building to the ground.

Marian was my soul mate, my heartbeat, my in-breath, and my best dreams. She was the first person to ever really love me. She was the last person who will ever really touch me. She was not my beginning or my end. She was my moment-by-moment assurance that love is real and life is good. I didn't spend nearly enough minutes with her, and through all the years we were together, I never spent a moment without her. I miss her. I miss her so much.

She was a devoted daughter, a faithful friend, a dedicated nurse, a caring stranger, a guiding light. She was not a perfect person. She sang to her cats way too loudly in the morning, she stole food off my plate, blankets off our bed, and every sweater I owned. Her jokes were terrible, which made them hysterical. She was so stubborn she would never give in, never give out, and never give up on me. You have stolen her from this world. The cost to us is staggering. The cost to you is worse.

The truth is, I always knew Marian was impermanent. We understood that someday one of us would leave this earth through death, and the other would be left behind. That awareness helped us love more deeply, communicate openly, and appreciate the small things that made the larger part of our life together. In loving her, I accepted I might someday lose her. It is the hardest part of love to know that death is the way of all things. But her death, at your hands, was too early, too violent, too wrong. This is not the age a healthy active woman should die. This is not the way someone who gave life to so many others should lose hers. Marian's death was unnatural. By employing the power to end a life before its time, you have rendered yourself unnatural as well.

You have condemned your innermost being to a cursed half-existence of soulless wandering, seeking a refuge that you will never find. A shadow has been cast around you no light can disperse. The arrogance and avarice which led to your actions that night will show themselves to be the fruit of a weak, insecure tree, something the inmates you are incarcerated with will find delectable as they devour you daily until there is nothing left but a mangled, empty pit. Incredibly, I feel a deep compassion and great swell of pity for you, Mr. Allen. That shows the real impact you have had on my life. By taking away my dear sweet love before her time, you have made me unnatural, too.

"Hey, Ms. Fine," Robyn calls, walking past the day officer in a raggedy T-shirt and faded gray sweatpants with a bright pink balloon reading "It's a girl!" and a baby shower gift bag bustling with glitter and ribbons. Luka skitters behind her, offering the floor a guilty smile as she holds a casserole dish in a cardboard box hastily decorated by markers that said "Happy Baby." The oddly shaped letters and strange cadence are not new to me. I've seen the lists Luka gave Marian when she needed something off the grounds of Virga.

Penelope's brow furrows, and she spreads her arms wide, then drops them as her mouth hangs half-way open. She only recovers from the sight when she realizes the Happy Baby casserole is really Luka's fabulous pot stickers and steamed broccoli.

"Um...what the..."

"News cameras caught Keith Allen's wife slipping back in the hospital this morning through the nurse's parking lot. Now there's cameras on both sides of the building. I thought this would be a good way to get us through the front door without drawing attention. I'm nobody, but they might recognize Luka from the news copter shots of the center. It worked like a charm."

Pen puts her hand on the back of the recliner to steady herself. The pink of the balloons swirls around her, then graduates through gray to black. She closes her eyes and opens them to an entirely different hospital room, filled with pink everything, smiling faces, and roses. So many roses. Propped up against the pillows with a newborn in her arms, the world could not have been a more welcoming, wonderful place. Bill sat in a chair beside her, running his finger up and down his daughter's tiny nose. The thin sheen of blond hair Rosie was born with parted naturally to the side, leaving a little bald spot Penelope kissed and nuzzled as the child slept in her arms.

"You are going to have the best life," Penelope whispered in her ear.

"What's with those scratches on your arms?" I asked five years later, as she sat in front of me for a weekly session. "Did you get a kitten?"

"Why would I do that? I can't keep a child alive, what chance would a kitten have?" Her eyes shifted from the chair legs to the bookcase and back, her head finding it impossible to raise more than twenty degrees.

"Look at me," I said gently, but with no room for argument. She bit her lower lip, sighed, and finally met my eyes. "The scratches?"

"I didn't cut myself to feel something. I feel everything. Every fucking feeling. I feel them. All. At the same time. I'm a damn train wreck of emotions. Happy? Are we done? Am I cured?"

"The scratches?"

One good thing about growing up with Hurricane Peggy, these little tirades Pen breaks into don't distract me at all. I just let the wind blow my hair back and hold my ground. The gale wears out eventually. That's when the real work of healing begins.

"I'm getting ready to sell the house. I was packing up boxes yesterday, and I came across Bill's garden things. He said to give anything he left to charity, but I'm not sure who the hell wants rusty clippers. So, I left them out by the trash." She stopped talking and began fidgeting with a prayer wheel on my desk as if this half-story is all she needed to offer. I don't know whether to laugh because she tried that, or be insulted she thought it would work on me.

"And they came in through an open window in the middle of the night and attacked you?"

She smirked, gave me that poisoned smile, and shook her head.

"I can ask stupid questions for an hour, or you can just tell me."

"Okay. On my way to the trash I saw the roses, the ones I planted outside...outside Rosie's window. I quit watering them. I quit feeding them. I had completely stopped caring for them but somehow, they bloomed. They all bloomed. My daughter is dead, and those goddamn roses were just shouting hallelujah to the sun. I grabbed that fucking bush and tried to pull it out of the ground with my bare hands. It wouldn't budge. So I stripped every petal I could grab off those vines. I bent the stems and I broke those bushes down until there was a red pile of mulch on the ground. If it wouldn't have depreciated the value of the house, I would have set fire to the whole thing. That's how I got these scratches."

I nodded as the energy consumed her, then bubbled back down after the boil, like my mamaw's fudge used to do. She wouldn't get square little pieces of heaven out of this batch. But it will, eventually, make her heart solid enough to hold.

"Well, I guess you were right about two things, Pen. You are feeling all the feelings. And you're not ready for a kitten."

Penelope burst out with laughter, honest and real, not the sarcastic chuckle she gives to others.

"I used to love roses," she said with a smile. Laughing feels good again, especially on a day after a night like that. "Now I loathe them."

"Why?" I asked, softening my voice and projecting my comfort to her in deep blue currents.

"Because they hurt."

"A lot of things hurt, Penelope. Going to the dentist hurts, but you don't set yours on fire. At least, not to my knowledge."

"They remind me."

"Of what?"

"Rosie."

"No. If they reminded you of Rosie, you'd have a million of them."

"Bill, then. The way it happened. The way he left."

"No. This is not about Bill. What do you see when you see a rose?"

"Joy."

"And..."

"There is no joy anymore. I loved her so much. I was so happy. She was so...I can't...I can't look at that joy and know it's gone forever." Her chest heaves in deep sobs, causing her head to drop as sorrow overwhelms her.

"No."

"And, they remind me," she gasps, the pitch of her voice high and strained as she struggles to talk between breaths. "I wasn't there. I was at work, doing a signing, chatting up strangers while my daughter was in pain. I was on a plane when she died."

"And?"

"It's my fault." Her breath puffs out of her in small bursts as she drops one tissue on the floor and reaches for another. "Every time I see a rose, it screams at me. It just says over and over 'you weren't there. You were not there.' I scheduled that signing because I needed to get out of the house. Bill and I were having trouble. Someone at a dinner introduced him as "Mr. Fine." He was furious. The tension had been rising. I spent every waking moment with Rosie just to avoid him. I thought I just needed the trip, to get some air. To give him some space. He had started doing photography again, thinking he could make a name—his name—for himself that way. That's what they were doing in the park. He was taking pictures. If I had stayed home. If I hadn't run away from the situation. If I wasn't such a..."

"Pen, stop. There's nothing wrong with you. It isn't about you. Death doesn't care who you are. Death doesn't care what your name is. Death doesn't judge. Death doesn't punish. Death just comes."

"That's so unfair."

"Yes. It is."

"So, that's it? Just—kids die. Go on? I tried that. I wrote a whole damn book about it."

"And that's why you loathe roses. Your suicide attempt failed because Death did not want you and will not take you to Rosie so you can apologize for being a human being. You can make all the book lists, trash all the roses, and hide behind those five hundred dollar sunglasses as you wave to people from inside your car, but none of it will give you any peace until you let go of this undeserved guilt."

"And how, exactly, am I supposed to do that? How do I forgive myself for not being there?"

"By being there. Wherever you are, whatever the next moment requires, you be there."

Our cook sets the box with the food on a chair beside Penelope, who lifts the lid to immerse herself in the spicy home-cooked aroma. It's the first food she's had that didn't come in plastic or taste like cardboard since this began.

"Mmmmm. Happy Baby, indeed."

Robyn fishes for utensils and brings out some bottled water and a travel mug of Pu-erh, the bittersweet tea we drink at the center, then hands the bag to Luka who sets up a little teapot and cup by my bed, thinking I'll be less lost at the crossroads of life with it near me. There is no tea in the vessel. How fitting.

"Did you say Pat Allen was 'slipping back into the hospital?' Where the hell did she go?"

"Dunno. It was on the local news. She was trying to make her way through the parking garage, and everyone was shouting questions."

"Did she answer any of them?"

"Hell, no."

"Shhhhhhh, the teacher," Luka admonishes. Robyn puts her fingers to her lips, then winks at my body.

"If there's anyone who enjoyed a good cuss word, it was Lyla," Penelope says. Luka rubs lotion on my peeling gray skin, gently nudging her fingers under the rim of my hospital gown. "She only said bad words when she was really frustrated or angry, which wasn't often, but she always used the most creative profanity."

"I know, right?!" Robyn claps her rough hands together as if she just remembered what her last wish from a genie would be. "Like how she used to call that fountain in the garden that always flooded the back porch 'Suckaphone.' I can still hear her out there mopping saying, 'that Suckaphone pump exploded again.'"

Luka chuckles as she whispers one of my favorite mantras into my ear, "All is well. All is well. Everything is a wreck, but all is well."

"My favorite was always 'bitchnose' for some reason. I don't know how or why she came up with that, but I always sorta loved it," Penelope says as a snow pea dangles from her mouth. She's trying not to devour her food in the first five minutes, but losing the battle.

Luka returns to her friends and takes the seat that once held the now-empty casserole dish. Penelope nods gratitude wiping the last of the sauce from her lips. Luka smiles at her. Robyn must be a good influence. I haven't seen Luka so at ease since Marian left this world behind.

"One time," Robyn holds her jiggling side as she begins chuckling to herself. "One time, Lyla was going to do a dharma teaching, and we were all gathering on the cushions to meditate before the teaching started. Lyla was in her office, the one with the rice paper door right behind the altar, and she was putting together one of those do-it-yourself bookshelves. She used every cuss word there was. Topaz went in to let her know we were all assembled and could hear her, but before she could say anything, we all heard Lyla scream, 'Do you know why these kits give you two free, shitfabulous Allen wrenches? So when you discover you just spent fifteen minutes screwing one side on backwards, you can throw one of these craptacles right out the door.'"

"Oh my," Penelope laughs.

"So Topaz just walks out and shrugs. But Luka here, she went and got Marian. Lyla was still in there, screwing and unscrewing, shouting about 'where the hell is side panel B,' and bam! Marian came stomping up the aisle, right through the cushions, and went back there. Her red hair was on fire. Everyone was just sitting on the edge of their seat waiting.

"'Ly-la-rose Gentry!' Marian said, just like a schoolteacher. 'If you don't stop this profanity right now, the Buddha himself is going to start drinking vodka out of the rain barrel.'

"Lyla didn't say a word.

"'Your class is waiting,' Marian said and stomped right back through the room. After about five minutes, the gong rings and Lyla steps out and bows, so slow and holy. She sits on her cushion and looks down at her notes, and no one was moving a muscle.

"'Today's teaching is...is...on...' She was giggling to herself so hard she could barely talk. '...on...today's class is on...equanimity... keeping calm...ummm...under...pressure.' Then she laughed out loud so hard she actually fell off her cushion and laid there on the floor cracking up. The whole room started laughing. It was the best class I ever went to."

The three share a hearty moment, even Luka, who always clued Marian in to my various crimes and misdemeanors. In all my years as a counselor and teacher, this was the only part I liked about hospital visitation—the stories people inevitably share. As long as we have these tales, no one will ever really die.

Robyn stretches her legs out and leans back, putting her rain soaked sneakers on the arm of Penelope's throne. Pen doesn't seem to notice. Now I know for sure this ordeal has worn her to the bone.

"That's what I always liked about Dr. Gentry," Robyn says. "She was real. She wasn't a monk or a nun. She was just a person, like the rest of us. She didn't pretend to know everything, or act like all you need to do is meditate and say three cheerful things a day and your life will be perfect. For her, mindfulness wasn't just some privileged new age club for rich people and bored housewives. It was gritty, in-the-trenches stuff. There weren't any sparkles or fairy wings on Lyla. She told us the first time I met her, at the halfway house, that life was hard, and meditation wasn't going to make it any less hard, but it would remind us we are equal to the task."

"Halfway house!" Penelope snaps her fingers. "I meant to tell you, you were right."

"Huh?"

"The thing you told me about the room and how it's not private, you were right. They were tapped in."

"Did you see it? Did she..."

"It's on the way. I'll find out soon enough."

Luka looks back at my body. Her lips move silently, and she closes her eyes, saying a prayer for the truth, or reciting from the book of the dead. I don't know which.

"Can I say something that might sound really horrible?" Robyn asks.

"Of course."

"It doesn't matter to me if she did it or not. And part of me sometimes hopes she did. Not the cops, but Allen. Every time the news shows that picture of his smug face when he's walking out of the courtroom, I'm like, 'Suffer and die, asshole.' I sorta hope she did it."

Pen leans forward with her inhale.

"You can't mean that. That would betray everything she is."

"Everything YOU think she is," Luka corrects. "We are all each other's projections."

"Yes, okay, everything I think she is."

"That's just the thing, Ms. Fine. I don't think people are just one day or one moment or one act. Dr. Gentry was so much more than this. She helped people. She healed people. She listened to phony wannabes selling mindfulness like a box of cookies, and she cried bullshit. But when you needed her, when I needed her, she was always right there. She didn't tell me what I wanted to hear. She told me what I needed to hear. Whether I wanted it or not. Why is she just that lump over there now? Even if she marched in there with a machine gun and took out the whole freaking pod, how is that her whole life? She came from somewhere. She belonged to someone. She belongs to us.

"I know Buddhism is all about being in the moment. But she's more than a moment. She's a whole goddamn life of moments, most of which, apparently nobody knew about. And that's okay. Everyone has a private side. Everyone. If you get that recording, and it shows her murdering that bastard with no mercy, it's not who she is. It's not what she believed. It's not what she taught. It's just her in a moment—giving him exactly what he deserves."

"I'm not sure she'd see it that way, and neither do I," Penelope answers through gritted teeth. "No matter how small a part of her life this is, it is a defining event, and it matters. I can't, I won't, believe she did this until I see it with my own eyes. I find it hard to accept two innocent guards are dead and she's in a coma over a moment of weakness."

"Not weakness," Luka says with rare force. "The teacher was never a weak person. Miss Marian told me once that she was in love with the teacher from the moment she saw her, because she had done something that took more strength and courage than most people will ever show in their lifetime. She said the teacher was the strongest person she had ever met. The teacher went to that prison to do whatever she felt she was required to do. Nothing more. Nothing less. Nothing right. Nothing wrong."

"Oh my god!" Robyn puts her hand over her mouth and laughs loudly, then leans over and drapes her arm across Luka's frail shoulders. "Girl, that's more words than I've heard you say in years. Damn, you can talk!"

Whatever argument Penelope plans as a response dissipates in the warm haze cast by Luka's awkward smile and Robyn's earthy goodness. I didn't know Marian told Luka that. I just thought she wanted to date me because I was so pathetic. I always considered myself her first stray cat. Now, I discover I was a lion. Her lion.

"I didn't mean to upset you, Ms. Fine. I guess I'm just saying everybody is like, 'If she did it, then it means this, and if she didn't, it means that...on and on.' I just think it is what it is. Murder or not, she's still my teacher, you know?"

Penelope nods as the sun shower deposits its last few drops on the ICU window, the final one leaving a clean streak through the grime that runs all the way to the edge.

18

Traditional Tibetan Buddhists believe there are six realms of rebirth. You can be reborn into any one of them, although some teachers suggest your karma may have a hand in determining the realm you enter. Human birth is considered the highest birth, which is incredible when you realize how much of this life we ignore or take for granted. However, it is the only birth that will allow you the opportunity to transition out of the endless cycle of rebirth and reach nirvana, a place of perfect rest. It is the only realm where you can "do better."

Modern, Western Buddhists, with the backing of ancient texts, don't always consider the six realms just to be literal afterlife destinations but psychological states. It doesn't take more than a casual glance to realize these are all stages every person goes through at some point in their time on the planet. People trapped in one always want to be in another, and everyone knows how that feels. Literal or not, the realms are real when you're in them, even if you didn't have to die to be there.

Just below human birth, is the Animal Realm. It's not a bad birth at all if you are a fluffy puppy or one of these weird neon fish who live near the deep blue ocean floor. I always wanted to come back as one of them. Knowing my luck, some research drone would net me, and I'd spend the rest of that life in a simulated tank, listening to a bored scientist tell me about how much he hates his mother-in-law living with them, and that's the real reason he works nights in the lab. The downside of the animal realm is you have no self-determinacy. Wild or domestic, you are at the complete mercy of the humans in this world. Like most people, my animal realm was adolescence. Filled with wild emotions and sporting a limber, though asthmatic, body, I was untamed and instinctive. Subject to the "my house, my rules" infrastructure of the teen years, a caged bird was the best I could become.

The Hell Realm is just what it sounds like—living hell. I was born into the Hell Realm, its fire fed by hurricane winds and desperately dry conditions. The lack of love, the dearth of hope, left us as nothing but roving tumbleweeds to be consumed in the clashes of passion and pride. Nice families don't live in the Hell Realm. The days after Marian was killed, I visited there for a while, but did not stay. Who hasn't been through hell at some point? Who would willingly go back?

The two God Realms work as twins with opposing problems. The Jealous God Realm is a world where you have everything you need, except one thing. You live a life consumed with envy and desire. The more you want your needful thing, the more you despise everyone who has it. It is a life of looking in the windows of others until you go insane with your lack. During the later years of my first life, I spent most of my time as a jealous god. I had shelter, sometimes food, school, goals, friends, but I lacked the one thing every other god seemed to have in bushels—love. Real love.

I watched people slam down the phone on loving parents because they weren't getting a ticket to a resort for spring break. I listened to my friends talk about how they were kicking a faithful, devoted boyfriend or girlfriend to the curb because they just weren't that exciting or hot. I once held the hand of a young man dying alone in an AIDS ward because his parents valued their religion over being with their gay son at the tragic end of his too-short life. The last thing he said to me was, "They aren't bad people. I love them." Everybody had so much love they could throw it around like confetti, but me.

When my first life ended with my blood soaked body lying on the ratty floor of my college apartment, I left the Jealous God Realm and woke up to my second life, reborn as a God. You'd think the God Realm would be higher than Human Birth, but it's not. In the God Realm, you still have everything you need and want, even that one thing the jealous god lacked, but because you have no pain, no need, you may end up with no compassion. Though it is the God Realm, it is not impervious to change, and it can be taken away from you in an instant. Many think the God Realm is the worst one of all, because no matter how happy you are, it is destined to end.

The morning I prepared to drive to The Bowl, with a weapon in my hand and murder on my mind, I knew which realm I was coming from. I'd been in it my entire third life—the Hungry Ghost Realm. Unlike the God Realms, the Hungry Ghosts have nothing but longing. Life in the Hungry Ghost Realm is barely living. You have nothing. You need everything. You are starving with a hole inside of you that cannot be filled. Your mind is thought-poor, your stomach is empty, and your soul is quicksand. I had walked like a ghost among the living through the trial and its aftermath, patiently putting on a smile for friends who gave good advice, dinner invitations, and encouragement. When I received the first letter from Keith Allen, an apology his lawyer got him to write for some future appeal, I just fed it to the craving abyss of my feelings and went on with the outward steps of living. Then, after several of those attempts failed to rouse the interest of my dampened embers, Pat Allen stood in my doorway.

"If you would see him, just once, and talk to him, I think you would recognize the power you two could have to heal each other," Pat said. "Keith is despondent, depressed, and giving up on ever being transferred to a unit where I could take the kids to see him. The sex offender unit is draining all hope of whatever life he could make in a real penitentiary. He told me the only thing he remembers from the sentencing hearing is what you said on the stand. He said your words haunt him. If they were strong enough to make an impact on him then, they are strong enough to reach him now. You teach compassion, Dr. Gentry. He did wrong by you, but can you look at his face and do wrong by him? If someone like you can't turn this around, what will it take for any of us to get back to right?"

My Hungry Ghost heart fed my grief-crazed mind the image of my fists pummeling Keith into the ground until he had to be squee-geed into a body bag with a mop. For the first time in my third life, I breathed real air and gave an authentic smile. Pat's colors were a mix of hope and deception, wrapped around each other like silken coils. I didn't let that stop me. This was the exit light I'd been waiting for, finally showing me the way out of this terrible realm. I didn't care where it led. I'd been through all the lower realms, so wherever it would take me would be home.

"I packed your singing bowl, Teacher, just the way it should be," Luka says, handing me the clear plastic case. In the early stages, the ice pick would get past the guards because of reverence. Now, it had made the trip enough to pass easily by familiarity.

"Thank you, Luka."

She reaches out and places her hand on my cheek, her soft brown eyes rimmed in bands of tempered steel. There was love in them, compassion, and fury.

"May you be well," she says.

"May you live with ease," I respond.

I walk through the main meditation room. Like me, the room is full of ghosts. Students laughing. Teaching happening. The day we sat Tonglen for a student who died of an overdose, tears running down our faces as we chanted and breathed. The night after everyone went home, Marian and I had a "pillow fight" while I was trying to clean the place up and ended up dancing arm in arm in a castle of cushions. Topaz sorting the mantra cards, singing the old-time gospel hymns her grandmother raised her on. The words of the Buddha, the mysteries of the dharma, the mantra for loving kindness all coated the walls of this room like a sheen of cigarette smoke on an old window.

"Luka," I turned toward her. During my life, I held back and threw away so many words as a way to protect myself and others. In that room, at the last goodbye, I didn't have any left. "If the ancients were right, and there is rebirth, I want to come back as your student."

"I want to come back as one of Miss Marian's cats."

And so it was with a genuine, grateful grin, this hungry ghost floated out of the Virga Center for Meditation and Renewal, toward a destination unknown.

"Thinking about the past, Dr. Gentry?" Keith asks, catching me staring off into space, waiting for Officer Johnson's attention to wander as he stands outside the door. "About how different everything would be if your wife hadn't gone out that night? Where would you be? Where would I be?"

I shake my head. "I don't spend a lot of time on the past, or the future. The most important moment in any life is the present moment. What has been will not change. What will come, will come.

Better to stay focused on the minute you're in."

"That's a pretty depressing way to look at life."

"Is it?"

"It doesn't leave any room for change. If you don't look at the past, how will you remember the soft, sweet lips of your pretty wife or the way she made you laugh or cry or coo? If you don't look at the future, how will you find your destiny?"

"It's not our job to find our destiny, Keith. Destiny finds us. I'm pretty sure mine knows exactly where I am at this moment."

"What? You surprise me, Doctor. No 'we rest in the hands of fate?' I'm disappointed. You're no deeper than a fortune cookie at the Noodle Shack in the airport."

I smile, sliding the singing bowl mallet to the perfect spot for me to grab it faster than lightning. Keith's mud brown aura lies in a static lump on his side of the table. A few amber sparkles bubble up when he sets out the traps baited with Marian's flesh, but he's confident to-day, comfortable. That relaxes me. As the wolf told Little Red Riding Hood, "All the better to eat you with."

"We might rest in the hand of fate, Keith, but make no mistake. We point its fingers."

"You're talking about karma? That thing where whatever you do in this life comes back to bite you in the ass?"

"That's not karma. That's payback, and as we all know, it's a bitch. Karma is a natural consequence of your actions. It is neutral in its energy and doesn't set out to teach or to punish, although you can certainly do both to yourself. If you plant tomato seeds, you get tomatoes. That's karma. If you plant good acts in your life, you will harvest a good response. You plant murder, you get prison—in body or in mind."

"Nan came to me for counseling because grad school was keeping her up at night, and she wanted someone to listen to her woes. All it brought her was my hard attention behind a skanky lezzy bar, where she ended up leading your wife to her death. Where's the karma in that?"

Keith's eyes loll to the side as he inhales deeply, drawing the perfume of his power, his tyranny of the profane, up his nostrils for a good strong high. It's better than cocaine, easier to get, and won't leave residue for the guards to find. Of all the forms of addiction recorded in the Diagnostic and Statistical Manual, this is the most pathetic.

"Karma isn't about what other people do to us. That's their karma. Karma is about what each person does, the actions each person sows into their garden. The truth is, no matter how terribly we hurt one another, the harm we really do is to ourselves."

"So is that why you're really here, Dr. Gentry? To get some of that good karma in your garden? Trying to dig up the resentment and anger you feel toward me for putting my hands on your woman and squeezing her so hard I could feel the tendon pop against my palm? Making lemonade out of lemons? Do you remember those coroner's pictures at the trial? My handiwork all over her throat, and all you could do was sit there and look so sad and soooo spiritual because every eye was on you. Not me, the taker. You, the loser."

"I'm not here for karma. I'm not here to be forgiving, or holy, or to heal my shattered heart. I'm beyond repair. You know that. You love it. Feeding off the wounds of others makes you so happy that causing you personal pain is the only way the universe will ever teach you compassion. I hope whatever karma has in store for you is going to be so crazy awful you end up owning the softest heart on the planet."

"That's not very nice," he stammers, squinting and trying to figure out what is so different about me today. He finger-combs his mop of damp, dull hair over his balding forehead and glances at me curiously. Why am I so virulent? Why am I talking so much? Why am I already leaning forward as if I'm about to stand up twenty minutes before our time is over? "Your garden is gonna get some weeds in it."

My entire body is a bowstring drawn back so impossibly far that, even if there were no arrow, the recoil of its release would cut through time. My jaw is locked and my heart is pounding. Breath comes through my nostrils like one of the bulls in Pamplona before running begins. The gate is about to open. My feet, restless hooves, push back against the cement floor. There are many demons in this room and so many runners who came before Keith, but today, I'm going to trap this fatuous sweating pig in front of me, and I'm going to gore him until there's nothing left but a greasy puddle.

"I told you. I am present in this moment. I'm not thinking about the past. I'm not working on the future. I'm not here for karma. I'm here for payback, and the moment is now."

"What?"

"Now!"

I spring forward and grab his dull-gray, prison-issued sweatshirt with my left hand, pulling him across the yellow line with a forward thrust so full of torque I could have miraculously picked him up and thrown him against the wall, like a mom who lifts a car to save her trapped child. But I don't throw him. I get a good solid grip before his brain can register anything but the chemtrail of my adrenaline, pulling him right up to my face. Then I take my right hand, the severed and sown fist, and with every ounce of energy I can steal from the world, I punch that bitchnose motherfucker right between the eyes.

"My name is Jeremy Fine. I'm here to see my aunt."

Penelope jumps out of the recliner, knocking her iPad to the floor. She bends quickly and picks it up, nearly toppling over the heels she kicked off in her sleep. Officer Brault groggily stands up and blinks. They'd both been nodding off for some time.

"My aunt," Jeremy points again to Penelope and nods, hoping his powers will persuade the half-awake officer to let him in the room un-challenged, even though he has a fanny pack big enough to conceal an oil barrel around his waist. It works. Genetics. They're stronger than people think.

"Sure, sure," Officer Brault says, stepping out of the doorway. "Are you okay, Ms. Fine?"

"Of course," she says, opening her arms wide as if the lanky young man in his mid-twenties with curly blond hair, wearing a plaid pocket shirt, is actually a five-year-old. "Come give your auntie a big kiss!"

Jeremy glares at her, then smiles. He's been beaten at his own con game. Make no mistake, grasshopper. You're good, but she's a mas-ter. He gives her a quick hug while she makes sloppy wet kissy noises against his cheek.

"Aunt Penelope, seriously," he mumbles, pulling away.

"Seriously? Jeremy FINE? Seriously?"

"I thought it would make it easier to get in. You said you were surrounded by cops."

"Night shift. And, I'll let it pass, this time. But, if you're gonna use my name, you'll have to dress better."

"Okay." He looks over at my body, his face pulled down by the gravity of the sight. "The Doc. God, she looks awful."

He makes eye contact for just as long as it takes for his mind to reconcile the carcass he sees in this bed with the living, breathing-without-help woman he saw not long ago. Then his eyes light up as he looks at the monitor and IV pump. He reaches out with a tentative finger.

"Don't touch that!" She calls.

"Do it, do it," I think, trying to get the words through his thick skull. That will knock this train off its trolley for sure.

He pulls his hands back and holds them up.

"I won't. How do they program this thing? Is it network assisted or an individual mainframe device?"

"The nurse comes in and pushes buttons. It beeps. She stays alive. If this is life."

"Cool, so it's individual. You know what would be great is if you could network these with a feedback sensor and split compilers so they could control everyone from one room and then..."

"Do you have what I asked for?" She whispers, looking toward the door to ensure their little family circus lulled Brault into a false sense of security. He nods and pats his fanny pack. She returns to the recliner and motions to the seat beside her. "Come tell me all about your Optimal Price."

"Optimus Prime."

"Yeah, that too."

Jeremy unzips the fanny pack so slowly the teeth of the zipper have time to kiss each other goodbye. He pulls out a red flash drive and slips it into Penelope's waiting hand.

"Here's your phone call. Whoever compressed it to send to you did a shit job. The audio is blurry, and you can't make out half of what he's saying."

"So you listened to it?"

"I thought there might be more information about their system than the notes you got from your friend. Man, he told that woman a truckload of confidential crap. We lucked out. The IT guy there is a fellow hacker. Didn't take too much money to get an encryption source from him. Bro code, you know. Besides, he says Hummel is a dick."

"Well, it doesn't have to stand up in court. Warden Hummel just has to think it will."

Jeremy nods. He's all for screwing the system, even if he doesn't exactly understand what the system is, or why it should be screwed. He swallows hard and hands her a black flash drive and an index card.

"You need to use your laptop, not the iPad. Open up the document on here. The first link is a VPN app, Virtual Private Network. It will make sure your IP address doesn't get out, or if you're using hospital wi-fi, their sensors don't get information about what you're doing. Don't get complacent, Aunt Penelope. When it comes to what we do online, everybody cares."

"Agreed."

"After you are on the VPN, use the second link to download Tor. It will give you protection and take you past the clear web without leaving a signature."

"The clear web?"

"The internet you see—Facebook, Google, Amazon—that's the clear web. It's only five percent of the whole web, but it's all most people will ever use."

"You put this on the dark web?"

Jeremy snorts in her face. He's a nice kid though, he doesn't laugh too loudly at her.

"No."

"Why not?"

He rolls his eyes. "Think a minute, Aunt Penelope. If you know about the dark web, it's not a secret, is it?"

She chuckles. Somehow, in the years she spent selling, hiding, and facing her grief, he went from brilliant, jerky kid to a wise young man while she wasn't looking.

"This is in the Black Hole. Deeper than the dark. Once you have Tor running, copy the final link on the document and plug it in. It will take you to a firewall." He points to the index card he handed her. "The video is .264 format. The URL is programmed to play it. You can't download it to anything else. To see the video, put in the first password."

"Snow White?"

"Yeah. I tried to pick passwords you'd remember. You need to use the password every time you hit the firewall, so if you close out but want back in, you have to retype. When you're finished, and I mean really finished, like this file needs to disappear, or if you decide not to watch it—go to the firewall and type in the second password."

"Rose Red."

Jeremy nods, biting his lip.

"That's what I used to call you and Rosie when you would visit us, remember? Snow White and Rose Red."

"I do." Penelope takes a deep breath, letting her memory settle into a grateful place in her heart, even if it stings on entry. Jeremy exhales, never lifting his eyes from his pant legs.

"It isn't a good idea to talk about it now because it will just upset you more, but I really miss Rosie. She was such...such a cool little kid."

"She was," Penelope joins him staring at the floor. Both on the verge, neither one willing to let the first tear fall. Genetics.

"Mom said you haven't been around because you said in your

book you were starting a new life and moving on, and I don't get how. I mean, I can't forget…"

"It was a lie, sweetie."

"What? Mom…?"

"The book was a lie. I wrote crap I didn't mean and pushed a bunch of fake positivity programs that didn't work for me or probably anyone else. I lost Rosie. I lost Bill. The books were all I had left that felt like mine. Lylarose was helping me be more honest, not just with my writing, but with my heart—accepting what happened, and trying to be authentic. Most of the time, I'm just like you in one of your cosplay costumes. Only, I forgot how to take mine off. I pulled away from everyone until I could get to a better place. I'm still kinda working on it. And now, this."

"But why did you…"

"Some things you do out of grief. Some things you do for money."

They both emit the exact same goldenrod color, momentarily so intertwined there is no beginning and no end. They are the same. That's the second time I've seen that happen since I told Luka goodbye. I don't know how common it is, but the world would be a better place if it happened more.

Jeremy stands to give his aunt a quick hug.

"Like I said, Aunt Penelope, if you decide not to watch it, use the second password. The whole URL will delete itself without a trace."

"Did you keep a copy?"

"Oh, hell no," he says. "This is a problem I don't need."

"Did you watch it?"

"Um…noooo, well, not really, yes, just a…"

"Jeremy?"

He nods, and looks over at me again, his eyes clouded with the event they can't unsee.

"And?"

"I don't think you should watch it. I mean, why do you have to watch it?"

"Because some things you do for love."

She hugs him again and gives him a real kiss on the cheek.

"My business manager will write you the check we agreed on. You'll get it in the mail soon."

"Yeah, cool."

"I'll have him add an extra three hundred dollars. Get us two tickets to the Comic-Con."

"Really?"

"Yes, now go. Before I remember what a dork you are."

She watches as Jeremy flashes a peace sign to Officer Brault, leaning back in his chair with his earbuds in. He nods and stretches his back before rejoining his show.

"What will I see, Lyla?" She asks me, staring at the black flash drive before turning on her laptop and downloading the path she's been warned not to travel. The IV bag drips on cue. The monitor beeps its steady rhythm. No clues. No help. Just life.

When the firewall comes up, she walks unsteadily to the bathroom, trying to hide her laptop and headphones behind her back. The door locks with a click as she sits on the narrow toilet, balancing the laptop on her knees and her sanity on the ledge without a net. That's the curse of the modern age. She has the technological ability to go into the deepest dark forest, but there's no breadcrumbs she can leave behind to mark the way back. There is no way back.

The flesh and cartilage of Keith's nose crushes under my fist with a satisfying deep tissue crunch. He screams like a teakettle shrieking the apocalypse. He tries to raise his murdering hands to his face, but I still have him by the collar. I lift him all the way out of his chair. There's a moment, a split second, when our eyes meet, his normally dim brown pupils popping large with terror. My soulless blue ghost eyes glow like an iceberg, the jagged hard surface going all the way to the deep pockets of an ocean filled with malice. Just when he thinks he's found the depth of me, my knee crashes into his crotch and the shriek becomes a grunt of lower guttural agony. I was ready for him to bend and raise my knee a second time, hitting him right in the chin. His teeth snap together as the blood from his nose pours down his chest. I hope he slips in it. I hope he drowns in it.

Dazed and hurting, he's easy to push up against the wall. He's nothing but a feather now. My anger, my hate, my symphony on the world's injustice plays through the room with the sounds of him choking, gasping, crying out. I am the conductor of this concerto of revenge. It's brutish and harsh, no blue notes, no rests for pacing, no chimes for mercy, just the clashing of cymbals and brash blaring brass of his reckoning. I hit him twice in quick succession, my fist against his cheekbone, the impact sending electric current up my forearm, then I wrap my ankle around his legs pulling his feet out from under him, listening for the air to push out of his lungs with a yelp when he lands flat on his back on the unforgiving cement floor.

The mallet is on the edge of the table. I grab it and flick my wrist, sending the decorated wooden top flying across the room. He starts to call for help but only gets to the "H" before I hit him again. The pod door opens as Officer Johnson gets his first full glimpse of the savage beating this weak, sinister pig is taking on the floor of law and order.

The shock stops him long enough to give me time to lunge at Keith's straining, red, sticky chest. Collecting my strength from every ounce of rage I have swallowed, stuffed, and stored for this moment, I raise on my tiptoes and drop my entire body on top of him, pinning his shoulders to the ground with my knees and pounding his abdomen against the floor with my hips. I slap him with my left hand hard enough for the skin-on-skin vibration to echo off the walls. I lean over and spit in his face.

My teeth are bared, my jaw is clenched, I breathe ragged snorts filled with mucus and menace covering him in a mist of acid. I want to show him the ice pick, let him feel the horror of knowing what's about to happen so the last minute he spends in the world is nothing but a searing, skin-stripping vat of terror that he will carry with him into every life he will ever know. There's no time. Johnson is fumbling at his holster, unable to get his fingers to push the unlocking buttons in the right sequence to release his gun. I hold the pick at the apex of Keith's neck for a second to get a rough estimate of where it needs to go to hit the jugular. He tries to squirm to the right. I lift my knees just high enough to drop them back on his shoulders, the sharp pain of his bruised collarbone reinforces his submission. I raise my arm, the sharpened pick gleaming in the harsh prison light. I hear Officer Johnson scream as my back arches and my spine solidifies harder than the concrete floor. I feel my shoulder pop when I've extended as far as my limb will go.

"Now!" I shout.

Colors. An explosion of colors. So many hues flood my vision I can't tell one from another. Rainbows made of every color imaginable erupt around me. Lightning of lavender, and waves of teal crash and cover Keith's body. A spectacle of a hundred shades of orange rise from the walls and swirl like a cyclone while bright yellow blades cut through my torso. Vibrant greens and reds with silver ribbons dance and play over Keith's head. Tan and blue snowflakes the size of softballs float around in an invisible wind sweeping me up in their majesty and awe. I'm awash in the spectrum, a prism of light pouring over me, stopping my thrust, stopping my heart, stopping time itself.

I look down to see Keith's brown and gray energy surrounding his body like dirty snow. He's frozen in fear. Then it hits me as indigo rain seems to torrent from the ceiling. These aren't his colors. They are mine. For the first time in my whole life, I can see my own aura and it is...everything.

Sparkling red circles rise from my hand cramped around the pick pointing towards Keith's neck. My arm is so high, so strained. In the flashing red blotches I see his hands grabbing my Marian by the neck, and the room goes black, then another crimson ball pops in my face. His hands become mine again, holding a steak knife, standing over the sink ready to sever my own gums in demented desperation. I close my eyes and open them to my mother's hand, raised in my college dorm, ready to strike me over and over, for the sins of her unhappy life. I shake her off. Not now. Not this time. Sucking in my breath, I see my father's arm raised with the exact angle and intention. The belt draped over his fist, his empty eyes, his pure unbridled fury.

So many hands, so much pain, such carnage. The history of our inhumanity is captured by our hands. Fingerprints of jealousy turned to murder, fear turned to power, ego turned to war, and insanity to genocide cover our human story from beginning to end. Raised hands, on picks, on spikes, on guns, on arrows made of fire—but there are no lotus left to fall in this world. Blood rains down instead of petals and poisons the soil our children walk over with their bare feet.

There's a snap, like the explosion of an old flash cube on a hand-held camera. In the bright light my lens reverses. I see my child body on the floor, curled in terror, covered in welts, begging my father to forgive me, to have mercy on me, to repossess his body with a human soul before I die beneath him. I see my mother, staring in the back bathroom mirror as silent tears fall over the washcloth she stuffed in her mouth so no one could hear her cry. Another new place. Another hollow horrid dinner party. More fake smiles. Lonely nights haunted by the dreams of a smart young woman that were sold for security like a handful of magic beans. She put her heart in the son who would not stay, and her sorrow in a daughter who couldn't leave fast enough. Nothing to do. Nowhere to go. Nice families don't live here anymore.

I see Penelope howling over the loss of her little girl, throwing everything on her dressing table at her husband. Where were you? Why didn't you hold her hand? Why didn't you know? Why didn't I know? Why? Why? Why? Why? Soon the perfume bottles hit a closed door in an empty room because he, too, is gone. I see Mrs. Rawls, sobbing at the grave of her daughter as her husband wraps his arms around her waist to keep the torn mother from jumping in the pit. The spirits of her ancestors shriek a banshee yell as the wind bends the trees.

I see Luka in an alley, bleeding out of so many stab wounds they wrap her entire body in compression bandages because they can't tell where all the blood is coming from. I see Topaz, overdoing it every day, desperate to make a bad start a better end. I see Shastri Nolan as a young man, sitting alone at a dirty bar in a different land, drinking sake out of a filthy cup because of the old woman who was shot for no reason other than she didn't come from the place his uniform was backing.

I see all of us—people I love—crumbling under an avalanche of suffering, and strangers I have not met crying on train station benches. Life has to be more than this. This pick, his neck, this relentless battle of right and wrong and tears and fear. This is not the end. This is not a beginning. This is the moment which makes the next moment and all the moments thereafter. Who am I in this moment? Who is he? What have we done to the world?

The gray puddle surrounding his body gleams with electric blue edges. Then I lose sight of the rim as Keith Allen is entirely covered in the same surging blue waves that are swallowing me whole. We are bound together, in this life, in this death, in this moment and we are... the same. A bright blue horizon takes over the ceiling when my mind is blasted by the thought, coming at me as if someone just walked into the darkest room of the house and, with a yank of a cord, pulled open the blinds so the unstoppable sun hits me straight in the eyes. My filter, that had been shielding me for most of my life, disintegrates. The light burns me and wakes me simultaneously.

You can love people. You can hate people. You can hurt them, heal them, embrace or expel them, but the one thing you cannot do is ever believe, at the essence of their being, they are any different than you. Every one of us, at some point, experiences isolation, fear, helplessness and shame. We are all a collection of experiences and choices, desires and ideas—some really great and some way lousy. Some people stay closer to their good core than others. Some get so lost, so addicted, so powerless, or so confused, their choices defy any suitable explanation. So we call them evil, monster, devil, or diseased. We blame them. We raise an army or a single calloused hand against them, and we spend the rest of our days pushing away the reality that we were, we are, and we always will be connected to them.

I gasp as I look down at my victim. How many times have I run this scenario in my mind, only to discover at the critical moment that it wasn't my mind after all? It was my pain, my sorrow, my own confusion transforming me into the lost, disoriented person he is, rather than the supporting, connected, life-giving woman I have always been. All my life. All. My. Life. I have said my family's legacy of violence would end with me. I'd stop it. I'd change it. A turquoise cord wraps around the pick and tethers itself to my heart, then snakes out in a hundred directions. To stab him is to stab myself. To kill him is to kill us all.

"No." I say, shaking my head.

My voice is low. It's solid. It's truth.

"This is not the way."

"DROP YOUR WEAPON!" Johnson shouts.

Keith stares at me, drying blood on his chin and a momentary wonder in his eyes.

I raise my other hand and drop the pick on the floor.

"KEEP YOUR HANDS UP!"

"He needs a doctor," I say, my legs shakily pushing me up as I stand. The colors ebb and recede from the room like an outgoing tide until all I can see in the harsh prison light is what I've done. "You need to call a doctor."

"DO NOT TURN AROUND." Johnson manages to release his gun and point it at me. Gasping, I feel my chest tighten, reminiscent of those childhood days when the asthma elephant decided to drop in for tea and inhalers.

"Honnnkkk." My hand instinctively drops to clutch my chest. I see Keith's blood on my fingers as I open my mouth and try to force some air into my exhausted lungs.

"PUT YOUR HANDS UP!!!" Johnson shrieks.

The asthma elephant reconsiders and thunderously runs for the hills.

"Shoot her!" Keith commands. It comes out through his broken nose as "soot huh" but it's pretty clear when he's trying to say. He rolls back and forth on the ground like an upside down red-belly turtle attempting to get up.

"WHAT?" Johnson shouts.

"You need to call..."

"SHOOT HER!"

"No. Call a..." My chest rising and falling, I struggle to project a thin, sharp, clear voice that can cut through the shouting in the room, but there's too many echoes pulling us under, like a deep ocean current that will not be displaced.

"For God's sake, SHOOT HER!"

"DO NOT TURN..." Johnson's shrieking unhinged voice swallows logic whole.

"Officer Johnson, you need to..."

"SHE TRIED TO KILL ME! SHOOT HER!" Keith's orders stifle any hope of reason, any chance of clarity.

With the colors gone, sounds clash around all of us, Johnson with his weapon drawn, his mind rapidly trying to figure out what to do, bays orders like a confused hound dog. Keith screams garbled instructions as he growls and groans. He tries to use his left arm to get up but it won't hold his weight. His right arm is still strong, able to do the job.

"Get help!" I cry out. Now I'm the prey. A frantic guard has his gun pointed at my back, and a furious murderer covered in blood with my spit drying on his cheek rises behind me. My body, overwhelmed by physical exertion and soul awakening fugue, is leaking strength like a colander. Take my word for it, when the tables turn, they don't fool around.

"DO NOT MOVE..."

"KILL HER!" Keith screams, spit and blood flying from his battered lips.

"OFFICER JOHNSON, LISTEN TO ME." Unable to drill through the din, I attempt to overcome the competition.

"GODDAMMIT, SHOOT!"

"LISTEN!"

"NOW! DO IT NOW!"

"NO!"

"NOW!" Keith cries

"WAIT! PLEASE WAIT!" The harried, raised voices of three desperate people locked in a struggle of confusion and control, life and death, bounce off the walls and ring in the singing bowl still sitting on the table. Like a rollercoaster plummeting from a marathon climb, the cacophony disorients us all into screaming, sightless, captive passengers on a one way trip through hell.

"SHUT UP!" Johnson finally manages to out-shout both of us. I can't see him, but if his body is quivering half as much as his voice, I'm in bigger trouble than I can handle. "EVERYBODY JUST SHUT UP!"

"Officer Johnson, I am not going to move."

"SHUT UP, DYKE! SHOOT HER!"

"Wait. What? I just..." Johnson becomes a small child pushed down a mountainside tumbling over and over and over, reaching for any branch that will catch him, but he can't slow down long enough to grab one.

Then a startling new voice, harsh and clear, enters the room and pulls the tormenting rolling ground out from under him as he falls off the cliff, into the sea.

"What the hell is happening in here?!"

BAM!

A deafening spear stabs me right through the brain. I cover my ears and collapse as the physical pain of the sound waves from the shot drives through my body like scissors cutting up the length of my spine. Keith, too, yells as he is propelled against the wall by the sudden sonic boom released in the concrete room.

Wing Supervisor, Lieutenant Cecilia Rhodes, drops to the floor.

Shot in the head.

19

"Oh my god, oh my god, oh my god," Brent Johnson whimpers in the seconds following the weapon's discharge. His ashen face and blank eyes make him appear to be a mere hologram of a man. "I shot her."

The wail of a siren and a constant battering honk, like a bicycle horn hooked up to a guitar amplifier set on twenty-five, begins to sound, making it even harder to overcome the physical pain in my ears from the gunshot. Metal doors start clanging and sealing the outer corridor.

"No!" I shriek, my voice lost in the siren's blurt. I crawl on my hands and knees to Wing Supervisor Rhodes. I didn't know her. She was just another guard to me. An athletic black woman with a sharply pressed uniform, eagle eyes that scanned each visitor, and an air of confidence as she walked up and down the long counselor-visitor corridor. I'd heard her bark an order or two at another correctional officer now and then, but other than that, she was simply a casual stranger whose spirit now rests heavily on my eternal slate. I feel her blood ooze over my hands like motor oil as I get close.

"Lieutenant Rhodes," I cry, uselessly. I see her vibrancy, a dark orange shield, surround her purposeful presence for a second, then disintegrate into small dots that drain of their color faster than I could reach her, until there was nothing. Nothing. She was gone. A wife, a mother, a friend, a co-worker, gone. I wrapped my arms around her body, blood still spurting in small dollops from the hole entering her temple. She was so heavy. So heavy. I rocked her back and forth, feeling her blood sink into my clothing, my skin, my soul.

"I shot Ceci. I shot her. I shot her," Johnson continues to whimper, standing over us with his gun still drawn. "Oh my god, I shot her."

Two large pneumatic doors close off the rest of the corridor, muting the echo of the blaring alarms, and lower the volume just a touch. The sound of boots and shouting of commands resound through the wing.

"Give me your gun," Keith says quickly.

"What?"

"Give me your damn gun!" Keith asserts. I'm in shock, Rhodes is dead, and Johnson is a glob of confusion. The dream Keith chased through every assault and violation he perpetrated in his life has finally come true. He has all the power in the world.

"Don't!" I shout, putting my blood soaked hand on the concrete so I can lay Officer Rhodes' head on something soft one last time.

"What? My gun?" Johnson backs against the wall.

"I'll take the blame," Keith says. "I'm already a murderer. I'll tell them I did it. I shot them both. Give me your gun, and you'll walk out of here to a three-week vacation. Review will clear you. Tell them I threatened you. I'll agree to anything you say. Just give me the gun."

"Officer Johnson, don't." I try to keep my voice calm, although I have to rush to get the words out before Keith talks over them.

"Give it to me. I swear to God. I'll eat the blame."

I slide my hand out from under Cecilia Rhodes's head and turn to see Johnson extend his arm, pointing the gun barrel to the floor with his hand on the slide, and turn the grip toward Keith to ensure what his firearms trainer called "the safe transfer of arms." He's back in the corner. I'm on my knees unable to rise fast enough to get anywhere near him, and Keith is only a foot away from the prize.

"No, no, no," I say.

"Give it to me," Keith seduces him.

Before I can counteract, my muscles loosen and a heavy veil lays over me. I sink back down to the floor, in the lotus position. I am flooded with an untimely, unusual sense of peace. My friend, Death, is here. I take a deep breath. It's over. It's all over. Soon my friend will come for me and wrap the warm blue blanket around me once and for all. I'm at the end of this life. There's nothing else to say. Nothing I can do. Inhale. Exhale. When he gets that gun, he will kill me. At last.

Johnson's hand lingers on the slide, and Keith covers the grip with his hand. I exhale, a tear of relief stinging the corner of my eye is the only pain left. Johnson lets go of his weapon.

"Pat didn't say anything about this," the officer stammers, his voice trembling.

"What?" Keith curls his hand around the grip. This gun is heavier than the one he owned. It causes his arm to drop for a moment. Then it rises.

"She said just to keep an eye on things. She didn't tell me about this. Nothing about this."

"You were with...what? You were with Pat? My Pat?"

"She told me. She told me to watch over you. To make sure this worked. She said do it for us. For all of us. She's so beautiful."

Keith looks over at me. I close my eyes. I'm calm. I'm open. It's time.

Fire splits the air amid an explosion of thunder as two shots ring out in quick succession. A scream begins but never finishes. The room goes red. I open my eyes to see Johnson's blood splatter against the walls as his body crumbles.

"That BITCH!" Keith screams.

"OFFICER DOWN. TWO OFFICERS DOWN!" A voice from

the corridor shouts as I sit there. "GET READY SQUAD A. ON THREE. GO ON THREE.

"That fucking bitch," Keith howls, walking around in a circle, waving the gun, trying to clear his head from the sound shock of the latest shots. Inhale. Exhale.

"Come on, dyke," he says before I can take a last breath on my own. He grabs me by the hair. My mouth drops open at the scalding sting of my scalp. He twists my body like I'm a wind chime. A groan comes from his throat as his sore left arm gathers around my chest. Pressing his body against the back wall, his left arm a cobra squeezing me against him, I become his shield. His right arm points the gun at the door.

"We're going down together. But not alone," he hisses in my ear, the smell of his blood and spittle assaults my nose as his spit tickles my ear.

"ONE!" The wing commander calls. Boots shuffle and body shields raise in response.

Lieutenant Rhodes's blood leaks out into the hallway, no doubt ramping up their lust for action. Johnson's gathers in a puddle around him as he pants for air. His chest rises and falls, but his eyes have no light. How many more am I willing to lead through the valley of death before this ends?

I exhale fully, feeling my boneless body shrink as I let go of everything, everyone, every hope, every joy, every fear, every desire, every love, every life. There's nothing left of me to hold. I slip through Keith's grip.

"TWO!"

I turn in Keith's arms, kicking at his calf, willing myself back to this world, back to this place, if only for a moment. I pull in all the strength I can scrape up, from every pocket of my will, and smash

Keith's cheek with my elbow, bringing forth a fresh shower of blood and shock. It stuns him, but not enough to loosen his hold on the gun. I think of Marian launching herself at this murderous bastard. You were right, my love. All in.

I become a beast. Frantically, I begin kicking, scratching, slapping at him. I lean over and bite his forearm, his yelp, bubbling through his bloody nose, sprays both of us. I grab at the gun. Just when my hand gets to the slide, he pulls the trigger, shooting the floor about 6 inches from my foot. A sharp nip, like a hornet sting, spreads through my hand as the slide runs over it, cutting me. A hot dart singes me when the shell lands against my neck. I reach back down with my now bloody thumb to grab the gun again as we both recoil from the force of the shot.

"THREE! THREE! THREE!"

Armed guards pour into the room. My back to the door, I can only see shadows, but their presence—uniformed, armed, and locked on target—is impossible to ignore. Keith tries to raise the weapon, but I've got my hand on his wrist, putting my full body weight against his charge. We stand here, eye to eye, bound together in life, in death, and though we are opposing forces, we are still the same.

I feel a push, like I've been shoved from behind, before the crack of the rifle reaches my ears. Then a burning pain as if a metal spike, bright orange and fresh from the flames, impales me. Gasping, I look down to a spreading puddle of red blossoming on my chest like a burgeoning carnation. I see a smaller bud opening under Keith's shoulder, then I hit the floor.

My body bounces on the concrete and lands with a thud, the noise swallowed by gunfire as three more shots enter Keith's body. One, notoriously, hits him right between the legs. I turn my face to the side, my eyes unable to see much in the red film covering them.

The asthma elephant returns, this time hugging me with a jacket of knives, making each attempted breath both painful and impossible. The last thing my physical eyes see lies fourteen inches to my right: a sawed off, sharpened ice pick beside a hollow, wooden mallet head, covered in lotus.

A plaintive whine, like the whimper of a wounded puppy calling out from the side of the road, escapes the thin walls of Penelope's hideaway. Somehow, she manages to watch all the way to the end. Her hand grips the sides of her face, covering her mouth to hold in a scream of sheer horror as my life drains in front of her eyes. She watches the stretchers take the guards away first. She listens to a squad member grab Brent Johnson's hand, trying to encourage the officer to hold on to life while his body convulses, his spirit long past gone.

Reaching out with a shaking finger, she touches the screen of her laptop as they lift me to a gurney, putting pressure on my chest, while everyone seems to be shouting directions or explanations into their various electronic devices. The warden walks in, angrily taking stock of the carnage in the red soaked room and asks for a briefing from the wing commander, the man who shot me in the back. He looks directly at the small bubble on the ceiling, right beside the light fixture. The screen goes black.

"Oh, Lyla," she says in a breathy cry. Her arms wrap around her abdomen as if she's been punched in the gut. The laptop clatters against the tile floor. "Lyla."

Pressing against the sink to pull herself up, Penelope staggers out of the bathroom like the lone survivor of a plane crash, wandering through the woods in a fog. Small sniffs and gasps leak out of her. She makes it to the chair by my bed before the strength in her legs runs out and she collapses onto the hard plastic covered seat. She's watched them lower the rails enough to know exactly where the metal latch works to release them. When she removes the barrier, she leans over and gently places her head on my shoulder. Her arm snakes under the ventilator tube holding, as best as she can, all that is left of me. Her whimper breaks through the last wall and she erupts in blurting, hoarse, heaving sobs.

"Nurse!" Officer Brault yells to the station. "Nurse, something's wrong!"

The nurse pads into the room quickly, although the only alarm sounding is the wail signifying the breaking of Penelope's heart. The rhythm of mine is as steady as time. Dutifully, she checks the vitals and looks over all the equipment, tracing the spaghetti of wires from port to post. She hovers her hand over the writer whose face is pressed against me as she cries, but decides not to touch her. It's one of the first things you learn working in the ICU. Some things need intervention, others must run their course.

"The patient is stable," she says to Officer Brault. The visitor? Well, that's his business.

Pen runs her fingers through my hair, placing her hand on my cool cheek, seeking confirmation for her frayed mind that this is truly me, and what she saw was real. She places her head back on me, letting gallons of denial flow out of her at the breakpoint of the dam. Showing amazing stealth for a large man in a starched uniform covered in cords and tools, Brault folds in behind her and puts a comforting hand on her back.

"Ms. Fine? Are you okay?"

"No." She shakes her head, her hands gripping the bed. The officer keeps his hand on her, letting her cry in peace, but never leaving her side.

"She didn't do it," Penelope mumbles over and over. "She couldn't. She couldn't do it. She couldn't do it."

"Shhhh, now. Just catch your breath."

"She stopped. She stopped. She didn't kill those cops. She didn't shoot him. She caught herself. She stopped herself. I knew. I knew. I knew."

"Ms. Fine, I know there's a lot of distrust about small town cops these days, and some of it, maybe, is deserved. I haven't spent any time with Greg Putnicki, but I know Steve Mesa, and I went to high school with Denise Markel. There's not a smarter cop in the world than Denise. Or more honest. If Dr. Gentry is innocent, she'll find the evidence. She'll clear her. You can count on it."

"She's not innocent," Penelope mumbles into the bed foam. "She's not. But she's not a murderer. She didn't shoot them."

A fresh round of tears and coughs blurts out of Penelope as she speaks. My heart aches for her. It shatters at her pain, at everyone's pain. No matter what the heart monitor says right now, mine is absolutely crushed.

She's right, of course. I'm not innocent. I didn't pull the trigger on that gun one time. But I am absolutely responsible for the deaths of Cecilia Rhodes and Brent Johnson. I am the reason Keith Allen lies across the hall sedated and brutalized. I am the person to blame for the shakes the wing commander experiences late at night when his mind goes over the scene again and again, wondering if he did the right thing. It is all on me. Lost in the dark forest of grief, I burned down countless acres trying to forge a road home.

When you're lost in the depths of a death, the confusion of mania, the craving of addiction, or the euphoria of infatuation—you don't know you're lost. You come across stop signs and trail markers, and you have fleeting moments of clarity where you realize you've doubled back or the terrain doesn't look like it should. Eventually, the people who love you stand in the corners of your life (because that's as close as you let them get) and shout, "You are lost! You are lost!" Still, you wander. Sometimes you meet people so "found" that you follow them, only to discover later that they, too, are lost. Yet, you carry on. As long as you can take one more step, make one more choice, take one more breath—dig deep, reach out, listen, learn. The last minute is still a good minute to find your way.

Officer Brault pats her on the back again and looks down at me. He doesn't know me from Eve, and yet, he places his other hand on my arm, as if to assure me that justice will prevail. I'm restored by his goodness.

"I'm so sorry. I shouldn't be crying all over you," Penelope says, picking up her head and wiping as many tears from her red eyes as she can catch. "I must look like a mess."

"Nah, you look...," he pauses for dramatic effect, "...fine."

She chuckles, in spite of herself, ejecting the last few tears in the queue.

"That was bad," she whispers.

"Made you laugh," he responds. "And it's okay for you to cry. Famous people got tears in them, just like everyone else. Rumor has it, under all that makeup, you're a real person—with better lighting."

She nods. "I'm going to remember that."

"It's like I said about cops. There are some bad ones, and there are a lot of good ones, but mostly we are all just human beings, trying to make it through the day. Some days, it's harder than others. Same with celebrities. Same with her." He pats my arm as he stands, then points to his badge. "Sue and I tell Courtney all the time that we make choices, and those choices have a consequence. But once you go deeper than the choices, maybe nobody's all bad or all good, totally innocent or completely guilty. Maybe we're all just here."

The cycle of lives is complete. Here, in my short, silent, fourth life, I have arrived at the realm of human birth.

Pen points to the microphone on his shoulder.

"Can you call your boss or whoever? I need to talk to the lead investigators and Warden Hummel again. I need all three of them back here, now."

"That's not gonna happen," he says, offering his hand to help her up from the chair.

"Tell them I have information about the crime I'm ready to share. But I'll only share it with Hummel in the room. They need to get in here."

"It won't matter if Jesus, Peter, and Paul are in the room. Not happening," he says, trying to guide her to the recliner. "Why don't you get some sleep?"

"I don't understand." She swerves out of his arm, suddenly aware of her laptop lying on the bathroom floor with her illegally obtained evidence blinking on the screen.

"You've got night shift syndrome," he laughs, allowing her to pull away. "It's three in the morning. Ain't nobody coming here now. Even the reporters are asleep."

"Oh."

"I'll tell dispatch you want to see Putnicki and Markel in the morning once they clear briefing."

"I won't talk without Hummel here."

"Well, the Warden is his own man," the officer advises as he moves back to his chair, noticing Pen as she spreads her arms, blocking the bathroom door. "But if Denise tells him to get here, he'll get here. He wants this cleaned up as much as anyone, I figure."

"I doubt that," she says, but nods. "You're right, though, a nap would do me a world of good."

He returns to his seat, motioning to the corrections officer outside of Keith's room that everything is okay. Penelope scoops up her laptop, happy to see the sleep mode somehow bounced her out of the connection and the firewall is the only thing on the screen. After a thankful sigh, she opens the door, tucking her laptop under her arm like a schoolbook.

"Officer Brault?"

"Yes, ma'am?"

"Thank you."

20

One of the only things Penelope and I actually have in common, besides our shared humanity and love of Luka's cooking, is our absolute hatred for mornings. Marian was the quintessential morning person. Bright eyes open at 5:00 a.m., chattering nonstop about her plans while gathering scoops of cat food for the bowls strategically placed on the grounds. It was horrible. By the time I would stagger out of bed at nine or ten, she'd be saying, "Today's half over!" I didn't realize Penelope shared the trait until one day when the yoga teacher was gathering guests to have a "sunrise session" and accidentally knocked on Penelope's door.

"Here's my sun salutation," the disheveled writer with an eye mask just barely propped up on her brows said, and then held up her middle finger for the yogi to see before slamming the door. After that, every time she tried to argue or pull a fast one on me, I'd say, "I've got a sun salutation for you, lady." It never failed to diffuse the moment.

Today, however, she's up before the camera crews. Although her laptop was secured in its case, the file kept playing in her mind like a horror film on a loop. She eventually shut down long enough for a quick recharge, but it was a troubled rest. Still, a woman on a mission can see nothing but the goal, not even a clock. The shower went on before daybreak, causing the night nurses to murmur.

"How many showers does she take a day?"

"I don't know, but she must have a miracle cream to keep her skin that smooth."

"Her makeup box is the size of a carry-on suitcase. What do you expect?"

"She spent twenty minutes looking at the travel rack in the corner picking what to wear, just to sit here all day, reading emails and watching the news. It's ridiculous."

"Allen's wife makes a lot of demands, but at least she comes and goes. I seriously don't think Ms. Fine has left the floor other than trips to the cafeteria. Even then, she brings the tray up here."

Just as they are about to begin a sonnet describing Penelope's various annoyances, she opens the door and glides into the center of the room.

"Mother of pearl," the nurse changing my IV bag whispers as the other blatantly gawks. For the first time since their unit was taken over by cops and robbers, the nurses see Penelope at her zenith. The sight momentarily blinds them and any complaint they may have imagined vaporizes instantly.

Her long blonde hair glistens with a stylized sheen, the sides curled lightly but not swept back. Her makeup, usually applied under the "you want me" philosophy, reveals a different intention. Her normally prominent lips are downplayed as the blush guides you straight to her sharp eyes. It's the palette she would have used for a boardroom proposal, not the cover of Writer's Digest. She picked the only power dress Topaz managed to snag in her hasty trip with supplies, a mid-length black Paola fitted dress from Et Ochs, which not only accentuates her well-toned body, but also the discipline and strength it takes to carry off this look. Although she expects to sit through much of her conference, she dons Stuart Weitzman ankle strap stilettos, disappointed Topaz only brought her four inch heels. The six inch would have made a better impression. Still, it's an oddly welcomed homecoming for her feet after days in comfy black flats.

"Good morning," Penelope says with a smile, measuring the effect her appearance has on her captive subjects. Shocked into silence, they just stare at her, unable to look away—like a car accident, with better accessories. This will work.

"Are you expecting someone, Ms. Fine?"

"Warden Hummel and the detectives are coming to talk to me this morning. I thought it would help my mood to dress more like a professional author and less like an urban squatter living in a hospital room. I so appreciate all the indulgences you've allowed me, and of course, your constant care of my teacher. Gratitude."

They nod, melting in her cauldron as the spell bubbles around them.

"Can we get you anything?"

"Not right now. Thank you, both."

By the time they get to the nurses' station, Penelope will have risen like the morning star, and Pat Allen will go back to being "that pushy witch."

"Don't even start with me," Penolope snaps her finger in my direction as she pushes the recliner to the corner and sets up the four hard-back chairs she snagged from the waiting room, placing her laptop on a bedside table where everyone can see it. "You got us into this, Lylarose Gentry, and I'm going to get us out." The sun has been saluted.

There's a triple blip on my heart monitor, then it goes back to normal. That's been happening more and more frequently. Almost enough to be noticed. In this room, on this day, however, there is only one thing that will be seen.

"Hello, Ms. Fine," Greg Putnicki says as he walks in to find her standing beside the chairs. She knew he was here. We could both smell his cologne as soon as the elevator doors opened. Instead of the slacks and polo ensemble he had on in the last interview, it's business casual today, with a blazer and open collar dress shirt. Seems like he had a chance to change clothes between his briefing and the hospital.

"Where's everyone else?"

"Oh, the warden stopped to answer a reporter's question, and Denise stayed behind to...um...help him do that. She's good with that kind of thing."

Later, when Penelope reviews the *News Now* feed, she'll see nothing but Detective Markel pulling Hummel by the sleeve as he blathers about meeting with the review board, saying "No comment" as the answer to everything.

Detective Markel stops for a second as she enters the room, taking in Penelope's full profile. She offers the writer an imaginary hat tip. Markel is in the same beige blazer she wore the last time, with a police union button on the lapel, a blue shell blouse, and some Dockers. Her gun rests in a shoulder holster opposite her dominant hand, and her badge is nothing but a bulge in a leather wallet inside the blazer's inner pocket. Her hair, a more earthy, serviceable blonde than Penelope sports, is braided down the back. She came to play hard. Penelope may have the detective's king in check, but there's plenty of room for Markel to maneuver.

Hummel wanders in behind Markel, the designated loser of this morning's power lottery. Between being grilled about security by the prison review board, ridiculed at the hands of every arm-chair scholar freshly graduated from Google School of Prison Administration, and the polite regrets of several agencies he once asked for a political endorsement, the Warden looks, as Ma Gentry might say, "like two cents, waitin' on change."

"Please be seated," Penelope gestures to the chairs and waits for them to sit before taking her own.

"This isn't a courtesy I intend to extend again," Detective Markel says. "You need to tell us everything you have to say, once and for all."

"How are you, Ms. Fine? How is Dr. Gentry?" The warden interjects. He offers her the most charming smile he can come up with. It crashes against Pen like a bird hitting a skyscraper window.

"I have something I want you to watch. After you see it, we'll discuss exactly how and when you are publically clearing Dr. Gentry of murder."

"Wait a minute," Markel starts before Putnicki puts his hand on her arm.

"Let's just hear her out," he smiles at Pen with a side nod of the head. She never takes her eyes off Markel. Typing her password in the firewall, she turns the laptop around for their first look at me and Keith, meditating at the prison table.

"Oh my god," Warden Hummel mumbles. "Where did you...? How did you...?"

"What the hell is this?" Markel leans over to get as close to the laptop as she can.

"Stop it! I demand you stop this right now!" Hummel reaches out to grab the laptop, but Penelope pulls it away. "Ms. Fine, I demand an explanation! Who gave you access to..."

Penelope hits the pause on the laptop. It actually got thirty seconds farther than she expected. "There's always someone who wants to talk through the movie."

"I'm actually on the warden's side," Markel says, crossing her arms. "I want an explanation before I watch another frame. What is that? Why does it look like a surveillance cam? Where did it come from? How do I know it's real?"

"Should I tell her, Warden Hummel, or do you want to do it?"

Seething, the warden locks his jaw and looks down, taking a deep breath.

"Well, somebody better tell me something, and fast, because I'm getting pissed."

Checkmate. Markel had some good moves, but Penelope's cool-under-pressure demeanor put the detective in a corner. Anger can be an opening, but rage never wins.

"Seems the counseling room was a little less confidential than anybody really knew." Pen shifts her eyes to the warden, but all she can see is the top of his head as he struggles to come up with an impossible answer that will stop the avalanche already in progress.

"You had a camera in C-pod?" Markel hisses at the warden.

He nods.

"Just a precaution. We don't usually turn it on for counseling, but I was worried. I wanted to give this a chance to work, but I knew it could go south."

"You had a CAMERA in C-POD that recorded this crime?"

Another nod.

"And you gave it to HER?!"

His eyes finally rise to face his accuser. "No! Not her! I don't know how the hell she got this. I didn't...I haven't..."

Markel turns to her partner. "Did you know about this?"

Another head drops. Putnicki is at least smart enough to know there's no way out.

"I knew he had video. I haven't seen it."

"What?!"

"He told me Rhodes was a misfire. Friendly fire. But if we stuck with the ice pick, we could bring it back to Gentry. No need to ruin Johnson. He said Gentry's probably gonna die anyway. He said it wasn't really Johnson's fault. His widow, you know. He said you were never married. You wouldn't understand."

"Wha..." Markel puts both of her hands in the air.

"I will have you arrested," Warden Hummel seethes. "You and whoever gave you this file. Cybercrime is a serious offense, Ms. Fine."

"I'm not sure that you will." The Cheshire cat smile spreads across her face as she holds up the red flash drive Jeremy gave her.

"Oh, god, what's that?" Markel says. Her colors explode in thirty different hues as she tries to wrap her head around any of this.

"It's a phone conversation," Penelope answers, keeping her hand just out of Hummel's reach. "Between Warden Hummel and my friend Trinity Marsh. A long conversation, very detailed. Mrs. Marsh will be happy to verify its authenticity to any court in the land."

"Son of a bitch," Hummel whispers.

"Trinity Marsh? The writer?"

Warden Hummel shakes his head like a man watching his own death from behind.

"She said she needed technical advice, for a movie," he mumbles. "It had to be based on real life. I told her some privileged information. She said she'd keep it to herself."

"A movie." Denise Markel lets out a sinister snicker. "You illegally placed a camera in a safe room where you illegally taped a crime, illegally hid the tape from law enforcement, fraudulently gave this jackass inaccurate information to set up an arrest, and then told the truth to a couple of bubblegum writers for a movie. Warden?"

"It's not how it sounds," he defends.

"It's exactly how it sounds," Penelope counters.

"I hadn't made any decisions, Denise. I was just following the ice pick, like he said. I was going to tell you.It wasn't a total set up. I didn't accuse, I didn't fabricate anything," Putnicki babbles.

"I don't want to hear one...More...Word ...from your mouth," Markel says declaratively. "We will talk later."

The detective turns her attention to Penelope. "And how did you get this evidence?"

"Magic."

"What?"

"I magically became aware that the counseling pods at The Bowl were bugged. I then snapped my irrelevant little writer fingers, and a link to the tape appeared on my screen and only my screen. I dreamed of the password that grants access and another that is the only word that can make it disappear forever. I've exclusively participated in this amazing supernatural event."

"In other words, you aren't going to tell me."

"My version sounds better, but yeah."

"I can take your laptop."

"Do you have a warrant?"

"Not yet."

"Well, I'd love to be in the room when you tell a judge why you want a warrant for the laptop of a private citizen with a very public fan base and a social media footprint the size of King Kong. That should be fun." Penelope squints as she smiles at Markel. And she wonders why Luka calls her "The Movie Star."

"It's not even on her laptop," Greg Putnicki's voice rattles like dice in a tumbler. "Look at the private browser. It's a linked feed. She can access it from anywhere, and we could take every machine she owns and never get to it."

"Did I ask you?" The detective glares at her partner who retreats back into the silent penalty box of his chair.

"I was trying to control the fallout, that's all," Hummel takes another shot. His spineless back is so bent over he appears to be a pretzel. "You know what the media does to corrections officers caught in friendly fire. They'd take them both down, in front of God and everyone. They already paid with their lives. No point making their family pay more."

"How patriotic," Penelope coos. "And the part where you're shielding a convicted rapist from his third murder because you don't want anyone to know your prisoner ran amok? What was that about? Blame the outsider, protect your 'tough on crime' image?"

"I was just looking out for my people, that's all."

"What a crock of shit," Markel snarls as she looks back at him, then sighs, realizing she's the only responsible adult on her side of the room. "I guess I don't need to ask if this is real. Let's have a look."

There are three signs of an awakened mind: compassion, wisdom, and power. Markel watches me straddle Keith Allen with the death blow all but certain, then stop. The camera did not catch the kaleidoscope of colors and revelations as they filtered through my mind, but it showed me halt, my face transforming from monstrous to merciful, my eyes clearing, my grip opening, my mind healing. The detective leans back in her chair when I drop the pick and stand, my hands in the air in total surrender to enlightenment and authority.

"She kicked his ass," Detective Markel says to Putnicki, then turns back to the screen when she remembers she's mad at him. Her eyes dart back and forth like a tennis match as we both try to get Johnson on our side.

"Fuck," she gasps when Lieutenant Rhodes is shot upon entry, having startled the confused officer. She doesn't look away when I hold the supervisor's body to my own breast as her life pours over my arms, but she does look over at my body. Watching Keith seduce Johnson into handing him the weapon, she leans forward, pawing at the laptop to back up and review the few seconds before Keith sends two bullets through the shell-shocked guard.

"I wish I could see his face. Is there another angle on this?"

"No," Warden Hummel answers, averting his eyes from the entire presentation.

"And I should believe you because..."

"Because if there was another view, my source would have found it," Penelope adds.

"The Blue Fairy?" Markel sneers.

"Something like that, yes."

Then, the detective with nearly fifteen years on the force witnesses something she's never seen before: a woman faces her certain violent death with the same calm as someone waiting for a friend to come through the airport gate. Pale green curiosity turns to clear intention when she recognizes the signs of Keith setting himself up for a firefight, only to watch me slither through his grasp like an eel and rise a water dragon. Power is not the capacity to win, to devour, to persuade—power in its purest form is simply the ability to rise.

"Can you turn the sound up?" She says as Warden Hummel literally steps around the body of Cecilia Rhodes to talk to the wing commander. Penelope answers the request, the setting on her face changing to stone.

"Who shot the doctor?" Hummel asked.

"I did, sir," the wing commander says, his face mask hanging below his chin. "I saw a weapon, and I fired."

"You saw her holding the weapon?"

"No, sir. I just saw the gun."

"But it was Dr. Gentry holding the gun?"

"I don't know, sir. I believe they were fighting over the weapon. I wasn't sure which hand it was in."

"So it could have been Dr. Gentry?"

"It's possible. I saw the gun, and I opened fire."

"Your report is that when you walked in, you saw Dr. Gentry with the weapon, and you opened fire. That's what you're telling me, right?"

"Yes, sir."

"Who shot him in the dick?"

"I don't know, sir. Right flank opened fire when he didn't go down like she did."

"Hope it was Jennifer," the warden laughs.

"Me too, sir," the commander answers.

Detective Markel clucks her tongue at the warden. "Review is going to have so many questions about that conversation."

"You can't show this tape. Not to them. Not to anyone. Give Ms. Fine what she wants, and let's be done with this."

"You don't really believe I'm as dumb as my asshole partner, and I'm not going to report this to Sheriff Wright, do you?"

"You can't." Hummel turns to her. "No one can know about this. Not Paul Wright, not the review board, and certainly not the public."

"It's a little late to get camera shy, Warden." Markel looks back at the laptop and at Penelope. "Run this back to where Allen plugs Johnson. Can you loop it?"

"And they call me 'princess,'" Pen says jokingly to the warden, who is in no mood for a smile. "I can't do anything to it, just watch it or delete it, but I can take you to the time marker."

"This isn't about you, Denise," Detective Putnicki brings a closed fist down on his legs. "Dammit. Listen for a change. You can't disclose this."

"Hell yes, I can." Markel watches the precise moment Keith shoots Brent Johnson and the angry little circle he walked in afterward two more times, softly whispering the word "bitch" to herself over and over.

Snap! The laptop closes in front of her nose when Penelope decides she's had enough.

"Hey!"

"My toys, my rules," Penelope says. "And, for once, Ding and Dong here are right. If you make this public, I'm still going to get what I want. The world will know Lylarose didn't actually kill anyone. But, not you. All you're going to get is a one way ticket off the job."

"You're a fortune teller now?"

"No, I'm still a bubblegum writer, but I can do simple things, like math. Warden Hummel told Trinity that the counseling wing was built around five years ago. Lyla spent an hour every other week for about five months in that room, so ten counseling hours. That leaves roughly 8,700 hours—per year—for other inmates to use that room. A lowball guess would be at least 500 inmates have spilled their secrets over the last five years. That's a lot of court cases over prisoner rights violations. Now, the warden may not have taped all of them, but how do you prove what you did not do?"

"Holy shit," Markel says, biting her lip.

"By the time the state of Maryland pays for all those cases, overturns good convictions, investigates police officers who were involved in said cases, and resets from the PR nightmare, there won't really be enough money to pay for a high level thinker, like yourself. Plus, you'll have just been instrumental in releasing a gaggle of known murderers and sex offenders back into society. I'm not thinking the police union will appreciate that too much."

Markel holds the bridge of her nose with her right hand, exhaling slowly. In my thoughts, I rise from slumber, cross the room, and wrap my arms around her stiffening shoulders. I hug her as hard as I can and whisper in her ear, "I understand, Detective. I've been dealing with her for years."

"What do you want?"

"You are going to hold a press conference where you announce that your investigation has concluded that Dr. Lylarose Gentry did not shoot anyone in that room. She is not a suspect, and she will not be charged with murder."

"I don't lie."

"I'm not asking you to say she's innocent. I am asking you to get the facts straight. Whatever else you say about her is your prerogative."

"I need time to investigate some things, verify, and make arrangements. I can't just walk out of this room and hold a press conference."

Pen emits a crack of jaded laughter that hangs in the air. "Really, because I could hold one on my way to the candy machine. There's a flock of reporters right outside the door."

Markel sighs, glaring at the warden who suddenly finds the tops of his shoes incredibly interesting.

"Okay," Pen relents. The lack of sleep must be affecting her. She's not usually this workable. "Twenty-four hours. At ten o'clock tomorrow, there will be a press conference in this hospital. Either you will stand up and clear my teacher, or I will stand up there, with this video, and do it myself."

"You'd let the world see the queen of peace over there savagely beat a seated inmate? I don't think so. They'd call her a hypocrite."

"That's better than cop killer. Besides, I saw you smile when she kneed him in the chin. I think most people might do the same. This isn't David and Goliath. It's more like Drano and a toilet clog."

Markel sucks her teeth as if they taste like old vinegar and nods.

"Good, it's settled." Warden Hummel stands up, brushing imaginary dust off his suit pants, washing his hands of the discussion. "What happens to the file? I can't be looking over my shoulders for the rest of my life."

"Too late," Markel coughs into her fist.

"As soon as the conference ends, I'll type in the magic word and my copy of this will miraculously, and permanently, disappear. Whatever happens to the original file is up to you. The phone call, however, I'm going to keep for a while. If I'm threatened in any way, or an IT person gets fired, or a fake account of what happens shows up online, well..."

"Understood," Hummel says, walking away with his eyes on the ground.

"You did the right thing, Denise." Detective Putnicki stands and opens his arms to let Markel walk in front of him. "What do you want to verify? What do I need to do?"

"The only thing you need to do," she says, puffing little bursts of air, like pug snorts, through her nose, "is figure out how you're getting back to the station. Because you're never fucking riding in my car again."

He leaves, much like the warden, deflated but grateful it wasn't worse.

"Sheriff Wright isn't going to let me do a conference without an arrest," the detective advises Penelope as they walk to the door.

"So, arrest someone."

"I intend to," Markel says, dropping her voice to a lower register. "Believe me, I intend to."

The minute Markel disappears into the elevator, Penelope runs for her iPad to see the pack of wild hounds bark questions and attempt to get a treat from all three of the officials as they emerge, grim and gray, from the meeting. All they manage to turn up is a barrel of "no comments" and a long shot of Greg Putnicki waiting near the nurses' entrance for a patrol car to pick him up. She pushes back her recliner and stretches out her legs, slipping off her shoes.

"Just one more thing, and I can take off my face," she says to me. The energy it took to generate that much persuasion drained her reserve tank. She doesn't have much left. My heart monitor gives three quick beeps. She looks up, seeing the steady rhythm that follows, and breathes a sigh of relief. "I know you hate this, but it's the only way. This isn't who I am anymore, Lyla. I promise. Robyn was right. It's just a moment. Don't give up on me."

She navigates through her texts until she finds a number channeled from her publicist, taps her phone and waits.

"*News Now,*" a deep male voice, made a gravel and exhaustion, answers.

"I need to speak to Laura."

"She's busy."

"This is Penelope Fine."

"Message?"

"Tell her where you'd like to work. Maybe she'll give you a reference."

"What?"

"Because when she learns that Penelope Fine called, and you didn't immediately patch me through, you're gonna need a new job."

"One moment."

"Ms. Fine?" There is so much hopeful thrust in the reporter's voice the phone shimmies.

"Laura, I've been meaning to answer your requests for so long. It's just nonstop here. I've been watching your coverage. I smell an award."

"Can I get an exclusive with you? It doesn't have to be inside Dr. Gentry's room. We can set up anywhere you want. I can get the local studio if you're more comfortable with the lighting. I'll let you preview the questions."

"Off the record. I can't do an interview, but I have a tip for you."

"I'm listening," the reporter whispers.

"Tomorrow at ten, the cops are making an announcement. They're ready to put this to bed. Get your best guys here."

"What do you know? Did they arrest someone? Allen die? What's the angle?"

"I can't say, but as a courtesy for your patience, I can tell you this. I'd drop the "guru from the dark side" storyline and start backing Team Gentry. Get me?"

"What about..."

"Oh, there's the doctor. Bye now."

"Done and done," Pen says, looking through her case for skin cleaner and some moisturizer. "It's like you always say, Lyla. You can't change what happened on the road, but you can take the wreckage and make a bullet, or a bridge. It's all up to you."

21

Penelope's spine isn't straight, but it started that way. Her legs were perfectly crossed in a lotus position. Now one leans to the left and the other has fallen off the recliner completely. Her closed eyes were once open. Her hands lie helplessly at her side. When she awakes, her phone app will show she meditated for three hours and fifteen minutes. Of course, she was only awake for four of those. For meditation, that's about right.

It's not that everyone falls asleep meditating (although it happens to all meditators at some point), but we spend so much of our lives spiritually asleep that meditation becomes nothing but the act of sitting with good posture while we do it. The purpose of meditation isn't to regulate your blood pressure, reduce your stress from a ten to a two, or open your third eye to the mysteries of the great unknown. Those are just happy side-effects. Meditation exists for one reason only. To connect yourself to the human being you have always been—the person deeper than your social programming, your pain, your aspirations, your memories, your mistakes.

Inside everyone—me, Keith, Pen, the nurses, the doctors, the reporters—there is a core being so beautiful, knowledgeable, and complete we would scarcely recognize it if we saw it in the mirror. Meditation is about renouncing everything but your breath and following it to that center. Sometimes we have to see the surface we are stripping away in order to let it go, other times, it simply fades from view. The position, the cushion, the timer, even the breath itself, are all building blocks, nothing more. You can sit for four hours and still not experience meditation, or breathe for ten minutes and have a life changing session because real meditation happens in one exact moment—the space between breaths. It's the moment you are neither inhaling, nor exhaling, coming or going. It's the moment you are no longer running away.

"Ahem," Officer Brault coughs ominously, trying to wake Pen before the squad of officers arrive on the floor. It's nearly too late. By the time her heavy eyelids have risen halfway, the sound of hard soled shoes coming up the stairwell can be heard. The elevator dings synonymously with the stairwell door opening. Two officers, guns out of the holster, stay back and guard the stairwell. Four others fan out on the unit. A plain-clothes policeman covers the nurses' station, encouraging them to step into a side room for a moment. Phones are stowed in back pockets. The guard by Keith's door rips his earbuds out so fast, he actually puts his finger in his ear to touch where the skin used to be.

The squad leader guides two additional patrolmen toward our room, one flanking each side of the door. Sheriff Wright must have called every cop in Oakland for this event. I don't have to wonder if Pen can see them. Her normally light violet hue transforms to such a deep purple it could easily be mistaken for black. No red. No panic. Just a long, heavy exhale. She turns the timer off on her phone, chuckling at the overly long mediation it recorded.

Detective Markel stops in the doorway, standing beside Brault. She's wearing the same blazer she wore ten hours ago, and the lines under her eyes show exactly how long it's been. If Pen were more herself, she'd be sure to mention to the detective that night shift is not her "beauty zone."

Pen casually looks around for her laptop, knowing it is far too late. She wouldn't have time to get the browser open, let alone type in the safe code. She tucks her phone in the pocket of her yoga pants. If the police don't already have Jeremy in custody and she could tell him to type in the code, there's a chance she'd get bail pending trial.

Detective Mesa is the next to arrive, never looking up from the clipboard in his hands until he nearly trips over Markel's big foot. He shows her something, and they excitedly discuss whatever the factoid on the paper reveals. Markel nods and smiles. Mesa smiles back, then nods to Brault.

"Ms. Fine," Officer Brault calls. "Would you come here, please?"

You know that mom instinct that kicks in when you want to strangle your kids for doing something stupid, but at the same time you'd be more than willing to stand in front of a firing squad instead of them? Gurus have that too. I can't stand up. I can't turn or scream or...anything. My heart beeps three times in succession, evens out, then blurts again. No one notices, except Pen. She turns to me and places her hand on my leg in solemn repose.

"I have to go now, Lyla," her soft voice quivers. There's no fake accent. There's no fake anything. "It's not a choice. I will be back as soon as I can. But if you should...well...if you should leave before I..." She stops, gasping, closes her eyes, then opens them. "If you do, I just want you to know...I love you."

It's the first time she's said those words since the day she kissed Rosie at the airport, then waved goodbye to her daughter, who was standing in the lobby smiling, holding her father's hand. They aren't quite as foreign or dry in her mouth as she thought they'd be. Who knows when she'll ever be brave enough to say them again.

"Ms. Fine," Officer Brault calls again.

Penelope walks to the door, swallowing hard. She looks at Detective Markel and nods. This time, it's her turn to give a hat tip. Officer Brault reaches down and unsnaps the handcuff pocket on the back of his uniform belt, handing the silver circles to Detective Mesa. Stunned, Mesa turns to face the lead detective.

"Me?" He asks.

"You hooked her, reel her in," Markel says with a side smile. "I'm in the market for a new partner. Let's see what you've got."

Mesa looks back at Penelope as Officer Brault gets close to her side and puts his hand loosely on her back. The same hand that comforted her after she came face to face with the horror at The Bowl now holds her captive, leading her to a place she'd never thought she'd go. I know exactly how that feels.

"I'm ready," she says, her wrists moving slightly forward. Her head is high, with a tear trailing down her cheek from our farewell, but her body is fluid, accepting. A gambler who doesn't understand, up front, that she can lose it all should never roll the dice. She is more honest and accepting in this moment than she's been since the day she was born into this world.

Mesa hands the clipboard to Detective Markel and turns in another direction, taking quick steps toward the triangular nurses' station and around the back. A cry or protest and shock comes from Keith's room. Markel chuckles to herself as a confused Pen looks at Brault, squinting, her mouth frozen halfway between open and closed. He pats her back with the same comforting presence he had before. Some roads always lead home.

"It's not me?" Pen asks through her mental vertigo.

"Not this time," Markel responds. "Bigger fish to fry."

"Patricia Allen," Mesa says loud enough to be heard by the emergency helicopter on the roof. "You are under arrest as an accessory before the fact in the murders of Lieutenant Cecilia Rhodes and

Correctional Officer Brent Johnson, and the aggravated wounding of Keith Allen and Dr. Lylarose Gentry. You are further charged with bank transfer and wire fraud, bribery of a state correctional officer, and violating prison policy."

"No! This can't be happening! I wasn't even there! I had nothing..."

Pat tries to pull out of Mesa's grasp, but he has her wrists behind her before the rest of the sentence degenerates into profanity and nonsensical protestations of innocence.

"I don't understand." Penelope looks at Denise Markel, too terrified to do anything but tremble.

"Murder charges won't stick," Markel says, either oblivious to or enjoying Penelope's neuropathic meltdown. "There was no way she could have known Johnson would freak out and plug Rhodes, and no jury would buy the argument she thought your guru over there was going to spring on her hubby with an ice pick, just because she set them up to be together."

"Charges? Set them up? What?"

"Once those get tossed, she'll definitely get time for the wire fraud, and bribery, although Hummel may put in enough golf games with the Sheriff to get that dropped if she takes a plea that covers both. I'd say three-to-five to out by two. Financial crimes never bring much time. People don't take money as seriously as blood. At least, on this end of the gun."

Pen stares wordlessly at the detective.

"You said to arrest someone," Markel murmurs. "Aren't you used to getting what you want?"

The author starts to giggle in small maniacal blurts, shaking her head and trying to catch her breath. "Not this quickly or distressingly."

Mesa gives the cuffs a little jerk to quiet Pat down so she can hear that "right to remain silent" part again. She's still pulling against him as they breach the door. Keith's body lies like a book on a desk, holding a story he cannot yet tell.

"It will go better for you in the press if he doesn't have to drag you," Detective Markel calls when they get closer, then she turns her attention to Mesa. "Walk her out the front door, Steve, nice and slow."

"Perp walk," Brault sings with a low whistle.

"Someone's got to pay for Rhodes," Markel replies.

"Could we just start this over? I'm really lost." Penelope asks.

Markel holds the bridge of her nose again, then exhales with a puff. If she'd have known police work meant so much people work, she'd have followed another path.

"EMT and ER personnel both reported when Allen was brought in he kept screaming, 'bitch, that bitch.' We all thought it was about Gentry, and him trying to tell us it was her. Turns out, he didn't call her 'bitch.' After this morning, I talked to witnesses at the prison who saw them interact regularly. They never heard that word. 'Dyke,' yes, but not bitch. So I decided to run that unknown set of prints on Johnson's gun."

"Detective Mesa told me it was probably his wife, handing him the gun in the morning as he was getting dressed."

"Well, not his wife, exactly, but someone who got out of bed with him. They were a match to Mrs. Allen."

"Allen and Johnson?"

"Not for the fun, I assure you. The money."

"Johnson had money?"

"No." Markel frowns at Pen's inept conclusions. "Don't quit your day job."

"Don't worry."

"Steve Mesa knew Johnson was dirty. He smelled it. He looked for a money trail but couldn't find anything in the main account. Then he noticed Johnson had a very active secondary email attached to multiple FundFinders pages. Johnson would set up a fake cause, a donor would drop a bundle, and it would close out. The SSN he used for the banking feature was Allen's, and the bank offshore."

"FundFinders. Detective Mesa was asking our director about that and if Lyla gave to them."

"Since we thought Dr. Gentry was the pivot, Steve guessed she was the donor, paying him to let her get close enough to kill. Accounting went through every record you guys had. You were whistle clean. It was Patricia Allen moving funds overseas through the accounts. Gentry had nothing to do with Johnson. Nobody was more shocked when she busted out with a weapon than Johnson. Well, except maybe Keith Allen. He looked pretty damn surprised when her fist met his face.

"Anyway, my asshole partner was supposed to be getting Johnson's computer and checking it out, but he spent his time chasing around ice pick receipts and eating at Dairy Queen with the warden. This morning after our meeting, Johnson's wife gave me his laptop, so we got half the story. Not only did we find the accounts, there was a hidden Dropbox folder shared with Patricia full of links, codes, and love notes. Good thing. By the time we got a warrant to pick up her computer, it was gone. House was as empty as an Amish barn. We couldn't even find a power cord."

"That's where she went, when the reporters caught her coming back into the hospital," Penelope adds.

"Probably. So far, what Mesa pieced together from naughty notes in Dropbox was that Patricia convinced Johnson she wanted Keith off the sex offender's unit and in gen-pop at a regular prison."

"That's exactly what she told Lyla. She wanted Keith off the sex offender's unit so she could take her kids."

"Well, the kid part was bullshit. They've been living in another state with her parents since Allen was arrested for murder. Safer for them. The offender's unit is a pretty protected environment. Regular prisons eat molesters and rapists for lunch. She wanted him in general population because someone as soft, stupid, and reeking of privilege as Keith Allen wouldn't make it three months before he was found hanging in his cell. She told Johnson once Keith was completely out of the picture, they could be together. So, he was supposed to watch over Gentry's sessions and make sure they worked. Patricia really believed Dr. Gentry could get Keith's mental status upgraded, and he'd be approved for a move."

"I know what you saw of Lylarose in that recording didn't look like it, but she's an excellent counselor, and if this had been a different time in her life, and Allen had picked a different victim, she could have." Penelope looks back into the room at my body, remembering the me that was and would never be again.

"If. If. If. Anyway, The Allens' practice is facing a shit-ton of lawsuits, so I guess she thought getting him killed would make a difference. They co-owned, so she's liable, but without the thrill of revenge, some victims would take a cheap settlement and move on. In the meantime, Patricia was slowly moving her assets out of harm's way through Johnson's FundFinders scheme. She was just using him as a means to an end."

"That bitch." Penelope puts her hands on her hips.

"Exactly."

"Excuse me, Detective, but I don't think that's why she wanted him in gen-pop," Officer Brault says, bowing his head with respect to his superior. He puts his hands behind his back, like a boy afraid of getting a swat for speaking out of turn.

"What's your theory?"

"Even with him dead, she would have to pay the suits, and they could always class-action her. I've been married a long time, and I've seen others crash and burn. A woman will put up with a lot of shit for the sake of her kids or her lifestyle. Cheating, lying, laziness—she'll take it all and make it work. But one day, when she's had enough, all that betrayal, all those lies, are going to come back up and demand payment. There's no guarantee he was gonna get killed in gen-pop, but if not, his life would have been a daily living hell. He'd be a pod-boy before his cot assignment got made. Either way, she was going to sip margaritas with her offshore nest egg and drink to every time he hurt her. That's what I think."

Markel nods approval. "That's a good tip, Brault. I'll keep it in mind. When Steve comes with me, we'll need a scene guy."

The night cop taps the back of his chair. "No, thanks. I like what I do."

"You're good at it," Penelope adds, then hits him on the shoulder with a fake slap. "You scared me!"

He points at Detective Markel and looks at the ground.

"Detective!" Penelope's wide eyes make everyone giggle. Even me.

"Before I moved to homicide, I was a traffic cop," Markel says, a low evil chuckle accentuating her own devil's grin. "Consider that your warning ticket."

Penelope presses her lips together and nods.

"From now on, drive safely, Ms. Fine."

"Yes, ma'am."

The patrolmen slip out of the unit as quickly as they arrived. The only one who said a word was the squad leader who asked Markel if the assignment could count as their quarterly drill since they suited up and ran a pattern. Markel just shook her head. Officer Brault folded his chair and left it by the nurses' station, waving goodbye to the guards left to watch Keith and call the station when he, too, could be charged with murder. Unlike his wife, Keith's charge will stick.

When Markel was the only one left, Penelope motioned for her to come into the room. She made a point of holding her iPad so the detective could see the *News Now* "Memories of an Inspired Teacher" video on the sidebar, featuring commentary from people who had "benefited" from my insight. If I had Topaz run a guest list from Virga, only about a fourth of them would have even been there.

"About tomorrow," Penelope says. "I've decided I'd much rather spend the morning with Lylarose than go down to the conference room. Their coffee is dreadful, by the way. So, if I could get a preview, I'd probably just watch from up here."

"I wouldn't bother coming," Markel replies. "It's not going to last long. Bottom line is, for reasons known only to herself, Dr. Gentry took a restricted object into the counseling pod, although there is no evidence it was used in the commission of any crime. When an altercation arose between Gentry and Mr. Allen, Correctional Officer Johnson lost control of the scene and accidentally shot Wing Supervisor Cecilia Rhodes in the chaos. The legally obtained footage from the hallway camera, just recently turned over to the Prison Review Board, shows Rhodes's body in the doorway and Dr. Gentry sitting with her during the next shots. We can conclude Allen was able to obtain Johnson's gun and murder the officer. Wing Command gave an appropriate armed response at the sight of a weapon, grievously wounding both Dr. Gentry and Mr. Allen. In the aftermath, an inappropriate financial and personal relationship between Johnson and Patricia Allen was discovered. All there is to it."

In other words, "that went wrong."

"What about Hummel? Does he just get to walk away from this?"

"No comment."

"I'm sorry about your partner," Pen says.

"You work with someone a long time, you think you know them. It stings."

"Yes, it does."

Formal meditation, the intentional type where you sit up straight, try to forget about what you had for breakfast, and follow your breath to the heart of your inner world, starts and ends with a bell. Or, here in the ICU, a heart monitor's beep.

One beep.

Inhale.

Exhale.

Two beeps.

Inhale.

Exhale.

Three beeps.

Inhale.

Exhale.

Three beeps.

Three beeps.

Three more.

"Trip-i-let, Trip-i-let," Penelope says, looking over blueprints on her laptop, echoing every first grade music teacher everywhere. She signs off on the estimate for rebranding Virga as "The Gardens: A Meditation and Retreat Center for Grief Recovery." The house Marian and I shared will become the Director's Office for Topaz to rule her new queendom. Luka asked to stay in the small room off the kitchen we built for her years ago. Meditation teachers and licensed psychologists specializing in grief were offered positions on staff. The new logo has a gilded circle and in the center—a blooming red rose.

We've settled into a new normal here in Room Five. Without Officer Brault's nightly sandwich, the recycled air has gone back to the delightful odor that alternates between acetone cleanser and Penelope's "fragrance-free" lotion, which smells anything but free. She eats in the cafeteria a little more and has showered at Virga at least twice, after Topaz meticulously removed any evidence of crime tape from the center. Luka arrives each morning, with Robyn in tow, to change one empty tea cup for another. Devotion: it doesn't have to make sense, it just is as it is.

A few news outlets left an intern behind to report any developments, but the circus left town as the grateful people of Oakland waved goodbye with their left hand and counted the till with their right.

Three beeps.

Three more.

Faster.

More.

Faster.

Penelope closes her laptop.

"Lyla?"

Three beeps, no, four.

More. More. More.

"WEEEEEEEEEEEEEEEEEE," A shrill ear-piercing sound,

pitched slightly below dog-whistle, shrieks warnings bigger than a hurricane.

"Lyla!" Penelope stands and looks at the monitor, squinting against the pain of the alarm. "NURSE!"

There's no need to shout, they are already in the room. As soon as the wail erupted, a team of these amazing professionals who spend most of their time calmly turning, testing, checking tubing, and monitoring my skin, hustled in and fanned out, each taking a station and setting about a task. It's not a dance, exactly, but a choreographed art form all its own.

"Get the backboard," one calls over the sound.

"Roll on three."

"CODE BLUE, ROOM FIVE, CODE BLUE, ROOM FIVE." The overhead announcement, calm as a sunrise, speaks in weird juxtaposition to the shrieking organized chaos around me. More people, hurried but not harried, enter the little beige box of wonder holding my fourth life.

"Ms. Fine, if you'd like to go to the waiting room, we'll come and..."

"I'm not leaving," Penelope answers, the stern, solid edge in her voice erasing any temptation to argue.

"That's fine, but we need to focus on the patient right now."

Penelope moves to the corner. She never looks away.

"I'll bag, you compress," one nurse says to another. She removes the thick blue tube that's been my lifeline and places a hand-held pump over my mouth, forcing air into my cavernous shell while her coworker pounds on my chest. There's another blue presence in the room, one I've known longer than anyone here.

"Rhythm?" The doctor asks.

"V.Fib." A nurse answers.

"Charge it," the doctor says, motioning to the defibrillator. A rising hum fills the air like a radio controlled drone ascending to a new height.

"Ready." The respiratory therapist calls and moves out of the doctor's path. It's amazing how many people surround you with such skill and purpose during a death. If only we did that while we were living, how much less suffering there would be in the world.

The shock rockets through my body, my torso jerking upward. It's a violent, rupturing pulse. Somewhere in the corner of the room, Penelope emits a breathy, wavering whimper.

"Epi," the doctor says as they stare at the monitor, and the bag returns over my mouth. The nurses change positions, each with a new station, and a constant focus. Twice more the cycle of CPR and shock plays through.

"Bolus of Amio," the doctor calls.

"No pulse," the nurse advises.

"Rhythm?"

"Asystole," comes the reply, a dropping deep-toned word.

"Now?"

"Nothing."

"What?"

"There's nothing."

"We've gone as far as we can," the doctor says loud enough for Pen to hear.

"CPR ended, fourteen thirty-five," the recording nurse repeats, making a notation to be put in the chart.

One by one, the machines go off. The sounds evaporate into one final tone. Then, silence.

This meditation is over.

"I'm so sorry, Ms. Fine," the nurse gingerly moves toward Penelope, standing beside her recliner.

"Thank you," she whispers. The virga that has hung over this room remains no longer. Gentle rain falls down Pen's cheeks.

"If you'd like to step out, we will clean her up for you to say goodbye."

"I'll stay," Pen chokes, but averts her eyes as the nurses go about the gruesome business of separating woman from machine.

Penelope looks back when they leave and nods to my friend, Death, with unblinking acceptance, a tree standing before the axe. Death, who took her daughter without asking, and pocketed her marriage as it floated through the ER doors, now collects her teacher. She doesn't fight. She doesn't flee. She was, as she promised to be, as she needed to be, simply present.

All human beings are prone to wander in the grand buffet of life and choose between the delicacies of miracle and mistake. I was wounded. I was healed. I found friends. I lost blood. I stood for peace. I fell in love. I have been tempted by error more often than I wish to admit. Yet now, with the last heartbeat forged by the worst decision of my lives, I was able to set a feast of choice before my dear student, knowing she has made her way to the table with a good heart and a strong mind. Teacher to student, friend to friend, lover to loved, parent to child, that is the greatest gift we have to give one another—a way out or a way in, a way to endure, a way to forgive, a way to move, a way to breathe, a way to live, a way to end, a way to begin again.

There is always a way.

ABOUT THE AUTHOR

Kellie Schorr is a writer and Buddhist yogi in the Nyingma lineage of Tibetan Buddhism. She lives and works in rural Virginia with her partner, Cathy, and their beloved beagles. Her favorite word is chiaroscuro.

www.ingramcontent.com/pod-product-compliance
Lightning Source LLC
Chambersburg PA
CBHW021028310726
48969CB00006B/1592